THE ANNOUNCEMENT

...Tonight, we are informing those people outside of our island nation that the Bandung is in control and demands immediate recognition. To insure that this demand is met, all members of the United Nations delegation presently in Jakarta have been taken hostage. They will be held hostage until the Bandung receives official recognition from each of the member countries involved, as well as their assurance that the Bandung government will be recognized as the official government of Java and that there will be no retaliatory response to this action. Immediate and positive response will insure that no harm will come to the members of the delegation. However, if that response is delayed, at precisely twelve o'clock noon Jakarta time tomorrow, one member of the UN delegation will be sacrificed and the body placed on the doorstep of the Mandarin Plaza Hotel for all to witness.

...We await the world's response.

Other *Leisure* books by R. Karl Largent:

THE BAJA CONSPIRACY
RED RAIN
THE ASSASSIN
THE SEA
RED WIND
RED SAND
RED SKIES
BLACK DEATH
RED ICE
THE LAKE
THE PROMETHEUS PROJECT
RED TIDE
THE WITCH OF SIXKILL
ANCIENTS
PAGODA

THE JAKARTA PLOT

R. KARL LARGENT

LEISURE BOOKS NEW YORK CITY

A LEISURE BOOK®

October 2006

Published by

Dorchester Publishing Co., Inc.
200 Madison Avenue
New York, NY 10016

ISBN 0-8439-4568-0

Printed in the United States of America.

THE JAKARTA PLOT

PART 1

Chapter One

Day Minus 3: Time 1241LT
Glodok Section, Jakarta

Teuwen Ng was a fidgety little man whose perpetually edgy condition was further exacerbated by the documents he was carrying in his valise. By arriving thirty minutes early, and ordering an unpretentious meal consisting of *sate* and *tahu* with a filling of vegetables, he had hoped to settle his stomach and avoid appearing like what he was—a man waiting to peddle sensitive documents.

To make matters worse, and there was always something that made matters worse for Ng, he had no idea what the man he was supposed to meet, a man by the name of Che Nagarajan, looked like. True, Nagarajan had told him to look for a man wearing glasses, a red tie, a dark three-piece suit, and carrying a raincoat, but so far, Ng had spotted no less than three different men who could have fit that description.

Equally disconcerting for the little man was the fact that the corner table Ng had selected was flanked by mirrors on two sides. If he looked up, he was unavoidably confronted by his own image. Anyone in the room who knew him would have found it easy to spot him. Ng disliked being both so visible and, by his own assessment, so vulnerable.

Finally a man in a red tie approached the table. To Ng's relief he fit Nagarajan's description. "The restaurant is rather crowded," the man said. "Do you mind if I join you?"

Ng nodded and gestured for the man to take a seat. "An unpleasant day," he offered, secretly wondering if such an opening was appropriate for someone who was on the verge of becoming an operative for a foreign government. "I mean, of course, because of the monsoons," he added. After he said it, he realized how superfluous his opening sounded. Everyone knew how hard it was raining.

The man extended his hand and introduced himself. "Che Nagarajan, Investment Counseling, Lippobank here in Jakarta." He spoke with confidence. Even more important, Ng thought he sounded like an investment banker.

Ng had practiced his own response. It was the one Nagarajan had told him to use. "Teuwen Ng," he said, offering the man his hand. "I am an administrative assistant." They were not the words Ng would have used to describe what he did, but if anyone who knew him had overheard him, they would not have disputed it.

Nagarajan pulled out a chair and sat down. To Ng's surprise, the man appeared to be in no particular hurry;

he lit a cigarette and studied the one-page menu. Then Ng realized that the man was talking to him. He spoke in a muted voice, almost a monotone, asking questions about the documents. Finally he said, "How do I know these documents are what you claim them to be?"

Ng was caught off guard by the question. More to the point, he was uncertain about how to answer. "I spoke to the woman at the hotel," he blurted. "She said I should contact you. She gave me the telephone number."

"Do you want me to repeat the question?" Nagarajan asked.

"You may examine them if you wish," Ng said. His chest hurt, and he was already wishing he had not made the initial call. From the outset, Teuwen Ng had been surprised at how casually the whole affair had escalated to its present level. He had always assumed that the people who operated in such a clandestine profession were layered in secret passwords, wore disguises, responded only to code names, and had an arsenal of sophisticated weapons at their disposal. Nagarajan appeared to have none of these.

"Back to the woman," Nagarajan pressed.

"She is the assistant concierge at the hotel?"

"Fina Tu," Nagarajan confirmed.

Ng wondered why Nagarajan had not whispered the woman's name. He nodded confirmation.

"Bright girl," Nagarajan assessed. "Her only problem is, she works both sides of the street. I've learned to be careful when I'm dealing with her."

The small talk was making Ng even more nervous than usual. "I have the documents in my valise," he admitted. "Would you like to see them?"

Nagarajan's answer astonished him. "All I wish to see is the first three pages, Mr. Ng. Based on those three pages I will be able to judge whether or not my people will be interested in the rest of the documents."

"But how do I get them to you?"

Nagarajan shrugged and snuffed out his cigarette. "If it were me, I'd open my briefcase, count off three pages, and hand them to me. No one who is watching us will think there is anything clandestine about a simple exchange of documents. After all, I am a banker and you are seeking advice from my bank. Right?"

Ng hesitated, glanced twice around the room, and finally began fumbling through his papers. Meanwhile, Nagarajan casually looked over the menu. Finally, Ng found what he was looking for, counted out three pages, and handed them to Nagarajan. "When will I hear from you again?" the little man asked.

Che Nagarajan ignored the question. This time he leaned forward before he spoke. "If these papers contain the information you claim, Mr. Ng, my government is prepared to comply with your wishes as you stated them in our phone conversation the other day. You will be flown to the United States and granted political asylum. It will simply be a matter of a phone call telling you where and when to pick up your ticket. You will board a Garuda flight, fly to Singapore, where a representative of my government will meet you, escort you through customs, and accompany you on to San Francisco."

Ng swallowed hard and his eyes darted about the restaurant. It was too simple. "How do I get the rest of my papers to you?" he asked.

"That won't be necessary, Mr. Ng. You will be taking the documents with you. Any further meetings between the two of us just might be the thing that arouses that suspicion you seem so concerned about. Perhaps I should caution you, though; it has been my experience that the only people who arouse suspicion are people who act in a suspicious manner."

Ng continued to lean forward, shielding his mouth with his hand. His voice had a skittish dimension to it. "You will please pardon my apprehension—I am certain you realize that I am in a very delicate position. My wife and children are—"

"I am not concerned with your wife and children, Mr. Ng. I am only concerned with the authenticity of the documents. However, I must ask; are you getting cold feet?"

From the expression on Teuwen Ng's face, it was obvious he did not understand what Nagarajan had said.

"I mean," Nagarajan explained, "are you saying you want to back out?"

Ng shook his head.

"Good, because if you did, now that I am reasonably certain you have what my people are looking for, if you were unwilling to turn it over to me, I would have to take it—and in the process I would probably have to kill you." Nagarajan tried to smile to soften the impact of what he had said, but Ng was too nervous to notice.

Ng watched while the man took the three pages, casually folded them, stuffed them in his pocket, and stood up. "You will be hearing from me," Nagarajan said. "There would be wisdom in staying close to the telephone. When things begin to happen we will have to move swiftly."

For the next several minutes, Teuwen Ng sat at the table trying to regain his composure. The meeting with Nagarajan had not gone at all the way he had anticipated. He had expected something different, something more conspiratorial, something far more arcane. He took a deep breath to steady himself, closed his valise, stood up, and started for the door. Only then did he remember that he had forgotten to finish his meal.

Day 0: Time 2240LT
Chinatown, Glodok,
Jakarta

Abon Sodong was a cloddish man of fleshy proportions. Moreover, he was bored. He lit a cigarette and waited impatiently for a large cockroach to reach eye level before he reached out and squashed it with the heel of his hand.

Then he laughed; even his laugh was obese, a muted, unpleasant, guttural sound. Still, he was pleased; he had managed the unfortunate creature's demise without in any way exerting himself.

Abon Sodong seldom did anything that required exertion and that included thinking. Nevertheless, it had occurred to him that if he did not have more important things to concern himself with, he might have counted the number of times he had reduced cockroaches to brownish wet smears on the dingy corridor wall.

But Abon Sodong did have more important things to do—like warn Chan and Shawad if anyone was coming or if he saw anything suspicious. After all, it was well known that the prostitutes who worked the cheap hotels and restaurants in the Glodok this time of night were quick to complain to management if their clients were distracted. Sometimes they even complained if they heard strange noises. The women were convinced that such disturbances cost them both time and money.

In addition, it was also well known that some of the prostitutes doubled as *politsos*. Politsos were paid informants of the Jakarta police encouraged to report anything or anyone they suspected of being associated with the Bandung. The Bandung, as Sodong assumed everyone knew, was the militant arm of the PKI, the Communist Party in Java. Officially, the PKI was a legal, recognized political entity in Java. The Bandung, however, was known to be populated with party radicals. To the Kujon government's consternation, they were tolerated, and on occasion even admired, by the disenfranchised. In Jakarta and throughout Java, that amounted to several million people.

Abon heard sounds and hurried to the stairwell at the end of the hall. One level down, a young prostitute, her back against the wall, legs entwined around his waist, was encouraging a youth of no more than twelve or thirteen years of age to perform. The boy was fumbling and inept, and Abon reasoned that the youth was not only inexperienced, but disappointed in the surroundings of his first encounter.

Abon watched from the shadows for several minutes, put out his cigarette, and finally went back to his post outside the door leading to the room where Chan and Shawad were working.

Inside that room, Zakir Chan and Od Shawad stood over a man reputed to be an agent of the CIA who fronted as a representative of the Lippobank. His name was Che Nagarajan. It had taken Chan and Shawad seven hours of what their leader, Bojoni Sarawak, would have termed an "appropriate interrogation" to force the man to admit that he had arranged to forward certain information to the American CIA.

Zakir Chan paused and appraised his work much as Sodong had assessed his earlier efforts in the hall—with a certain degree of satisfaction. He had part of the information he needed, but not all of it. Nagarajan, for the second time in the past thirty minutes, had passed out. His breathing was shallow, and his face, bloated and swollen into a pulpy, discolored montage of lacerations and bruises from the beating, would have made him unrecognizable even to those most intimate with him.

Chan, the smaller of Nagarajan's two interrogators, rested and congratulated his Party comrade. Then he reached for the telephone. "What we have learned only confirms what Sarawak suspected," he said. "He must be informed."

Like his colleague's, Shawad found his breathing was returning to normal; it was no longer labored. And like Chan, he also assessed his work, but with a far more critical eye. He considered himself as much of a craftsman as one of the unfortunates who ran booths in the winding lanes and back-alley shops south of the Jl Pancoran. He had beaten the admissions out of the man first with the leather strap with nails, and finally the small lead club, the *spada,* that all Bandung members carried.

As Zakir Chan dialed the number with one hand, he grabbed Nagarajan's hair with the other and lifted the man's head. This time, however, there was no longer any sign of breathing. He let the man's head drop when he heard the voice on the other end of the line. "I would speak with Sarawak," he said.

There was a delay of several seconds before he again heard someone on the other end of the line. "This is Sarawak."

"Comrade General, this is Zakir. We have confirmed your suspicions. . . ."

As always, Sarawak's voice was confident, rich with the element of intonation and clarity that men in power are prone to cultivate. "And?"

"Nagarajan has admitted that he arranged for the information to be passed on."

"Passed on to . . . ?"

Zakir Chan was reluctant to anger his leader. He hesitated. Now he would be forced to admit that Nagarajan was dead—and unfortunately for both him and Shawad, the man had died before revealing anything about how he intended to pass the information on. "We do not know, General," he finally admitted.

Sarawak's tone changed. Suddenly he sounded impatient. "Then you must continue to interrogate Mr. Nagarajan until we know what he has thus far refused to divulge."

Zakir Chan could feel the words and he could hear what they sounded like; still, it was difficult to actually say them. Finally, he found the courage. "Nagarajan is dead, Comrade General."

Sarawak's silence was deafening. Zakir Chan could feel his own heart beating, and wished that were still the case with Nagarajan.

When Sarawak spoke again his voice was measured. "You found nothing on his person that would indicate who he has spoken to or who he has been dealing with?"

Chan looked at the small clutter of personal papers and belongings of the dead man scattered on the table in front of him. "Only this," he admitted, "a series of incoherent scribblings on a small piece of paper—a name and a Garuda flight number . . . "

"Continue," Sarawak insisted.

"It means nothing—just scratchings," Chan protested.

"You say a name appears on that piece of paper," Sarawak demanded. "What is it?"

Chan squinted in the dim light of the single sixty-watt bulb hanging from a cotton cord in the ceiling. "The name is that of someone called Ng. It is dated with tomorrow's date, the ninth—"

Sarawak cut Chan off before he could finish. "Find out," he said. "We must know if the name Ng appears on the passenger manifest of any Garuda flight departing tomorrow. If you find that to be the case, the plane must not arrive at its destination."

"That will be difficult," Chan protested. It was unlike him to inveigh his leader's orders.

"Difficult? Of course it will be difficult, Comrade Chan—but not impossible." With that, the Bandung leader paused for a moment. When the sound of his voice came through to Chan again, it was even more emphatic than before. "I repeat, Comrade, you must see that the Garuda flight carrying Mr. Ng does not reach its destination."

At that point Zakir Chan knew that Sarawak had said all he intended to say. He placed the receiver back in its cradle, went to the door, opened it, and motioned to Sodong, who was again standing at the top of the stairwell.

"It would appear that our Mr. Nagarajan is no longer of any use to us," Chan said. "You will assist Comrade Shawad in disposing of the body."

Sodong shrugged, and lumbered down the hall and into the room. His demeanor was that of a man both slightly annoyed at having been summoned to do strenuous work, and at the same time preoccupied. Neither Chan nor Shawad had any way of knowing that the sight of Nagarajan's battered body slumped over in the chair was of little consequence to their bovine colleague. Sodong was still daydreaming, entertaining an assortment of sordid fantasies about the young prostitute.

Sodong hefted the body of the bank official, threw him over his shoulder, and waited for Shawad to open the door. "There is a refuse bin in the alley," Chan informed him. "Put him there. Let someone else worry about disposing of the body."

Day 1: Time 0503LT
Chinatown, Glodok,
Jakarta

Toko Remi, a student by day, and employed at the Balai Seni Rupa as a combination custodian and security man at night, picked up the newspaper and headed for the elevator. It was his custom to finish his work early and take the museum's copy of the *Jakarta Post* with him to the rooftop. An English-language newspaper, it not only gave him an opportunity to read the paper and practice his English, but it also gave him something he felt he needed, further insight into the strange Occidental culture.

On this particular morning, there was a second reason for his morning ritual. The rains had stopped—for the time being at least. The nightlong downpour the Malays called the monsoons had ceased and the skies had at least partially cleared. Because of this, Toko Remi hoped for a rare sight in the monsoon season: a glimpse of a sunrise.

He stepped from the elevator, went through the service door, and walked out onto the roof. The sky was evolving from darkness into a pleasing terra-cotta complexion, not unlike the color of the Majapahit creations in the museum at the university. He found his chair and positioned it so that he could watch the sunrise; he would read his paper when it was light enough. For the moment, however, he allowed himself to absorb the sounds and inhale the smells of the city. To Remi these sensations were pleasant—if for no other reason than that they were the essence of Jakarta, the marrow and quintessence of his first nineteen years.

He stayed that way for several minutes, sitting and listening to the commotion made by the street hawkers setting up their stands and the first blush of the early morning traffic. In the distance he was aware of the thunder of the huge jets at Soekarno-Hatta airport. It was the first wave of early morning international flights leaving for distant lands that, for the present, Toko Remi could only dream and occasionally study about. He counted: one, two, three flights; giant birds stretching their immense wings, reaching for a netherworld; a Nirvana, a Utopia.

Then it happened. Suddenly there was a giant ball of fire, an unbelievable eruption in the sky, a great thunder—and then silence as pieces of flaming debris rained down on what he knew to be the vast waters beyond the harbor at Tanjung Priok.

Forty-three-year-old Chean Ajan stepped down from the crowded bus with his hand still in his pocket. At an early age, Chean had been taught to always carry one hand in his pocket—over his billfold. He still did it. It was his way of deterring the pickpockets that seemed to flourish in the crowded early morning buses in and out of Merdeka Square.

He stepped in a puddle along the curb and felt the water seep into his shoe. It was but another in a string of early morning annoyances. The difference was that this one was one he would have to endure for several hours. The young *shimon* with the blaring boom box who had ridden the bus all the way into the Square from Punta had been even more vexing, but he was gone now—just like the sweaty, crowded bus. Chean's wet foot would be with him all day.

Across the street from the bus stop was the Bali Restaurant, where Chean Ajan had been the day cook for the past twenty years—an accomplishment of note, because Chean had been born with only one leg. The days were long and the work arduous, but there were those that said the Bali Restaurant was one of the finest places to eat in the entire market area.

Chean Ajan took great pride in that fact. It was he,

most folks said, who was responsible for the restaurant's excellent reputation.

But now there was a small handful of people, some of them vendors, others early morning customers of the Bali, milling around in the street, looking up into the gray dawn sky.

"Did you see it?" an old woman asked.

Chean Ajan shook his head. "See what?"

"There was an explosion," another declared. "I looked up and I saw fire falling from the sky."

Chean Ajan scanned the open sky over the monument in the square. Admittedly there were minor smudges on the lens of his glasses, but he saw nothing. A few traces of smoke perhaps, but was that not the infamous pollution of Jakarta? He shrugged, looked up and down the street, and as was his custom, uttered a short prayer before entering the restaurant.

Unlike Toko Remi, Chean Ajan did not witness the Garuda Airlines Boeing 747 in its death throes. And at that point, neither man had any way of knowing that one man, with the surname of Ng, along with 240-some others, had perished in that crash. Chean merely turned up his collar against the weather and went into the restaurant. To his dismay, it was raining again.

Day 2: Time 0713LT
Hooker's Bar and Grille,
Key Largo

Gideon Stone hadn't shaved in three days. The reason was, when he decided to explain why—*if* he decided to explain why—simply preference. On the other hand, Hooker Herman, who had known Gideon since their high school days, would have argued that with Gideon Stone even a small matter like not shaving was actually part of his ongoing rebellion. Hooker claimed that since Gideon had resigned from the Agency, he'd rebelled against anything that even hinted at convention. Not shaving was his protest against organizational protocol and an example of his anti-establishment behavior. In all fairness, however, Hooker was equally quick to point out that most of the clientele who frequented his establishment leaned toward that kind of behavior.

Hooker Herman was a big man; big in the sense of most portly specimens who eat too much and drink even more. It was said, with some pride by those who knew him, that Hooker could drink anyone, man, beast, or creature, under the table. He had demonstrated that prowess by frequently outlasting some of the biggest imbibers in south Florida.

Hooker Herman had a forty-six-inch waist and a neck like a Green Bay linebacker—which is another way of saying he had no neck at all. Yet despite his girth and three-hundred-pound presence, it was Hooker's smile and ingratiating style that impressed his customers and endeared him to everyone that walked through the door of Hooker's Bar and Grille.

"Know what those folks said?" Hooker beamed as he started back down to the end of the bar where Gideon was perched. "They said they liked this place well enough to stick around for another couple of days. How about that?"

Gideon Stone grumbled something about Largo already being overcrowded, and stared down at his coffee. Hooker knew his old friend well enough to know that Gideon's brain didn't kick into gear until after the third or fourth cup, and he didn't get social until almost dinner time. Until then, about the best anyone could hope for was an occasional shrug, and if Stone was really listening, an acknowledging nod of the head.

"Maybe I ought to sell them this place, huh?"

Gideon looked up and rubbed his eyes, but there was no response, and Hooker poured him another cup of coffee.

"Marie would like that," Hooker continued, "selling the place, I mean."

"Who's Marie?" Gideon managed to ask. It was his first semi-coherent utterance of the day.

"My wife, dammit. You know that."

"I thought her name was Corona."

Hooker leaned back against the cabinets behind the bar and folded his arms. He reminded Gideon of a sumo wrestler. "For Christ's sake, Gideon, Corona is the one that bailed out on me two years ago. Marie came along and we figured what the hell—so we got married."

Gideon nodded and went back to his coffee. On two cups of coffee and at this hour of the day, he was not about to try to follow his old friend through one of his tangled tales of Largo logic. He turned his attention instead to the man who had just walked through the front door. He was wearing a suit and carrying a briefcase. Gideon began mentally ticking off what the man wasn't. He wasn't a tourist. He wasn't a guy looking for a fishing charter—and he wasn't a local. The only time locals suffered through the torture of wearing a suit in Key Largo was when they were getting married or going to a funeral. And sometimes they didn't even dress up for those occasions.

He watched while Hooker greeted the man and the newcomer handed him a card. Then he heard Hooker say, "He's down there, at the end of the bar."

By the time the man reached him, Gideon had sized

him up. He was tall, trim, clean-shaven, and whatever was in the briefcase was fairly heavy. There was a barely perceptible tilt to one side. The man had a look of eagerness, and the disgusting look of convention.

"Gideon Stone?" the man asked. He was sticking out his hand. "My name is Williams, Jack Williams."

Before Gideon could acknowledge him, Williams had reached in his pocket, flipped open a compact black wallet, and produced a badge. Stone glanced at it, frowned, and turned back to his coffee. "I don't care what you say, I was not fishing without a license. I came through the channel at an idle, and the lady I was with last night was over twenty-one. So what's the hassle?"

Williams smiled. "There's an empty booth over there, Colonel Stone. Mind if we move over there so we can talk?"

"It's Mr. Stone," Gideon said. "That 'Colonel' thing is a long time in the past. Besides, I was a lieutenant colonel."

"What I have to say is very private," the man persisted. "A booth would be quieter."

Gideon shrugged, picked up his cup, and moved to the nearest booth. Williams was still settling in when Gideon asked, "So what's the Agency sending people to Florida for these days?"

Williams was the smiling type. It occurred to Gideon that Jack Williams would make a good insurance agent if he ever got out of the Agency business. "Jake Ruppert told me you'd be a little testy, especially in the morning. So I figured what the hell, I might as well see if I could talk to you at your worst. Somewhere in my 201 file it says I like challenges."

"You got one," Gideon mumbled, then added, "How is that old pirate?"

"Up to his ass in alligators," Williams admitted, "and he's the reason I'm here."

Gideon signaled for another cup of coffee, slumped back against the back of the booth, and waited.

"How long have you been out now?" Williams asked. Both men knew he was referring to Gideon's resignation from the CRU, the Covert Response Unit, of the CIA.

Gideon tried to conjure up his first smile of the day. It came out more like a half smirk. "You know damn well how long it's been. In fact, I'd wager you've got everything from my name, rank, and horsepower to the type of gasoline I buy in that damn briefcase of yours."

Williams continued to smile, opened his briefcase, and laid a manila file folder on the table. When he opened the case, Gideon caught a glimpse of a military-issue .45. "It says here, Gideon Stone, forty years old, ex-Air Force, ex-provost marshal for General Berning, and most recently, ex-CIA, CRU to be more specific—now retired. According to your file, you left because you claimed to be 'burnt out.'"

"There's a helluva lot more than that—like a strong distaste for bureaucratic bullshit, too damn many starched collars, and a tendency to throw up at 'must attend' cocktail parties. For two years now I've been saying I'd rather take a beating in a Singapore alley than ever have to listen again to some damn overstuffed general's wife tell me about her gallbladder problems." Gideon made a sweeping gesture with his hand. "Look around you, Mr. Williams. Just in case you hadn't noticed it—not a trace of the aforementioned can be found anywhere on Largo—not even if you poke around under the covers."

Williams took a sip of his coffee and set his cup down. "I read somewhere in your files that you've got the curiosity of an alley cat. So when do you get around to asking me why I'm here?"

"Couldn't care less. My so-called 'curious nature' has been stifled by two years of south Florida fun in the sun and a boatload of stiff margaritas. I'm what the locals call a 'happy camper.' And I have every intention of staying that way."

Williams opened the file. "Ever hear of a man by the name of Bojoni Sarawak?"

"Who hasn't? Last time I heard, Sarawak was a big red hemorrhoid on the ass of the Sarni Kujon government."

"He's more than that now. It seems that Comrade Sarawak has elevated his game. Two weeks ago, the bureau began hearing rumors of a coup attempt in Java."

"By Sarawak?"

Williams nodded. "Three days ago, our operative in Jakarta confirmed it. In exchange for political asylum, we arranged for one of Sarawak's insiders to be flown to the United States. Supposedly this guy had all the details of the impending coup; where, when, how, etc."

"You said 'supposedly.' "

"So I did. I said supposedly because he never made it. His plane went down in the Java Sea shortly after takeoff."

Gideon Stone frowned. "Was it that Garuda flight out of Soekarno-Hatta a couple of days ago?"

"That's the one. Not only that, we've been informed by the Jakarta police that the body of one Che Nagarajan was found out behind some back-alley, fleabag hotel in the Glodok section the same day the plane went down. Nagarajan was the guy who made arrangements for our informant. The Jakarta police say there wasn't much left of Nagarajan. The JPD says it looks like they put him through hell before he talked. And we know he talked because Sarawak had no way of knowing how we were hustling an informant out of the country if he hadn't."

"This guy Nagarajan, he was our operative?"

Williams nodded. "Graduated from UCLA with honors."

Gideon pushed his cup away, leaned forward with his arms on the table, and lowered his voice. The early morning south Florida sun was pouring through a window over Williams's shoulder and a couple, obviously tourists, had slipped into the next booth. "I find this all very interesting, Mr. Williams. It's too bad about Nagarajan, but the way I hear it, the big money and big risks go hand in hand. It sounds like he gambled and lost."

Williams removed another file from his briefcase and shoved it across the table. "Here, read it. It'll save us both time."

Gideon opened the file. It was from Ruppert, the text of the fax Williams had received the previous evening.

> *You'll find Stone someplace on Key Largo. He doesn't have a phone and the only way we know to get in touch with him is through his post office box. Tell him I want him to go to Jakarta and put a crimp in Sarawak's tail. If he's interested, he'll have to come to Washington first for a briefing. Tell him he'd be doing an old friend a favor. . . .*

Gideon laughed and pushed the piece of paper back across the table. It was his first real laugh of the day—this one sounded much more sincere than his earlier effort. "Let me tell you what I think you should do, Mr. Williams. You should call Jake Ruppert and tell him I still love him. Then tell him I said no way. Those days are behind me and I intend to keep it that way. I'm out of shape and I'm not interested. Besides, why the hell would I want to go to Java? It's the monsoon season over there. I like the weather down here in Largo just fine."

"Jake told me to tell you he would make it worth your time."

Gideon Stone shook his head. "You tell Jake the damn Agency doesn't have enough money in its annual budget to pry me out of here."

"Is that final?"

Gideon nodded. "Real final."

It was a few minutes after seven that same evening when Gideon Stone sat in Hooker's place, staring at the telephone. The day, despite its promise, had been a disappointment. His plans to do a little Yellowjack fishing had had to be canceled because a low-pressure area north and east of Cuba was kicking up six-foot waves—and the sun had disappeared early in the day when the clouds draped the Largo sky in a slate-colored overcast. As far as Gideon was concerned, the latter made the day even worse because it was a situation that deprived him of one of his cherished sunsets.

To top it off, Carrie, the girl he had met at the party aboard Sam Creighton's yacht, *The Pandora,* two days earlier, had called Hooker's and left a message. She was canceling their dinner engagement—no reason given. Against that backdrop, even Hooker's world-famous margaritas had ended up tasting flat.

Oblivious to the world around him, Gideon was unaware that Hooker had been watching him. "Never saw you sit and stare at a telephone before, Gid; must be expecting a call, huh?"

Gideon shook his head. "Quite the contrary, Hook, my

friend. I'm sitting here trying to come up with a list of reasons why I shouldn't make a call."

"Some dame?" Hooker inquired.

"Same as, a friend who needs help. Equally compelling."

"I've never known you to resist a damsel in distress or a friend in need," Hooker said. He pushed the phone across the bar and grinned. "Ease your conscience—make the call."

Gideon hesitated, reached for the receiver, and dialed, not in the least surprised by the fact that he remembered Jake and Alice Ruppert's number after all these years.

Alice Ruppert picked up the phone after two rings, and didn't seem at all caught off guard to hear his voice. She squealed with delight, they exchanged a string of pleasantries, and there was a round of small talk before he finally got around to asking for Jake.

"He's already left for Miami," Alice informed him. "He told me to tell you he would meet you in the lobby at the Park-Langley at ten o'clock tomorrow."

Before she hung up, Alice told him again how nice it was to hear from him and how glad she was that he and Jake would be working together again.

As he put the telephone back in its cradle, Gideon Stone looked at his old friend. "Jesus, Hook, am I that damn predictable?"

Hooker Herman looked at him. "Sometimes," he said with a grin. Then he looked at his watch. "I was listening. If you hustle, you can still catch the nine o'clock shuttle flight up to Miami."

Chapter Two

Day 3: Time 1004LT
Park-Langley Hotel,
Miami

The lobby of the Park-Langley had all the accoutrements of a big hotel without actually being one. Around the perimeter of the lobby there was the predictable string of boutiques, a newsstand, and one of those stand-up, hurry-up bars with a bald-headed bartender. He was a man with a reputation for knowing more scuttlebutt about the Marlins, Dolphins, and Heat than most of the beat writers professed to know.

Gideon found Jake Ruppert at the bar. Despite the hour, the acting director of the agency's covert-activities wing was nursing a martini and looking worried. Their initial exchange consisted mostly of *"how the hell have you been?"* and a barrage of secondary questions that took even less time to play out. Three minutes later Jake hustled them off to a quiet corner of a nearby coffee shop where they could talk.

Jake Ruppert was sixty, looked older, had been Gideon's mentor in the early days, and had been the agency's main CRU man for the past ten years. In more recent months he had been named acting head of the Agency while Chet Harms, the new director appointed by President Weimer, was undergoing the usual round of Senate approvals. Williams, new to the agency, had no way of knowing it, but Jake Ruppert always talked like a man who was "up to his ass in alligators."

"Glad you could make it, Gideon," he started. "It's nice to talk to some whiskers. They've got me surrounded by a bunch of hot young law school grads who couldn't work their way through a maze on Sesame Street."

Without saying so, Gideon concurred. He had heard the same grumblings from some of his old colleagues still slugging it out in the trenches. "From everything I read in the newspapers, it sounds like the Agency has seen better days," he finally said.

Ruppert agreed, and out of habit, looked apprehensively around the crowded room; the alligator syndrome. "Every time I turn around, I see a hole in the damn system, Gideon. It's getting so you can't trust anyone to do their jobs. Everyone seems to have their own agenda."

Gideon cleared his throat. "Why is it I don't think you had me meet you here so that you could complain about your staffing problems, Jake?"

"Obviously, that's not why we're here," Ruppert admitted, "so let me do us both a favor and get straight to the point. Two days ago, a Garuda 747 went down near a small atoll some fifteen miles off the coast of Java. What you probably read in the papers is that a lot of people lost their lives in that crash. What you may or may not know is that we had arranged for political asylum for one of the passengers on board that flight. Supposedly, that man was carrying the full details of how the PRC had funded and equipped Bojoni Sarawak's planned coup against the current government of Lieutenant General Sarni Kujon."

"Wait a minute, last I heard we were opposed to the Kujon government."

Ruppert lit his pipe, took a puff, and laid it down. "I have to admit, Kujon would have a hard time winning a popularity contest in Washington these days. But everyone would have to admit that he's a whole lot better than having Sarawak and his bunch of Bandung thugs in power.

"For the last several months we've been getting reports from our sources in Beijing. The PRC generals have been loading Sarawak up with supplies. Our satellite photos confirm he's been stockpiling weapons and ammunition on the island of Karimunjawa. Bottom line: The Agency's analysts now believe he has enough trained men and arms to pull off a coup any time he wants to. The way we see it, it's no longer a question of if—it's a question of when."

"I still don't see where—"

"Let's cut straight to the chase, Gideon. Chet Harms, even though he hasn't been officially blessed, has started calling the shots, and he has authorized me to hire you to go in there, retrieve that information, and find out what Sarawak has up his sleeve."

Gideon laughed. "Me? Why me? Unless I'm missing something, you still have—"

Jake Ruppert held up his hand and lowered his voice.

"Hold on. You're absolutely right, we still have our Asian monitoring ship; *Bo Jac* is still in the area. Currently it's disguised as a logistical support vessel for Universal Oil's exploration fleet in the area."

"Fine. Then let them retrieve the information."

"Not so fast. True, the horse is sound. We've got the equipment to retrieve what we're looking for, all right, Gideon, but not the jockey. Wormack assures me he's got twenty-seven of the best computer hacks and administrative types aboard that ship that money can buy. Unfortunately, none of them is qualified to take on a mission like this one."

"Then get the damn Navy to do it."

"Can't trust 'em, Gideon. The last thing we need is for some saber-rattling, hotshot admiral to listen to some of Sarawak's rhetoric and decide he's going to take on the bastard. If someone goes charging in there with guns blazing, the whole damn thing could blow up in our face."

Gideon took a sip of coffee. "Read my lips, Jake, *not in-ter-est-ed*."

"You haven't heard the deal."

"It wouldn't make any difference. I'm not interested."

"Then why the hell did you fly up here?"

"Because I owe you that much. Alice told me you had already left for Miami. I couldn't bear the thought of you drinking all by yourself."

Ruppert reached into his coat pocket and laid a slip of paper on the table. There was a number with a dollar sign scrawled in front of it and it was signed by Chet Harms, the man soon to be named Agency Director.

Gideon Stone picked it up, looked at it, and laid it back on the table. There was a twenty-seven-footer in slip seventeen in Powell's marina that the money Ruppert was authorized to pay him could put within the realm of possibility. Gideon shook his head. "Tempting," he admitted, "but no dice."

Jake Ruppert grunted, wadded up the piece of paper, put it back in his pocket, and frowned. "Are you saying there's nothing I can say to get you to change your mind?" Gideon nodded. "That's precisely what I'm saying."

Ruppert picked his attaché case up off the seat and laid it on the table in front of him. "I've been thinking, Gideon, if life is that good down there in Largo, maybe Alice and I ought to rethink our retirement plans." There was both a trace of sarcasm in his voice—and a trace of admiration. Ruppert had intended both.

"Out of curiosity, Jake, how long do you think this little chore is going to take?" Gideon asked. The moment he said it he realized he had just given Jake Ruppert the impetus to push harder.

Jake waited. He was baiting Gideon, and his former number-one troubleshooter knew it. "Our best guess is that it won't take more than three or four days. We know where the plane went down; it's just a matter of going down there and getting what we're after."

"Three or four days, huh? That's all?"

"Four days max," Ruppert repeated. He lit his pipe again to give Gideon time to think.

"Question. What if the bodies have all been recovered by the time you attempt your little recovery operation?"

"Not a chance. Our sources tell us they don't have the resources. On the other hand, if they have, we can kiss the effort off and you'll be money ahead."

Gideon Stone hesitated. He looked at Ruppert and studied the face of the man who had been both a tutor and a friend. Finally he said, "Give me that damn piece of paper. If anything happens to you, I want proof of just exactly how much money is coming to me."

Ruppert grinned.

"You just bought yourself one Gideon Stone for the sum total of four days. Got that? Four days. If we haven't recovered the bodies by then, I'm telling the captain of that damn support ship of yours that I'm on the next helicopter flight out of there. Agreed?"

Ruppert smiled, and handed him the piece of paper and an envelope.

"What's this?" Gideon asked.

"Your airline ticket. You're booked on an American flight. It leaves Miami at noon. Your connecting flight for Kuala Lumpur leaves LAX at 1800. Our man will meet you at the airport and arrange for you to get out to the *Bo Jac*." With that, Ruppert glanced at his watch and started to get up. Then he paused. "The way I calculate it, you've got just enough time to catch your flight."

Gideon Stone looked at the envelope and opened it. There were five new one-hundred-dollar bills paper-clipped to the ticket.

"I figure you'll need a toothbrush and some other goodies," Jake offered.

Gideon Stone shook his head. "Actually, I don't need anything," he admitted. "I packed everything I figured I'd need before I left Largo."

Day 4: Time 0831LT
The Bo Jac, *Java Sea*

It had been exactly thirty-four hours between the time Gideon Stone had lumbered aboard the American Airlines flight in Miami and the time he stepped down from the Kaman SH-2 Seasprite helicopter onto the monsoon-swept helideck of the *Bo Jac*. In that short amount of time he had traveled halfway around the world, and had stopped just long enough to be thoroughly briefed with background information on the downed Garuda flight by the CIA's resident agent in Kuala Lumpur.

He was familiar with the *Bo Jac*. It was the eyes, ears, and nerve center of the CIA's Asian operations. Built by the Swedes, it weighed four thousand tons, was 366 feet long, and had a beam of sixty-seven feet. It was said that the ship was so stable that it was capable of intricate "station-keeping" maneuvers that enabled it to hold its position in a Force 9 gale of forty-one to forty-seven knots.

In addition to keeping tabs on activities throughout Indonesia, it was the Agency's watchdog for most of the eastern portions of China as well. What made the operation of the *Bo Jac* even more remarkable was the fact that it was right there for all the world to see—if anyone had bothered to look. It was cleverly disguised as a commonplace support vessel in Universal Oil's exploration fleet.

The seven-story superstructure contained the fire station, the helideck, wardrooms, forward wheelhouse, and most of the ship's sophisticated electronics. A three-man-capacity DSRRV, the *Indon IV*, a multi-purpose vessel, was housed along with the stores area and decompression chambers aft—along with a twenty-ton crane.

Less than thirty minutes after landing on the monsoon-battered helipad, a tired and irritable Gideon Stone was hustled into a wardroom on the second deck of a spy ship that even the President of the United States had denied existed less than a week earlier.

"Not bad," Gideon drawled. He settled himself at the eight-foot-long conference table and surveyed his surroundings. "I mean, considering the fact that most folks, including the President, don't even know this floating intelligence tub exists."

"We like it," Parker Wormack admitted. There was not a trace of a smile on the face of the man Jake Ruppert had termed one of the best OICs in the business.

Gideon Stone was already forming his own opinion about his host. It was easy; Jake Ruppert's briefing hadn't left anything out. It even included the fact that the *Bo Jac*'s OIC had been short-changed when it came to a sense of humor. Parker Wormack had a clipped moustache, silver hair, wore tiny wire-rimmed glasses and a no-nonsense expression. In describing him, Ruppert had used such terms as dependable, thorough, and knowledgeable. All in all, the cadre of attributes Gideon and the Agency would have wanted in the man who would be calling the shots on the recovery effort.

Now, just a few minutes after shaking hands with Wormack, Gideon had to admit Ruppert had his OIC pegged. He was humorless, military-straight, gaunt, and had made it abundantly clear from the outset that he had little patience with small talk.

"I suppose if the President had a need to know," Wormack said, "someone in the Agency would have informed him." Then, almost as an afterthought, he inquired if Gideon would like coffee. When Gideon nodded, Wormack pressed a small button at the end of the table and a white-coated attendant appeared, served them, and promptly left the room.

"Nice touch," Gideon observed. "Like I said, looks like you people have all the comforts of home out here."

"The man's name is Pang," Wormack said, "recruited from the locals. Maylay by birth, and when required, quite capable of serving as an excellent interpreter. You can report to Mr. Ruppert he is quite worth the money we pay him."

Gideon nodded, busied himself thumbing through some old magazines lying on the table, and waited. Thus far he hadn't been able to make up his mind whether Wormack was one of those people who explained things because he couldn't stand a void in the conversation, or if he was the kind of man who was simply a bit uneasy because he knew why Gideon was there. "I trust your trip was a pleasant one, Colonel Stone," Wormack said. He had a clipped manner of speaking that was consistent with his thin lips and betrayed his British boarding-school background. Somewhere along the line he had developed the nervous habit of twisting the small gold band on the ring finger of his left hand. It occurred to Gideon that nervous habits and tics probably went with the situation. Any man serving an eighteen-month tour on the *Bo Jac,* isolated from his family, was bound to be putting one helluva strain on his psyche as well as his marriage.

"Tolerable," Gideon grunted. "I never did learn to like flying in foul weather."

"Unfortunately, you arrived just as the monsoon season is swinging into high gear, Colonel. For the next several weeks, I'm afraid you will have little to look forward to except a great deal of rain and even more wind. At times, I fear, even the spy business can get rather boring."

"I won't have time to get bored. That's another way of telling you I won't be here that long," Gideon said. "My orders are to get this little chore wrapped up and get out of here."

Wormack arched his eyebrow, and Gideon saw what he decided passed for amusement in the Englishman's expression. "I detect a certain eagerness to get on with why you are here, then. Is that correct?"

"Let me lay it on the line, Parker. Jake Ruppert bought four days of my time—that's all. The way I see it, the moment I put a foot down on that damn helipad of yours, the meter started. Whether we recover this guy's body or not, I have every intention of being long gone the morning of the fifth day."

Wormack looked even more amused. "That may be difficult, Colonel. While it is true that our magnatometer readings and sonar have successfully pinpointed the site of the major portion of the wreckage, there is a great deal of debris to contend with—not to mention the rather unsavory aspect of sorting through, according to the manifest, two hundred and forty-seven bodies."

"Do we know what kind of condition the plane is in?"

Wormack nodded. He appeared to be relieved that the conversation had finally worked its way around to Gideon's mission. "Without actually sending one of our men down to verify the precise condition of the craft, we have accumulated enough data to be reasonably certain that the aircraft exploded and broke up in mid-air. All of this, of course, ties in with what we have heard from observers and recorded on sonar profiles. The wreckage appears to be in three large and wholly separate sections in water depths that vary from one hundred and fifty to more than three hundred feet. The crash site is close to a small island, and the sea floor there slopes away from what you Americans would term a small atoll. All of which could mean that when you take into account tide action and the time since the crash, the wreckage may be spread over a very large area. With all of that in mind, Colonel, I believe you can see why I think four days is a bit optimistic."

Throughout Wormack's assessment Gideon's expression had continued to deteriorate. He hated to admit it, but Wormack was probably right. They would be damn lucky to pull it off in four days. He studied the *Bo Jac*'s OIC and thought about his deal with Ruppert. It didn't take him long to come to the conclusion that Parker Wormack was not the kind of man who would see the humor in a phone call to Ruppert telling him to stick the whole mission up his rectal cavity. "I guess the only question then is, where and when do we start?"

This time Wormack stood up, went to the door of the wardroom, and summoned two people who had obviously been waiting in the corridor. He introduced them as Agents Taylor and Preston. Taylor was the taller of the two, appeared to be older, and was decidedly more athletic-looking than his colleague, a diminutive, auburn-haired woman with snapping green eyes. She instructed Gideon to call her Jessie. Wormack referred to her as Ms. Preston. Gideon had already skimmed the personnel records of both.

The three shook hands and Taylor took a seat across the table from Gideon.

"What limited knowledge any of my people have," Wormack began, "relative to the use and capability of our DSSRV equipment, the *Indon IV,* lies with Agents Taylor and Preston. Having said that, I'll let them take it from here."

Unlike that of his OIC, Morris Taylor's face had been encompassed in a big ingratiating grin since he entered the room. "What Parker means by that," he drawled, "is that I manage to make myself a nuisance. I go down with the *Indon* anytime she's launched—but the Navy has always supplied the pilot. All in all, Colonel, I'd say I'm pretty damned handy when it comes to following instructions. They tell me what button to push and I push it."

Wormack cleared his throat. "Before we get into the

actual operation of the *Indon IV,* I've asked Morris and Ms. Preston to brief you on what we think we've been able to confirm thus far."

Gideon watched the woman get up from the table and go through a methodical routine that consisted mostly of pressing a series of buttons and activating switches. As she did, the lights faded, the drapes in the wardroom closed, a wall display was illuminated, and a detailed schematic of a 747 materialized. "This should give you a quick refresher course, Colonel Stone."

"I keep hearing the word 'colonel.' Let's set the record straight, Ms. Preston. That's Civilian Stone. Lieutenant Colonel Stone is now retired and has been for some time. Good enough?" Gideon was certain that everyone in the room was cognizant of the fact he had put emphasis on the word "retired." But he was equally sure his request fell on deaf ears.

"I'll try to remember that," Preston said with a smile and turned her attention to the schematic. "I thought it best to start by familiarizing everyone with the layout of the aircraft. Note that the forward section includes the flight deck, avionics equipment, crew bunks, and the food storage and food preparation area, along with some first-class seating. The midsection is primarily devoted to passenger seating, luggage storage, and the main cargo area below. The aft section is more of the same along with the plane's auxiliary power units."

The woman paused long enough to play with the switches on the panel at the speaker's rostrum again, and the schematic of the intact aircraft dissolved into a crude sketch of it—but now there was a difference. This one illustrated how the magnatometer and the side-scan sonar trailing from the *Bo Jac* viewed what remained of the Garuda flight.

"The forward section is here," she said, "and the aft section is here." She pointed to the two sections of the aircraft near the atoll. "From here on it's simple geometry; calculating the size and distance of the feedback impulse and the configuration of the target, we have, accurately we believe, concluded that these two sections of the aircraft are almost a mile apart—parallel with each other and in the shallower water of the atoll."

"What about the center section?" Gideon pressed.

"Here," Preston indicated, "roughly five hundred yards west of the cabin section. Water depth here varies from one to four hundred feet. The variation is attributable to a large sandbar and reef that runs parallel with the entrance to the atoll. Our profile charts of the atoll indicate there is a sharp drop-off to somewhere around six hundred feet several hundred yards beyond that point."

"How steep is that drop-off?" Gideon asked.

"Somewhere in the neighborhood of thirty degrees."

"Any chance that some of the passengers may have been carried away into that drop-off by the tide?"

"There is always that chance, Colonel."

Gideon leaned back in his chair and frowned. There was that word again. "Now comes the big question. How the hell are we going to find the body of one individual with parts of two hundred and forty-seven people floating around down there? According to Ruppert, Nagarajan was instructed to book this guy's reservations, hand him his ticket, and let our man in Kuala Lumpur know their seat assignments. When the plane landed in Kuala Lumpur, our man was instructed to intercept him at the airport before he got off the plane."

"That may not be as difficult as you first imagined, Colonel," Preston said. "There are several things you couldn't possibly know. First, I talked to Nagarajan by telephone two nights before he was captured by the Bandung. Even then he was concerned about trying to get the information out of Jakarta without Sarawak knowing it. He said he was convinced Teuwen Ng was playing games with us. By that he meant Ng had given us some of details of the coup—but not all of them. It seems Mr. Ng was reluctant to reveal everything he knew about Sarawak's coup attempt because he didn't trust us. He was convinced that if we already knew everything he knew, we would not help him escape."

Wormack cleared his throat. "What Agent Preston hasn't told you, Colonel, is that we assisted Nagarajan with his efforts to help Mr. Ng get out of Jakarta—and we took a few precautions that even Mr. Nagarajan wasn't aware of."

Gideon leaned forward. "What kind of precautions?"

Jessie Preston turned off the projector and took a seat at the conference table next to Gideon. She was wearing perfume, not too much—just enough.

"In the past, Colonel" Wormack replied, "we have had informants change their mind after we delivered our part of the bargain. We figured that could be the case with Mr. Ng after he had put distance between himself and the Bandung. So we bugged his briefcase."

"And?"

"To be more specific," Wormack said, "we inserted a very small but very dependable transmitter in the lining of his briefcase and instructed him to hand the case over to our man in Kuala Lumpur when he landed. Mr. Ng was led to believe he would not get our full cooperation nor the money if he did not hand over the briefcase. He was told that if he did not have that briefcase handcuffed to his wrist when he landed, our man would not be able to identify him and would not make contact with him. We are reasonably certain that Mr. Ng understood that the briefcase was his ticket out of Jakarta and his escape from the Bandung."

"No briefcase, no contact, no money," Preston added. "Under those circumstances, we feel certain he followed instructions."

"And the transmitter is working?" Gideon asked.

"We released a monitor buoy at the crash site. We were still receiving a reaffirmation of signal less than twenty minutes before I came in here to attend this briefing," she said.

Wormack edged forward in his chair. "Quite obviously, Colonel, both our success and the ease and speed with which we are able to locate Mr. Ng's body will in large part be determined by whether or not the briefcase was handcuffed to Ng when the plane went down. If it was, that transmitter signal could expedite this whole search effort and make it a great deal more rewarding. If it wasn't, all bets are off and your four days on the *Bo Jac* could be an exercise in futility."

Day 4: Time 1431LT
The Bo Jac, *Java Sea*

By two-thirty that afternoon, Gideon Stone had managed to grab a bite to eat and a three-hour nap. He had spiraled into a deep sleep—yet he had been somehow still aware of the strong winds and heavy rains buffeting the *Bo Jac*. Now he was sitting on the edge of his bunk trying to shake off the aftereffects of the last two days. He thought momentarily about the twenty-seven-footer in slip seventeen at Powell's marina and Carrie, the girl who had canceled out on their dinner engagement, before gradually slipping into an awareness of where he was and what he was supposed to be doing. He was still mired in that train of fragmented thoughts when it was derailed by a knock on his cabin door. "It's open," he grumbled.

Jessie Preston pushed the door open and poked her head into the darkened cabin. "Sleep well?" she asked. Unlike Wormack, her reserve came with a personality. She had a ready smile. She stepped into the cabin and perched herself on the corner of a small desk that held a computer and video display. Gideon had already deduced that it wasn't all business on the *Bo Jac*; there was a stack of game cartridges piled beside it. "Preston thought maybe you would like me to show you around before we get started."

Gideon grunted, pulled on his trousers, and fumbled through the few personal items he had purchased before climbing on the plane in Miami. He was looking for a shirt. "From the sound of your accent I'd judge you to be from Great Britain," he said.

"More specifically, London," she said. "I'm surprised you asked. I was told you were the kind who knew everything there was to know about the people on your team."

"Your name is Jessica Penelope Craft Preston. Born in 1962 in Keldy. Graduated in 1982 from Telford with a degree in physics. Married that same year, divorced a year later, and joined M a year after that. You're checked out in three different kinds of choppers and you speak three different languages—one of which is Maylay. More?"

"Apparently the file neglects to mention the fact that I am an excellent cook."

"No file is complete."

Preston waited. It was obvious she was comfortable with their sparring. Finally she asked, "Are you ready?"

"What's the agenda?"

"Wormack thought it would be a good idea if I introduced you to the rest of the crew—then we could head below and I'll give you a run-through on the *Indon*. Wormack has the crew working on the prelaunch. It will take something less than three hours to make ready."

Gideon stood up and followed the woman out of his cabin, through a maze of corridors, and finally down two flights of steps to the main deck. Aft of the superstructure they passed the diving-bell winch, the heave-compensating system for the bell, the actual winches, and the bell itself.

"This whole area is geared to supporting the diving bell and the DSSRV," she said. "The dive area consists of five levels and can accommodate the activity of up to twelve divers. We lower the bell through a hatch in the ship's bottom; the ready area is called the monopool. The bell can work down to fifteen hundred feet."

"If the wreckage is spread over a two-to-three-mile area like your colleague says it is, I'm afraid that diving bell won't be of much use to us—unless, that is, we can isolate the radio signal and lower the bell right over it."

As Jessie walked she listened; her route took them the length of the lower deck down a long corridor past the diesel-electric generators, a fenced area containing the gas-storage bottles for the divers, the twin decompression chambers, and finally the launch area where the *Indon IV* was contained. She shouldered her way through a series of restraining gates into the capture bay, and Gideon saw two technicians look up in surprise.

"Colonel Stone, I want you to meet Zeke Marshal and Buster Kelly. These are the people who make this little jewel tick."

Marshal grinned, wiped his hands on his overalls, and shook Stone's hand. Kelly was less gregarious; he nodded a greeting from the other side of the bay and went back to his work.

Jessie made a sweeping gesture with her right hand. "Well, here she is, Colonel, all forty-eight feet and fifteen lovely tons of her. Meet the *Indon IV, DSSRV 49785*."

Gideon had seen pictures of the *Indon IV* in Ruppert's office. That meant the pride of the *Bo Jac* had to be at least four years old—because it had been that long since Gideon's last trip to Washington. In those days the Navy's *Osprey II* was the state of the art in deep-sea salvage and recovery vehicles—and it was the forerunner of the prestigious *Indon IV*. Even more important, Gideon had cut his teeth on a DSSRV when he piloted the *Osprey* on two separate occasions, both recovery efforts, but both admittedly decidedly smaller in scale than working the wreckage of the Garuda flight.

The *Indon IV* was a multi-capability DSRRV designed to be crewed by two operators. A third station was available to accommodate medical or technical personnel when the mission dictated such a need. Gray-green in color, it was forty-eight feet long and ten-foot-nine athwartship. It weighed a little over fifteen tons. "And," Preston said as she concluded her walk-around, "most of her equipment is the type used aboard the *Arca Dino*; basically it's a large-object salvage system. You'll be working with the latest ICAD system—sonar, closed-circuit television, four cameras, four recorders, and the sweetest navigational devices your government knows how to build, two 4-11's and a magna-chrome 17-180."

If Jessie Preston had been asked, she would have admitted that she was impressed. Gideon Stone seemed to be absorbing everything she was telling him. She was throwing a lot at the man some wag in the Agency had once said was capable of finding anything—even a zit on a supermodel. Even then, Gideon was urging her to get on with it.

"One of your Navy officers who piloted her said it's a whole lot like crawling into the cockpit of an F-16," Jessie added. "Everyone tells me you will love her even more once you get behind the A panel."

"Batteries?" Stone finally asked.

"Four six-packs. You can operate all systems for two hours or at fifty-percent load for four. You have a load calculator on your A panel run by an off-line computer. It will work your reserve out to a tenth of a second."

" And when we find the body?" Gideon was tempted to add, *"If we find the body."*

Jessie leaned back against the wall of the transfer chamber with her arms folded. She slipped out of her role of instructor and paused for a moment. "I've been thinking about that aspect of this mission ever since I heard you were coming aboard to ramrod this project, Colonel."

"And?"

"Best guess?"

"Go ahead."

"I believe we are likely to encounter one of two scenarios. If that transmitter signal leads us right to Ng and it's a clean situation, we can use the bow manipulator arm to bring the body on board. If not, in all probability we are faced with an OVA mission. It will be necessary for one of us to activate the decompression chamber, stand down all the unnecessary equipment to conserve power, maintain position—and when you're ready, you go out there and get Mr. Ng, briefcase and all."

"Me?"

"You are the only one qualified."

Gideon thought for a moment. "That sounds like a scenario that requires three sets of hands."

"If you think we need him, Taylor has logged fourteen hours of mission time. I've observed him—he knows what he's doing. The problem is—everything we've been involved in up until now has been in a support role. Neither Agent Taylor nor I have been checked out to pilot this craft. A rather unsettling thought, don't you think? If anything should happen to you . . . " She let her voice trail off.

"What's our procedural backup if we have to do an OVA?"

"We have a Newtsuit on board and anything else you might need, if that's what you mean."

Gideon nodded and glanced at his watch. "How soon will we be ready?"

Jessie Preston looked at the two technicians. Marshal indicated the prep would take at least another hour. Kelly seemed reluctant to say how long it would take him before he was ready.

"I've still got a valve to replace on the breathing gas source in case you have an OVA," Kelly said.

Gideon returned to his study of the configuration and placement of instruments in the A panel. The A panel was the control deck. From the layout in the A seat he could control almost everything, including the variable beam ballast and trim tanks. The forward thruster, thruster ducts, hydraulic and propulsion controls, all could be controlled by his left hand even though they were on B panel.

Jessie watched him. "Look familiar?" she finally asked.

"An hour should give me just about enough time to get familiar with everything," Gideon admitted.

"Good enough," she replied. "I can use that time to make certain we have all the sector charts we'll need in the computers. The last thing we need is a computer glitch while we're down there. Anything else?"

Gideon pushed himself back from the controls, leaned back in his chair, folded his arms, and shook his head. "All we need now is a strong signal from Ng's transmitter."

Through the *Indon*'s forward A panel observation port, he watched the two technicians continue their prelaunch check. As Marshal and Kelly continued to plod methodically through their routine, he knew he needed a whole lot more than a strong transmitter signal. If the *Indon* was going to find a human needle in a haystack, he needed a helluva lot of luck to go along with it.

Chapter Three

Day 4: Time 1621LT
The Indon

Gideon synchronized his watch with the *Indon*'s chronometer, and corrected for error. Each prelaunch command was preceded by a brief hesitation as he double-checked the sequence. The ready room crew had advised him that the *Indon* was ready. The launch would come on the thirty-minute mark of zero hour when he activated the computers for the projected two-hour mission. If they accomplished nothing else in those first two hours, Gideon figured that the run would get him used to the equipment and the terrain.

He had just crawled into the command chair when the launch crew sealed the hatches. His ears suddenly felt as though they were clogged and he could feel the change in pressure.

Kelly had already stepped back, and Marshal's voice filtered through the com sys into the control cube. "We're opening the sea valves, Colonel. You'll feel the buffeting as the monopool fills. When she's full you'll feel the free drift."

Jessie waited until the last minute before she climbed into the number-two chair. She began punching the latest surface weather conditions into the GL computer. Next to her, Gideon watched the information stream across his number 2 support monitor.

. . . 1630 launch observation—waves eight to ten, horizontal visibility less than a mile, surface winds 37 gusting to 48 . . .

Taylor was standing behind them. "Damn barometer is falling again," he complained. "The boys topside are staring a shitty afternoon in the face."

"Shitty," Gideon repeated with a grin. "Is that one of those words you learn growing up in Big Springs?"

"Pretty good word," Taylor confirmed. "A well-articulated *'shitty'* can cover about everythin' from bad weather to bad food."

Gideon turned back to the panel and asked for verification and confirmation of each of the launch commands. "Dive trim indicator on. Diving planes bow and stern, vertical and in the off position. OP computers up. On the mark, give me a systems check."

Out of the corner of his eye he could see Jessie Preston studying the instruments. "She's all decked out like a gal goin' to her first prom," Taylor confirmed. "Trim and proper."

There was a momentary but pronounced oscillation, more buffeting, and as they watched, the seawater began gushing over the obs ports. "She's all yours, Colonel," Marshal informed him over the ship-to-DSSRV com sys. "Don't forget to bring something home for us, Daddy."

"16:30:11," Gideon recited. "Mark your DT." Then he remembered to add, "Thank you, launch control. All indications are we're watertight and all systems appear to be functioning. We've got a *go green* on both A and B."

Gideon secured the lockdown on Panel A, depressing the A-2, A-7, and A-11 switches, and felt a sudden lurch and then the sensation of buoyancy. He depressed the initial phase button on the computer-generated voice monitor. It was sequencing—dutifully repeating instructions.

> *. . . all systems control configurations logged and engaged . . . dive trim actuator on automatic . . . advise confirming audit of air mixture . . .*

The *Indon* began yawing, and Gideon corrected as Jessie started her scroll through the computer's index of situation displays.

"Give me an update," Gideon barked.

"Fathometer, three zero and descending . . . "

"Punch up the first grid . . . "

Jessie scanned the four monitors, looking for a reading. "We have it, first zone, third reference—on the grid. We're in sync. Let her down."

Directly in front of Gideon and above the A panel was a six-inch-thick carsdan acrylic lens thirty inches long and fifteen inches in height. Beyond it was the tattletale and frothy, gray-on-gray world that revealed that topside the crew of the *Bo Jac* was contending with the havoc caused by the monsoon.

Gideon tweaked the magnification on the center display, then sealed off, retracted, and coiled the trailing AAt snorkel. The cabin lights went red, and he activated the side illuminators. Shadows suddenly became areas of color and movement.

"Reading . . ."

Jessie Preston scanned both instruments. "Corrected to four seven." Then she pointed at the starboard side monitor. "Got something on the video display. Colonel."

Gideon peered into the darkness and brought the *Indon* into a slow and easy 180. Just over a small reef he saw what at first appeared to be only a shadow. As the *Indon* approached, it materialized from vague shadows into a jagged piece of aluminum, and Gideon slowly rotated the CA1-4 over the object to determine the dimensions.

Jessie waited until the readings were confirmed and read the digits aloud. "Four-four-five-seven-seven-three." The indexing computer flashed the image on the number-four monitor and filled in the voids. What only micro seconds earlier had been an unidentifiable and misshapen piece of metal quickly became, according to the computer, a twisted section of aluminum aileron.

Jessie, still straining, saw something beneath it, adjusted the beam of the starboard CA1-4, leaned forward, then recoiled. Taylor leaned over her shoulder. "Oh shit," he groaned, "I was hoping to hell I wouldn't see somethin' like that."

Gideon had seen it as well. For the next several seconds he squeezed his eyes shut as though the gesture might erase the image from his mind. They had discovered the bloated body of a woman. The woman's head and one arm were missing.

* * *

At 17:30:03 the EMT indicators on both of the *Indon*'s A and B control panels recorded the sixtieth minute of mission time. At that same moment, the DSSRV moved cautiously from the B into the C sector and hovered over grids C-6i and C-6k where the crew of the *Bo Jac* had indicated the transmitter signal had been the strongest on the surface.

"Looking at the bottom grid," Jessie said, "it would appear that between C-6i-e and C-6k-e, we have a significant downslope, Colonel—indications are it could be as much as a 60-or-65-degree drop off. If that's the case, we might find what we're looking for in the bottom near the base below the slope."

Jessie scanned the lagoon bottom directly ahead of them and watched it drop away before disappearing into an expanse of darkness. Gideon throttled back, inched the DSSRV over the edge of the drop-off, and dropped the nose of the *Indon* into an easy, unpowered glide downward.

"Declivity?" Gideon barked. The digital readout on the A panel had gone into a free fall.

"Sixty—that's six zero degrees," Jessie replied.

"Fathometer?"

"One hundred and sixty––now sixty-five—now seventy—now settling . . . "

Gideon glanced over at his copilot in the *Indon*'s second seat. There was a thin, decidedly green sheen of sweat on her forehead. The illusion had been created by the panel lights reflecting off beads of perspiration. "How's your stomach holding out?" he asked.

Jessie Preston nodded. "You haven't lost me yet, Colonel. At least not completely." She was making a fight of it. So far her stomach was still holding up—but the outcome was still in doubt. The decapitated body under the aileron had triggered the first wave of nausea. The second had hit her when they uncovered the center section where most of the passengers were seated; they had come upon an area where Sarawak's carnage defied description. All Jessie could do at that point was keep her eyes fixed on the instruments and refuse to look out at the tangle of ballooned bodies, most of whom were still strapped in their seats.

As Gideon watched, the *Indon* was gliding over the section of the fuselage aft of that portion of the cabin located earlier. "How's our signal?"

"Steady and strong, Colonel. This could be it." Jessie was forcing herself to look up and out through the viewing port above the B panel. Gideon was slowly rotating the craft's forward illuminator over another scene of wholesale slaughter directly beneath them. The view through both ports was a tortured tangle of twisted metal and debris. There were suitcases, articles of clothing, books, someone's personal computer, a doll, a toy truck, a woman's purse, and hundreds of other personal items strewn about the area. Some of the objects were half buried in the sand; others looked as though they had been neatly arranged for anyone wishing to peruse the area and take inventory.

Finally, and Jessie saw it before she could avoid seeing it, there was the body of a small child. It undulated in the turbulence created by the *Indon*'s shrouded aft prop. She was unable to determine if the child was a little boy or a little girl—the fish had already done a number on the body. Most of the soft tissue had already been eaten away.

Jessie Preston swallowed hard, forcing the acid taste of the bile back down her throat. "I'm putting the coordinates into the computer, Colonel. When you took that little excursion around the center section, the signal became slightly weaker. It dropped all the way off to a 7.04. Right now I'm getting a steady 7.53. We might be showing the effects of power usage."

Gideon hovered the *Indon* over that portion of the cabin where the giant 747's wing connected to the fuselage. It had been ripped open just forward of the third cargo area and behind the wheel housing. "Make your mark," he said, "then we're out of here."

Jessie looked at him. "But we've got the transmitter located—"

Gideon pointed at the ET readout. "Our friend Mr. Ng will have to wait. We're running out of juice. We've got less than twenty minutes to make it back to the *Bo Jac*."

Day 4: Time 2041LT
The Bo Jac

The *Bo Jac*'s recovery of *Indon IV* had come off without a hitch. Now, about two hours after returning to the ship, Gideon, Jessie, and Moe Taylor were briefing Wormack on the results of their first dive. Taylor was sketching the layout of the debris-littered bottom where the signal in Ng's briefcase had been the strongest.

"The location is here," Taylor said, "right smack dab on this grid line between C-6l-e and C-6k-e. At that point, the signal strength maxed out at 7.53 pulses . . . "

Wormack stared across the table at Jessie Preston. She was frowning. "All right, Jessie, you're our expert, how do you read that?"

One of only four women aboard the *Bo Jac,* Jessie Preston shrugged and focused on Taylor's drawing. "Actually, Parker, it could mean any one of a number of things. It could be that the integrity of the transmitting device has been somehow compromised—like a crack in the casing—or running low on power—or maybe it's buried in the mud and sand. It's been down there less than a week—which tells me that if it was out in the open and if the casing was still intact we should be getting a stronger signal."

"Let's assume the worst," Wormack said. "Let's assume that the transmitter is losing power; how long do we have?"

"If it's 7.53 now and not buried, that would indicate that it is deteriorating rapidly," Jessie informed him. "It should be reading somewhere in the neighborhood of 9.5 to 10.0. Which is another way of saying it won't last more than two or three more days."

Wormack looked at Gideon. "The next question is equally critical. Now that you've located the signal and had a chance to view the area, do you think you can get to the briefcase?"

Gideon hesitated, and Taylor began sketching again. "It depends," Gideon said. "We've got a rather large section of one of the wings here and one of the turbo-jet engines here—not more than ten to fifteen feet from it. The engine is half buried in the muck, but even with the agitation in the water, we could see the exhaust nozzle, the cone, and the shroud. We figure the rest of it was probably swallowed up when she plowed in."

"What else?" Wormack pressed.

"Pretty much what you'd expect," Gideon said. "A garbage dump. Flotation devices, passenger seats, luggage—but curiously enough, no bodies in that particular area."

Wormack leaned back in his chair with his arms folded. "From here on out it's your show, Colonel," he said. "You tell me what you need and I'll see if I can round it up."

Gideon stood up and moved around the table. "With three pairs of hands I think we've got everything we need. We need someone on each of the control panels if we do an OVA. Right now it looks like we'll have to do a little grunt work outside the capsule."

"Can you do the OVA?" Wormack asked.

Gideon nodded. "That's probably why Ruppert hired me. "I've got a sneaking suspicion he anticipated as much."

"On the other hand, I've been told those extendable manipulators can move mountains," Wormack said. "Are you certain an OVA is necessary?"

Gideon Stone unrolled the grid chart. "Maybe they can, but here's what we're fighting. The engine and the wing section Taylor sketched are on a fifty-eight-degree downslope. At fifty-eight degrees, the slightest bit of turbulence could cause that debris to shift at any minute. From a salvage and recovery standpoint, that whole area looks like an accident waiting to happen. Not only that, we've got a bottom current that's working against us—at times we had an LI reading of 2.5 knots."

Wormack looked around the table. "All right. You three are the closest thing we have to experts. Anyone have any ideas?"

Gideon grunted. "Several, but there's no guarantee any of them will work. If Morris can work the manipulators and we can move some of the larger sections of debris around, I can crawl outside the capsule, and poke around."

"Sounds risky," Wormack ventured. "What if something happens to you? How does Jessie get the *Indon* back to the ship?"

"Glad to hear you're so damned concerned about my welfare," Gideon grunted.

"You, Colonel, are the mercenary. I feel certain you anticipated certain risks when you accepted this assignment. My concern is for my people and the equipment."

"I believe I know which buttons to push to get her back to the surface," Jessie interjected. "From there Marshal and Kelly can talk me back to the ship."

The expression on Wormack's face manifested his skepticism. "What else do you need beside an extra pair of hands, Colonel?"

Gideon Stone pointed to the layout of the *Indon.* "We need something more than the two hours of max-up mission time those batteries give us."

Wormack shook his head and looked at Preston and Taylor. "Can that be done?"

Jessie hesitated. "I—I think it can," she speculated. "Gideon and I talked about it. First, assuming we can shift that debris around, locate Ng and his briefcase, and get him aboard, we will have done so without appreciably adding to the gross weight. Second, we can strip out some of the equipment we won't be needing and further reduce the GVW. Lastly, we can run on half power until we get to the probe site and return to half power after we make the recovery."

"What does that buy you in time?"

"We think we can accomplish that by wiring in two extra standby batteries," Gideon added. "Those two batteries should buy us an extra hour—if we need it."

"As for space, Parker"—Taylor edged forward in his chair and began sketching again—"we stack 'em against the compression wall between the cockpit area and the dive chamber. I'll run the cables into the CPU. We'll use them only if we need them."

"Think it'll work?" Wormack asked. He directed his question at Gideon.

"If I didn't think it would work I wouldn't go along with it."

"How about you, Jessie?"

"I've been down in that contraption dozens of times, Parker. If something happens to Colonel Stone, I think I know what needs to be done."

Gideon looked across the table at her. "Thinking and knowing are two different things, Ms. Preston. I don't intend to be crawling around out there on the bottom of that junkyard with someone at the controls who *thinks* they know what to do next."

Jessie Preston forced a smile. "And I, Colonel, wouldn't have offered if I wasn't one hundred percent convinced I knew what I was doing."

Wormack closed his folder and looked at his watch. "The next question has to be *when*?"

"Kelly and Marshal say they can have the *Indon* ready to go back down by 2200," Gideon said. "We'll be ready."

Day 4: Time 2114LT
The Kjody Hoptem

It was a small second-floor room with stained plywood walls, a single hinged window held shut by a bent wire coat hanger, and an aged ceiling fan that only served to agitate the dank and humid air in the room. The cot, with its frayed, once-white muslin sheets, sagged under the weight of the man who had been trying for more than an hour to sleep.

The solace for Bojoni Sarawak was the fact that the wait would soon be over. The years of planning were behind him—the day of implementation had finally arrived. Everything was ready. In a matter of hours he would set into action the plan that would fulfill his destiny—he would become the principal figure in a drama that would hold the world beyond Java in rapt wariness.

Still, he was apprehensive. Beyond the thin walls of the decrepit old hotel, the night rains hammered down, making the stagnant air in his room even more unbearable, and the winds continued to rape the old wooden structure with unrelenting hostility.

Across the room, in the darkness, the girl now slept, entangled in an array of makeshift bedding on the straw mattress she had brought with her. As a concession to the heat, she wore no clothing, and in the occasional light that crept into the room from passing cars, Sarawak could see her lean, hard, and still-youthful body.

What was her name? How old was she? Where did she come form? He would have asked, but the truth of the matter was it did not matter. Most of them were sent by their fathers, by their brothers, even by their husbands—all trying desperately to win favor with the man who would soon be the new president.

In the darkness he permitted himself a small smile. They were all fools. None of these things mattered. The only thing that mattered now was the hour and the day—and the fact that soon it would be done.

There were lights again in the narrow street under the window, and he could see the girl and the pan of tepid water along with the sponge she had used to try to cool what she termed his fever. Sarawak repeated the word fever and laughed aloud. It was a muted, throaty sound, and he wondered if the girl had ever heard the word malaria. Even if she had, would she have understood if he had described the parasites that frequently ravaged his blood and made him weak with chills and fever? He doubted it.

Bojoni Sarawak's thoughts slowly made the transition

again from the young woman who slept across the room to the events that were about to unfold. Mentally he was rehearsing his first radio broadcast. There would be no television for that—a simple radio message would do, short on theatrics, long on impact. Of such things he was a master.

He had just started to roll over on the narrow cot to seek sleep again when he heard a knock on the door. He reached down to the floor, cradled the .45 in his hand, slipped his finger past the trigger guard, and inched it forward until it coiled around the trigger. The voice at the door called his name.

"General Sarawak, it is time."

Sarawak swung his feet over the edge of the cot, laid the automatic down, and pulled on his shirt before he stood up. For the most part the attack had passed; the quinine had helped. He walked across the room and nudged the woman with his toe. "We are leaving," he said. "You must go."

The woman was startled, and she sat up. "No, I will go with you," she said. Her voice was small and fragile.

"No, go," Sarawak said. "Tell your husband—"

"I have no husband. I am alone."

Sarawak doubted her, but he knelt down and touched her face. "You were not sent here by someone?"

The woman shook her head. "I was told you were here," she said. "I came because I believe in what you are doing."

"And what is it you think I am doing, little one?"

"I come from a small village near Cipanos. There they say you are preparing to rid us of the oppression of the aging Sarni Kujon."

Sarawak's fingers paused in their caressing, lingering on the softness of the young woman's throat. Despite the heat and the closeness in the room, she was trembling. "How did you get in?" he asked.

Her voice became perceptibly stronger when he touched her. "I told the men in the alley that you had sent for me—just as you had sent for others before."

"Do you remember the names of the men that let you in?"

The woman shook her head. "I do not know, General. They wore the uniform of the revolutionary militia."

Sarawak sighed, stood up, walked back across the room, and put on his trousers. Then he sat down to pull on his boots. When he was finished, he picked up the automatic, stuffed it in his belt, and started toward the door. "You would be wise to go now," he said, "while you have the opportunity."

"No. I will follow you, General," she said, scurrying to her feet.

Sarawak did not wait. He opened the door, stepped out into the dimly lit hall, and descended the stairs to the alley. Assasio Muta, the one who had awakened him, was waiting, huddled back in the doorway of the service entrance out of the rain. Less than twenty feet from where they stood, the truck was waiting. The lights were on and the motor was running.

"The hour, it has finally come, eh, General? We have waited a long time for this day." Muta's voice was coarse and edgy.

Sarawak nodded. "Who was on duty when you arrived?"

"Sodong and Chan," Muta said.

"Dispose of them," Sarawak said. "They cannot be trusted."

"But they have been loyal," Muta protested. "They have been with us since—"

"They are stupid and careless," Sarawak growled. "There is no place for stupidity, carelessness, and insubordination in the new, revitalized People's Republic of Java. Dispose of them."

Muta offered no further objections. He started down the alley toward the spot where the two men had been standing guard. Like him, they too had sought refuge from the rain; they were huddled in a doorway behind a small restaurant next to the Kjody Hoptem. When Muta looked back, he saw Sarawak walking toward the truck. Then he saw a woman hurrying through the shadows to catch up with him.

As General Bojoni Sarawak crawled into the cab of the truck, he heard two shots. Muta had followed his instructions.

Day 4: Time 2247LT
The Indon

Morris Taylor had been staring at the red indicator light, assessing both the strength and location of the transmitter signal. For the last several minutes he had been frowning. Finally he admitted what Gideon had feared: The signal was deteriorating. "Damn it, it's getting weaker, Colonel—and according to the GI we're right on target."

Gideon glanced up at the grid indicator. The screen was evenly divided: C-61-e and C-6k-e. "How weak?"

"Pulse 5.0, no, make that a 4.9."

Gideon looked back at Jessie Preston, standing in the doorway between the control pod and the chamber. She was shaking her head. "How long do we have?" he asked her.

"The casing must have cracked open—and if that's the case, we don't have long. The pulse has deteriorated from

7.53 to 4.9 in less than six hours. The weaker it gets, the faster it will erode."

Gideon pushed himself away from the A panel, stood up, and instructed Jessie to take his seat. "She's all yours. I think I'll take a walk in the park out there and see what's under the damn pile of junk. We're getting a steady downdrift from the lagoon. Last check at MT0037 we had an NW current, 334 at a steady 1.7 k. It shouldn't be a problem but you'll have to watch it closely."

Jessie moved in and took over the controls while Gideon activated both forward illuminators and flooded the target area with a ghostly white light. The green-gray world outside the *Indon* evolved out of the darkness, and they were confronted with a world of spooked gracher fish with iridescent silver stripes down their sides. Beyond them was a forest of tangled seaweed, and a trashed landscape cluttered with broken and fragmented parts of the Garuda airliner.

The lights in the cabin dimmed as he flipped the on switch and activated the two power-draining extensible manipulators. The crablike claws opened and seemed to take on a life of their own.

At the same time Gideon began barking out commands. "All right, Ms. Preston, this is where you earn your keep. Cut the power to everything we won't be needing—save all the energy you can. I want the nose camera up and running—get a picture of everything those manipulators churn up, and make damn certain we're getting everything on video. I'm going to attempt to get that wing section out of the way so we can see what's under it."

"Cameras on, Colonel," the woman confirmed, "video on—recorders on—we're transmitting back to the *Bo Jac* and TC indicates they are recording as well."

Gideon waited while Taylor maneuvered the *Indon* into position and settled on the bottom with the manipulators pointing downslope toward the wing section. As he did, the side thrusters kicked up a soupy storm of silt and seaweed, instantly reducing the visibility forward of the viewing area to a murky zero.

"Give her a second to settle," Gideon ordered, "and give me the readings."

Taylor, still monitoring the B panel, squinted through the port into the darkness. With the personnel lights off in the control pod, both panels were bathed in a spectral red-and-green glow. He adjusted the mike, leaned forward, and began reciting. "Pitch and trim control—on automatic. Acoustic transmission—up. Photo cameras—up. Video—on and recording. All telemanipulation systems—functioning. MT—we're one hour and thirty-seven minutes into it. According to the computer, Colonel, with those spare batteries we've got 127.5 minutes until we should be initiating docking procedure—that's one-two-seven-point five and mark."

Gideon hit the PTT. "You getting all this, Parker?"

Wormack's voice boomed into the control area from the *Bo Jac* overhead. "Loud and clear—the audio quality is excellent . . . but we're picking up some thermocline distortion on your video transmission."

"Keep your eyes peeled," Gideon said. "We're going to see if we can flip that wing section over and see what's under it." He looked at Preston. "Did you pick up Wormack's comment about video signal erosion?"

"At the moment I'm more concerned about Ng's transmitter," she said. "We're losing the signal fast—it's down to 4.1."

Gideon shoved the starboard manipulator arm down and forward, wedging it under a section of the broken wing. The claw head burrowed through the muck until it was buried. "Okay, sweetie," he grunted, "let's see what the old girl was hiding under there." He pushed the extensible arm into the full up position—and pulled back. The wing section lifted, teetered on its edge momentarily—then dropped back into place. The silt and debris swirled again. Jessie Preston heard him mutter.

Gideon retracted the starboard arm, flipped the synchro switch, and locked both extensible into the full automatic mode. Taylor leaned forward again as the silt began to settle. "You know, Colonel," he said, "it occurs to me that the boys at Lockheed never dreamed we'd be using these fancy multi-million-dollar manipulators of theirs to pry a damned chunk of a 747 wing section out of the mud."

"All we have to do is get it started," Gideon grunted. He pushed the arms forward again. This time they were operating in tandem—eight feet apart—digging into the bottom under the wing section. They could hear the extensible arms straining.

"Check your gauges on the servomechanisms, Colonel," Jessie called out. "The starboard extensible is already off the dial. If you keep pushing, it'll burn out."

Gideon continued to press down. "Nudge the damn thing," he ordered.

Jessie hesitated. "You mean . . . ?"

"I said nudge it, dammit. Cozy the nose shield right up against the wing section and start pushing."

"But what if . . . ?" The words choked back in her throat as Jessie responded to Gideon's command. He activated the rear thruster and brought the shrouded prop up to "ahead-slow."

The wing section lifted, hung precariously for several moments on the manipulator claws, teetered—and finally toppled on over. When it did, it slipped down on the slope below the area on the grid where Ng's transmitter signal had been strongest.

Taylor let out a whoop and leaned forward, pressing his forehead against the largest of the three obs pod ports. The sledding section of the plane's wing had stirred up the silt again, momentarily obscuring the *Indon*'s viewing area with a swirling cloud of sandy residue. When the sand began to settle and the scene finally cleared enough to begin filming again, it took another several moments for him to decide what he was looking at. By the time he did, it was too late. His stomach had already revolted and spiraled into a slow roll. For several moments there was that awful interval when he wasn't at all certain he would be able to control what happened next. "Holy shi—" he started to say—but before the word could get past the bile taste in his mouth, his throat had constricted and his brain had gone into the denial mode.

Gideon and the Preston woman saw it at the same time. Jessie Preston closed her eyes, somehow managed to muffle her scream, and turned away; Gideon was tempted to do the same. Instead, he stared at the tangle of carnage until the images began to crystalize.

A chunk of the downslope's bottom had been gouged out—probably, he figured, by the impact of the nearby housing of one of the turbo engines. Entangled in the shards of metal was a seat platform with four seats ripped out of the plane's passenger section. The passengers, or what was left of them, were still strapped in their seats.

Gideon swallowed hard and slowly routed the beam of the forward obs halogen back and forth over the scene. When he finally managed to get the words out, he realized they sounded stilted and mechanical.

"All right, let's get busy. Remember, we're not here to do a damn body count or worry about things we can't do anything about. We're here to recover Ng's briefcase. That's what this little exercise is all about. Start by giving me readings. Are we still picking up Ng's signal?"

"We're locked on," Jessie said. "Steady like a heartbeat at 4.1—but very weak." She grabbed the printout and scanned it. "No erosion in signal strength for at least the last seven minutes."

"When do we lose it altogether?" Gideon asked.

"At 3.0 we won't be able to detect it unless we're sitting on top of it."

Taylor had managed to regain a modicum of control over his stomach, but Jessie could hear him struggling for air. "Suppose one of those poor slobs is Ng?" he finally asked.

Gideon grunted and began again methodically playing the obs light over each of the victims. The reef fish had been busy. The lips, eyes, and most of the soft-tissue facial features had been eaten away on two of the passengers. In one case the fish had managed to completely destroy the person's identity. Next to him, the passenger's chest cavity had been ripped open and hollowed out. There was a mocking, sightless, empty-socketed expression of disinterest at the untimely intrusion by the crew of the *Indon*.

"What now, Colonel?" Jessie Preston pressed. "That transmitter is out there—I'm still getting a 4.1 pulse. . . . "

"Can we get any closer?" Gideon wanted to know. "Can we isolate it any further?"

Jessie shook her head. "I think we're getting all we're going to get."

Wormack's voice boomed in on the obs pod speaker over the A panel. "What the hell is going on down there?

We still aren't getting any video and the audio is breaking up every ten seconds or so."

Gideon had been hoping to avoid the inevitable. "In a perfect world, Parker, that damn briefcase of Ng's would have been lying out there in the mud and all we would have had to do was scoop it up with the manipulators."

"In a perfect world, Colonel," Jessie reminded him, "we wouldn't even be here because there wouldn't have been an airplane down here in the first place."

Gideon looked at her and then Taylor. "What's our elapsed MT?"

"Less than seventy minutes to go," Taylor said, " . . . 69.31. That's six-nine-three-one and mark."

Gideon Stone headed for the dive chamber. "You kids amuse yourself, I'm going out there to dig around. If your little tracking gizmo is working, Ms. Preston, and we're sitting right on top of that transmitter, then I damn sure ought to be able to find it."

"I'm going with you," Jessie said. "Four hands are better than two."

"You stay here and mind the store," Gideon ordered.

Day 4: Time 2311LT
Mandarin-Plaza Hotel

Bojoni Sarawak glanced at his watch as the truck rounded the corner onto the deserted Jl Thamrin and headed for the Welcome Statue. They passed a Hard Rock Cafe and a Kentucky Fried Chicken before moving into the heart of the hotel district. The lights were off in both. From time to time Sarawak saw evidence that Ketan Sabo had stationed Bandung militia men at strategic locations along the way. Sarawak was pleased; the entire event was unfolding just as he had envisioned it.

The truck, along with two staff cars, pulled into the courtyard of the Mandarin-Plaza and Sarawak stepped out. He instructed the woman to wait until he sent for her. Muta hurried from the second of the two cars and joined him. Even though the rain's intensity had momentarily subsided, the gusting winds whipped what rain there was into an irritating frenzy.

The portico of the Mandarin-Plaza was already lined with Bandung militia men when Sarawak marched up the stairs into the hotel's ornate lobby. The furniture and appointments were in disarray and the hotel's night staff had been rounded up and herded into a small alcove. Bandung militia men were guarding them with a ragtag assortment of weapons.

"Report," Sarawak ordered.

Captain Ketan Sabo motioned for a young man among the handful of guards to step forward. Like Sarawak and Sabo, the youth was dressed in the Chinese-supplied standard Bandung uniform of two-piece field camouflage. He wore a holstered Che Pan .45-caliber automatic on his hip, and carried his automatic rifle by the charge handle. His salute was clumsy. Sabo repeated the order. "Report, Lieutenant Boh."

Boh, Sarawak decided, could have been no more than twenty years of age. Like so many of the Bandung regulars, most of whom were recruited from the small villages at the western end of the island, it was obvious Boh relished even his limited authority. His manner mirrored his admiration for Sarawak, and at the same time revealed a certain swagger that came from being entrusted with the role of leadership.

Boh's voice cracked and he chose his words carefully. "The members of the delegation have all been rounded up and confined to their rooms," he said. "I have taken the precaution of placing guards outside each room. All seven floors as well as each entrance have been secured."

"And the hotel's staff?" Sarawak questioned.

Boh nodded in the direction of the group of nervous people milling about in a crowded alcove adjacent to the hotel's lobby. "We have accounted for everyone except one night cook," Boh admitted.

"What about the American Vice President?" Sarawak continued.

"As you ordered, General, he and one of the other hostages are being detained in the dining room. The American has been most uncooperative. The delegate from Great Britain is with him."

Sarawak smiled. "Excellent, Lieutenant Boh, excellent." Sarawak surveyed the entrance to the hotel's dining room. "And now, Comrade Captain Sabo, let us savor the moment. Perhaps we should go into the dining room and hear what the American Vice President thinks of his mission now."

Sabo followed the rebel leader into the spacious dining room. Like his general, he was keenly aware of the moment.

Day 4: Time 2315LT
The Indon

Gideon opened the sea valve and stepped to the side of the chamber as the water began gushing in. He was going through his predive checklist for the second time and Jessie Preston's voice was filtering into his headset through the PEA.

"Give me a signal when you're ready, Colonel."

Gideon held out his hand with the thumb inverted. "Now's as good a time as any," he said. As he did, the platform beneath him began to lower him from the dive pod and the woman saw him give the OK sign.

"All systems functioning," he assured her. Then there was silence.

To Jessie Preston it seemed like an eternity before she saw Gideon swim out of the shadows of the DC and around to where he could be seen from the obs ports at the front of the *Indon*. Even then he was still more than thirty feet from the passenger platform where the signal was the strongest.

Suddenly the words "Can you hear me?" crackled through the UW com.

"Affirmative, Colonel, loud and clear. We can hear you and we now have visual. The signal coordinates are directly ahead of you." As she said it, she caught a hurried look at Taylor. Tiny beads of sweat were again reflecting the array of panel lights in front of him.

"Damn silt is making it hard to see," Gideon complained. "If my compass is working, that passenger platform should be just ahead—correct?" He shoved the beam of his handheld halogen ahead of him and activated the helmet illuminator.

The crew in the *Indon* watched as Gideon threaded his way through a jungle of seaweed and finally past an outcropping that they speculated was either lava rock or reef. As they watched, Taylor continued to play the forward obs halogen back and forth like a searchlight. "It should be right in front of you, Colonel," Jessie said.

Gideon emerged from the snarl of spiralweed, checked his depth gauge, adjusted his buoyancy belt, and moved into the impact area. The small receiver on his wrist was emitting an intermittent pulse. "Check your reading, I'm losing my signal."

"If that casing has been compromised, we're out of luck. Our only hope is you find it before it goes dead," she warned him. In the background Gideon could hear Wormack's voice booming into the *Indon*'s obs pod.

Directly ahead of him he could see the seat platform where it had torn loose from the decking in the 747's interior. Like many of the others, the bodies of the four passengers were still strapped in their seats. What made it even worse was that he realized there were some 240 others floating around in the same area—and any minute he could literally stumble over another one.

As Gideon moved in close enough to touch the bodies of the four passengers, he could feel his own stomach do a slow pirouette. Through it all, Jessie was keeping up a steady stream of chatter. He was grateful—in her own strange way, Jessie Preston was providing his only thread of connection with the world of the living. "How bad is it?" she asked.

Gideon knew he didn't have the stomach or the words to describe what he was seeing. Still, he tried. "Everything is pretty well butchered up. From the looks of things—these might have been the seats right behind the galley. At first pass, I'd guess I've got three men—and a woman—at least I think it's a woman. . . . " His words were starting to become jumbled, almost unintelligible. Jessie could hear him trying to regain control of his breathing. "Lots of hair—some jewelry—here's something that looks like it could have been a necklace. . . . "

"Keep your focus, Colonel—we're looking for a man with a briefcase and a security chain."

Gideon grunted. "Not so far—wait, I do see something—it's buried in the mud." He knelt down in the wreckage and clawed his way past a remnant of the luggage rack and a three-foot segment of the honeycomb material beneath the skin of the fuselage. He pulled the object out of the mud and she heard him mutter again.

"What is it?"

"False alarm—it's the damn door off one of the microwave ovens." He dropped the piece of glass back into the muck and looked back at the capsule. "How are we doing on MT?"

Jessie Preston glanced up and ran a quick check on the gauges. "We're in good shape, Colonel—lots of time." She wondered if he could detect the element of concern in her voice. Ng's transmitter signal was growing weaker by the second.

Suddenly Jessie heard what sounded like a loud peel of thunder; the *Indon* began to vibrate and she felt a series of tremors. The cameras caught Gideon as he was suddenly enveloped in a swirling cloud of bottom debris and torqued backward before slamming him into the cowling of one of the Garuda flight's engines.

Jessie felt the seat go out from under her, pitching her backward into the center console. The *Indon* spiraled up on its nose, pitched backward, and yawed out of control. At the same time she saw Taylor topple sideways out of the B panel command chair and slide along the floor until his head slammed against the bulkhead. She heard him moan, saw the blood begin to spew from a gash in his forehead and begin to pool under his head.

The capsule settled momentarily, then began shuddering again. The second tremor lasted less than five seconds. It was less violent then the first. As she scrambled to her feet, there was a series of flash fires in the obs pod and the acrid smell of burning wiring. Both control panels were smoking. The warning light above the B panel was flashing, and she could smell the stench of burning plastic and insulation.

Still dazed, she heard Wormack's voice booming through the obs pod speakers. "*Indon,* do you read me? *Indon,* this is *Bo Jac*. Do you read me?"

Jessie clawed her way back to the console and the radio. "Parker, it's Jessie. We just took a hit of some kind. It must have been swarm quakes. We've got damage—can't tell how much—there's smoke in the obs pod. Taylor is hurt. . . . "

"How bad?"

"I can't tell, I think he's unconscious and he's bleeding. . . . "

"Where the hell is Gideon?"

"He's OV. The last we saw him he was digging around in the wreckage."

"Can you see him?"

"Not yet. I heard the rumble, felt the ground shake, looked out the obs port, and saw a wall of muck and sand start sliding down the slope. Gideon was trying to get out of the way."

Chapter Four

Day 4: Time 2341
The Indon

Gideon Stone knew he hadn't lost consciousness, but he had lost time and he was both dazed and disoriented. The cloud of silt that surrounded him was starting to diminish, and the only thing he had to contend with now was the still-swirling murky water. His vision was still obscured, and as he had been taught when he learned to dive, he began to count. He had already been through the initial period of panic and he had air—that much was certain—the mouthpiece hadn't been dislodged. But he had lost his handheld halogen, his helmet illuminator had been knocked out, and for the moment at least, he was operating in total darkness.

The turbid water continued to create an almost opaque barrier to visibility in every direction. He knew the procedure—and despite the fact that he had already conducted one 360-degree revolution, there was still no sign of the lights from the *Indon*.

He began lecturing himself. All right, Stone, keep your head—check your equipment—keep counting—wait for the water to clear—and regulate your breathing. He began mentally going through the check list; start with the demand valve—make sure it's working—you don't know where you are—you don't know whether or not that wall of whatever it was carried you downslope into deeper water or what. Find out how much air you've got. He felt his heart skip a beat when he realized that the pressure gauge measuring the air in the cylinder was broken.

He was still trying to get his thinking oriented when he heard the word "Colonel" filter into his headset. The second time he heard it, it was even clearer.

"Colonel, do you read me?"

His mike was dead. Gideon pressed the response button on his transmitter twice in rapid succession. Their prearranged signal in the event voice transmission failed called for two depressions if his response was affirmative and one for a negative.

Voice communication was all one-way now—and it was in the hands of Jessie Preston. She had to talk him back—she had to ask the right questions. She had made contact; that was the first step. It was her show now. Gideon was banking on the fact that she was as calm under fire as Wormack and that damn personnel dossier had indicated.

Her first attempt was right on target. "Are you all right?"

Gideon responded.

"From where you are, can you see the lights of the *Indon*?"

In the capsule, the light on the com set panel blinked once, and Gideon could hear the woman suck in her breath. "Do you have any idea how far or where you are in relation to the impact area?"

Gideon pressed the transmit button once, and heard Wormack's voice boom in the obs pod speakers. "Jessie, tell Gideon you're going to turn on every damn light you can get your hands on: your forward obs lights, the sweep, even the shroud lights—then start banging on the hull. It's a long shot, but if he can't see the lights, the audio sensors on his pinger may be able to pick up the direction the sound is coming from."

The next voice he heard was Jessie's. "Did you get any of that, Colonel?"

Gideon pressed the response button twice and initiated the slow and methodical 360-degree maneuver for the second time. He was operating on a combination of instinct and logic. There was still no sign of the *Indon*'s lights, and to make matters worse, as he made his turn, he realized the wall of water that had swept him down the slope had deposited him in a forest of thick, head-high sea grass and zonalweed. There was a kind of iridescence to the water, and he began to understand it was not just a case of waiting for the silt to settle—the same series of tremors had also stirred up tons of microscopic phytoplankton. Until that settled, there was no way he would be able to see the lights of the *Indon*—and the reverse was equally true—there was no way the *Indon* could see him. Even worse, until he knew which direction he had to go, there was a good chance that if he moved at all he might be getting himself into even more trouble.

Jessie's voice sifted through again. "Do you see the lights, Colonel?"

Gideon's response was another negative. But even as he responded he could hear the dialogue between Wormack and Preston. The woman was describing Taylor's condition and the fact that several of the internal systems aboard the *Indon* had been knocked out by the swarm quakes. He heard Wormack ask if she believed the craft was operational. There was no answer. Finally, the unnerving silence ended when Jessie Preston's voice came through again.

"Still with me, Colonel? If you are, I've got an idea. It's a long shot, but it might work. Look in your rescue pack. There should be a couple of FC-71 underwater incendiary flares in the panpack. If you have them, give me a signal—same code, two for yes, one for no."

Gideon rummaged through the cylindrical aluminum rescue container strapped to his leg until he located the brace of phosphor fatotic flares. Jessie was right; two of them had been tucked in the side pocket of the panpack. They were the small ones, the kind that lasted no more than two to three minutes—but they had one advantage, they were easy to light. All he had to do was twist off the friction cap. He signaled back to the *Indon*.

"Read you, Colonel. Okay—we're going for it. Let's give it our best shot. Even if I don't see the flare, there's a good chance one of the scanner sensors or cameras will pick you up and burp."

Gideon unscrewed the cap, ignited the fuse, held his breath, and lifted the flare high in the water over his head. For the next several seconds the red-orange phosphor-based torch flickered, struggling with the even deeper recesses in the lagoon's darkness. Finally, it flared and illuminated the area around him.

Gideon Stone realized that the unscripted prayer that followed probably bordered on sacrilegious. It was certainly not well thought out. It was totally involuntary, lacked eloquence, had been conjured up almost as afterthought—and was laced with profanity. But it was sincere and it was enthusiastic. Only later would he wonder what Hooker and some of his poker buddies back on Largo would think of that.

The first flare flickered and died out. Gideon counted to thirty and lit the second.

"I see it," Jessie shouted, and suddenly the redirected beam of the forward obs halogen became visible as it penetrated the soupy darkness. "Start walking toward the light, Colonel—and if you'll take back some of those chauvinistic remarks you made earlier today, I'll even leave the porch light on for you and we'll have a homecoming party."

Jessie Penelope Preston, Gideon thought, you've got yourself a deal. But as he started in the direction of the faint lights of the *Indon,* he could hear her inform Wormack that Taylor's breathing had become irregular and was becoming more and more shallow by the second. For the second time in less than ten minutes he tried to conjure up a suitable prayer.

Day 5: Time 0017LT
Mandarin-Plaza Hotel

Franklin Nelson had never impressed Bojoni Sarawak, even during Sarawak's student days at UCLA when Nelson was the Lieutenant Governor of California. Now, in the middle of the Jakarta night with the wind-whipped rain assaulting the city from every angle, an unshaved Nelson impressed him even less.

The American Vice President was a small man with a sparse crop of dingy gray hair, a thin mustache, and owlish eyes that hid behind tinted glasses. He was still dressed in pajamas and a robe after being rousted out of bed by Bandung militiamen earlier that evening. He looked like anything but a man qualified to hold the second-highest elected office in the land that had educated Sarawak.

Sarawak lit a cigar while Nelson, seated next to the British representative, Sir Edward Peel, fidgeted in his chair. Finally Sarawak spoke. "Gentlemen, you may as well make yourself comfortable. I am afraid that your ordeal, as I have heard Sir Edward so delicately state it, is just beginning."

Nelson, annoyed by the smoke from Sarawak's cigar, pushed himself away from the table and stood up. "This is outrageous," he protested.

Sarawak smiled. The photographs Nelson carried in his dossier on the general did not do him justice. He was a handsome man with—on the surface at least—a pleasing demeanor. He had a luxurious thatch of wavy black hair and brown, often penetrating eyes. As one American journalist had pointed out, the combination of looks, smile, and rhetoric had made him a folk hero to millions of Maylays. "Before this affair ends, my esteemed guests," Sarawak said, "I fear both of you, as well as the rest of your unfortunate colleagues, will regard these next several hours, perhaps even days, as more than a mere tribulation. More than likely you will use such words as distressing, perhaps even calamitous, to refer to your experience."

"And just how long do you intend to detain us?" Nelson demanded. He was still standing. At five feet, ten inches in height he was not all that impressive.

Sarawak lifted his head and exhaled a thick slate-blue cloud of smoke. It hung over his head like an annulation. "The answer to that, of course, depends solely on how your individual governments react to my demands."

"Exactly what is the meaning of all of this?" Peel fumed. It was the first time he had spoken since he entered the room.

Sarawak sighed, contemplated his cigar for several moments, and finally looked at the two Bandung staff officers who had accompanied him into the Mandarin Plaza dining room. Captain Ketan Sabo sat on his right and Major Asassio Muta stood to his left.

"Tell me, Sir Edward, I am curious, do you read *Time* magazine?"

"On occasion."

Sarawak continued to look amused. "You will excuse my obvious amusement, Sir Edward—but early on I learned that one can never be quite certain what the British read. Nevertheless, since you do, you are no doubt aware that I have been dubbed the voice of the disenchanted—the unfortunates and the disenfranchised in my native Java. More recently, I have become more than that to these people; the people have elected me their vehicle of change—of hope, of a new tomorrow. All, of course, because of my opposition to the oppressive Sarni Kujon government."

"Preposterous," Peel sniffed. "You have not been named or elected anything. You have appointed yourself. Any mandate you profess to have is nothing more than your own self-anointed sense of importance. You are, and the world knows it, nothing more than a pawn of the Beijing regime."

Sarawak's smile was slowly dissolving. "I would caution you, Sir Edward, it is unwise to irritate me. As for you and your colleagues, while you may be somewhat inconvenienced during the next several hours—you will not be harmed. Unless, of course, the American government refuses to see the folly of their continued intervention in Indonesian affairs."

"Just exactly what do you mean by that?" Nelson fumed.

"I will spare you the boring plague of redundancy, Mr. Vice President. In precisely one hour, I will go on the air to inform the American government and its sycophant friends of my demands. Demands that I assure you your capitalist leaders will find difficult to accept, but quite necessary."

"My government will not tolerate—" Nelson started to say, but Sarawak cut him off.

"You, Franklin Nelson, are not in a position to say what your government will or will not tolerate. You see, this is all quite simple; my demands will be met—my conditions accepted—or you will pay the consequences. Those consequences, gentlemen, are your lives."

Peel, the antithesis of his American associate, tall and angular, with finely chiselled features, appraised the Bandung leader for several moments before he spoke. When he did, his words were measured, matter-of-fact. "You are playing with fire, General Sarawak. I can assure you, if anything happens to any member of this delegation, you and your band of Bandung thugs will suffer dire consequences. The United Nations has no tolerance for men of your ilk."

Rather than agitated, Sarawak appeared to be amused.

He stood up and walked slowly around the table until he was standing directly behind Peel and Nelson. "Over the years I have found it most advantageous to be an ardent student of history, gentlemen. For example, I am not unaware that Americans have been held hostage before—and that the fumbling American leaders did not believe the Iranian government was serious. Why? Because the Iranians did not take strong enough initial action. I will not make that mistake. I will impress upon the leaders of your countries that the Bandung is very, very serious—and that there will be dire implications if my demands are not met."

"Are you saying we are being held hostage, General?" Nelson demanded.

Sarawak smiled, shook his head, and finally laughed. "Hostage, prisoner, pawn; whatever you choose to call it, Mr. Nelson. However, I think it only fair to caution you that before you begin to express indignation and bravado, you are in no position to do so." Sarawak paused. "Look around you. As you can see, both Major Muta and Captain Sabo are heavily armed—and perhaps I should also warn you, they are fortified with some forty of my finest Bandung militiamen here in this hotel at this very moment. In addition, there are over two hundred militiamen stationed at key checkpoints throughout the city, and a thousand well-armed Bandung troops bivouacked just a few miles outside of Jakarta. To a man, they are eager to see the day when the new People's Republic of Java takes over. Needless to say, they are ready and eagerly waiting for my call."

Nelson stared back at his Bandung captor in disbelief. When he finally worked up the courage to speak, his voice betrayed him. The words were strong, but the officiousness, the prior air of indignation, and the outrage had all diminished. "I feel it is only fair to warn you, General, my government will respond with vigor. If you do not call this shameful charade off, you will regret the day you conceived of this insane idea."

Sarawak took his time, walked slowly back around the table until he was facing the hostages, sat down, and ordered the guards to escort Nelson and Peel to their rooms. "Make certain," he said, as an afterthought, "that our guests hear my broadcast." Then, as the hostages were led from the room, Sarawak signaled to a young lieutenant who had been standing just outside the door. "Inform the radio people that I am ready."

"Yes, Comrade General," the young officer said. He saluted and left. Sarawak relit his cigar, stood up, walked to the window, and stared out at the rain. In his mind he was going over his speech again.

Day 5: Time 0057LT
The Bo Jac

Gideon Stone was into his second cup of coffee. Jessie Preston had resorted to tea. They were waiting for Parker Wormack to return from the *Bo Jac*'s sick bay where Taylor had been taken when the *Indon* returned to its berth in the monopool.

They had been sitting in silence for several minutes before Gideon spoke up. "Just in case I didn't say it before, that was quick thinking down there. Well done. If it hadn't been for you, this whole mission could have turned out a helluva lot worse than it did."

Jessie set her cup down. "Acknowledgement appreciated, Colonel—but I assure you, not necessary. I've gotten quite used to men thinking I might not be able to hold up my end of the bargain because I'm a woman. I've had to prove myself everywhere I've ever been. First it was my ability to fly, then the Agency, and after I was assigned to the *Bo Jac*, it was a long time before Wormack finally accepted me."

"So, tell me—is proving yourself what makes Jessie Preston tick?" Gideon's question caught her off guard.

"I was trained as a pilot," she began, "but ended up being a desk jockey in the AGO section. I had a wing commander who had an aversion to giving women responsibility. So I decided to prove myself; I attended every special weapons and tactics school I could get my hands on."

It had occurred to Gideon that the only thing he knew about the woman was what he had read in her file. That plus the fact that Wormack had assured him she was more than capable of meeting any emergency that was likely to arise. An out-and-out acceptance of anyone's blanket assessment wasn't like Gideon Stone. He had long made it a practice to know everything he possibly could about the people he worked with. As Jake Ruppert often said, "If you're going to depend on someone, you better know what makes 'em tick."

He got up, walked over to the sideboard, and poured himself another cup of coffee. "All the same—thanks."

Jessie Preston leaned forward in her chair and drummed her pencil on the table. "You asked a civilized question—you deserve a civilized answer. Let's start with the fact that even though my papers say I'm British, I was born here in Java. My father was a career diplomat, my mother was Indonesian. Before he retired from the diplomatic service, I saw the world. I went to a women's preparatory school in Germany, attended college in London, and actually came back to Jakarta for a time. I guess that was when I was going through one of those 'trying to find my identity' periods. When that didn't work out, I joined up."

"What about the Agency?"

"M? They recruited me. Four years later, when I heard about the *Bo Jac,* I put in for it. I guess it was one of those 'roots' things. Anyway, they approved it and I've been on loan to your government ever since—just like Wormack."

Gideon looked around the room, aware of the waves pounding the hull of the vessel. "It's just an off-hand observation, of course, but it looks like a pretty dull assignment, day in and day out confined to this tin can."

Jessie Preston waited before she answered. "Apparently you didn't get a very good look at me, Colonel. The fact is, I look like millions of other Indonesian women except for the green eyes and red hair. That's a plus. All I have to do is slip in some tinted contacts and put on a wig. Within the last thirty days I've been in Jakarta at least four times—always on official business. My mother made certain I paid due homage to my heritage. I not only speak the language and several of the regional dialects, I know Jakarta like the back of my hand."

Gideon was intrigued. Given the opportunity, he would have probed further but Parker Wormack had returned. The *Bo Jac*'s section chief looked harried.

"How's Moe?" Jessie asked.

"Severe concussion, seven stitches, and weak; he lost a lot of blood. Crimmins says he'll be all right, but it'll take some time, three days, before the doc wants him up and around, and another week or so before he returns to his duty station."

Gideon took a sip of coffee and waited for Wormack to continue.

"Now," Wormack said after clearing his throat, "suppose you tell me what happened down there."

Jessie Preston did most of the talking. "Bad luck," she said with a shrug. "According to our computers, we had the *Indon* sitting right on top of Ng's signal when the swarm quakes hit. But that's as close as we got. It was one of those 'now or never' situations—the signal was getting weaker by the minute. When the debris settled—no more signal."

Wormack looked disappointed. "Any chance we could locate it again?"

"Hell, yes. There's always a way," Gideon replied, "but it'll take divers, lots of 'em. We'd have to rake and sift through every piece of wreckage, every body, and every piece of anything that didn't look like it belonged down there. Then we'd have to hoist it to the surface and sort through it. It's a long shot—real, real long."

Wormack sighed. "What do I tell Ruppert?"

Gideon shrugged. "Don't tell, ask. Ask him how much time we have and how much money the Agency is willing to spend. And while you're at it, remind him I've got three days left on my contract. Three days, that's all."

Before Wormack could respond, there was a knock at the wardroom door.

"Come in."

The man was one of the data analysts Gideon had seen earlier when Taylor was giving him a tour of the *Bo Jac*. The man's face was flushed. "We began picking up a radio broadcast just a couple of minutes ago, Parker. It's Bojoni Sarawak. We think you better hear it. . . ."

Day 5: Time 0123LT
Mandarin-Plaza Hotel

Flanked by Captain Sabo and Major Assasio Muta, in a crowded, smoke-filled room on the sixth floor of the Mandarin-Plaza Hotel, Bojoni Sarawak took his seat in front of the microphone of Radio Republik Indonesia. On the desk in front of him was a copy of the speech he had labored over for the past several weeks.

Two technicians from the national radio station scurried about the room, making final preparations, while a representative of the hotel brought in a pitcher of water and attended to last-minute details. "Will the general require anything else?" the man inquired.

Sarawak waved him off and pulled the microphone closer to him. The moment had finally arrived. Four years of planning was about to come to fruition. One of the two engineers approached and nervously instructed Sarawak to watch his hands for the signal. "When the light goes on, I will point to you and you may begin, General."

Sarawak wetted his lips and waited. Finally the signal was given.

My friends and fellow countrymen, all people of Java, at precisely one o'clock this morning, less than thirty minutes ago, on the fourteenth day of October, the members of your Bandung Party became the official government of the island nation of Java.

At that time, former President Sarni Kujon and cabinet members of his Loyalist Party were informed of this action and encouraged to step down in a peaceful and timely manner—thereby avoiding bloodshed and recognizing the Party of the People's Republic of Java as the party now in control of this island nation's destiny.

At the same time, I am using this opportunity to

inform supporters of the Kujon government, both here and afar, that the Party of the People's Republic of Java will no longer tolerate or abide foreign intervention in Javanese affairs.

To insure that the immediate withdrawal of the Kujon government is accomplished in a non-violent and timely fashion, the Bandung military wing of the RPJ is, at this time, implementing a state of national emergency in Java. Until such time that this state of national emergency is lifted, Javanese borders will be closed and no transportation will be permitted into or out of the country.

Sarawak paused briefly to take a sip of water. When he continued, his voice had become even more somber.

As many of you know, a delegation of the United Nations is currently in Java in an unwarranted and unwanted capitalist attempt to influence the former Kujon government to take actions necessary to stifle the voice of the Bandung. Their mission in our country serves only one purpose, to insure that the efforts of the Bandung are rendered ineffective.

We cannot and will not allow that to happen. The Bandung is the true voice of the people of Java. The mission of the Bandung is to rid the people of the oppressive Kujon government and its foreign influences.

Because of this, the Bandung must take definitive measures to insure that the transition of governments is complete, prompt, and void of foreign intervention.

Tonight, and to that end, we are informing those

people outside of our island nation that the Bandung is in control and demands immediate recognition.

To insure that this demand is met, all members of the United Nations delegation presently in Jakarta have been taken hostage. They will be held hostage until the Bandung receives official recognition from each of the member countries involved, as well as their assurance that the Bandung government will be recognized as the official government of Java and that there will be no retaliatory response to this action.

Immediate and positive response will insure that no harm will come to the members of the delegation. However, if that response is delayed, at precisely twelve o'clock, noon, Jakarta time today, one member of the UN delegation will be sacrificed and the body placed on the doorstep of the Mandarin Plaza Hotel for all to witness.

Sarawak paused.

We await the world's response.

Only then did Sarawak pull back from the microphone and look around the crowded room. As he did, the officers of the Bandung Militia began to cheer.

Day 5: Time 1438LT
Langley, Virginia

Chet Harms, the Agency's newly appointed director, along with department heads Jake Ruppert, Sam Peterson, and Mike English, were all there as were most of their resource people. There was a steady, nervous, yet subdued din of conversation throughout the room until Harms asked for their attention.

Harms, a long-time member of the CIA, was still awaiting his anointment by a Senate committee as the new Agency Director. He was a popular choice with Agency insiders, but this was the first real crisis the Agency had faced since his nomination. It was, as Ruppert had put it when he heard the text of Sarawak's speech, "the new chief's first real test under fire."

"All right, I think we all know why we're here. By now most of you have heard a tape of Sarawak's speech and many of you have even had an opportunity to go over the transcript word by word. Our people in the area assure us that there isn't any doubt Sarawak means business.

"But since this whole Indonesian thing falls under Jake Ruppert's jurisdiction and he's on top of it, I'm going to ask him to bring you up to speed."

Jake Ruppert cleared his throat, methodically shuffled the stack of papers in front of him, carefully aligned them, and made certain all the edges were neat before he began. All the while, his eyes repeatedly scanned the long conference table as he endeavored to make eye contact with every person in the room.

"I'm certain all of you know our government has long been convinced that the People's Republic of China in Beijing has been backing the Sarawak-led Bandung forces on the island of Java.

"However, belief is one thing—documented proof of the PRC's involvement is quite another. To say the least, that proof has been difficult to come by.

"Up until two weeks ago, the only thing we had in the way of proof Sarawak was doing more than bending our ears with unceasing rhetoric were some satellite photographs of the Bandung's weapons buildup on Karimunjawa. Even with those photographs, there was no way to prove the money to buy those weapons and supplies was coming from Beijing.

"Then we got lucky. Our man in Jakarta was contacted by a man by the name of Teuwen Ng. Ng is or was a minor official with a company in Danau-Toba. That company was doing business with the Bandung. Mr. Ng contacted us with an interesting proposition. In exchange for political asylum in the United States, and a certain sum of money, he was willing to provide us with documents that proved Beijing was shelling out money for Sarawak to buy his toys.

"The reason the funds were so hard to track is because they were wired halfway around Europe before they ever got into Sarawak's hands. One week it was deutschmarks, another it was Swiss francs, and according to Ng, the last transfer of funds was made in Dutch gilders.

"You know how it worked from there. Sarawak and his Bandung thugs have been buying weapons from North Korea, Vietnam, and the PRC. Eventually the monies filtered back into Beijing and the cycle started all over again. The difference is, three months ago, Mr. Ng just happened to stumble across the paper trail of these transactions."

At that point Harms took over. "And that's when our man in Jakarta, Che Nagarajan, bought airline tickets for Ng on a Garuda flight. That flight would have eventually brought him and the documentation we have been looking for to the United States. Nagarajan was convinced that documentation was sufficient to persuade some of our more recalcitrant friends in the United Nations to back us when we wanted to impose sanctions on the Beijing government for supporting Sarawak."

"And where's that documentation now?" The question came from the far end of the table.

"Unfortunately, it's at the bottom of the Java Sea," Ruppert answered, "and based on the report I received less than an hour ago from Parker Wormack aboard the *Bo Jac,* it's likely to remain there. We had the briefcase isolated, but it seems the crash site has been struck with a series of ongoing swarm quakes that has further scattered the wreckage and again concealed the whereabouts of the briefcase containing the documentation. When I spoke to Parker Wormack just a short time ago, his assessment of the situation was that the likelihood of recovering Ng's briefcase and the documents is, and I quote, 'highly improbable.' "

"In other words," Harms added, "we have nothing to take to the Security Council and no way to support our claim. The proof that we almost had in our hands less than twenty-four hours ago is now languishing at the bottom of the Java Sea. Needless to say, we've got a sticky situation on our hands. My gut feeling is that things are going to get a lot worse."

Day 5: Time 1640LT
Washington

Shuler Huntine was the antithesis of conventionality, a throwback to the fifties. Jake Ruppert wouldn't have been in the least surprised if, sooner or later, the President's senior aide had shown up for one of their meetings wearing jeans, a white T-shirt with a pack of cigarettes rolled up in the sleeve, and penny loafers. It was a known fact that Shuler Huntine had even gone so far as to name his first son Elvis, and his second after Jimmy Dean.

This time, however, Jake was destined to be surprised; there was Huntine, on time and disgustingly conventional—regaled in a blue pinstripe suit, white shirt, button-down collar, and wing tips. His only connection to his preoccupation with a time four decades earlier was his haircut: high and tight. He had worn it that way since his Marine Corps days.

Ruppert found him poring over a street map of Jakarta. There was a cardboard cup of coffee in front of him and the radio station was playing golden oldies. "Come on in, Jake," he said without looking up.

Ruppert dropped down in the nearest chair and threw his raincoat over the chair next to him. Other than the three chairs, a kidney-shaped table, and a brace of telephones, the office was bare: no pictures, no plants, none of the conventional accoutrements of an office. It was still leased in the name of an accountant who had vacated it some two years earlier.

Shuler Huntine had a fetish for secrecy. About his seldom-used and secret Georgia Building office he was often heard to say, "when I unlock the door I know no one is taping the goddamn conversation." Now he was looking at Jake and stamping out his cigarette. "I hear you hauled Gideon Stone out of mothballs for this one," Huntine began.

"Harms said to give it our best shot. Our best shot is Gideon. Any objections?"

"Matter of fact, I consider it a stroke of genius. I talked to the President. He agrees."

"He knows?"

"That's my job—to make damn sure he knows."

"Then he's up to speed?"

Huntine nodded, leaned back, and crossed his legs.

Ruppert couldn't tell whether he had paused to listen to an old Julie London recording on the radio or to further reduce what he was about to say to the fewest possible words. Saying something in the fewest possible words was an obsession with the man who was reputed to be as close to David Weimer as anyone in the President's cabinet. "Confession time, Jake; what do you know about this guy Sarawak that I don't know?"

Ruppert opened his briefcase and pulled out Sarawak's dossier. It was several inches thick. "Here's everything we've got on him," Jake said.

"Good, then we don't need to spend any time on his background. Let's talk about what the President wants. Right now the main man has a full plate—not to mention an election coming up. As far as the President is concerned, Sarawak's announcement last night is about as welcome as a sudden case of jock itch. He wants us to get this thing resolved as quickly as possible. That's item one; item two is Nelson. I think you know Weimer's relationship with the Vice President; bottom line—he considers Frank Nelson one step below a chicken fucker. However, that's not the way he's viewed by the voters in California. Those silly bastards like him. He delivered the California vote in the last election—and the President figures he's going to need Nelson's help again—maybe even more so this time around."

"So he wants to get Nelson out of there—alive?"

Huntine took a sip of his coffee. "Alive is the key word. At the same time, we can't make it look like Sarawak is making the President of the United States jump through hoops."

"Meaning?"

"We respond—but at the same time we make it look like we're playing hardball. This is Carter and the damn

Iranians all over again. It's the Kennedy and Castro game. We don't blink—understand?"

"I take it you have a plan?"

Huntine nodded. "I give you the outline—you fill in the details. Send Gideon Stone in to get him. We'll get some special forces people in there to back him up. In the meantime, we'll start the negotiating—we'll get the Navy to position itself just outside the harbor at Tanjung Priok—and we'll do some flyovers and show Sarawak a little muscle."

"So, while Sarawak is preoccupied with our posturing, he'll start maneuvering to counter our move and meanwhile Stone slips in the back door."

"Simple, huh? Hey, all you have to do is figure out how that gets accomplished. Now, the next question is: What kind of resources have you got on that damn floating spy-trap of yours that one no one is supposed to know anything about?"

"In the way of personnel, mostly computer jocks. We don't have much need for anything else. We do have a multi-talented chopper pilot by the name of Jessie Preston that we hustle in and out of Jakarta on a regular basis. She's on loan from M. We got her because she knows the area and she knows Sarawak. She knows how he walks, how he talks, and how he thinks."

"This Preston, can she contribute?"

"She did a tour in the Falklands; flew one of their gunships, thirty-one missions. You be the judge."

"Think Stone can handle it? He's been on the shelf for a while."

"If he'll keep the bit in his mouth. The question with Gideon is, can we keep him under contract long enough to get the job done?"

"That's your problem." Huntine grinned. "In the meantime, get him geared up. I'll have the rest of his support team on the deck of the *Bo Jac* in twenty-four hours. Okay?"

Ruppert knew that was it. As far as Shuler Huntine was concerned, he had said everything he had wanted to say—and everything that needed to be said. The "okay" was his closer. He folded up his map, straightened his papers, and stuffed them back in his briefcase. As he did, he looked at Ruppert.

"I'd buy you a drink, Jake, but I've got to get back to the office. The President wants me to report back on our little meeting."

Jake Ruppert grunted and picked up his coat. It was rush hour and it was raining. By the time he got back to his office in Langley and made contact with his people aboard the *Bo Jac,* he would be staring at another long night.

Day 5: Time 1202LT
Mandarin-Plaza Hotel

Bojoni Sarawak sat in his room staring down into the deserted hotel courtyard. The rain had driven everyone inside, the pool furniture had been hurriedly stacked in alcoves to save it from the wind, and the poolside bar was shuttered and abandoned.

Outside his room, in the hotel's corridor, he could hear the muted voices of Ketan Sabo talking to one of his militiamen. Sabo had waited until he was finished with the young woman who had come to his bed earlier that night. Like the others, he did not know her name. It was enough, he decided, that she knew his.

Finally, thinking that Sabo had not wanted to disturb him with news while he slept, he dressed and went to the door. Ketan Sabo broke away from his conversation with the young militiaman. Sabo was frowning. "There has been no response, General," he said. "I am told that the American consular representative in Bali is out of the country."

Sarawak scowled. Sabo's news was troubling. There had been more than enough time for a response. He had expected to hear something by now. It had been almost twelve hours since his radio broadcast—more than enough time for even the fumbling Americans to formulate one of their carefully worded replies.

"Perhaps the American leaders have not been told of—" Sabo started to suggest.

Sarawak did not wait for his young captain to finish. Instead he went back into the room and picked up the telephone. "I would speak with Major Assasio Muta," he said.

There was a delay of several moments before Muta came on the line. "Yes, General."

"The time has come," Sarawak said. "We have received no response. Select a victim—anyone but the American Vice President. As revolting as I find the little man, he is our biggest bargaining chip. We will spare him for the time being." After a pause, he added, "I remind you, Major, it is imperative that the world knows that we mean business. Therefore, I prefer that you carry out your orders under the portico at the front of the hotel."

"I will take care of it, General," Muta answered. He hung up and looked around the room where the members of the U.N. delegation had been detained. "That one," he said, pointing at Peel. "Take the Britisher out to the front of the hotel."

At 1231 Jakarta time, Sir Edward Peel was led through the open portico into the street in front of the Mandarin-

Plaza Hotel and instructed to kneel down with his hands behind his back. Peel's brief protest was cut short when Muta brought his .45 down on the man's shoulder, sending him sprawling on the rain-soaked brick pavement in the drive leading up to the portico.

Muta waited until he was certain that news people and television crews were recording the event. Then he buried the muzzle of the .45 in the back of Peel's head and fired.

Chapter Five

Day 5: Time 1303LT
The Bo Jac

Less than ten minutes after seeing Peel's assassination on CNN, Jake Ruppert managed to get through to the *Bo Jac* by phone. In those ten minutes, the *Bo Jac*'s crew had already watched the event three times on three different network feeds. By the time Ruppert's second call got through, he had spent another ten minutes on a conference call with both Huntine and the President.

"All right, here's the latest on this end," Ruppert began. His voice was tired. He had both Wormack and Stone on the line. "The President goes on the air in about thirty minutes. He and the Secretary of State have already been in touch with most of the countries involved. They are informing them that we are ordering the aircraft carrier Shenandoah into the area, and that the President will be addressing his remarks directly to Sarawak. I'm told that CNN and the rest of the White House press corps have been alerted and they are setting up their cameras now.

"In the meantime, we're getting ready to put an Apache gunship on the helipad of the *Bo Jac*. When it arrives, there will be a five-man handpicked special forces team on board. They've already been informed that Stone will be in charge—and they've been instructed they are there to help him go in and get the Vice President.

"In the meantime, be prepared for anything. Huntine says the President is already taking heat—first from the British Embassy, and then from the Russians. Everyone wants to know what the hell we're doing about this situation."

"How about an ETA on that Apache?" Gideon asked.

"It'll take a while, she's traveling heavy, sixteen laser-guided Hellfire missiles and a 30mm Hughes Chain Gun, plus your support personnel and their equipment. Huntine assures me she's already airborne. We had to strip out some of the backup avionics to get the personnel in there, and she has to make it through some nasty weather, but our best estimate on an ETA would be two hours—"

"One question," Gideon interrupted. "What happens to my paycheck if we don't pull this off?"

"Harms said to tell you we'll send it to your favorite charity."

"You're upping the ante, right?"

"I'll double it. We'll arm wrestle for anything over that when you get back to the ZI."

Gideon heard the click in his ear. By the time he nestled the receiver back in its cradle, he had already directed his first question at Jessie Preston. "You heard all of that?"

"Most of it. Where do we start?"

"Wormack says you know Jakarta like the back of your hand. What do you know about the Mandarin Plaza?"

Jessie had to think for a minute. "Sprawling structure, two hundred and eighty rooms, the east wing was recently renovated. That's the VIP area and that's probably where Sarawak is keeping the hostages. Six—no—seven stories counting the old ballroom on the top floor. But the hotel hasn't used that ballroom in years."

"What's on each side of the hotel?"

"Shops on one side—none of which are more than two or three stories. The old German embassy is on the other. It's been closed for years. Some Indonesian heavyweight financier bought it a couple of years ago and it has been undergoing extensive renovation."

"In front and in back?"

"A parking area in the rear along with the hotel's courtyard. In front is one of the city's main thoroughfares, lots of traffic—congested most of the time. Even more so with the press and TV crews camped out there—not to mention the gawkers."

"Even in this weather?" Gideon asked.

"Everyone is used to it." Jessie smiled. "Monsoons are a way of life in this part of the world."

Parker Wormack looked puzzled. "I don't quite see what you're getting at."

Gideon thought for a moment. "Let's pose a hypothetical situation, Parker. Suppose you were trying to secure a building in a densely populated, modern city like Jakarta. And at the same time, you were being distracted by an outsider making a show of power in your city's harbor. How would you respond?"

Wormack frowned. "Well, first I'd make certain my flank was protected. I'd post my guards at every entrance, making certain all sides of the building were covered—and I'd most likely spot a couple of lookouts on the roof."

Gideon nodded and looked at Jessie. "How many stories in that old embassy building?"

Jessie shrugged. "Three, maybe four. Why?"

"Think we could get into that old building?"

"You know what they say, Colonel, where there's a will, there's a way."

Gideon glanced at his watch and back at Jessie Preston. "According to Ruppert, that chopper with our handful of special forces personnel is less than two hours from touching down on the *Bo Jac*. That's just enough time for you to sketch the layout of the Mandarin-Plaza and the buildings in the adjacent area. The minute they get here, we go to work."

A slow smile was beginning to play with the corners of Jessie Preston's mouth. She looked at Wormack, then at Gideon. "It seems to me, Colonel, that I recall a rather emphatic four-days-out-and-out-of-here speech when you first arrived. What happened?"

Gideon laughed. "I take it neither of you have played poker with Jake Ruppert?" Both Wormack and Preston shook their heads. "I have, too many times—the old boy's a pussycat. He bluffs easy. All I had to do was pause before I answered, and he sweetened the stakes."

Day 5: Time 1537LT
The Bo Jac

According to Gideon's watch, the Apache had been on the helipad for something less then fifteen minutes when one of the *Bo Jac*'s deck crew ushered the five-man special forces team into the wardroom. Wormack wasted no time getting down to business. He introduced Gideon and Jessie and went around the table as each of the men recited his name, rank, and specialty code. None of them wore any indication of rank or insignia. Gideon decided that either Huntine could be credited with careful planning or he had lucked out; two of the men, Casio Butcher and Sheban Geronimo, either were or could have passed for Malays.

The Apache's pilot was Captain Jeris Alan, and Gunnery Sergeant Butch Miller was responsible for handling the bird's armament. Alan was obviously a product of the Academy. Both men had combat experience, and the three enlisted men all had that mean look Gideon liked.

When they were finally settled in, Gideon went to the front of the wardroom, pulled down the screen, and turned on the overhead projector to show them Jessie's sketches. It had been a long time since he had conducted a briefing.

"What you are looking at, gentlemen, is a drawing of the Mandarin-Plaza Hotel, where the hostages are being held. The drawing also indicates the proximity of the buildings immediately adjacent to the Plaza.

"We have every reason to believe the hostages are being detained in the east wing—but we can't be certain. Keep one thing in mind—if he's anything, our boy Sarawak is predictably unpredictable."

Gideon paused. "As you are no doubt aware, one of the hostages has already been taken out. That means there are six remaining; one of those hostages, of course, is the Vice President.

"To the west and immediately adjacent to the hotel is a four-story building currently undergoing renovation." Gideon stabbed at Jessie's drawing of the empty embassy building. "This is where we hit them first. By the time we put our plan in motion, the *Shenandoah* should be within spitting distance of their harbor, Tanjung Priok—and we think just close enough for the Bandung to know what's happening. All things being equal, the presence of the *Shenandoah* should cause Sarawak some indigestion—or at least give him something to think about.

"So, while that's occupying his thinking, this old embassy building becomes diversion number one and our first target. I want two of you to find a way into it and work your way to the top floor. Then I want you to plant an explosive big enough to blow a hole in the east wall of the embassy building and the west wall of the hotel."

"How big a hole, Colonel?" one of the men asked. The other members of his unit laughed.

"Don't mind Butcher, sir," Alan explained. "Somewhere along the line Casio got the impression God made him the world's foremost authority on blowing up things."

"It's not an impression, sir, it's a fact," Butcher assured his commander.

Gideon studied the ruddy-faced lance corporal for several moments. Butcher was just what the doctor ordered. He looked big enough and disagreeable enough to chew his way through the embassy wall. Plus, he had an attitude.

"I don't give a damn how big a charge you put in the wall of that old building, Corporal. But I want it big enough to get the job done and loud enough to create a major diversion. . . ."

Butcher was grinning.

"At the same time, it should be small enough to insure that it doesn't bring the whole damn roof down on the people. As far as we know, there are still a lot of guests other than the hostages in that hotel.

"And one other thing, Corporal Butcher, make damn certain you and your backup have cleared the building and are long gone before the device explodes. I don't want any exchange of gunfire.

"If this diversion is going to work, Sarawak's men have got to be caught off guard. And the only way that works is if they're chasing ghosts. Got it?"

Butcher nodded. "I've got just the thing you need in my little ditty bag, Colonel. It's my own special concoction."

"All right then, while Corporal Butcher is implementing his little surprise," Gideon continued, "the rest of us will be otherwise occupied. Captain, you and Gunnery Sergeant Miller will be creating a secondary diversion—you will be making certain that Apache of yours is getting lots of attention before, during, and after Butcher does his thing. Make several low-altitude passes back and forth over the city; low enough to be identified and disconcerting to Sarawak, high enough to avoid any small-arms fire.

"Your risk should be minimal. At this point it's doubtful Sarawak has anything inside the city proper that's big enough to do you any damage. It's too soon after the coup, and up until now he's had his hands full. The logic behind this is if he had come rolling into the city last night with anything bigger than some M-16's and a couple of handheld rocket launchers, the Sarni Kujon government would have been tipped off."

"What about the rest of us?" Geronimo asked.

Gideon turned off the projector and leaned on the rostrum. "CNN and TPI, Televisi Pendidikan Indonesia, have been covering the coup since Sarawak's first broadcast last night. Sarawak needs the media attention if he intends to pull this thing off.

"Despite the weather, both TPI and CNN, and maybe a couple of others, have had their news helicopters flying over the area most of the night and on through the morning. Ms. Preston here assures me these choppers are flying out of two small privately owned service terminals at the back of Soekarno-Hatta airport.

"Okay—why is this important? Because we need one of those small choppers to get into the hotel. That makes confiscating one of those news choppers our first order of business.

"After we get our hands on the chopper and get our timing synchronized, Jessie will use that chopper to put two of us down on the roof of the Mandarin. The timing has to be such that we get on that roof within minutes after Butcher has created his diversion. That's why I need a big boom, gentlemen—I'm betting Sarawak will hustle the guards on the roof of the hotel to help look for the people that planted the bomb.

"And that, gentlemen, is the plan. Any questions?"

Alan, the Apache's pilot, had the first. "How do we get Corporal Butcher and his partner into the heart of the city?"

Gideon hesitated and looked at Wormack. "We're in luck. Parker informs me that the assistant concierge at the Mandarin is on our payroll. She wasn't on duty last night when Sarawak took over the hotel—but she has to go in tonight. She checked in with us earlier today. She tells us the manager of the Mandarin has been in touch with her and she has been instructed to report for work tonight at 2100 hours to relieve her boss.

"The woman uses the hotel's service van to pick up the mail before she comes in when she works nights. So—we send the bomb squad, Butcher and Powers, in with her in the mail van. She assures us she can use some of the side streets and let them off in the proximity of the old embassy building. It should work—it'll be dark and in all likelihood, raining—that should be in our favor.

"While we don't have many, we do have one more thing in our favor. Jessie picked this little item up during one of the newscasts earlier today. In addition to the UN delegation, there were approximately one hundred and seventy other guests in the Mandarin when Sarawak took over last night. Some of them may have managed to get out, but we have to assume most of them are still there. That means Sarawak and his men have their hands full just keeping track of everyone."

Alan had waited until Gideon finished before he spoke up. "If you're going into that hotel, Colonel, you're going to need a backup. Who's going in with you?"

Gideon studied their faces. "You tell me. Who's the best man for the job?"

The answer came from the bull-shouldered man sitting next to the captain. "That would be me, sir, Sergeant Sheban Geronimo. Butcher may know his sticks, Colonel, but I can knock the eye out of goddamn turkey at fifty yards."

Gideon looked across the table at Jeris Alan for some kind of affirmation.

"I was told to assemble the best men I could find in the unit," Alan verified. "You're looking at them, Colonel. You can go to the bank with any of them. If Sergeant Geronimo says he wants to go into that hotel with you, he's the one I'd take."

Day 5: Time 0600LT
The White House

When David Weimer wanted privacy and secrecy, he held his meetings in a small twelve-by-fourteen room wedged between the Map Room and the Diplomatic Reception Area directly under the more famous Blue Room. It was bereft of the usual White House appointments and off-limits to the White House staff. The President and his two top aides had the only keys. When Jake Ruppert was summoned to the White House, the meetings usually took place in that small room—the one without a name.

Within minutes after Ruppert's arrival, he was escorted to the lower level, where he was intercepted by another agent who ushered him to that very room. Huntine, who had a reputation for being late no matter what the occasion, was already there, talking on the telephone. When he finished, he informed Ruppert that the President was on his way down.

Jake Ruppert was tired. As he had anticipated when he left his meeting with Shuler Huntine the previous afternoon, he had spent the rest day and well into the night on the telephone. When he wasn't involving himself with the details of the plans being laid on the *Bo Jac,* he was kept busy relaying information to both Chet Harms and Huntine. It was a little after four o'clock in the morning when he finally felt it was safe to grab some much-needed sleep. He called his wife, told her he wouldn't be home, and dozed off on the sofa in his office. An hour or so later, Huntine's call came through. The message was straight to the point. The President wanted to talk to him. There wasn't even time to shave.

Now Weimer's aide was handing him a piece of paper. it was a list of the UN representatives being held hostage in the Mandarin-Plaza. Jake Ruppert already knew the names, but he read it anyway.

Frank J. Nelson
Vladimir Lesni
Aduma Malaka
Mohammed Farah Makidid
Edward Peel
Boris Azinsiskov

A line had been scratched through Peel's name as though the person constructing the list had been informed of Peel's death after the list was prepared.

As far as Ruppert was concerned, the list of hostages was strange in still another way—none of the countries of the members of the delegation had been listed, nor had their titles.

"What about the Mexican representative?" Ruppert asked, "Dr. Miguel Cruz? I don't see his name. He was on the original list. Stone and Wormack are operating under the impression that Cruz is still being held hostage."

"Less than an hour ago we learned that Cruz somehow managed to escape and made it to the Spanish Embassy. For the time being they believe he is safe."

"*Time being* is the operative phrase," a voice said. When Ruppert looked up, the President was standing in the doorway. "By that I mean General Sarawak is the type who might just choose to disregard embassy sanctity."

Ruppert stood up, "Mr. President, I—"

Weimer waved him off. "At six o'clock in the morning, Jake, we screw the protocol. I appreciate you coming in at this ungodly hour."

David Weimer was a tall man, taller than either Ruppert and Huntine. At first glance he looked as if he might have been an athlete at one time or another. But that wasn't the case; as the result of an errant shot in a childhood hunting accident, he had a noticeable limp. Now, as he entered the room, he looked tired and the limp was even more pronounced. His eyes were bloodshot and his voice was hoarse.

"I suppose Shuler told you, Jake, I'm taking a lot of heat. Every damn country that has an embassy in this town and has a representative on that delegation in Jakarta has seen fit to come in here and complain in the last twelve hours. They all ask the same question; they all want to know what we're doing about Sarawak. That's why I had Shuler call you; he tells me the Agency has developed a plan. If that's the case, I want some assurances."

Ruppert wasn't sure how far back he needed to go to bring the President up to speed. He knew that the President had already been advised that Gideon Stone was on the scene and had been put in charge of the rescue effort. What he did not know was how the President knew Gideon. On the drive into the city from Langley, he had decided that this was not the time or place to ask.

"I spoke to Colonel Stone less than two hours ago, Mr. President. The special forces team has arrived on the *Bo Jac* and they are preparing to go in at 2100 Jakarta time. I went over the plan with them. It's sound—but it's risky."

"How risky?" Weimer pressed.

"On a scale of one to ten—maybe a nine."

"Will it work?"

"It can, sir," Ruppert said, "but like Colonel Stone said, no guarantees."

The President appraised him for several moments, rubbing his hand across the stubble on his chin and looking briefly at Shuler Huntine before he began again. "As Mr. Huntine has so indelicately put it, the whole world thinks we're sitting here with our thumbs up our asses. The way our friends see it, General Sarawak is mocking us and we aren't doing a helluva lot about it. Fortunately, they aren't either. All we need at this stage of the game is for some of our friends in the United Nations to start playing Rambo. If that happens, we'll have a helluva lot bigger problem on our hands than an attempted coup in Java."

Huntine waited for Weimer to finish. "I relayed your message, Mr. President. I told Jake the first order of business was to get the Vice President and the rest of the hostages out of there. Without them, Sarawak doesn't have any leverage. And I reminded him to tell Stone that it wasn't his job to get Sarawak."

Weimer slumped back in his chair. "Which is precisely why I wanted to talk to you, Jake. I wanted to remind you that both diplomatically and technically, General Sarawak is Kujon's problem. That situation is further compounded by the fact that up until now, Sarni Kujon continues to play ostrich. The man refuses to acknowledge that he even has a problem. Which leaves us no other choice but to interpret that as that the Kujon government is unwilling to tackle General Sarawak. The rest of our friends in the UN apparently share that view. That's why the delegation went there—to convince Kujon to deal with Sarawak before something like this happened.

"The bottom line on all of this is that I can station every damn ship in our fleet in that harbor and it won't help a bit. The Chinese aren't going to back out of their deal with Sarawak until and unless we can put some pressure directly on them. No pressure—no backing off. Those documents we lost when the plane went down would have given us the pressure point we needed. It's a damn shame Colonel Stone couldn't recover them. We would have had something to take to the Security Council and wave under the nose of the Beijing government."

"I take it then that the President knows what happened earlier today when the swarm quakes hit?" Ruppert said.

Huntine nodded.

The President leaned forward and lowered his voice for emphasis. "There's a lot riding on this. Officially, I'm telling you to send Stone in there to get Nelson and the rest of the hostages out of there. Personally and off the record, I would enjoy reading General Sarawak's obituary in the *Post* tomorrow morning. I can take the heat from our friends—all of whom are doing nothing more than trying to protect their collective political asses just like I am. Let's face it, none of us wants a confrontation with the Chinese; far, far too costly."

"I understand, Mr. President."

"At the same time, I don't want a goddamn bloodbath when Stone goes in there. It's a delicate line." Weimer hesitated again, weighing his words. "How do I wrap this up, Mr. Ruppert? Do I tell you I don't care how you do it—or do I just tell you to get it done?"

"We'll give it our best shot, Mr. President," Ruppert said.

"I know you will," Weimer said. "Let's just pray that our best shot is good enough to get the job done." He stood up and extended his hand. "Let's also hope that the next time we get together, it's at a far more reasonable hour."

The President had been gone for several minutes before Huntine had anything to say. It was an offhand question. "What do you think, Jake? Think Gideon can pull it off?"

"I think . . . " Jake hesitated. "The President is right—a little prayer couldn't hurt."

Day 5: Time 2107LT
Soekarno-Hatta
International Airport

After a choppy forty-minute flight from the helipad of the *Bo Jac,* Jeris Alan settled the Apache onto the darkened tarmac at Soekarno-Hatta airport. Following Gideon's instructions, he had put the AH-64 down in front of a seldom-used brace of service hangars belonging to Merpati Airlines and at the exact spot where the rendezvous with the young assistant concierge from the Mandarin-Plaza was scheduled. Gideon breathed a sigh of relief. The first stage of the plan had come off without a hitch.

The woman's name was Fina Tu, and she was swaddled in a bulky raincoat with her collar pulled high to protect her from the weather. Other than the fact that she was a woman, Gideon wasn't able to tell much about her. She was a small woman with an even smaller voice—and she spoke in a kind of half-Maylay-half-English dialect that Gideon found difficult to follow.

Jessie Preston saw what was happening and stepped in. "I keep telling you, Colonel, I can do other things besides fly choppers. Let me talk to her." She turned to the assistant concierge, and listened as Fina Tu went on to explain what was happening. "She's trying to tell you that that's the hotel's Toyota service van over there," Jessie relayed. "She says she brought the one without windows because she thought it would be safer. But—and get this—she also says Sarawak's men have set up roadblocks on all the major streets running into and out of downtown Jakarta."

"Ask her if she still thinks she can get through."

Jessie asked the question in Maylay, and repeated the woman's answer in English. "She thinks she will be able to avoid them by using side streets and alleys—but that it will take a little longer."

"Tell Ms. Fu or whatever the hell her name is," Gideon grumbled, "that I don't like the word 'think.' Can she get us through or can't she?"

Jessie translated for the woman.

When the woman nodded, Jessie began determining the amount of time it would take her to drive the thirty-five kilometers into the city. Gideon listened, and began revising the timing. The other members of the hostage rescue team were already busying themselves transferring their gear from the chopper to the hotel's van.

Gideon had supervised every step of the readying; Jeris Alan's preparations had been meticulous. Each of his men had been equipped with 45-caliber side arms, an MP-5N Heckler and Koch 9mm submachine gun, an ammo pack, a pack belt, and night-vision goggles. In addition, Butcher and Powers each hefted small tubular aluminum containers that included timing devices, electronic gear, and two packets of P1-at explosives. Butcher had explained the logic behind two containers by saying if one of them didn't make it, the other still had everything he needed.

As far as Gideon was concerned, the choice of P1-at was curious for a controlled explosion. A one-pound packet of P1-at was more than capable of leveling the entire four-story embassy building. Still, Butcher had twice defended his choice. "You run the show, Colonel, but you leave the bang to me. Okay?"

At the same time, Sheban Geronimo, Gideon's backup when they landed on the roof of the Mandarin, stood watch.

"Ask her where and how far it is to the hangar where the television helicopters are kept," Gideon said.

Jessie Preston slowly repeated the question in Maylay.

Fina Tu understood, and pointed east in the direction of the main terminal. Then she held up two fingers.

"She says it's two kilometers," Jessie reported.

"Good. Now tell her we want her to drive us to within a hundred yards or so of the TVRI hangar, find a dark place, and let us out."

As Jessie repeated the instructions to the woman in Maylay, Gideon turned to Jeris Alan. "Okay, Captain, it's up to you now. Check your watch. Give us exactly forty-five minutes. Then you start giving Sarawak something to think about. We'll take off five minutes later. We'll make two passes over the area at a low altitude so that they're used to seeing us and you know we're ready. If we play our cards right, they won't be paying much attention to us—they'll be too damn busy trying to figure out what you're up to. When we see Sarawak's men start scrambling toward the blast site, we're going in. Got it?"

Alan nodded. "We've got a few tricks up our sleeve that should add to their confusion, Colonel." Then he added, "Good luck."

Fina Tu brought the Toyota van to a gradual stop in the shadows of the overhang of a fueling shed near the TVRI hangar, and shut off the lights. In the short time it had taken them to leave the Merpati compound and arrive at the TVRI area, Gideon made note of the fact that the intensity of both the wind and the rain had increased. Some rain was good and some wind was good—it afforded them cover—but too much of either would make it even more difficult for Jessie to put the chopper down on the roof of the Mandarin.

He called for one last synchronization of watches before Jessie and Geronimo crawled out of the van and dashed for the deeper darkness behind the hangar. As Gideon crawled out, he glanced back at Butcher. "Big boom, Casio—got it? But not big enough to weaken the roof of that damned hotel. We still have to put a chopper down on it."

Even in the shadowy darkness, Gideon could see Casio Butcher grinning. "Like I said, Colonel, I'm your man; big booms are my specialty."

Gideon tapped the young woman on the shoulder, motioned for her to proceed, closed the door, and waited until the van disappeared down the service road and turned the corner. By the time he caught up with Jessie and Geronimo, Sheban had already checked out the area.

"It should be a piece of cake, Colonel," he whispered. "There are four doors in all, service doors on each side of the building plus the big hangar doors in front. They're closed. From what little I could see, it looks like there's two choppers in there along with some boxes and crates. The two choppers are both small ones."

"He's right," Jessie said. "I'm familiar with them. I saw them flying around the city when I was in Jakarta. All of the TV stations fly variations of the old West German MBB BO 105's. Most of the ones they use around here are built here in Indonesia."

"Think you can fly one of those crates in this kind of weather?" Gideon pushed.

Her answer surprised him; it came out sounding more like a snarl than a response. "Look, Colonel, just once—why don't you try forgetting I'm a woman. Those 105's in there are toys compared to what I'm used to. Would you feel better if I talked like one of your men and said I flew through shit a whole lot worse than this? Here it's a little rain and wind—over there it was groundfire and lots of smoke from burning fuel depots. Or have you forgotten?"

Gideon grinned, bit his lip, and looked at Geronimo. "How about the personnel in there?"

"I saw two, sir—both on the far side of the hangar. They look like they could be mechanics or maintenance types. They've got the radio cranked up and they're playing cards. It doesn't look to me like they're expecting any company."

Gideon was silent for a moment. "All right, this is the way we play it. Jessie, you go around to the service door and walk in, tell them you've been driving around out here because you're supposed to pick up someone at the Merpati Airlines maintenance shed. Then ask for directions. In the meantime, Sheban and I will slip around to the other side, come in through the west door and up behind them. Give us thirty seconds to get around to the other side of the building before you go in."

Jessie Preston nodded, stood up, headed for the door, and counted to thirty before she opened it. One of the two men looked up, the other stood.

"Can you help me?" she said. "I'm afraid I'm lost." When she saw the puzzled look on the men's faces, she realized her mistake. "*Saya mau pergi ke . . .* " she began, switching to Maylay.

"Siapa nama anda?" the man asked.

By the time Jessie repeated her question and started to answer his, Stone and Geronimo had emerged from the shadows behind the two men. Gideon took one out with a karate chop across the shoulder, and the man went to his knees. Geronimo used the butt of his .45 on the other. Neither of the two men had time to register surprise.

"Tie 'em up and gag 'em," Gideon ordered. "Jessie—get ready to get us out of here."

Casio Butcher and Kendall Powers crouched in the back of the Toyota van as it pulled out of the terminal area onto the main highway and headed into the city. Twice the Maylay woman slowed momentarily for traffic lights. When she did, the only sounds either of them could hear were their own breathing, the hum of the engine, and the persistent slap-slap sound of the van's windshield wipers.

Through it all, Butcher continued to work with the P1-at. While Powers occasionally monitored traffic, Butcher opened one of the two containers, measured out approximately half of the compound, wadded it into a crude ball, and carefully inserted two small copper wires just below the surface. Then he used a small gauging device to check the depth and placement of the wires. Finally, he attached a length of C-cord fusing; it was a three-foot coil of thin plastic wiring that was attached to the battery pack. Satisfied with his handiwork, he took out a roll of electrical tape, secured each connection, and held it up in the intermittent illumination of passing streetlights for Powers's inspection. "Pretty, huh?" he asked.

Butcher was inspecting the device for the third time when Fina Tu slowed again and finally brought the van to a complete halt.

"What the hell are we stopping here for?" Butcher whispered. "I don't see any damn stoplights."

The young woman managed to make the words "militiamen" understandable. Powers inched his way forward on the floor of the van past the mail sacks and peeked over the back of the driver's seat. Finally, he looked back at Butcher. "I think we got trouble," he muttered.

Powers watched Fina Tu roll the driver's window down as a man in a hooded raincoat approached the van. He was holding his right hand up in a halting motion. In the other he held a flashlight.

"Buka pinta," the militia man ordered. His voice was young and edgy.

Fina Tu was rattled and she hesitated. If the young soldier found the two Americans in the van, there was no telling what he would do. Fina Tu's hesitation was just enough to make the young man even more tense. He froze when she reached for the handle on the door. By the time she opened it, he had already reached in the pocket of his raincoat for a small revolver. With his other hand he began stabbing the beam of his flashlight in Fina Tu's eyes. As he did, he shouted back to another militiaman.

Up to that point, the young soldier's backup had been standing at the side of the road under the overhang of a bus stop. He was leaning on his rifle with his shoulders hunched against the weather, paying little attention. But now he had begun circling to the other side of the van with his rifle pointed at Fina Tu.

"Siapa nama anda," the first soldier demanded.

"F-Fina Tu Sayan," she stuttered. But by that time it was too late. She had waited too long to respond. The young militiaman lunged forward and shoved the revolver in her face.

Powers continued to watch. He was waiting until the last possible second—hoping to avoid a confrontation that was beginning to appear inevitable. He had no way of knowing where they were in relation to the hotel area and no way of knowing who would hear the shot. By the same token, he knew he couldn't afford to wait much longer. It was now or never. He pulled himself up, lurched forward, jammed his .45 through the open window, and fired. At something less than six inches from his target, the right side of the young man's face exploded and he was catapulted backward.

By the time Kendall Powers was able to spin around and squeeze off a second shot, the second militiaman had dropped to his knees and fired twice. He heard the first bullet rip through the cab of the van and he heard Fina Tu scream. The second gouged its way through sheet metal and whistled harmlessly past his head.

He waited until the man with the rifle stood up. Powers extended his arm, sighted, and squeezed off two more rounds. The glass in the passenger's-side window splintered, and he watched the man clutch at his stomach before he stumbled forward and slumped to the pavement.

It wasn't until he heard the back doors of the van swing open that he realized there was a third militiaman. The man had an automatic rifle and he opened fire. The hail of bullets ripped through Casio Butcher. He was still clutching the bomb, but the body of the man Gideon Stone was counting on to create the biggest diversion of all had been propelled backwards into the pile of mail sacks. His chest and his stomach were already a bloody smear, and he had never uttered a sound.

In that same volley, the militiaman had managed to bury one of the slugs in Powers's thigh—but unlike

Butcher, he managed to get off two shots of his own. The second one hit its target. The militiaman dropped his rifle, clutched at his throat, and slid to his knees. Powers crouched and spun again. Then he saw it the young Indonesian woman was slumped over the steering wheel. She was sobbing and holding her hand over her right shoulder. An ugly wet smear had saturated her raincoat just below the shoulder, and a thin trickle of blood had already searched its way down her arm and out from under her sleeve.

"How bad are you hit?" Powers shouted.

The young Indonesian woman understood him just well enough to stammer out, *"Sa—saya—saya baik . . . "*

"Dammit," Powers yelled, "speak English. How bad are you hit? Can you make it? Can you drive?"

She was still sobbing when Powers grabbed her by the arm and spun her around to get a better look at where she was hit. The woman saw past him, and screamed. In the surreal half-light of the street lamps, she had caught a fleeting glimpse of what was left of Casio Butcher. An oily stain had clawed its way out and over him. There were two gaping holes; one in his chest, the other in his stomach. He was still struggling, still trying vainly to suck in all the air he could—but it was an exercise in futility. The passage between nose and mouth and lungs had been blown away. The word "esophagus" ricocheted around in Powers's brain like a ping pong ball. Who gives a damn what they call it, he thought, the son of a bitch isn't there any more.

Powers knew even before he bent over his friend. Casio Butcher had fallen into the final spasm of a desperate and pointless struggle. Powers realized what was happening—but only because he had seen the terrifying spectacle before. He reached down and gently clamped his hand over his friend's face until all the sounds of dying ceased.

When it was over, Powers turned back to the woman. "Now, dammit, can you drive?"

Fina Tu's right arm hung limp at her side. She was trying desperately to choke back her sobs. She shook her head. The word *tidak* was barely audible.

"Does that mean no?"

Fina Tu nodded.

"Then crawl over into the passenger's seat," he ordered. He pointed to help her understand. "Before we do anything else, I've got to get rid of these bodies."

Kendall Powers jumped down out of the van, winced when the pain shot up his leg, and one by one, pulled the bodies of the three Bandung militiamen over to the side of the road and dumped them into a drainage ditch that was already choked with the runoff. When he was finished, he looked at the van for several moments before deciding to do the same with Butcher's body.

By the time he was able to pry the packet of explosives out of Casio's hand and lift his body out of the van, he had come to the realization that the bullet hole in his own leg had done more damage than he'd first thought.

He slipped the belt out of Butcher's pants, tied it around his leg, creating a tourniquet, lifted Butcher's body over his shoulder, and hobbled back to the side of the road. He muttered a quick prayer, rolled Butcher's body down the incline into the darkness, and went back to the Toyota.

As he crawled behind the steering wheel, he looked at the woman. "Don't try to talk. I'll drive—you point. Understand what I'm saying?"

The woman's eyes were glassy and she was staring

straight ahead through the shattered windshield. The sobs were less frequent now but, she was still trembling.

"Dammit!" Powers roared. "Answer me—do you understand?"

Finally Fina Tu nodded.

Chapter Six

Day 5: Time 0931LT
Indonesian Embassy,
Washington

Undersecretary of State Marshal Saalfrank stood in the vestibule of the Indonesian Embassy appraising, as he had many times before, the rich red, white, and bronze colors of the tulis batik wall hanging that had dominated the entrance to the building. It had been there for as long as he could remember. It was, he had decided on each of those previous visits, a bit too ornate for his Midwestern taste—and definitely different from anything he had studied in the one art appreciation class he had taken as an undergraduate at the University of Nebraska.

It had become a ritual. He pondered the work from a

distance, cocking his head sideways and hooding his eyes, hoping to gain some insight into the artist's intentions or the work's meaning.

When he heard footsteps behind him, he turned, expecting to greet one of the Indonesian ambassador's secretaries. On this occasion, however, he was welcomed by the ambassador himself.

"Beautiful, isn't it?" Keramat Koro said. The way he had phrased his question, it sounded as if he was looking for Saalfrank's approval of the work.

"Indeed, Mr. Ambassador, it is lovely," Saalfrank said, "but I have to admit that I believe I would appreciate it even more if I understood it better."

"There are centuries of history and folklore depicted in the work," Koro explained. Then he smiled and waited, as though he expected Saalfrank to confirm the obvious reason for calling so early in the morning.

When Undersecretary Saalfrank hesitated, Koro led him into his office, where a painting depicting a Balinese temple dominated an otherwise bare wall behind his desk. Marshal Saalfrank had always assumed that this work, unlike the other, had some sort of religious significance. He cleared his throat and began. "You sent for me, Mr. Ambassador?"

Koro nodded. Twice before, when Sarawak had first begun to flex his muscles on the island of Karimunjawa, the American's presence had been requested. "You are here because I requested your presence," Koro said. "Correct?"

"I am here, Mr. Ambassador, because of your request and the fact that General Sarawak has already taken the life of one member of the Security Council delegation, Sir Edward Peel, the representative from Great Britain. Now he is threatening to take the lives of others." At that point he hesitated, waiting for Koro to affirm his government's condolences. When the Indonesian ambassador remained silent, Saalfrank continued. "My government does not understand why the Sarni Kujon government remains mute—why they have not issued some kind of statement."

"What exactly would you have us say or do?" Koro asked. "Would you have us acquiesce and give into the rebel demands—or should we, as you Americans put it, stay the course? Which would you have us do?" Koro paused, opened the ornate pewter cigarette case on his desk, extracted a cigarette, and lit it. "Should I remind you that His Eminence Sarni Kujon is a man in his eighties, the rightful ruler of our nation and a god-king to our people. Should I also remind you that we are a peace-loving nation with only modest military resources; certainly not the kind of resources needed to rid ourselves of men like Sarawak and his Bandung movement."

Saalfrank listened. He knew where Koro was heading. The two men had held prior discussions about Sarawak. But he was equally aware that in recent months there had been little or no dialogue with the Kujon government about the matter. Now, Sarawak had announced his takeover.

"Frankly, we are somewhat perplexed by your country's actions, Secretary Saalfrank. First we hear the announcement by your President Weimer that he is sending in the powerful United States Navy—but I am more recently informed by reliable sources in Jakarta that your Navy sits outside of my country in international waters and takes no action."

Saalfrank weighed his words carefully. "No one understands the delicacy of this situation more than we do, Mr.

Ambassador. Unfortunately, the whole world is watching, including many of my country's biggest critics."

"Your concern is about your critics when men are dying?"

Saalfrank cleared his throat. "What I'm saying is, Sarawak has the backing of the Beijing government and he also has many followers in your country. Karimunjawa is no longer just a slumbering little Indonesian island with a handful of restless people protesting current Kujon government policies."

"We are aware of that," Koro snapped.

Saalfrank wasn't finished. "While your government ignores what is happening, Mr. Ambassador, General Sarawak, along with his Bandung terrorists, has accumulated enough arms, equipment, and men to become a very real threat to the balance of power in that part of the world. Today it is Java. We have every right to assume that his ambitions extend far beyond that one island."

Koro's expression was implacable, but his voice exhibited his concern. "Then why does your government not take action?"

"This is a very delicate matter, Mr. Ambassador." Saalfrank reached down, opened his briefcase, took out a large eight-by-eleven envelope, and laid it on the ambassador's desk. "We have satellite photos which show the magnitude of the arsenal General Sarawak is accumulating on the island of Karimunjawa and the training facilities where he is preparing his Bandung followers. It is quite obvious to us that Sarawak isn't preparing for a peaceful coup, Mr. Ambassador; he is preparing for an all-out confrontation with the Kujon government."

Koro put down his cigarette and stood with his hands clasped behind his back, ignoring the envelope. "I have also heard that your government claims to have documentation which proves that the Beijing government has been supplying Sarawak with money and arms. If you have such proof, why has it not been presented to the UN Security Council?"

Saalfrank hesitated.

Koro repeated his question. "Where is it? Why have you not shared it with the Security Council?"

Saalfrank's shoulders sagged. "Unfortunately, that documentation, Mr. Ambassador, was in the hands of one of our couriers, who was on his way to the United States. He was aboard the ill-fated Garuda flight that went down in the Java Sea one week ago. Since then we have been on the scene, attempting to recover those documents."

Finally, Koro took a seat. When he did, he leaned forward with his arms on the desk and tented his fingers. "I have learned many American expressions during my brief stay in your country, Secretary Saalfrank. Perhaps one of those sayings is appropriate now. Perhaps I should be asking, What do you intend to do about it?"

Saalfrank lowered his voice. "That's the real reason why I am here, Mr. Ambassador. As we speak, my government is initiating a plan to rescue the hostages. As soon as we have rescued them, we can deal with the larger issue, that of General Sarawak and his announced coup." Saalfrank paused and ran his fingers across his chin. "You are well aware that any large-scale military action on my government's part, such as our Navy going ashore now and taking action against Sarawak, would be misconstrued as simply one more case of American intervention in a situation that called for diplomacy.

"Bottom line, Mr. Ambassador, we believe it is too late for diplomacy. I am here to inform you and the Kujon government that we are going in after the hostages—and we will use force to achieve that objective. Our first priority is to get the hostages out of there; then we let the United Nations do the negotiating. If that fails, my government can see to it that the Kujon government has the necessary wherewithal to dispose of General Sarawak."

Koro was silent for quite some time. "Then I will inform my government of your intentions."

"No," Saalfrank said, "it is imperative that you say nothing of our intentions. With all due respect, Mr. Ambassador, we do not know who does and who does not sympathize with the Bandung. We are informing you of our intentions only out of courtesy to your government."

Day 5: Time 2207LT
Mandarin-Plaza Hotel

On two separate occasions between the dinner hour and ten o'clock, Bojoni Sarawak had tried to get some sleep. Each time the effort was aborted by distressing fits of sweat and nightmares. The attacks of fever, like the tide, ebbed and flowed; the bed linen was soaked, and each of the malaria episodes had been accompanied by brief but intense headaches.

Now, still suffering the aftereffects of his bouts with the fever, he was being briefed by Ketan Sabo. The young Bandung captain sat across from him in a small fourth-floor alcove that Sarawak had declared off-limits not only to the hotel staff and guests, but also to all Bandung militiamen except his immediate staff.

The hotel's kitchen staff, many of whom had professed to be sympathetic to the Bandung movement since Sarawak had taken over the hotel, had prepared a meal for him. As Sabo updated him, Sarawak devoured a dinner consisting of *kodok, lemper,* and *nasi rawon.* The *kodok,* or frog, was a favorite with Sarawak since his boyhood on Bali. The *nasi rawon,* a spicy beef soup liberally laced with fried onions, was a concoction he had only recently learned to enjoy.

"What have we heard from Kujon?" Sarawak asked.

Ketan Sabo shook his head. "The old one continues his silence, General. There has been no word from the palace, nor have we heard from his usually vocal emissaries."

Sarawak was perplexed by Kujon's continued silence. "Surely he knows what is happening."

"Our contacts in the palace claim the old one is waiting for a response from the Americans."

Sarawak listened, finished eating, and wiped off his mouth with a napkin. "I find that strange," he confided. "The old fool has never been one to hold his tongue. So far we have heard no expressions of outrage, of indignation, no pontificating—it is unlike him. Why now?"

Ketan Sabo, unlike his Bandung leader, was not the kind to concern himself with questions of behavior. To him, matters were either black or white. The reasons behind Kujon's reticence were of little interest to him. Instead of trying to find an answer to Sarawak's question, he contented himself with lighting a cigar that he had pilfered from the hotel's humidor in a first-floor gift shop. When he had exhaled his first draw on the cigar, he returned to his reporting mode.

"We now have confirmed reports that the American aircraft carrier *Shenandoah* is anchored some twenty-five miles from the harbor, General. One of our gunboats is monitoring its transmissions. It reports there has been little activity."

Sarawak listened to the wind howling outside his hotel

window. The rain hammered against the glass and he sneered. "Are we supposed to be impressed by this senseless display of power?" Then he added, "At a time like this, the monsoons are our ally."

"Nor has there been any response from the Americans other than the speech by their President," Sabo added. He pointed to the clock to remind Sarawak of the time. "Perhaps it will again be necessary to show them we have every intention of carrying out our threat."

Sarawak reflected for a moment. Finally he said, "Bring me the one from Checheno-Ingush, the one they call Lesni."

Vladimir Lesni, despite having achieved the advanced age of eighty-two, was still surprisingly robust and active. A former Communist Party leader in Checheno-Ingush, he described himself as a former Bolshevik who had thrown off the yoke of myopia to see the error of his ways. Now slightly stooped, but still standing over six feet in height, he was the only man in the UN delegation that could stand toe-to-toe with Sarawak and look the general in the eye.

Unlike the others in the delegation, when he was ushered into the room and ordered to stand in the presence of Sarawak, he showed no sign of apprehension.

Sarawak, still seated, appeared to contemplate the hostage for what Ketan Sabo regarded as a long time before he spoke. "You know, Comrade Lesni, I find it somewhat curious that a man of your stature and background would permit himself to be duped into an alliance such as—"

Lesni stood with his feet apart, his arms folded, staring back at the general. Sarawak knew the look of defiance. "I do not wish to be lectured," Lesni said, "before I become yet another victim in your futile bloodbath, General. Please spare me your simpering rhetoric about suppression of the masses and the corruption of capitalism."

Sarawak felt his face color, and he stood up. He circled the aging former Bolshevik before he began again. "You are a foolish man, Comrade. I was ready to offer you what we use to call when I was in college in America 'a deal.' In exchange for your willingness to try to convince the other members of your esteemed delegation to encourage the Kujon government to step down both promptly and peacefully, I would have been willing to grant you your freedom."

Lesni spat on the floor in front of Sarawak and stared past his tormentor. He moved easily from his native Russian language to Maylay. "You forget, Comrade General, I have already spent a lifetime witnessing what happens to men who allow themselves to become enslaved to totalitarian ideals and oppressive governments. I did that once; I do not wish to be a part of that nightmare again."

Sarawak had underestimated the aging Russian. Lesni was strong—much too strong. Strength among hostages was dangerous. "Send Major Muta in," he said, struggling to reveal his rage.

Moments later, Assasio Muta appeared at the door. Aware of the hour, he had been anticipating Sarawak's summons, and he was smiling. "Yes, General," he said.

"Ah, Major Muta, I have a small chore for you; the kind you relish. It would appear that our American friends need another reminder that the clock is ticking. Escort Comrade Lesni to the hotel's foyer and see that he joins his high-minded colleague, Mr. Peel."

"Yes, General," Muta answered. He crossed the room, walked up behind the Russian statesman, and poked the barrel of his Chinese 9mm automatic in the small of Lesni's back. *"Bisa berbicara bahasa Maylay?"* Muta asked.

"Da," Lesni uttered in Russian, and with Muta prodding him, he started toward the door.

Sarawak was still waiting for the two men to leave the room when the phone rang. Sabo answered. As he listened, his expression changed. "One moment," he said, "I will inform the general." He clamped his hand over the mouthpiece and looked at Sarawak. "Our patrols report that three of our men have been killed at one of the checkpoints on the Jl Merdeka."

Sarawak frowned. "When?"

"Only moments ago, General," Sabo said. "They also report that they found the body of an American. He was dressed in commando gear."

"So that is their game," Sarawak said. He was amused. "They resort to subterfuge. While we watch the front door, they come in the back door. Two can play that game, Captain. See that our guards are alerted."

Day 5: Time 2301LT
The Banjaran-Nepo,
Jakarta

For Kendall Powers, the darkened side streets and even darker alleyways of the Banjaran-Nepo section of Jakarta had become a mind-boggling maze. Still, the Malay woman continued to guide him. Moreover, twice within the last few minutes she had indicated that they were approaching the site of the deserted embassy building. It was a labyrinth of streets that seemed to lead nowhere and impassable too-narrow lanes.

Through it all, they had developed a system of workable hand signals. Powers turned when and where Fina Tu pointed, and slowed when she instructed him to slow. Twice they had been forced to stop while Powers loosened the tourniquet on his leg and checked the bleeding in her shoulder. Twice more they had been forced to alter their route when the young Indonesian woman spotted Bandung militiamen stationed at checkpoints along their intended route.

Finally they pulled into a narrow alley between two buildings, and Fina Tu pointed to an imposing structure at the end of it. *"Berhenti disini,"* she managed. Her voice was weak.

"That's it?" Powers asked.

"Ya," the woman said. She managed to open her door, crawled down out of the van, and motioned for Powers to follow. Powers hobbled after her, pulled his collar up against the rain, and peered up the alley into the darkness. Behind him two dogs were rummaging through a pile of garbage. The young Indonesian woman, with her right arm hanging limp at her side, was watching him. He motioned for her to stay back, and began working his way toward the embassy building.

Ahead of him was the building's loading dock with a single, ineffective incandescent bulb hanging over a rusty sign. Beyond it was a concrete loading dock littered with boards, broken pieces of drywall, and other construction debris. The thought occurred to him that the workers would have to start all over again after he had finished.

By the time he had managed to get to the ramp leading up to the dock, his leg was throbbing again and he was forced to stop and loosen the tourniquet. At the top of the ramp there were two doors: one a service door, the other a large overhead affair that had been chained and padlocked. Next to the service door was a window covered with a sheet of plywood. He pried the plywood off the window, opened it, shoved the small metal canister, his MP-5N, and other gear through, hefted his weight up on the sill, and despite the pain in his leg, pulled himself through. When he looked back down the alley, there was no sign of Fina Tu but the van was still there.

Inside now, Powers scanned the cluttered receiving area, waiting for his eyes to adjust to the darkness. He was on the ground floor, and he knew he had to work his way up at least three floors. That sounded a whole lot easier than it was going to be. His leg was pounding again, and each step brought with it a stabbing pain that rocketed up his spine and into the base of his skull. He groped around in the darkness until he located the stairway and started up. When he got to the landing at the top of the stairs he saw a light and heard voices. He knew it was too risky to use even the small penlight he carried. Instead he traced the tip of his fingers over the brass braille compass strapped to his left wrist, and was finally able to determine that the voices were coming from the north side or front of the building.

The one thing Kendall Powers wasn't able to determine was whether the men had been posted in the old building as guards, or if they had just stepped in to escape the weather. It made a difference. If they were guards and prone to any kind of discipline at all, they would probably be patrolling the building from time to time—and that could pose a problem. If they were simply using the old embassy as a shelter, in all probability they would stay right where they were until the rain abated or they were ordered elsewhere.

Again he waited, trying to regain his bearings before he started up the second flight of stairs. He was dragging his leg now and the numbness had not only slowed his progress, it was causing him to stumble. He fell and felt another sharp pain shoot up the length of his body. When he reached down to test his leg, he realized the blood had started to seep out over the top of the tourniquet. The leg was one problem—the voices were another. His concern now was that the voices had stopped.

He collected himself and lay there for several moments until he heard footsteps. The long penetrating beam of a flashlight was sweeping systematically back and forth across the floor, pausing now and then to probe into the darker corners. Powers tensed.

"Ke mana?" one of the voices asked.

"Saya mau pergi ke . . . " another answered. The second voice sounded to Powers as if it was still some distance from the first.

Powers pulled himself up on his knees, again felt the stabbing pain, somehow managed to stifle the urge to cry out, slipped his hand in his field packet, took out his garrote wire, tried to regain control of his breathing, and waited.

The footsteps came closer and the beam paused for a moment before it began plying back and forth at the bottom of the steps just inches below him.

"Apa kabar?" the second voice voice shouted. It sounded as though it had come from the other side of the open bay. Another beam of light, accompanied by labored breathing and footsteps, turned the corner and began probing its way up the stairs. Despite his leg, Powers coiled, waited for just the right moment, and lunged. His left hand clamped down on the man's mouth, his right forearm came up and lodged under the man's chin. The rest was training—three years of it. The man's head snapped to the right—then just as quickly back to the left.

There was a sickening splintering sound, and even though the man was still locked in Powers's grasp, his head lolled lazily to one side.

Kendall Powers held his breath for several seconds, and finally breathed a sigh of relief. When he did, he lowered the man's body to the floor, turned off the flashlight, and waited. Within a matter of moments, he could hear the approaching footsteps of the other guard. He was shouting something in Maylay. There was alarm in his voice, and it seemed to increase each time he failed to get a response. Powers managed to pull the body of the dead guard behind a stack of cartons, crouched, and again waited.

It wasn't long until he could see him—the light was pivoting back and forth and up and down. Powers had to give him credit, he was cautious, and even though the string of Maylay questions continued to go unanswered, he was moving closer.

Powers continued to wait.

The Maylay was almost close enough to touch.

Powers held his breath. His head was pounding and his leg was throbbing. Again he coiled, lunged, and caught the militiaman flush in the side. He could hear the air go out of him when they hit the floor.

Once again, the steady diet of training took over. All in one motion, Powers had landed on top of the man, wrapped the garrote wire around the guard's throat, and was tightening it. There was a profane, partially muted, short-lived protest, and a brief struggle,but the outcome was never in doubt. Powers continued to tighten the wire until the brief scuffle ended.

It was over—and when he was certain it was, Kendall Powers permitted himself the luxury of slumping to the floor and the chance to catch his breath.

* * *

Gideon Stone and Sheban Geronimo had been crammed in the back of the tiny MBB BO 105 chopper for almost thirty minutes when Jessie finally took off. Moments later they saw the Apache make its first pass over the city.

Alan and Miller had brought the craft in from the north, the direction of the harbor, circled the hotel twice and disappeared again back into the rain and darkness. Gideon estimated the Apache's first pass at something in excess of 1500 feet.

They had watched Sarawak's men gather in the street in front of the hotel. They were gesturing, waving their arms and running back and forth, but there was no groundfire.

Alan made his second pass even lower, and this time the Bandung were better prepared. The Apache dropped two NL flares, and the street in front of the Mandarin was temporarily awash in an eerie yellow-white phosphor light. By the time the militiamen's eyes had adjusted to the sudden glare of the flare and managed to open fire, the Apache had already disappeared.

"Nice touch," Jessie heard Gideon mutter. "If we get out of this damn thing alive, Preston, remind me to buy those two a drink."

Through it all, Jessie Preston continued to tweak the collective and hold the MBB BO in a steady hover a couple of hundred feet above the rooftops less than a block from the Mandarin-Plaza. The tiny turbine-engined craft had a plus that she hadn't anticipated; it was equipped with an electronic device that automatically enabled her to maintain the rotor rpm while she watched the drama unfold on the street below. "Looks like you were right,

Colonel," she said. "The Bandung militiamen aren't paying any attention to us. That Apache has them worried."

Gideon's eyes darted back at the EFT on the 105's control panel. The green light on the digital time display was flashing as the last digit in the sequence evolved into a zero instead of a one.

Gideon was watching. He inched his way closer to the cockpit. "That's it, Jessie, we're down to the short hair. If everything is on schedule, Alan's got time for one more pass before Butcher gives us our boom. Start praying."

Jessie Preston watched the array of muted lights on the flight panel and her hand hovered nervously over the cyclic stick. Geronimo grimaced, his lips sealed in a thin line as he checked and rechecked the clip on his MP-5N. He had already attached his AN/PVS-4 night-vision sighting device.

Day 5: Time 1151LT
Manny's Delicatessen,
Washington

Jake Ruppert waited for his old friend Sherman Shapiro to take the first bite of his corned beef sandwich and make his customary proclamation of excellence. It wasn't long in coming.

"I tell ya, Jake, my boy, for the life of me I don't know why I ever let you talk me into meeting you anyplace else. This, my friend, is what food is all about—it's a repast fit for a king. Nobody, absolutely nobody puts together a corned beef sandwich like your pal Manny."

Jake Ruppert was satisfied. He put his drink down and reached for his cigar. This was what lunch with Sherman Shapiro was all about.

Lunch with the newsstand owner was always a treat. Not only was Shapiro an old and trusted friend, equally important was the fact that, like Jake Ruppert, he too enjoyed a good cigar. Even more important, he had nothing to do with the Agency. With Sherman Shapiro there was never any danger of shop talk. Jake liked that. Sarawak's coup attempt in Java had made the last seven days more than a trifle intense on the Washington scene, and opportunities for Jake to get away from it had been few and far between. Even Alice wanted to talk about it when he went home at night.

Jake waited while his old friend took his second bite and went into his customary second fit of ecstasy before finally reaching for his own sandwich. He was about to take his first bite when out of the corner of his eye he saw Della approaching their table.

Della Eiseman was a fixture; she had been the day manager at Manny's for as long as anyone could remember. In some ways she was as famous as the delicatessen's larger-than-life owner.

"You have a phone call, Jake," she said.

Ruppert muttered something about no rest for the weary, excused himself, got up, and walked over to the telephone at the end of the room. "Jake here," he wheezed.

Shuler Huntine's raspy voice managed to bore its way in even over the noise of Manny's lunch crowd. "Are you watching CNN?"

Jake Ruppert glanced up at the television over the bar. "Naw, Della's got some game on—I think it's a replay. Why?"

"Sarawak just turned the heat up a couple of notches. Less than ten minutes ago one of Sarawak's stooges marched Vladimir Lesni, the Russian representative on the delegation, down to the hotel lobby and with every damned TV camera in Jakarta looking on, proceeded to blow Lesni's brains out."

For several seconds, Jake Ruppert had trouble swallowing. Finally he clamped his hand over the mouthpiece and shouted at Della. "Switch it over to CNN!"

By the time the woman complied, the cameras had pulled away from the scene and the commentator was talking about how at first the crowd around the Mandarin Hotel had cheered, but was now subdued.

Jake watched the scene in silence, and it was several seconds before he became aware of the fact that Huntine was talking again. " . . . the President was on the line less than thirty seconds after Lesni was shot. He wants to know what the hell is going on."

Jake Ruppert looked hurriedly around the room before he answered. "Stone is on his way in," he said. "At the moment that's all I can tell you."

Huntine wasn't satisfied. "Won't do, Jake. I need more information than that—a helluva lot more. Weimer's hot."

"I'll be back in the office in fifteen minutes. I'll get an update and get back to you as soon as I know something." As he nestled the receiver back in the cradle, he was already shouting at Della. "Give me one of those Bowser boxes, sweet thing, something's come up back at the office."

Day 5: Time 2353LT
German Embassy Building,
Jakarta

Twice more Kendall Powers found it necessary to stop and relieve the pressure on his leg. He had lost track of how many times he had been forced to do so, but it was at least the fifth or sixth time. The bullet had ripped its way through the meaty part of his thigh, entering in the front and exiting in the back. Blood had saturated his pant leg down past the knee, and if there had been anyone to ask, he would have informed them it was like walking on a stub—a very painful stub. Each step had become a form of torture, sending a clear message to his brain—and he winced aloud every time he took a step.

He was on third floor now, and if Jessie Preston's sketch was right, there was only one more floor to go. Even worse than the pain at the moment was the way that pain had affected his thinking. It was muddled and confused; time and again he found it necessary to keep checking and rechecking his equipment. At one point he came close to panic because his mind had begun playing tricks on him and he was convinced he had left the small canister containing the explosives on the first floor of the building.

Through it all, Kendall Powers had become more aware of the rising element of uncertainty that was also creeping into his brain. There was uncertainty about where the explosive should be placed, and even more uncertainty about how the fuse should be handled. He had the training—but Casio Butcher had always been the expert—not him—and even though Casio had carefully gone over the procedure with him, as they always did prior to a mission, Powers had never actually been required to step in and be the one to place and detonate the explosive. Butcher had always been there.

He loosened the belt that served as a tourniquet, slowly counted to ten, at first feeling relief and almost immediately thereafter, another surge of what was rapidly becoming an unbearable pain. He tightened the belt again, got slowly to his knees, caught his breath, picked up the canister and MP-5N, and stood up.

"One more flight of steps," he muttered, and started up again.

At the top of the stairs he stopped to try to regulate his breathing and as he did, he realized he had encountered another obstacle. The series of twists and turns in the stairs on the way up had confused him. Now he was in total darkness. There was no light at all. The windows had all been boarded up. On the lower floors he had at least had the benefit of the light that filtered in from the street lamps in front of the building. Now even that was gone.

Again he laid his equipment down and tried to run the tips of his fingers over the braille compass. His hands were shaking uncontrollably and he was shivering, but he was still reasonably certain that the east wall was directly ahead of him. That meant he would have to turn around and go back the other way.

The handful of Bandung officers that had assisted Bojoni Sarawak in his takeover of the Mandarin had been assembled in a smoky fifth-floor room. In total, there were seven of them, including Ketan Sabo and Assasio Muta. Sarawak studied their tired faces and tried to assess their frame of mind. He was well aware that fatigue had set in. To a man they were exhausted; most of them had gone without sleep for periods ranging from thirty-six to forty-eight hours.

To make matters even worse, the Bandung general had little to report that would encourage them. Thus far there had been no indication that the Sarni Kujon government was ready to step down and turn the fate of Java over to his coup. Kujon's unexpected silence was compounded by the fact that even though two members of the UN delegation had been assassinated, there had still been nothing to indicate that the rest of world was ready to recognize their effort.

Now, in addition to the fact that an American Apache gunship had penetrated their defenses and was making menacing passes over the city, there were two other pieces of disturbing news. The first was that the Americans had positioned one of their powerful aircraft carriers just outside the harbor at Tanjung Priok. Second was the report that the bodies of three Bandung militia men had been found in a ditch on the road leading in from the airport.

Sarawak paced back and forth in the room as he informed his men of what was happening. "American intervention is to be expected," he said. "It comes as no surprise. The Americans continue to do what they have for the last half century, meddle in the affairs of other countries. They assume the mantle of righteousness and take it upon themselves to determine what is best for other people. Once again the Americans have wrongfully appointed themselves enforcers of the status quo." He lit a cigarette and appraised the impact of his words before he continued. "I know you are tired. I tell you these things now only because we will be forced to redouble our vigilance and renew our commitment to show the world that the Bandung will never rest until we are able to overthrow and deliver the people of Java—and eventually all of our beloved island nation—from the oppressive Kujon regime. We are on the verge of making the People's Republic of Java a reality—we must not falter now."

When Sarawak finished his speech he went to the window, opened it, and pointed below at the garden courtyard in front of the hotel. The new People's Republic of Java flag, his flag, had been raised in front of the hotel.

As the officers of the Bandung filed out of the room, Sarawak turned to Assasio Muta. "Major Muta, I want the remaining hostages assembled in the room next to this one. Put two of your most trusted guards at the door. Under no circumstances are they to be allowed to talk to anyone or leave the room. I want them in a place where we know their every move. If one of them poses a problem . . . shoot him."

"Yes, General," Muta replied.

"As for the rest of the guests that are still in the hotel, Captain Sabo, see that they are evacuated immediately. I am afraid that our warmongering friends have something up their sleeve. If that is the case, I want to be prepared for them."

Chapter Seven

Day 5: Time 1211LT
Washington

Shuler Huntine's office, located in the lowest level of the White House, was considered one of the classic monuments to chaos. File folders were piled everywhere: on his desk, on top of file cabinets, in stacks in corners. His only concession to order was a small area in the center of his desk where he kept three telephones, each a different color, a fax machine, and a stack of yellow ruled legal tablets.

In the farthest corner of the room was a thirteen-inch black-and-white monitor that could, by pressing a single button, bring the horrors of the outside world into focus. The smoky screen could show everything from the White

House's internal security system, to the White House briefing room where the President held press conferences, to all the broadcast and cable channels.

Now, in the middle of the night Jakarta time, he was watching a bizarre spectacle: a stream of people, men and women and an occasional child, most burdened with luggage, filing out of the Mandarin Hotel. From all appearances, they were being peacefully escorted out into the rainy Jakarta night by several dozen Bandung militiamen.

Even though Shuler Huntine was watching the Mandarin's evacuation, he had turned the volume down so he could hear Ruppert better over the phone.

"We don't know what the hell is going on," Ruppert admitted. "In this case you're watching the same channel I am and you know as much about it as I do."

"What the hell is Parker Wormack telling you?" Huntine demanded.

"He says he doesn't know. There's been no announcements. Apparently Sarawak has instructed his people to keep their mouths shut. By now he has to be thinking we're up to something. Wormack says he has his people monitoring all the Indonesian TV and radio stations.

"One thing he did say—and that's causing some confusion around here—is that less than thirty minutes ago, a TVRI broadcast claimed that a Bandung militia patrol found three of their own and one American's body in a ditch along the highway leading in from the airport. According to the broadcast, all four of the men had been shot."

"No ID on the American, I assume?" Huntine pressed.

"No word on that. If it was one of the men that went in with Gideon, he wouldn't be carrying any ID," Ruppert assured him. "Bottom line: At this juncture we just don't know."

Huntine continued to watch the small screen. Ruppert heard him sigh. "Looks like I'll have to tell the President that neither you nor your people can add anything to what we already know. Is that it?"

Jake Ruppert hated to admit it, but this was a scenario being played out halfway around the world—and even though his own people were there they were either involved in the actual operation and unable to be contacted, or not close enough to the action to be able to give him a reading.

"I'm afraid that's it, Shuler," he finally admitted. "Just as soon as I have something concrete to report, I'll get back to you."

Shuler Huntine grunted, slammed the receiver back in its cradle, and turned up the volume on his television. It occurred to him that at that very moment, as little as he knew, he still knew more about what was going on with Sarawak and his coup attempt than the President. That bothered him.

While the rest of the world watched the slightly out-of-focus parade of images originating with TVRI in the rain-soaked streets of Jakarta, Huntine fumed. Then he picked up the telephone, this time the black one. Images passed on by satellite to CNN, the same images he knew the President was watching, continued to taunt him. What the hell was going on? There was no answer and he finally hung up.

Suddenly Shuler Huntine felt closed in. He got up from his desk and walked out of the room, and up the steps to the first floor. From where he stood at the window, he could look out over the Jacqueline Kennedy Garden on the east side of the White House. There was a garden there, all right, but on this sunny late October day, there wasn't much to see. All of the flowers had died—

and most of the leaves had fallen. It was an uncompromising scene. Huntine hated it when there was no room for compromise.

Day 6: Time 0014LT
Former German Embassy,
Jakarta

For Kendall Powers, the world had become an amorphous, gossamerlike universe of half-formed surreal images. Time was warped. Space had little, and sometimes no, definition. He came and he went—one moment he was forced to deal with the now and the reality of pain, the next he was a soldier residing in a boundless cosmos. It was all-inclusive, all-evasive—and all confusion.

Then, as in any return to consciousness, the awareness brought with it the ache that had compelled him to seek a temporary escape in the first place. He shook his head as if the gesture might help him over the last foggy hurdle, as if it might put him on a level playing field.

His leg continued to throb—or whatever word a man would use to describe something that had catapulted him into an arena that far exceeded what he knew as excruciating pain. He counted to ten, inhaled, held his breath, and again began groping in the darkness for his equipment. He was searching for the elongated canister containing the explosive, for an instrument he could use to chisel out the mortar—for a tool of some sort that would help him pry the bricks loose—then he could—

Finally there was no point in going on. He stopped altogether. He leaned forward on his hands and knees—knowing he was going to be sick. There was an aura—an aura that went with losing blood and with being sick to his stomach. He retched, not once but twice, emptying the contents of his stomach near the very place where he was working. Instead of feeling better, he felt weaker.

He closed his eyes. Why was he here? What was he doing? There was a purpose—right? If there was a purpose, what was it? He sat back on his haunches, tried to regulate his breathing, and waited for the sensation to pass. Finally the feeling subsided. He picked up the knife and began chipping away at the mortar again. The brick—that was it, the brick; he had to remove the brick. There was work to do. Time was of the essence—but why?

Still, he continued to whittle away—fragments, flakes, tiny, disklike wafers of crumbling dust—and suddenly, when he was on the verge of exhaustion, the brick was loose. He felt along the edges until he was able to pull it out and lay it on the floor in front of him. Through it all—or was it just in his mind—there was the odor of mildew, of something very old, of something dead—very, very dead.

He paused again—and then he began counting again.

Surprisingly, just closing his eyes for several moments made him feel better—and even if no one could hear him—he was laughing—he was happy—he was free of all encumbrances. He reached into the canister and took out the packet of explosive, straightened the thin spaghettilike wires, and carefully attached them to the lead terminals. Then he ran the leads to a small battery taped to an analog timer. He wound it twice, checked it, pressed the switch, and it began to tick.

Now, he thought, there's something else I believe I have to do. I have to go—I have to leave this place and go away—far away. But before he could get to his feet, he started to laugh and found himself being whisked away into his whirling, quixotic world again. He slumped back, laughing, against the wall, fumbled through his pockets until he found his pack of cigarettes, extracted one, and savored the smell of the tobacco. Only then did he conduct a search for his lighter.

It was the laughter that masked the sound of the cautious footsteps behind him. "Stay—where—you—are," the militiaman ordered. The man's English was broken, but his rifle was pointed at Powers's head.

Kendall Powers turned, looked at the intruder through hooded eyes, and slowly sagged to the floor with his back against the wall. He was in a sitting position with his knees tucked up against his chest and his arms wrapped around his legs.

"Siapa nama anda?" the guard demanded.

Powers had no idea what the man was talking about, but he laughed anyway.

"Siapa nama anda?" the man repeated. *"Bahasa Inggris?"*

Suddenly Kendall Powers stopped laughing and began counting. The words were only slightly slurred. "You're—you're about to get the surprise of your life, old buddy." Then he began counting again. "One thousand and six, one thousand and seven, one thousand and eight . . . "

The Maylay guard was holding a Chinese automatic rifle in one hand and a flashlight in the other.

Powers quit counting and started laughing again. "Did anyone ever tell you you're an ugly little son of a bitch?" he said with a giggle.

No one knew exactly what time it happened, but microseconds later the fourth floor of the old German embassy building next to the Mandarin-Plaza Hotel exploded. There was an instantaneous ball of fire, accompanied by flying shards of metal and debris—and finally, the stench of burning flesh. The floor buckled and sagged, portions of the old building's ceiling and roof caved in, and the world of Kendall Powers and an unknown May-lay militia man became an all-consuming inferno.

Despite the muffling sound of the chopper's rotor, the wind and rain, and the fact he was several hundred feet above the old embassy building when it exploded, Gideon Stone both heard it and saw it. The explosion was bigger, much bigger than he had anticipated. "All right, Jessie, now it's our turn."

Day 6: Time 0014LT
Mandarin-Plaza Hotel

Bone-weary and occasionally dozing at his post on the fifth floor of the Mandarin-Plaza when the bomb went off, Ketan Sabo was jarred into awareness and felt the floor of the Mandarin-Plaza Hotel shudder at the same moment. Then, for what seemed like an eternity, he was convinced the very floor he was standing on would give way under him.

There was instantaneous chaos as the dust and smoke billowed up from the floor below. He could hear people shouting, and the two militiamen he had stationed in front of the door to the room where the hostages were being detained dropped their rifles and fled.

The door to Sarawak's room flew open and the Bandung revolutionary leader stepped into the corridor, staring in disbelief at the pandemonium. At the same time, Assasio Muta emerged from the room across the hall from Sarawak with his tunic unbuttoned and his automatic drawn. A frightened young woman, only partially dressed, cowered behind him.

Sabo, trying to restore order, saw another Bandung

militiaman emerge from the turmoil in the stairwell. The man was bleeding and dazed. "A bomb," he shouted, " . . . a bomb and there is—is—there is fire."

Initially, Sarawak could only smell the smoke. But now it was billowing up from the floor below. He went back into his room and raced to the window. Five stories below, people were spilling out of the hotel's entrance into the streets and his Bandung militiamen were making no effort to stop them. Many of the militiamen appeared to be fleeing.

"Captain Sabo," Sarawak ordered, "round up some of your men and find out what happened. Report back to me."

Ketan Sabo acknowledged his general's order, motioned for the first four men he saw to follow him, and charged down the smoke-filled stairs to the floor below. Only three obeyed, while the fourth bolted for the stairs and what he believed was safety.

Sabo had felt the blast and knew it was powerful, but it had wreaked far more devastation than he was prepared for. The corridor of the floor below was congested with smoke; there were piles of smoldering rubble and debris. Doors had been blown off their hinges and the ceiling near the elevator was on fire. Within moments he could hear the forlorn, mocking wail of the hotel's fire alarm and the cries of two men who had apparently been too close to the site of the blast. They were stunned and frightened. One of them had lost an arm.

Then Sabo saw it; there was gaping hole in the fourth-floor west wall of the hotel and a roaring barrier of flame both in front of and just beyond it. He scrambled, half crawling, half clawing his way over piles of smoldering wreckage, ignoring the heat, disregarding the choking smoke, then found a way through and signaled for his men to follow. A handful of the beams that had been supporting the roof of the old embassy building had already given way; some had snapped, others had collapsed through a hole in the floor to the level below. Sabo saw one of his men stop and recoil. In the smoky aftermath of confusion, the man had blundered into the decimated remains of one of his fellow militiamen. All that was left of the former soldier was a charred and dismembered torso; anything beyond that was unrecognizable.

Just beyond that body, there was another. This one was partially buried under burning litter, already scorched beyond any hope of recognition. Sabo caught a glimpse of the submachine gun the man had been carrying. He did not recognize the make.

Even though the thick, acrid smoke had almost forced him to turn back, Ketan Sabo finally managed to make it to the landing at the top of the stairs in the old embassy building. He looked down, and again motioned for his men to follow. Only then did he realize that just two of the three men were with him.

Jessie Preston was nervous—more nervous than she dared to admit. She could sense it in the familiar little twinge she felt in her palms and the soles of her feet—the only two places on her body that betrayed her at times like this. She lowered the collective to start the helicopter's descent, and adjusted the cyclic to insure that she was maintaining just enough airspeed for the approach through the clouds of billowing smoke. This one was going to be tricky and she knew it.

While they had waited, Sheban Geronimo had crawled up to the 105's flight deck and into the chair beside her. The stock of his HK was tucked in the crotch of his shoulder as he peered down into the darkness.

Other than the unceasing noise of the buffeting wind, the unrelenting sounds of the monsoon, and the 105's air-thumping rotor, their wait had brought with it a disturbing furtiveness in the aircraft's cramped cabin. For the last several minutes, neither Geronimo nor Stone had spoken. It was as if both men realized that Jessie Preston was doing something she had never done before, something, in fact, she had never dreamed she would have to do. There had been no simulations—no scenarios like this one back in her flight school days.

In the midst of those buffeting winds and the unceasing rain, she was attempting to land an aircraft she had never flown before onto the roof of a hotel that didn't have a helipad, without lights and with nothing to judge space and distance with but a pair of night-vision goggles designed primarily for a man carrying an M-16. To top it off, the landing area had just been rocked by an explosion and there were no guarantees. The roof of the hotel appeared to be intact, but they knew it could give way under the weight of the 105 the moment it touched down.

She eased the aft cyclic to decrease her speed and start the landing flare. She was nursing the collective as the 105's airspeed dropped below the transitional lift, and she used the forward cyclic and collective to pull up and hold at a hover level over the landing area.

Gideon held his breath and watched the former combat pilot deftly manipulate the controls until he felt the reassuring bottoming-out sensation of the skids making contact with the roof. Only then did he allow himself to breathe.

The moment the 105 touched down, Gideon Stone kicked the door open, leaped down to the roof, and dropped to one knee. Geronimo was right behind him.

They were in luck on two counts. First, the roof was

still partially intact. Second, if Sarawak had militiamen posted on the roof, they had run for safety when they felt the explosion. Above him, Jessie throttled back on the 105's power, waiting for Stone to give her the all-clear signal.

Just as he did, the roof started to give way directly in front of the craft and angry orange-red flames began shooting up from the inferno below.

"Get the hell out of here before she caves in!" Gideon shouted.

"What about you and Geronimo?" Jessie screamed.

"If we can find Nelson and the rest of the hostages and get back to the roof, we'll set off a flare to give you a signal. If the roof goes, hightail it back to the ship and tell Wormack what happened. We'll find another way out."

Gideon jumped back and crouched as Jessie shoved the throttle controls to the takeoff power setting. The 105 lifted into a hover, escaping the flames, and Jessie held the craft in a nose-down attitude until Gideon heard the rotor motor rev to a climbing speed. He was still watching when the 105 spiraled up and disappeared into the swirling smoke and rain.

By the time Gideon turned around, Geronimo had already inspected the elevator and the service stairway leading down into the old ballroom. His face was covered with soot and his eyes were tearing from the smoke.

"We got us one king-size problem, Colonel; the damn updraft in the elevator shaft is feeding the flames. The smoke is pouring out of the goddamn thing like a cheap chimney. We can try the stairs down to the ballroom, but the whole sixth floor appears to be an inferno."

"Is there a fire escape?"

Geronimo shook his head. "Didn't see one, Colonel."

"How do you feel about heights, Corporal?"

From the way Stone had phrased the question, Sheban Geronimo knew what was coming next. With both the elevator and stairways impassable, there was only one other way down; they would have to go over the side and rappel their way down the side of the building until they were sure they had worked their way past the flames.

"Don't like 'em, Colonel—but what the hell, I don't like snakes either and they're thicker than flies where I come from."

Gideon picked up his gear, and the two men began carefully circling that section of roof where the flames had already chewed their way through, working their way toward the back of the hotel where the smoke wasn't quite as dense.

Gideon uncoiled the rope, secured it to the base of the hotel's TV tower, shouldered the strap of his HK, swung it around to his back, and crawled over the side of the building. To his left he could see flames leaping out of the window on the floor directly below him, but beyond that he could see nothing. The combination of dense smoke, darkness, and rain obscured the rest.

"Keep your eyes peeled," he shouted. "As soon as I find a place to get in, I'll release the tension on the rope. Got it?"

Geronimo nodded, felt the dryness in his mouth, spun around, pinned his back against the wall, and watched Gideon go over the side.

Gideon Stone took a deep breath, carefully pushed himself over the top of the fire wall, shimmied down several feet, felt the weight pull on his arms, and tried to stabilize himself. The coarse surface of the bricks had already begun to abrade the sleeves of his jacket, and he groped in his confusion for a toehold. He had believed it would all come rushing back to him, but it wasn't. It had been too long—he was out of shape and he was having trouble breathing; even worse, he was having trouble holding on. At the worst possible moment, Gideon Stone's brain was suddenly overloaded with a cadre of doubts and uncertainties. The keen edge was gone—and all the wrong things were coming back to him—like the fact that it was situations like this that had made him decide to get out of the CIA business in the first place.

He began counting again, glanced down to calculate his next drop, gathered himself, tensed, kicked out, and felt the soles of his boots grate the brick surface as his body came to a halt again. He tied off, reached out, grabbed the steel casing of a sixth-floor window, and using the tips of his fingers like a claw in the mortar between the bricks, began working his way toward it. Geronimo was right, the ballroom of the Mandarin-Plaza was a write-off—there wasn't much left of it. If they were going to find a way in to get Nelson and the rest of the hostages, they weren't going to find it on the sixth floor.

Gideon sucked in, took a deep breath, loosened the tie-off, and wondered if the fifth floor would be any better. Even then he would still be one floor above where Butcher and Powers had detonated the bomb—but with any luck at all, he could find a way in.

Somewhere off in the distance, he could hear fire sirens. He glanced down, saw nothing but smoke, kicked his feet against the wall, shoved his weight out and away from the wall—and released. This time the drop was a good eight feet.

Ketan Sabo was finally able to breathe again by the time he reached the first floor of the embassy building. He was still coughing and his eyes burned. The smoke, thick and acrid on the upper floors, was starting to filter down, but the worst of it still hadn't reached the lowest levels.

"Search this area," he ordered. "They may still be in the building."

While Sabo waited, one of his men threaded his way through the piles of construction material to the west side of the building and discovered the broken window. "Over here, Captain," the man shouted.

Sabo gathered himself, worked his way to the window, peered out over the loading dock, and spotted the hotel's service van still parked at the entrance to the alley. He forced the lock on the service door, motioned for one of his men to follow him, and instructed the other to continue his search.

Moments later, the two men had worked their way from the old embassy building's loading dock down the length of the cluttered back street until they were less than twenty feet from the darkened vehicle. Even in the half-light, Sabo could see someone sitting behind the steering wheel.

He waited, twice used the sleeve of his tunic to wipe the combination of smoke and rain from his eyes, and finally approached the van. The figure behind the wheel still hadn't moved, and he stabbed the beam of his flashlight into the cab. It was a woman.

Sabo jammed the barrel of his revolver through the bullet-shattered window. *"Siapa nama anda?"* he shouted.

The woman raised her head and tried to look at him, but it was a transitory gesture. Her lips appeared to be trying to form some kind of response to his question, but her voice was failing her. She was wearing a coat, and the sleeve and shoulder area was saturated with a red-brown oily smear.

The Bandung captain waited—then slowly traced the beam of his flashlight down the length of the woman's body until it culminated in a puddle of congealed blood on the floor board near her feet.

"Siapa nama anda?" he demanded again.

The woman leaned her head back and closed her eyes. "Fina Tu," she finally managed. *"Mi nama Fina Tu."*

"What are you doing here?"

The woman shook her head, and this time the gesture was almost imperceptible. Her breathing was shallow, and even the simple act of swallowing had become painfully difficult for her. She opened her eyes briefly, looked at him, then closed them again. "Fina Tu," she repeated, "Fina . . . Fina Tu . . . "

Ketan Sabo opened the van's door and crawled up in the cab of the Toyota beside the woman. There were bullet holes in the windshield and the driver's-side window was shattered. He reached down and took the woman by the wrist to check her pulse. She offered no resistance.

The young militia guard who had accompanied him from the embassy building had been standing on the other side of the van, waiting, with his rifle pointed through the window at the woman's head.

Sabo reached over and pushed the barrel of the rifle away. "There is no need, Corporal," he said. "She is dead."

Acting on Sarawak's orders, Assasio Muta had rounded up the four remaining hostages from the UN delegation and herded them into the central fifth-floor hotel corridor. Aduma Malaka, the representative from Turkey, was balky and given to coughing fits because of the smoke. Mohammed Farah Makidad, the Jordanian representative from Amman, unlike the others, had decided to be cooperative. Muta recalled that he was the only one in the delegation who, in his conversations with Sarawak, had claimed to be sympathetic to the Bandung movement.

Both men were led to a stairway at the far eastern end of the hotel, where there was little evidence of the fire. There a young Bandung lieutenant kept them covered and instructed them to wait until the others caught up with them.

Muta himself had taken charge of the Bulgarian, Boris Azinsiskov, and the American Vice President, Franklin Nelson, detaining both of them while he waited for Sarawak. Of the four, only Nelson had been gagged with his hands tied behind his back. Muta, following the Bandung leader's orders, had taped Nelson's mouth shut.

"A feeble effort," Sarawak said as he approached the PRJ major and his two captives. He ignored Azinsiskov and looked directly at Nelson. "I appreciate your indulgence, gentlemen," he said evenly, "but as you can plainly see, your American friends have bungled matters again."

Azinsiskov stiffened. "I demand to know where you are taking us."

Sarawak laughed. "As I have already pointed out, the American effort at disruption has resulted in little more than a minor inconvenience, my Bulgarian friend. However, I have instructed Major Muta to escort you and your colleagues to safety until the fire can be contained. It will do us no good if we allow you to perish. Of course, if the fire cannot be contained, you will be transported to safety elsewhere. You and your American colleague are much too valuable to—"

"And if I refuse to cooperate?" Azinsiskov snapped.

Sarawak smiled. "That would be most unfortunate, my Bulgarian friend. I would caution you, do not overestimate your value as a hostage. I have little patience with such matters. If you refuse to cooperate, I will simply order Major Muta to shoot you."

Muta unbuttoned his holster, drew his automatic, and moved closer.

The Bulgarian drew himself up. "I will not be cowed by the threats of a half-savage madman," Azinsiskov said.

"Very well," Sarawak said, "but I must warn you, your refusal to cooperate, Comrade Azinsiskov, will earn you no medals. Quite the contrary, if your objective is to die like a hero, your choice of time and place is most unfortunate. For all your countrymen will ever know, you died like a sniveling dog." Sarawak stepped back and continued to smile. "Do you wish to reconsider?"

Azinsiskov glared back at him.

"Very well," Sarawak said. "Shoot him."

Assasio Muta smiled, nodded, buried the barrel of his automatic in the back of the Bulgarian's neck just above the tunic collar, and pulled the trigger.

Gideon kicked out the glass, hung precariously for several moments, and finally shoved out. The kick propelled him out and away from the building—then back again like a pendulum. It was one of the things he hadn't forgotten—burying his face in the crook of his elbow to shield it from broken glass when he crashed through the window. He landed on the floor, rolled over into a semicrouch, and dropped to one knee with his HK poised. He had done it before—not always with good results. This time he was in luck; there was smoke everywhere but no sign of flames, no splinters of glass in his face—and better yet, no sign of any of Sarawak's militiamen.

He checked again, waited until he was certain, then reached back through the window and tugged twice on the rope. He felt the rope go slack, then taut, and he knew Geronimo had picked up his signal; he was on his way down.

When Gideon stood up, he pinned his back against the corridor wall, peeled out of his poncho, waited for Geronimo, and breathed a sigh of relief when he saw his backup crawl through the window. "Now comes the tough part," he whispered, " . . . finding those damn hostages."

Geronimo nodded. "We check every room, fifth floor down, right?"

"Either that or we find one of Sarawak's goons and make the son of a bitch talk."

"That shouldn't be too hard, Colonel. This damn place must be crawling with 'em."

Day 6: Time 1311LT
Langley, Virginia

Jake Ruppert nestled the receiver back in its cradle, picked up the remote, turned on the television, took a sip of his cold coffee, and switched channels to CNN. The scene unfolding on the monsoon-swept streets of the Javanese capital for the world television audience was a bizarre one.

One of Jakarta's landmarks, the prestigious old Mandarin-Plaza Hotel, was on fire and Bojoni Sarawak's Bandung militiamen were holding the firefighters at bay.

The reporter on the scene was using terms like strange, odd, and outlandish as he hunted for words to describe the events unfolding in what had become an ordeal for the world as well as the Security Council hostages. As Ruppert watched and listened, the newsman struggled to paint an accurate word picture to go along with the image.

Sources close to what has been developing here in the last hour have confirmed that almost an hour ago, an explosive device of considerable magnitude went off on the fourth floor of the former German embassy building. That building is adjacent to and immediately west of the hotel. These sources say that is where the fire started.

Shortly after, perhaps less than fifteen minutes later, there was an exodus by what is believed to be the handful of remaining guests that were still registered at the Mandarin-Plaza at the time of the blast. Their departure coincided with the arrival of a number of fire engines.

However, when the firefighters attempted to enter the hotel, a small contingent of Bandung militiamen, which, from what we are able to see here from our vantage point in front of the hotel, now seems to number no more than perhaps twenty or thirty men, refused to allow them access.

I was able to talk briefly with one member of the hotel's staff as she was escorted out of the hotel after the blast, and she told me she was not aware of any casualties—although she did say she was told the flames appeared to be centered in the top three floors of the hotel. . . .

Ruppert took another sip of coffee, frowned, and changed channels. On the local NBC affiliate, the scene was being broadcast from a newscopter cam circling over the hotel. Because of the rain and darkness, it was difficult to make out any detail. What he was able to see was little more than occasional flames coming from the old embassy building. Beyond that, the dense clouds of smoke spiraling up and out of the burning complex made it difficult to determine the extent of the damage. He watched it for several minutes, and was about to switch back to CNN when the phone rang.

"Ruppert here."

Wormack's voice crackled through. "We just got confirmation from Apache. Alan's been in radio contact with Jessie Preston. She told him she was able to put Stone and Geronimo down on the roof of the hotel shortly after the blast. She said she waited around for several minutes, then hightailed it out of there."

Ruppert tensed. "Anything else?"

"Both Alan and Preston are attempting to monitor the Jakarta police and fire frequencies. Apparently one of the fire trucks was trying to get through some back street behind the hotel, and they found a Toyota van less than a block from the site of the fire. Alan says there's a lot of chatter and he can't make out everything they're saying—but from what he was able to make of it, the van was all shot up and the driver was dead."

"Could they tell whether it's the hotel van? The one that took Butcher and Powers in?"

"That's what we got out of it," Wormack said. His voice was breaking up.

"Then how the hell are we going to get those two out of there?"

Wormack hesitated. "I'm afraid we don't have an answer for that one, Chief. Unfortunately, that's not the worst of it. Preston told Alan that the roof of the hotel where she intended to land to pick up Stone and the hostages had collapsed and there's no way she can put the 105 down to recover them."

Jake Ruppert grumbled. Jake Ruppert always grumbled when things were going bad. "So—what's our recovery plan now?"

There was a long pause before Wormack answered. Long enough that Ruppert knew he wasn't going to like what Wormack had to say. "We give them the name of a seldom-used contact in the Glodok section in case they had trouble—but for the time being they're on their own."

"What the hell do we do now?"

Wormack hesitated. "There's not much we can do except wait—and pray."

Day 6: Time 0112LT
Mandarin-Plaza Hotel,
Jakarta

It was Gideon who discovered the body of Boris Azinsiskov sprawled out at the top of the stairs leading down to the fourth floor of the hotel's east wing. Muta's bullet had ravaged a hole in the back of the man's neck just below the base of the brain, and exited through his lower jaw. By the time Gideon stumbled across him, the Bulgarian, bleeding profusely, had managed to claw his way the length of the corridor from where he was shot. He was weak—but he was still alive. Gideon cradled Azinsiskov's head in his hand as the man tried to speak.

"You—you are—the Americans?" Azinsiskov managed to ask. His voice was all but inaudible, muted by the string of blood clots clogging his throat. "They—they—they said you were—were coming . . . "

Gideon cautioned the man not to speak, and did what he could to make him comfortable. "We're here," he finally said. The moment he said it he realized the words sounded shallow and meaningless. It was like showing up a day late for a funeral. Nothing he could say or do was going to change the outcome.

"Th—they—they have—have taken the—the members of my—my delegation away," Azinsiskov was finally able to cough out. Even shallow breathing had become a chore. His brain formed words, but he choked as he tried to articulate them, and a thin stream of the telltale ravages going on inside his body began trickling from the corner of his mouth. The mutilated lower half of his face was a mask of carnage caused by Muta's bullet.

Gideon bent closer, putting his mouth nearer to the man's ear. "Where are the rest of the hostages?"

"They—they—they took—took them—them away."

"Where? Do you know where they took them?" He had enunciated each of the words slowly and carefully in an attempt to make it easier for the man to understand him.

Azinsiskov's eyes drifted shut. "I hear—I hear rain. In my—in my—my homeland near the Black Sea when it rains there is—"

"Where did they take the hostages?" Gideon repeated.

The Bulgarian opened his eyes. For one fleeting moment he looked at Gideon with the clear, coherent gaze of a man who knew where he was and what was happening to him. "They—they separated us."

"The American, Nelson. Where is he?"

"Sar—Sar—Sarawak."

"Sarawak has him?"

The Bulgarian nodded.

"Do you know where they took him?"

"I—I—I hear rain. We—we are—are almost home. Yes?"

"Do you know where they took Nelson?" Gideon pressed.

What followed was one brief moment when Gideon thought Azinsiskov's tortured face tried to reflect the peace he felt. Then the grimace and the hurt returned. Finally, his eyes drifted shut and the pain began to subside. He had closed his eyes without answering Gideon. He took one last deep breath, and then he stopped breathing altogether.

Chapter Eight

Day 6: Time 0130LT
Mandarin-Plaza Hotel,
Jakarta

A handful of Bojoni Sarawak's officers and men milled aimlessly around the Bandung leader in the smoky confusion of the hotel's grand lobby. Sarawak, seemingly immune to the volatility of the situation, continued to confer with two of his officers and the hotel's manager. Meanwhile, the hotel employees were being instructed to save as many of the ornate old building's paintings and artifacts as possible. Most of the items, however, were being carted from the hotel and stacked in the rain-swept drive in front of the building. The few remaining Bandung militiamen, preoccupied with keeping the firefighters out, paid little attention to a growing legion of looters. The treasures were disappearing almost as fast as the hotel employees carted them to supposed safety.

The combination of sporadic gunfire by Bandung militiamen and the unceasing rains had earlier taken a toll on the crowd. The crowd had diminished with darkness—but the spectacle of the fire had again swelled their number.

Now the firefighters, unable to enter the building and fearing for the safety of bystanders, did what they could to move the crowd further back from the scene. Even the news crews had retreated to safety.

Less than twenty minutes earlier, Sarawak had sent for the Vietnamese ambassador in Jakarta, and now Nhon Dak, a moon-faced man wearing a gray-green trench coat with his collar pulled high around his neck, was standing in front of him along with his interpreter. The pair, whose arrival on the scene had been delayed while Dak checked with his superiors in Hanoi, had twice apologized for the fact that the Vietnamese ambassador had been called away, and expressed the hope that he, Dak, "a mere third secretary," could accommodate General Sarawak's wishes.

Sarawak listened impatiently through the rigors of protocol, and finally instructed Major Muta to escort two of the three remaining hostages from a nearby room. Both Aduma Malaka and Mohammed Farah Makidad were still blindfolded and gagged as they were led into the room at gunpoint.

"Under the circumstances, I have no further need for them," Sarawak announced. "Are you familiar with the game of chess, Mr. Dak?"

Following the interpreter's translation, Dak nodded.

"Then you realize that this is not unlike a chess match.

There are times when it is necessary to change one's strategy and sacrifice pawns to achieve one's objective. Under the circumstances, both Mr. Malaka and Mr. Makidad's importance has been mitigated by the foolish attempt of the American government to ignore my demands. Their attempt to rescue the hostages and their refusal to recognize the new government of the People's Republic of Java have not only exacerbated the situation, they have reduced our efforts to something I had hoped to avoid, a power struggle."

Sarawak waited for the interpreter to relay what he was saying. When the interpreter finished, the minor Vietnamese official again nodded his understanding.

"Take Mr. Malaka and Mr. Makidad to your embassy and inform their respective governments that they are safe. But inform them only after you have waited until 0600 hours. In the meantime, Major Muta will escort you and the hostages to your car and my soldiers will see that you are permitted to drive out without interference."

Dak again listened as the interpreter repeated Sarawak's instructions. When the man finished, Dak nodded and smiled. "I am ready to comply with your wishes." Then he added, "Whenever you are ready, General."

Sarawak waited until Muta ushered the four men through the lobby, through the entrance, and finally out into the hotel's portico before he turned to his attention to the hotel's manager. Sarawak took the man aside so that no one could overhear them. His name was Teraha; he was a short, thin-lipped, slightly pompous little man who had been without sleep for two days. Teraha resented the fact that he had been reduced to the role of Sarawak's lackey in front of his employees during the hotel's occupation.

Sarawak lowered his voice. "I am told that there is a network of passageways and tunnels beneath the hotel. Is that correct?"

"It is true, General," Teraha said. Then, by way of explanation, he added, "When the Welcome Monument was erected several years ago, the engineers devised a series of service and maintenance tunnels to accommodate the—"

"The purpose of the tunnels does not interest me," Sarawak said, interrupting. "Where do they lead?"

"There is a stone building near the monument area to accommodate maintenance and controls. The tunnels can be accessed from there."

Sarawak, obviously pleased, turned from the hotel's manager to Assasio Muta. The Bandung officer had returned from the hotel's portico and was awaiting orders. "And now, Major," Sarawak said, "bring me the American Vice President."

When Muta returned, he was prodding the Californian with the barrel of his 9mm automatic. Unlike Malaka and Makidad, Nelson's blindfold had been removed and only the gag remained in place. He had been stripped of his glasses and his hands were still tied behind his back. Unshaven and cat-eyed, he blinked in the sudden harsh light of the lobby. When he struggled to protest, Muta buried the barrel of the weapon deeper in the small of his back. "You will speak only when you are spoken to," Muta ordered.

Bojoni Sarawak hesitated. Gradually his intense frown became a smile again. He knew now how a cat felt when it toyed with a terrified mouse. He had visions of the insolent Nelson both cowering and pleading before he was through with him. "How do you feel about leaving?" Sarawak said.

Muta reached around the frail frame of the Vice President, ripped the tape away from Nelson's mouth, and prodded him again with the automatic.

Nelson drew himself up. Despite his worsening situation, he still somehow managed to sound officious. "Shall I assume you have finally come to your senses, General, and that you are ready to give up this senseless—"

The frown returned. "You do not have the luxury of pontificating, little man," Sarawak snapped. "I have asked you a simple question. You will do me the courtesy of answering it."

Nelson hesitated. "If the general is asking whether or not I am ready to be released, I can assure you that—"

"Do not try my patience. I was simply inquiring whether or not you are ready to leave Jakarta." Sarawak weighed his words. "You see, I have found it necessary to alter my plans. My new plan, unfortunately for you, requires your continued involvement and further necessitates relocating you to a more secure location."

"Where are you taking me?"

Sarawak nodded in the direction of the hotel's manager. "Mr. Teraha, our most gracious host for the past few days, has agreed to show us a way out of the hotel that is both convenient and—I stress this—inconspicuous. While the television cameras posted outside the hotel continue to record the arrivals and departures for all the world to see—they will be unable to record the fact that we have taken our leave."

Finished with Nelson, Sarawak waited several moments before he again turned his attention to the openly recalcitrant little hotel manager. "And now, Mr. Teraha, if you would be so kind, please show us the way to the tunnel." He paused again. "And just to make certain you are not tempted to try to mislead us, I have asked Major Muta and several of his men to accompany us." Sarawak's smile intensified. "I believe you have had ample opportunity to see Major Muta demonstrate his considerable expertise on several occasions in the last two days."

Teraha slowly surveyed the grim faces of the Bandung militiamen surrounding him. The hotel was burning, his career was in ruins. He saw no alternative, and no reason not to cooperate.

A pall of heavy, thick smoke had already begun creeping into the second-floor landing where Gideon Stone waited. Less than ten feet from him, Sheban Geronimo, his face still streaked with sweat and dirt, had just completed his search of the rooms in the second floor's east wing.

"Struck out, Colonel. The damn place appears to be deserted. If the hostages are still here, they're either dead, Sarawak is hiding them, or they're on one of the floors below us."

Gideon glanced up and down the hall one last time, straining to peer through the nearly opaque cloud of swirling gray-black smoke. So far, it hadn't been at all what he had expected; between the two of them they had conducted a room-by-room search of each of the floors and they had come up empty-handed. No hostages, no Sarawak, and even more curious, no further sign of his Bandung militia. Thus far they had encountered only a small handful of Sarawak's men, all on the upper floors. Choked with smoke and frightened, they had put up little resistance. At the first sight of the Americans they had thrown down their weapons and fled.

"Looks like we'll have to forget about Sarawak, Sheban. At the moment I'm a helluva lot more concerned about the safety of the Vice President."

"No sign of the other hostages either?" Geronimo asked.

Gideon shook his head. He was scowling. "Before he died, Azinsiskov said Sarawak had separated them. If they're still hiding on any of the floors above us, we flat out missed 'em—and if that's the case, we're too late to save them. With the wind feeding the fire in the elevator shafts and the west stairway blocked off by flames, this is their only way out."

Geronimo peered up the stairway into the swirling smoke. It was growing thicker by the minute. "It's strange we didn't see any sign of Sarawak or any of his men, Colonel, and it appears that most of the hotel's guests that managed to get this far made it all the way out. What now?"

Gideon continued to squint, doing what he could to shield his eyes from the smoke. "We search the damn lobby and anything else we can uncover. If we don't find anything, we get the hell out of here."

A disoriented Teraha, with Sarawak following, and Muta immediately behind, the barrel of his automatic burrowed in Nelson's back, groped their way through the dimly lit service tunnels two levels below the hotel complex. Four Bandung militiamen, instructed to cover Sarawak's escape, trailed behind them at distances ranging at times from fifty to several hundred feet.

The smoke from the out-of-control fire three levels above them continued to spread, and had now begun to thread its way into the tunnel's ventilation system. On two separate occasions, the smoke had confused the nervous Teraha and forced him to backtrack. Each time he attempted to retrace his way through the labyrinth of passageways as he searched for the tunnel access that would lead them to the monument exit.

For Sarawak, the increasing astringency of the smoke was further compounded by torrents of rainwater gushing through the overtaxed sewer drains into the tunnels. Through it all, Teraha continued to assure them they were more than halfway to the monument exit. For Nelson, it was a bewildering maze of darkened tunnels where the inadequate lighting had already failed and the rush of water swirled around his thighs. Overhead, in the maze of electrical conduits lacing the ceiling of the tunnel, he could hear the agitated sound of hordes of rats scurrying from one island of safety to another.

Finally, Teraha stopped to catch his breath. The little man was drenched with sweat as he leaned against the coarse concrete wall and shoved the beam of his flashlight ahead of him, searching for some sign they had somehow stumbled back into the central tunnel leading to the monument. His confusion betrayed him. Where he had once been certain he was on the right track, now he was riddled with doubt. Behind him he could hear Sarawak growing increasingly more impatient with their progress.

Twice, the American hostage guarded by the Bandung major had fallen. Each time, Muta had dragged him to his feet and prodded him forward. Even in the faint light, Teraha could see that the American's face was now a montage of tiny cuts, bruises, and lacerations. To compound matters, he was having difficulty breathing.

Finally Teraha heard Sarawak speak. Despite the general's growing agitation, his demeanor still masked his concern. Even now, his voice remained surprisingly calm and unruffled. He was looking at Muta. "Bring the prisoner to me," he said.

Sarawak thrust the beam of his flashlight into Nelson's face and studied his captive for several seconds before he turned to face Muta again. "It would appear that our hostage no longer has the will to continue, Major. His frailties impede our progress. Perhaps we should continue without him."

"You would leave him here?" Muta asked.

Sarawak thought for a moment. "Quite the contrary, Comrade, we still have use for him. There is another way. You will accompany Mr. Teraha, and perhaps with a little persuasion you will be able to encourage him to hasten his efforts. I will remain here with our hostage. I am beginning to believe Mr. Teraha believes he has something to gain by detaining us here in the tunnel with his confusing pattern of twists and turns."

Muta frowned.

"I suggest you show him the error of his ways, Major. Impress upon our Mr. Teraha that he will find it in his best interests to redouble his efforts to quickly extricate us from this maze he has so foolishly led us into."

"The general is wrong," Teraha said. "I have been in these tunnels only once before—I am confused by the smoke and lack of light—"

"And if he doesn't?" Muta asked his leader, ignoring Teraha's protestations.

"I think you know what to do," Sarawak said. "Kill him."

Despite the rampant confusion in the hotel's lobby, it had taken Gideon Stone and Sheban Geronimo less than twenty minutes to search it and the shops on the hotel's main floor. Their task would have been even easier if it hadn't been for the added chaos caused by the squadron of firefighters and their equipment. The handful of Bandung militiamen that had been holding the firefighters at bay had now disappeared into the Jakarta night.

It had taken another ten minutes for Geronimo to locate one of the few remaining members of the hotel staff that could speak English. She was a small woman who had been detained by the Bandung and forced to remain at her post for the duration of the siege. She was frightened and unnerved as she was led toward Gideon, and her face mirrored the exhaustion and mental strain she had been under for the last forty-eight hours. Gideon did what he could to put her at ease before he began. "Nothing is going to happen to you," he assured her. "All I want is some information. Do you understand?"

The woman's acknowledgement was a barely perceptible nod.

"My name is Stone," he said. "Lieutenant Colonel Stone. I'm an American. My government sent me here to help rescue the hostages. We've searched the rooms on the upper floors but we couldn't locate them." He waited several seconds to make certain she had understood him. "Have you seen the hostages?"

The woman hesitated.

"Have you seen the hostages, or do you know where they are?" Gideon repeated.

"Only—only a few of them," she finally managed. Then she attempted to clarify what she had said by adding, "Not all of them."

"Have you seen the one they call the American Vice President?"

"Yes," she said. Her voice was still tentative, and Gideon repeated the question to make certain she understood him.

"I have seen him—only a few minutes ago."

"Do you know where he is now?"

"Sarawak . . . " she began, then looked away. She suddenly sounded frightened and her voice trailed off, as though she had thought better of continuing.

"What about Sarawak?" Gideon pushed.

Again the woman seemed reluctant. Finally she said, "The American one—he is with Sarawak."

"Where?"

"I—I—I was not supposed to overhear them. General Sarawak was being very cautious—very secretive. He wanted Mr. Teraha to show him the tunnels. . . . "

"What tunnels?"

The woman was beginning to regain her composure, but her voice was still thin. Gideon was finding it difficult to understand her. "There . . . there are many . . . many tunnels beneath the hotel . . . "

"Where do these tunnels go?"

"I do not know," the woman said.

"Can you show me where these tunnels are?" Gideon persisted.

The woman seemed to deliberate before she finally indicated a willingness to show them. "You will not make me go with you?" she asked.

"You show me where those tunnels are," Gideon said, "and I'll see that you get out of here."

With Assasio Muta behind him, repeatedly prodding him with the barrel of his automatic, Teraha continued to careen his way through the surging waters swirling in the maze of tunnels beneath the hotel complex. Twice, Muta had allowed him to rest, both times just long enough for the hotel's manager to regulate his breathing.

Each time, when he started out again, Teraha prodded

the beam of his flashlight at objects well ahead of him, hoping to find some indication that they were in the right tunnel and headed in the direction of the monument. Finally, he saw it.

"There, up ahead," he said, pointing, "there is the ladder. It leads up into the basement of the service building located in the base of the monument."

Muta elbowed his way past the little man, sloshed through the water, grabbed the highest rung on the ladder, and pulled himself up. He opened the trapdoor at the top of the ladder and danced his light around the enclosure. It was exactly as the Mandarin-Plaza's little manager had indicated: a service area housing the lighting controls and a series of pipes and valves that governed the water flow to the fountain in the monument. It was exactly the opposite of everything they had been forced to endure since entering the tunnels: dry, out of the monsoon winds, and free from smoke. Muta waited several seconds, took several deep breaths in an attempt to clear his lungs, and climbed back down into the tunnel.

"I was right, was I not?" Teraha asked. "It is a way out, right?" There was a trace of triumph in his voice.

Assasio Muta's face was expressionless as Teraha started to move past him and reach for the ladder. Muta released the snap on his holster and took out his automatic. It took several seconds for the little man with the thick glasses to realize what was happening. When he did, he tried to step away, but there was no place to hide. If he intended to protest, the words lodged somewhere in his throat and never quite materialized.

Muta squeezed the trigger and two shots reverberated through the tunnel in rapid succession.

Only one had been necessary. Tehara's body recoiled,

slamming back against the wall of the tunnel before slumping forward, face-down in the turbid water.

Muta took a moment to appraise his handiwork, holstered his automatic, and paused. He lit a cigarette and took several drags before systematically retracing his steps back to where Sarawak waited with the hostage.

Now deep in the tunnel, Gideon stopped, stood motionless and held up his hand. "Kill the light," he whispered. Sheban Geronimo turned off his halogen lantern and looped the handle back through his belt. When he did, the only remaining illumination came from a flickering bulb some forty or fifty feet ahead of them. "I hear something. . . . "

Geronimo squinted down the darkened tunnel in front of them. "I think I heard it too, Colonel," he whispered. "Think they're just ahead of us?"

Gideon shook his head. "Can't be certain where it's coming from. Just ahead of us, though, another damn service passage leads off to the right." As Gideon checked his compass, he heard noise and voices. This time the voices had been clear enough that he could even detect their twitchy nature. "Whoever they are—they sound a tad nervous," he said with a grin.

"How many do you figure there are, Colonel?"

"At least two, maybe more, can't tell."

"Think it's Sarawak?"

Gideon shook his head. "So far we haven't been that lucky."

"Which tunnel?" Geronimo whispered.

"You take the one to the right, I'll take the one straight ahead. We're still going down; the water's getting deeper. That means we still haven't reached the halfway point in this damn thing."

Sheban Geronimo knew the routine. The years of training took over. He removed his night-vision goggles from the carrying case, discarded his field cap, pulled the device down over his face, removed the lens cap, and turned on the rotary switch. When the green glow materialized, he checked the IR illuminator, removed the goggles, and let them hang around his neck. "Water's getting deep, Colonel. I sure hope these damn tunnels start heading up soon."

Gideon watched the corporal shoulder his way into the mouth of the cutoff, slip around the corner, staying close to the wall, and start down the tube. It took less than ten seconds for the blackness to fold around him as he disappeared. Then, while Gideon continued counting, he went through his own prep-check: pulling on his PVS-5, changing clips, and slapping a thirty-round magazine in his HK. Finally he opened the double-tap, and paused just long enough to determine whether or not he could still hear the voices. He could, and the fact that he could made him all the more cautious. They were no closer or further away than they had been. If what he was hearing was Sarawak and his hostage, why wasn't the Bandung leader making any progress toward the other end of the maze of tunnels? There were two possibilities, he told himself. Either Sarawak's escape efforts had hit a snag—or more likely, he had instructed some of his men to lay back and bring up the rear in the event someone had followed him into the tunnel.

Gideon counted to ten, collected himself, took a deep breath, crouched, felt the water swirl up and around his chest, and began inching his way forward. The light was less than twenty feet ahead of him when he stopped again, checked for the voices, and heard enough to be convinced that they didn't suspect anything. There was a muted conversation and a half-laugh—all in front of him. Behind him there was a cacophony of other distant sounds, all seemingly stifled and suffocated by the din of rushing water.

It took several seconds, but he managed to make his way past the light without being detected. The voices were louder now and he came out of his crouch, straightened up, wrapped his field cap around his hand, gripped the bulb, and unscrewed it. The moment he did, the voices stopped. He reached down and let the bulb slide out of his hand, and it was quickly carried away by the water.

There was more waiting. When he did hear voices, they were little more than a whisper. Gideon pulled the night-vision device up, slipped the band around his head, removed the lens caps, adjusted the field range, and waited.

"Berhenti disini!" he heard one of the voices shout.

"Kebakaran!" another screamed. Simultaneous with the man's order to "fire" there was the deadly sound of a submachine gun burping a hail of hot lead into the darkness around him. He heard slugs ricochet off the concrete walls of the tunnel and slice through the water. He dropped to one knee, squeezed off one burst, and saw the eerie green infrared image of one of the militiamen spin around, clutching at his midsection. Gideon had no way of knowing how many of them there were to start with, but now he was sure of one thing—there was one less. The man slumped, let go with what sounded like a string of Maylay profanity, and disappeared beneath the water.

As far as Gideon was concerned, he had already paid the penalty for losing his edge—and he knew he had been lucky; one of the Bandung bullets had nicked him, creased his cheek just below his right eye, and a thin trickle of blood was already tracing its way down into the corner of his mouth. He knew he was lucky because if the bullet had been a quarter inch to the left he could have kissed Largo, the fishing boat, and whatever her name was good-bye. Already he could taste a salty residue—one more thing to be grateful for—at least he was still around to taste.

There was no element of surprise now. If plan one didn't work, he had to go to plan two. He dropped to one knee, voiced a loud scream, closed his eyes, and plowed face-forward in the water, still clutching his HK. Now he had to depend on what he could hear.

He closed his eyes, lay motionless, and listened. The water transmitted and magnified every sound. He could hear them—still some distance away; one, no—two of them, sloshing through the water toward him.

The shooting had stopped, and Gideon held his breath. There was that old familiar pounding and clawing sensation in his chest, and the water created swirling, phantasmic images in the lens of his NVG when he opened his eyes.

Even then, with the element of surprise now on his side, there were those same old fleeting fears to contend with. They came and they confronted him—and he tried to put them out of his mind by focusing on his count. Yet when one image began to fade, another seized him even before the previous one had completely withered away; the damn battery pack in the goggles would fail, the seal would break, water would somehow damage the HK and foul the firing mechanism, or the militiamen would be too savvy to drop their guard.

One thousand and ten, one thousand and eleven. Between counts he could hear the sound of the men sloshing their way toward him—growing louder.

Gideon waited.

He continued the count. One thousand and thirteen. One thousand and fourteen. One thousand and . . .

Were the bastards getting closer?

He could no longer taste the blood.

He held his breath and a montage of images, snapshots in his mind, apprehensions, impressions, and symbols began cartwheeling through his brain. Now his heart was hammering. There was a throbbing sensation in his chest.

They were close now—damn close—they had to be. Were they suspicious, or had they let down their guard?

Gideon was counting on them being overconfident. He was banking on the darkness and on the shadows, on the ghosts and fears that plague men's minds when they are stalking each other. He was counting on every little thing that plays with a man's mind when he is threatened.

He inched the barrel of the submachine gun up until the tip of the barrel was just below the surface of the water.

Would they see it and open fire?

One thousand and twenty. One thousand and twenty-one. Close enough, damn it.

Squeeze.

Continue to squeeze.

The sound was exaggerated, arrogant, haughty; a string of violent explosions magnified by the wrath of the swirling water. Gideon shoved his head above the surface and heard their screams. Through the lens they were black-on-black icons silhouetted in a pale and distant green watery light, bizarre half images of wounded marionettes. One had already sunk to his knees. The other was trying to claw his way out of his own personal hell, clutching at the wet walls, but all the time sinking down.

Beyond them, still some thirty or forty feet away, was another. He was holding a flashlight. The muscles in Gideon's arm tightened, the trigger finger constricted, and he held on until he had emptied the clip.

The light went out.

Gideon sucked in and held his breath. Then he felt it. Pain. He had been hit. At times like this he had been taught to assess, to take inventory; and now he wasn't doing it. Behind him he could hear someone creeping toward him.

Where the hell was Geronimo?

He sagged back against the cold, damp, concrete surface of the tunnel wall and realized he was powerless to stop the ensuing spiral—a whirling plunge into another, even darker dimension.

"Colonel." The voice was hissing at him through layers of gauzy chaos. " . . . it's me, Corporal Geronimo . . . "

But Gideon Stone never heard him; he had already passed out. He had sought his escape in an empty, encompassing unconsciousness.

PART 2

Chapter Nine

Day 6: Time 1555LT
Bethesda, Maryland

Jake Ruppert had noticed that by the time the calendar got around to reflecting the fact that it was the dying days of October, the old and prestigious Brookhaven Club of Bethesda had usually forfeited most of its autumnal charm. This year was no different. The trees had shed most of their foliage, the two golf courses had been buttoned up for the winter, the gardens were bare, buried under blankets of thick mulch, and what little groundskeeping activity there was appeared to be focused on preparing for the inevitable arrival of winter.

Under the circumstances, Jake Ruppert wasn't at all certain what to expect. With Chet Harms still fighting a rear-guard action with a Senate committee regarding his appointment as the permanent head of the Agency, Ruppert was on a treadmill, again filling in; this time being ushered into and expected to perform in another unfamiliar arena.

On the plus side, he was glad Shuler Huntine was going to be running the show. The President's aide would do most of the talking and cut the deals—if, that is, there were deals to be cut. On the negative side, Jake Ruppert wasn't sure what his role was in all of this.

He was on his way to a meeting, a meeting Shuler Huntine had suggested he not discuss with anyone until they knew what was on Fong's mind. Now, as Ruppert drove up the meandering, barren tree-lined road toward the club's sprawling main house, he passed saddle barns, tennis courts, and the polo grounds; all appeared to be deserted. Obviously the people who were interested in such things had found something else to occupy their time.

At the entrance, he left his car with a young valet who seemed surprised someone actually required his services, went inside, and found Shuler Huntine waiting in the club's great room. The ex-Marine was standing with his back to the fireplace, and in typical Shuler Huntine style, he began briefing Ruppert before the head of the CIA's CA crew had even managed to get his coat off.

"Let me give you thirty seconds of background on Fong before we go in there," Huntine said. It was vintage Shuler Huntine, the subject's name, rank, and horsepower—with personal observations kept to a minimum. "His full name is Fong Lu Chek. He's Beijing's official off-the-record voice over here."

Ruppert repeated Fong's full name before asking, "Just for the hell of it, why don't you tell me what this meeting is all about?"

Huntine shrugged. His apology sounded insincere. "I got a call from Fong's personal secretary two hours ago. He said Fong wanted me to meet him here. He indicated Fong had some information for us."

"What's this guy's official title?" Ruppert asked.

"Doesn't have one. When we tried to run a background check on the old boy, we came up with a big zero in an empty box. We know where he lives, where he banks, and we've had a peek at his health records. Outside of that, he's a nonentity. His dues here at the club are paid through a bank in Singapore. The one thing we have learned is that when he speaks for the Dung government, you can go to the bank on it."

"Inscrutability plus, huh?"

"Exactly."

Given more time, Jake Ruppert would have probed further, but at that point a heavyset Asian stepped into the foyer from a nearby room. He looked like something out of a James Bond movie. "Mr. Fong will see you now," the man said.

Fong Lu Chek was slender, elegant, and articulate. He wore a meticulously tailored three-piece dark-blue silk suit, and sported a diamond ring on his right hand that Jake figured was wholly inconsistent with Party paradigms. He had straight black hair and wore rimless glasses. From the outset it was obvious that he and Huntine had not only met but worked together before. To Jake's surprise, the greeting was more cordial than formal. Huntine introduced Ruppert, and the three men seated themselves at a carefully buffed antique oval table that had the pleasing aroma of furniture polish.

"I hope I have not inconvenienced you," Fong began. He nodded in Huntine's direction, then fixed his eyes on Jake as though he were contemplating what he was about to say. "As for you, Mr. Ruppert, I trust your esteemed colleague has already told you—what we discuss here today should be held in the utmost confidence."

"The utmost confidence," Ruppert assured him.

"You may speak freely," Huntine said. "I asked Mr. Ruppert to join us because he is the one who is most familiar with—"

Fong finished the sentence for him. "The unfortunate situation in Java. Am I correct?" Without waiting for either of his guests to confirm his assumption, Fong turned and looked out the window. "I have observed that often your weather here is not unlike the first stages of a monsoon."

Huntine and Ruppert waited. Already Fong had exhibited an inclination to be surprisingly direct. Fong leaned forward, propped his elbows on the table, tented his fingers, and peered through them like a child playing a game. "If one lives in my part of the world long enough, one can learn to ignore the minor inconveniences of the rainy season," he said. "Unfortunately, one cannot ignore other things—such as the matter of General Sarawak."

"Your government has been supplying the general with arms and supplies for some time now," Huntine said. "We have satellite photos that confirm the buildup on Karimunjawa."

"Under the circumstances, then, it would be foolish of me to refute the accusation," Fong replied. There was the trace of a smile on his face. "You Americans have a saying: A picture is worth a thousand words. However, we are not here to discuss ideology—whether one form of government is superior to another. We are here to discuss the man."

"That's precisely why I asked Mr. Ruppert to attend

this meeting," Huntine confirmed. "He is directing the activities of our people in Java."

It was Fong's turn to wait. When he remained silent, Ruppert leaned forward in his chair. "Perhaps you know something that we don't know, Mr. Fong," Ruppert said, "but based on the latest reports from our people on the scene in Jakarta, we now know that General Sarawak, along with his sole remaining hostage, the Vice President of the United States, has escaped. We also know that the Mandarin-Plaza Hotel has incurred extensive damage as the result of the fire—but the Jakarta police and soldiers from the Sarni Kujon army have moved in and it is no longer under Bandung control. Our immediate concern then is not Sarawak, but the whereabouts of Vice President Nelson."

Fong's frown deepened. "I find it somewhat curious that you have waited until now to mention the matter of the hostages and what I would assume to be most important to you, the safety of your Vice President."

"The two matters are inseparable," Huntine said.

"Let me put your concerns regarding your Vice President to rest," Fong said. "I too received a late dispatch from my comrades. General Sarawak was in touch with Beijing within moments after returning to Karimunjawa."

"Then he has returned to Karimunjawa?"

"He has," Fong confirmed, "and as for the matter of your Vice President, he is still in Sarawak's custody."

"Then Nelson is still alive?" Ruppert said.

"He is," Fong confirmed. "That is—how do you Americans say it, the good news? The bad news is that my government would view any attempt on your part to rescue your Vice President through force as an act of aggression on a third world country."

It was Huntine's turn to lean forward with his arms on the table. He was frowning. "And just exactly how do you suggest we liberate our Vice President, Mr. Fong?"

"Negotiate," Fong said.

Huntine began shaking his head. "No way." His voice sounded abrupt, and he attempted to soften it. "I'm afraid that negotiation is out of the question. If we negotiate with Sarawak and make even the slightest concession, we open ourselves up to every maniac who thinks he can get what he wants from us with an act of terrorism."

Fong's expression didn't change. He stood up, walked to the window, and stared out at the rain for several moments. When he turned around again, he was smiling. "We know each other quite well, my friend. I suspected that might be the case. That is why I have suggested that we have this little talk. You see, my government also has a problem, Mr. Huntine. And our problem, curiously enough, is also General Bojoni Sarawak."

Huntine glanced across the table at Ruppert. "And this is what you came to tell us, correct?"

"You are most astute, my American friend." There was a pause before he continued. "As you have already indicated, my government has a policy of supplying arms and equipment to the people of any country endeavoring to throw off the yoke of imperialistic and oppressive government. That, by definition, is the Sarni Kujon government in Indonesia. But the timing and manner with which General Sarawak has chosen to initiate his efforts is the subject of much discussion with Chairman Dung and his comrades."

"What you are telling us is Sarawak forgot to clear this coup attempt with the Party leaders in Beijing," Huntine guessed.

"You have a way of speaking most succinctly," Fong said. "It is a trait I admire—and it saves time."

"And you are also trying to tell us that Chairman Dung is beginning to regard General Sarawak as a loose cannon. Correct?"

Fong folded his hands behind his back and turned slowly to stare out the window again. "Precisely," he said.

Jake Ruppert couldn't believe what he was hearing. To him it sounded as if Dung had instructed Fong to sell Sarawak down the river. He started to ask for clarification, but Huntine held up his hand.

"With your permission, Mr. Fong, I would like to rephrase for Mr. Ruppert what I believe you just said. Mr. Fong is telling us that General Sarawak has lost favor with the Party officials in China. And he's also saying they don't care how we handle it as long as we don't drag them into some kind of situation where they will be forced to condemn aggressive behavior on our part."

Ruppert could see Fong's reflection in the window. The off-the-record spokesman for the powers in Beijing appeared to be pleased with Huntine's interpretation—he was smiling again. While Jake had gotten one message—that Fong was pleased with Huntine's summary of their meeting thus far—he had missed another—that in Fong's opinion at least, the meeting was over. The same scowling Asian who had ushered them into the room less than thirty minutes earlier was now handing them their coats.

Their departure was only slightly more ritualized than their arrival. Fong shook hands with both men; they were escorted out of the room, and were left standing in the great room again before Huntine said anything.

"Puts a whole different slant on it, doesn't it?" Huntine observed.

"What do I tell Stone?"

"Nothing until I've talked to the President."

Day 6: Time 0736LT
The Bo Jac

Parker Wormack had assembled the entire Covert Action crew in the officer's mess. The Apache pilot, Captain Jeris Alan, and his gunner, Butch Miller, were standing near the door to the galley. Taylor, released from sick bay but still not cleared for duty, was flanked on one side of the table by Jessie Preston and Wormack. Sheban Geronimo and Gideon Stone were across the table from them.

"Looks like everyone is here," Wormack began, "so let's get started. As you all know it's standard CA practice to give everyone a chance to go over our mission. Before we start, however, I'd have to say, from my perspective, we gave it a bloody good effort—but the bottom line is, we did not accomplish what we set out to do. The Bandung, while no longer holding the rest of the delegation captive, is, according to what Ruppert has been told, still holding the Vice President hostage."

"We're going on the word of someone we know very little about," Gideon reminded them. "All Huntine and Ruppert were told is that Sarawak managed to escape and took Nelson with him. But that was a good four or five hours ago. Nelson may be dead by now for all we know."

"True," Wormack admitted, "but for the time being we are operating on the assumption that the Vice President is still alive. And we will continue to operate and plan on that assumption until we have definitive proof otherwise."

"What's the word on Butcher and Powers?" Alan asked. "Any confirmation?"

Wormack took a sip of tea before he answered. "The Jakarta police have asked for assistance in identifying the American found in the drainage ditch along with the three Bandung militia men. The *Shenandoah* is sending a forensic team ashore to help them identify bodies. Obviously, we can't intervene because officially we don't even exist."

Jeris Alan stared down into his cup before he spoke. "I know my men, Colonel, and I know it's not my job to speculate, but it's my guess Corporal Butcher never made it to that old embassy building. Whoever set that blast off wasn't exactly an explosives connoisseur—and I would have to assume that what we had was Corporal Powers simply doing his damnedest to pull off the mission."

"It was a helluva lot bigger than we anticipated," Gideon agreed. "If it was Powers, he saved our ass. Without that explosion, Sarawak's people would have picked us off like flies."

Alan waited before asking, "So what's our status now?"

Wormack sighed. "Officially, we're in a stand-down. According to Ruppert, Huntine tells him the President is taking a great deal of flak. At the moment the press is all over this like a cat in heat. They've got him boxed in. He can't deny that we made some sort of an attempt at a rescue effort because they've got the body of an unidentified American in commando garb to prove that we were involved in something. In so many words, they're saying that we stepped on our dingus. Added to that, of course, is the fact that while we now know three members of the Security Council delegation are safe, the press is also pointing out that they also know three are dead: Lesni, Peel, and Azinsiskov."

Alan looked across the table. "What about you,

Colonel, what do you think? Could Sarawak have found a way out? And if he did, could he have taken the Vice President with him?"

Gideon shook his head. "Geronimo and I were told Sarawak and a handful of his men were attempting to escape through the service tunnels under the hotel. Maybe they were, maybe they weren't. We tried to follow, but those tunnels were flooding fast and all we ever really encountered was a squad of Bandung militiamen. That's when I took this hit in the shoulder. The question is, did Sarawak leave them behind to cover his tail—or were they trying to escape themselves and got lost in that maze of tunnels like we did? If Sarawak and Nelson were down there, we never saw them. According to Ruppert, the Chinese are saying they managed to escape. When Corporal Geronimo found me, the damn place was crawling with Kujon's troops. Maybe they found him. If they did, maybe they're not telling us."

Wormack was pensive. "I agree with you, Colonel, it is an intriguing possibility. However, that possibility only raises more questions. We know the Kujon government isn't all that happy with our presence in Indonesia. They would like nothing better than to see us close our military installations over here and clear out. There's nothing to stop Sarni Kujon from putting a bullet in Sarawak and telling us the threat is over."

"Either that or put a bullet in him, blame it on us, and let Kujon try to convince his people that the Americans bungled the situation," Jessie speculated.

"That could be very dangerous," Taylor interjected. It was the first time he had said anything. "Keep this in mind . . . whatever he is to us and the rest of the world, Bojoni Sarawak is a charismatic leader and his followers number in the millions. The back streets and alleys of

Jakarta are crawling with people that see him, the whole Bandung movement, and the People's Republic of Java Party as the only way out of their misery and poverty. If the people thought that Kujon murdered him rather than be forced to face him in an eventual election—that could lead to another coup attempt against Kujon. And a second coup attempt just might end up being a helluva lot bloodier than this one."

Before Taylor had the opportunity to elaborate on his theory, there was a knock on the door. Gideon did not recognize the young ensign who poked his head in and made an announcement. "It's Sarawak, sir," the man said. "PRI is replaying a tape that they received less than thirty minutes ago."

In his cluttered office in the lower levels of the White House, Shuler Huntine reached across his desk and hit the button that turned up the volume on his television. He was picking up a CNN feed of Sarawak's tape. The newscaster was indicating it had been received only minutes earlier.

To Huntine's surprise, Sarawak's voice was even more collected and arrogant than before. He sounded none the worse despite the ordeal of his failed coup attempt.

> *My fellow Javanese, the Party of the People's Republic of Java and its Bandung leaders greet you from Karimunjawa.*
>
> *As most of you are aware by now, unwarranted American intervention in the affairs of the Javanese people has resulted in the untimely death of fourteen Bandung militiamen—and as yet uncounted scores more of innocent Javanese bystanders. These deaths occurred during the Americans' ill-advised attempt*

to exert force on your Bandung leaders and bring to an untimely end the PRJ's attempt to oust the corrupt American lackey leaders of the Sarni Kujon government.

While it is true that the recent PRJ coup attempt has been aborted, our efforts to rid the Javanese people of the yoke of repression will be renewed in an even more vigorous fashion within a matter of hours.

We, the Bandung leaders of the People's Republic's great and glorious independent island nation, renew our commitment to rid the people of the Kujon government's oppression.

To achieve that end, I have ordered Bandung militia men to prepare to launch M-72 missiles at key Kujon government installations throughout our beloved island nation. . . .

Bojoni Sarawak was still posturing when Huntine turned down the volume and dialed Jake Ruppert's office. "I assume you've been listening to our boy Sarawak," he said. "If you haven't, you've been missing quite a show." Huntine glanced at his watch. "He's been at it for the last twenty minutes."

"We've been listening," Ruppert admitted. "I've got my people assembled and we're preparing to go over his inventory and discuss just exactly what he has stockpiled on that island fortress of his."

"Good, get back to me as soon as you have a handle on things."

Wormack put his pipe down and said, "What I'm looking for from each of you is your best analysis of the situation. Anytime you hear an assessment by someone that you disagree with, I want you to jump in. That goes for everyone at the table, regardless of your area of expertise. Sarawak may be bluffing about a missile launch, but we're in no position to take chances. We'll start with you, Ben, you've been monitoring his buildup. Is he making threats he can't back up, or does he have the missile capability?"

Ben Tillston, who had joined the meeting with other Agency specialists, adjusted his glasses, opened an oversized manilla envelope, and spilled the contents out on the table. "These are the latest satellite photos, Parker. Most of what you see here were taken in the last thirty days when we began to see activity on some launch pads that have been essentially dormant for the past two years. The Bandung built these pads five years ago and nothing happened. Then, three months ago, activity started up again. Sarawak said he was prepared to launch M-72 missiles, and we would have to agree that he has that capability." Tillston passed around the photographs of the launch pads. "These photos indicate he has four launch sites, and from the size and location of those sites, those pads are capable of handling M-72's or something in that range."

Gideon studied the photos and laid them back on the table. "Refresh me—M-72's?"

Tillston settled back in his chair. "The M-72 is an updated version of the old Soviet family ME-1-e short-to-intermediate-range vehicle using a standard KK-4 warhead. Russian design throughout, typical Russian approach; they utilize pretty much standard off-the-shelf hardware. The lads in the Pentagon would classify them as damn near antiques. Nothing sophisticated—effective range seven to nine hundred kilometers—but very dependable and very, very deadly. Quite obviously, their range defines their target location. All of which tells us that Sarawak's target selection is limited to any major target in the vicinity of the eastern end of the island."

Franz Kilborn, the newest member of the *Bo Jac* team, began pointing to the map of the island. "Ben is right. An effective range of seven hundred to nine hundred kilometers puts several key Javanese cities within range, among them Kujon's installations at Surabaya and Yogyakata, both of which just happen to be rail centers. If Sarawak goes after them, he is obviously hoping to take out and cripple Kujon's ability to retaliate in the east. The downside for Sarawak is, he'll be taking out some key population centers as well."

"Would he do that?" Taylor asked, "considering the fact that he gets the majority of his support from the population centers east of central Java? If he launches missiles at any one of those population centers, he's cutting into his own manpower base."

Wormack looked around the gathering. "Moe raises a good question. Does Sarawak alienate his own people if he goes after Kujon's installations in Surabaya and Yogyakata? There's bound to be fallout and civilian casualties."

"I don't think that's a consideration with Sarawak," Jessie said. "This is the same man we saw assassinating unarmed UN officials for an international television audience."

"Jessie's right," Gideon agreed. "The fact that it's his own people won't slow him down."

"Then there's the other side of the coin," Kilborn cut in. "We've just watched Kujon stonewall it for four days. If Sarawak wants a response out of Kujon, he may figure he has to haul out the heavy equipment."

"What about you, Sylvia?" Wormack probed. "You've

been analyzing his strengths and weaknesses; what do you think?"

Dr. Sylvia Martin was one of only four women assigned to the *Bo Jac*. Attractive, in her late forties, she was often heard to jokingly claim she had come by her somewhat dubious assignment because she had two advantages most of Wormack's people didn't have. First, as a former citizen of Ukraine and a behavioral psychologist, she had spent most of her professional career studying the behavior of men who embraced Communist ideology. That helped—but second, and even more important, she liked to say, was the fact she was married to the ship's second officer—and unlike the other women assigned to the *Bo Jac,* she knew exactly where her husband was at all times.

"General Sarawak's profile is well known to everyone on this ship," she said, "and outside of Chairman Dung, he is perhaps the most complex person in our computer. He was a student activist while attending UCLA in America and a member of the Young Socialist Party. He returned to Java at the age of twenty-seven and became a member of the PKI, the Indonesian Communist Party.

"Ten years ago he more or less took over the island of Karimunjawa, ran the local officials out, formed the Bandung movement, and established it as the military arm of the new People's Republic of Java. He's been getting money and supplies from the Dung regime in Beijing ever since. The coup attempt that we witnessed in the past week was inevitable. But, and I need to stress this, there's something about this whole affair and the way it was handled that is inconsistent with what we know about Dung."

"I have wondered the same thing, Doctor," Tillston said. "Do you think this initial coup attempt had Beijing's blessing?"

Sylvia Martin removed her glasses and waited several moments before she answered. "There is always a danger in basing decision on speculation," she admitted, "but if I'm forced to conjecture, I would venture to guess that General Sarawak undertook this initial coup attempt with Dung's blessing. I doubt, however, that Chairman Dung approves of the way he handled the hostage situation. Unlike previous Chinese leaders, Chairman Dung seems to be sensitive about what the rest of the world thinks. Not because he's any humanitarian, mind you, but because he recognizes what it will take to get Taiwan back into the fold and keep his country solvent in an increasingly complex and interdependent global economy."

As Wormack looked around the room, several people were nodding agreement with her analysis of the situation. Eventually he turned his attention back to Ben Tillston.

"Two questions, Ben. One, assuming the Chinese are telling the truth and Nelson is still alive, where do you think Sarawak is keeping him? Two, what's the best way to get him out of there?"

Tillston thumbed through his papers again, and this time produced a detailed pencil sketch of the Bandung base on Karimunjawa. "What I've done here," he said, holding the drawing up to the light, "is copy this off of the satellite photos. But I have attempted to clarify certain features of the installation and eliminate some of the confusion in the shaded areas which are of little concern to us.

"As we all know, Sarawak's base on Karimunjawa covers the entire island. That means the base itself, not counting some of the more desolate areas where there is no discernible activity, covers somewhere in the neighborhood of eighty-five to eighty-seven square kilometers. There are no security fences as we know them; a heavily patrolled shoreline constitutes his first line of defense. He has manned and armed guard towers every two hundred meters." Tillston passed out more photographs. "These pictures were taken from one of our small patrol boats disguised as a Maylayan fishing vessel. When we had these pictures enlarged, we learned that each of these towers is manned with two guards." Tillston was pointing at the detail in the photographs again. "If you look closely you'll be able to identify mortars and handheld rocket launchers in each of the towers. So, if you're thinking about putting some kind of rescue squad ashore, Parker, it will take some planning."

Wormack nodded.

Tillston continued. "The main part of the base is located on the north side of the island and actually surrounds the only deep-water harbor on Karimunjawa. The Chinese have supplied Sarawak with four updated Houjian fast-attack missile boats. These replace the old Huangdeng and Hegu-class FACs that most of us associate with the Chinese.

"These Houjians are equipped with two triple YJ-8 SSM launchers, one twin 37mm-type automatic machine gun, and two twin 30mm-type 69 AA guns. These are quite similar to the ones we saw in Hong Kong after the 1997 handover from Great Britain."

Gideon studied each of the photos and passed them on to Geronimo.

"Note also that one of the photos shows an old Luda III with 15km-range CY-1-ASW-missile capability in the harbor. This photo was taken less than a month ago. Our best thinking is that it was there on a training mission. It was only there for three days—and it's probably not part of the Sarawak arsenal."

Gideon moved around the table to get a second look at

the photos. "The harbor's proximity to the main base is what?"

Tillston pondered Gideon's question. "If I understand your question, Colonel, everything that is absolutely essential to Sarawak's operation is in the immediate vicinity; the airstrip, fuel depot, supply buildings, even the barracks are all in a five-square-kilometer cluster that surrounds the harbor area."

"What about aircraft?" Gideon pressed.

"Not what you'd expect in this day and age," Tillston offered. "Some, but not many. We do know that he has four Bell 206A COIN helicopters, two Bell 212's, and two SA 365 Dauphins. There is an old C-54 and an even older C-47 sitting adjacent to the main hangar. We have not been able to determine what's in a smaller hangar a few hundred yards from the main administration building—which, incidentally, is the long low-profile building perpendicular to the east-west runway."

Gideon was frowning. "Okay—now comes the big question, Ben. You appear to know what Sarawak has in his pocket as well as anyone. If you were going in after Nelson, what's the best and quickest way to get in there?"

Tillston mulled the question over in his mind several moments before he answered. "Best and quickest are probably two different things, Colonel. You could have Captain Alan drop you and your team in one of the more remote locations on the island—but you would be faced with working your way down out of the mountains. That would be the safest way—but it would take a great deal of time. Or we could figure a way to sneak you in the front door somehow."

"And how would you do that?" Gideon pushed.

Gideon could tell by the expression on Tillston's face that he was conjuring up mental images, discarding some, keeping others. "Why not take the direct approach, Colonel? Walk right in the front door . . . where they least expect you."

"The harbor?" Gideon asked. "Why not? It just might work."

Gideon Stone looked around the room before leaning back in his chair. "You only said one thing that bothers me, Ben. It's that word *might*."

Tillston smiled. "If you were General Sarawak, Colonel, where would you feel the least vulnerable?"

"I gotta admit, I sure as sure as hell wouldn't figure on anyone coming in through the front door."

Across the table Sylvia Martin was smiling. "I think Ben may have something," she said. "The only thing bigger than Bojoni Sarawak's ambition is his ego—and that's already taken one big hit when his coup attempt failed. As far as he's concerned, he's thrown down the gauntlet. He's telling Kujon to step down and get out of the way or he's going to start hurling missiles at him. If you were making those threats, Colonel, what would you be doing now?"

Gideon was still thinking. "I'd either be getting ready to fire those missiles, or I'd damn sure be making it look like I was getting ready."

"Precisely, and if Sarawak was giving any thought at all to what Kujon might be doing, or the fact that he might be contemplating some kind of retaliatory measure—where would you think he would try it?"

"Either by air or coming in through the back door?" Tillston guessed.

Sylvia Martin continued to smile. "Right. Most assuredly he would not be expecting anyone to confront him where he feels he is strongest."

Gideon stood up again and began walking slowly

around the wardroom table. His hands worried a pencil. From time to time he stopped and closed his eyes as he conjured up and discarded possibilities. Everyone in the room realized he was the one who had juggle the uncertainties, the odds against success or failure, and in the final analysis, weigh those factors against the risks involved. Twice he looked at the maps and charts, only to return again to study Tillston's sketches and the satellite photos. Each time he calculated the distances and time involved. When he was finished, he looked at Jessie Preston.

"If I could come up with a way to get us into the Karimunjawa harbor in the *Indon,* do you think you could pilot her back out?"

"A word of caution, Colonel," Kilborn interjected. "From everything we've been able to observe, the mouth of that harbor is extremely narrow and quite shallow. Narrow enough and shallow enough, in fact, that on two separate occasions our satellites have been able to photograph medium-tonnage Chinese freighters unloading outside the harbor. In both cases Sarawak was using shuttle barges to bring his supplies ashore."

"Duly noted, Mr. Kilborn," Gideon said, "which means we'll have to be doubly alert."

"More than alert, Colonel. In an ingress that tight, there is no reason for us not to assume that the mouth of the harbor is also heavily mined. That's standard practice with the Chinese, and that's where General Sarawak obtained most of his training."

"Franz is right, Gideon," Wormack said. "Your radar would be useless. The first time they heard an unidentified ping, the element of surprise would be lost."

"All right—no radar," Gideon said with a sigh. He was watching Jessie Preston to see how she reacted. So far she hadn't flinched—but he wasn't sure they had heard the worst of it yet. "What kind of mines?" he finally asked.

"My guess," Kilborn ventured, "compression-type. They're cheap, plentiful—and easy to anchor in a shallow harbor. Little or no drift. Sarawak's people don't need a hell of a lot of skill to plant them or to be able to get in and out of the harbor; all they have to do is pay attention to their harbor charts."

"Okay—so it will be difficult. What is it you told me the other day, Jessie?" Gideon grinned.

"I think I said, 'Where there's a will there's a way,' Colonel."

"Exactly," Gideon said. "If we're determined to get this done, we'll find a way." At that point he decided to refrain from asking any further questions, and came back to the table and took his seat. He spread out the photographs, the maps, the harbor charts, and the computer printouts detailing dates and time of ship arrivals. He studied each of them for several minutes and finally looked up. "All right, Parker, suppose I said I need four people. With four people I think we can get in there and get the job done. I need Jessie to pilot the *Indon* out of there after we make it in. Then I need Corporal Geronimo to help me retrieve Nelson. And I'll need a fourth to make damn sure they can't follow us when we leave."

The room was quiet. Finally Jeris Alan held up his hand. "I don't know what the hell is wrong with me. I guess I'm a slow learner. My pappy always said never volunteer, but something tells me I'd like to get a look at this operation up close and personal, Colonel. Count me in."

"Suppose you tell us how you intend to get us into that harbor without blowing ourselves to kingdom come," Jessie said. "Or have you already figured that one out too, Colonel?"

Gideon shook his head. "Not yet—but I'm working on it. Tell me, Franz, just exactly how much traffic does go in and out of that harbor?"

"It's a busy place, Colonel. The big ships seem to show up every week or so. The locals are in and out of there several times a day, every day. Why?"

"Lots of traffic? Every day?"

Kilborn nodded.

Gideon glowered. The details still weren't clear in his mind. He knew all too well that the acid test of any idea was the ability to articulate it. If it didn't sound like a half-assed scheme after the air got to it—it just might work.

"Why? Because we're going to poke the *Indon*'s nose right up under the stern of one of those local supply ships and follow it in—right through the minefield. Think you can handle that, Jessie?"

"Why not? We called it 'follow the leader' when I was a little girl. I was pretty good at it."

"Good. Then, when we get inside the harbor, the three of us, Geronimo, Alan, and me, all bail out—Jessie bides her time, lays low, and either waits for a ship she can follow out or reverses her computer profiles."

"Question." Kilborn frowned. "We're a long way from the harbor at Karimunjawa, Colonel; way out of the *Indon*'s range. If the *Bo Jac* takes up a position anywhere near that island, Sarawak's people are going to be wondering what one of the ships from the Universal Oil fleet is doing in their waters. They're bound to be suspicious."

Gideon looked across the table at Wormack. "How about it, Parker? Think Ruppert can get one of those heavy-duty choppers from the *Shenandoah* in here?"

"Possibly. What's your plan?"

"Simple, if Fleet can get one of those big Sikorsky

Super Stallions in here, it can pick up the *Indon* and put it down just far enough offshore that Sarawak won't even know we're out there."

"We can use the rain and darkness as cover," Alan added.

Gideon nodded. "Alan's right. I still don't have all of the details worked out, but it's starting to come together."

"It could work," Wormack agreed.

"It damn sure better work," Gideon said. "We'll follow one of the supply barges in and while Corporal Geronimo and I go ashore to find Nelson, Captain Alan here makes damn certain those gunboats of Sarawak can't follow us when we're hightailing it out of there. I don't want someone shooting at us during the attempted recovery of the *Indon*."

"You, me, Captain Alan, Corporal Geronimo, and when you find him, the Vice President," Jessie reminded him. "That's five people, Colonel. Think we can get 'em all in that little jewel?"

"It'll be tight," Gideon admitted. As he said it, he was looking up and down the length of the table. "Now, one last question. We've talked about the base and the harbor; what else do we need to know?"

Ben Tillston looked across the table. "This may be irrelevant to our plan, Colonel, but there is a complex consisting of several small buildings located on an inlet approximately five kilometers east of the base itself. On the surface at least, it doesn't appear to be anything significant, and we have never photographed any activity there. Still, you should be aware of it. It's located there on the map." Tillston pointed out the location and leaned-back in his chair again. "However, there is a small cruiser, no apparent armament, tied up at the pier."

"Duly noted," Gideon said. "Anyone else?"

Wormack sagged back in his chair, removed his glasses, and rubbed his eyes. "How's the shoulder?"

"It wouldn't stop me from going fishing if I was back in Largo," Gideon drawled. "I don't figure it'll stop me now."

Wormack took one last pass around the table. "Speak up now if any of you see any holes in this plan. Otherwise we're all agreeing we think Colonel Stone's plan will work."

"It damn sure better work," Gideon grumbled.

Chapter Ten

Day 7: Time 0231LT
The Bo Jac

Gideon Stone shoved open the side port, felt the rain pelt his face and peered out into the churning slurry of wind-whipped rain and surface-hugging clouds. The weather had deteriorated, and the horizontal visibility was limited now to no more than thirty or forty yards. At the same time he was keeping an edgy vigil on the three powerful 4,380-hp turboshaft engines of the Sikorsky CH-53E Super Stallion. He sucked in his breath and held it. He had already logged one bad experience in weather like this in the frenzied skies over Tanken when the Stallion went down. Once was enough; he wasn't looking forward to another.

The Stallion's main rotor blade continued to whip the Indonesian night into an aberration as the giant craft hovered just off the stern of the *Bo Jac*. Gideon exhaled. His mouth was dry. So far, so good. This time it would be different. This time the pilot hadn't taken a direct hit just minutes before he started to land. This time Gideon had Jeris Alan looking over his shoulder, assuring him that the chopper was right where it was supposed to be. "Couldn't do better myself," Alan admitted.

Even with that assurance, Gideon continued to monitor the sequence of events like a nervous groom. The *Bo Jac*'s monopool had been flooded an hour earlier, the *Indon* launched, subsequently tethered, and finally collared with a flotation device that made the DSSRV bounce like a cork on a endless succession of seven-to-nine-foot swells. Now it was up to the skill of the chopper pilot. He had to hold the CH-53E steady while the crew of the giant helicopter dropped a hook, captured the high-priced fifteen-plus-ton bundle of technology known as the *Indon,* and wrenched it out of the water for the flight to Karimunjawa.

The *Indon*'s baby-sitters, Zeke Marshal and Buster Kelly, had gone into the water when the vehicle was launched. Despite the size of the waves, the pair had manually cajoled and coaxed the vehicle into snare position with a set of remote controls designed for just such a capture operation. Through it all, the two men had monitored their multi-million-dollar, high-tech ward like a couple of rookie surgeons sweating out their first operation. Now, with the hook and harness dangling close to the triangularly configurated fore and aft four-point D rings on the hull exterior, Gideon knew Zeke Marshal was looking up into the wind-whipped rain waiting for the cable to slacken. As soon as it did, he was prepared to climb aboard and go to work.

Despite Alan's assurances, Gideon felt himself growing tense. Waves continued to hammer the small craft, often swelling high enough to crash over the *Indon*'s conning tower and elevated fore air tank. Still, like some kind of double-jointed acrobat, Marshal was able to scurry up and onto the deck platform and reach for the lift hook. Twice he tried and twice he failed. On the third try, he was able to grab it. Then came the struggle to engage the hooks; three times Gideon heard him shout into his com pak for more slack. Finally, on the third try, he made the connection.

There was more chatter. Gideon heard the voice of the *Indon*'s maintenance chief crackle the length of the cavernous fuselage of the Stallion giving the signal for the lift. Suddenly there was a decidedly more powerful pitch to the roar of the three General Electric engines, and the giant Sikorsky began a slow and gradual rotation into a climb. He heard a round of cheers and from that moment on, Gideon could see nothing; the scene below him was wiped out by the wash of the powerful rotor.

Finally, when there was nothing left to see, Gideon turned away and dropped to his haunches to sift through his tac pak. He was checking his gear for the third, fourth, or maybe even the fifth time; he had lost count. Out of the corner of his eye he could see both Jeris Alan and Sheban Geronimo going through the same ritual. It was the same for them as it was Gideon; a way to stay occupied—a way to keep the unknown elements of such an undertaking from playing with their minds.

Their inventory had been carefully laid out, checked, and double-checked back on the *Bo Jac*. Each of the three who were going ashore were carrying MP-5N Heckler and Koch 9mm submachine guns. Each of the HKs was outfitted with a flashlight and laser, both operated by a pair of pressure switches custom-fitted into the pistol grip. In addition, each of the weapons was rigged with a three-round trigger option and thirty-round magazines. Each man carried a tac pak and each of the paks contained another five clips.

The bulky tac paks were watertight, collared with a buoyancy ring, and contained an aux belt with a .45-caliber automatic, extra ammo, a six-inch GAR knife, a couple of Nl-7s's, and two sedative grenades. Plus, Jeris Alan had brought along what he called his personal security blanket, a couple of thirty-six-inch-long pieces of stainless-steel wire and an HK69A1 grenade launcher.

"How much time have we got?" Alan asked. It was the third time he had asked. The Apache pilot was understandably tense. In recent months, his missions had all had been confined to flying. Now he was being thrust back into a covert-action. He was rusty and he knew it. He had confided to Gideon that he wondered how sharp he would be—how well he would perform.

Jessie Preston checked her watch before she answered. She was giving Gideon a chance to reassure him. "ETA is 0309. That gives us another twenty-five minutes before the drop."

At Gideon listened, he squinted into the darkness of the Sikorsky's cargo space and began to pull on his gear. All four of them had donned their wet suits back on the *Bo Jac,* and now it was time to put on their dive gear. Gideon snapped into his weight belt and harness, slipped the buoyancy compensator over his head, and synchronized his watch with the others. He wore a compass on the left wrist, depth gauge on the right, with a detachable halogen light clipped to his aux belt.

"We're in luck, Colonel," Jessie shouted over the thumping sound of the rotor. "Wormack has Tillston monitoring the harbor transmissions in and out of Karimunjawa. Tillston says that a Chinese tanker, the *Ti Win,* is requesting an off-loading barge."

"The gods are smiling on us. Get a position," Gideon ordered.

Jessie Preston repeated the order and waited. Finally she turned back toward Gideon and shrugged. The smile had faded. "Tillston says he's lost contact, Colonel. But he thinks from the sound of things, the captain of the *Ti Win* is waiting for some kind of response from harbor control."

"Tell him to stay with it," Gideon said, "and tell him all we need to know now is what time they intend to tie up with that barge and how long it's going to take them to get off-loaded. If we know that, we can estimate when the barge expects to be headed back into the supply docks on Karimunjawa."

Jessie went forward to the flight deck to check their position. She returned with the news that the Sikorsky's pilot had been able to locate the *Ti Win*'s broadcast frequency. "The pilot says to tell you he's picking up the *Ti Win*'s signal now. We're getting close, Colonel."

Gideon nodded, checked his watch, and began going over the deployment plan. "Okay—we're in luck. He can lock on and follow their frequency in. Weather permitting, he can take us down to within twenty to twenty-five feet of the surface for the drop. My guess is that with this weather and this time of night, we can get within six to seven hundred yards of the target without being detected. The freighter crew will be busy unloading the ship, and the rain and the wind should pretty much mask any of our equipment noise."

Gideon signaled for others to gather around him. "Okay, here's the jump order—I'll go first, Geronimo follows, Jessie goes third, and you bring up the rear, Captain. Each of us is responsible for our own tac pak, so double-check the seal before you jump. Jessie will kick out the flotation collar before she jumps. Geronimo and I will retrieve it, get it inflated, attached, and secured around the *Indon* before we put anyone aboard. Clear?

"When we're ready to go aboard, Jessie goes first. As soon as she gets on board, she'll fire up the onboard computers, activate all systems, establish contact with the drop vehicle, and start purging the air tanks. Alan, you go in second. Geronimo and I will tidy up outside, deflate and detach the flotation collar, and make damn certain we don't leave anything floating around in case the weather clears. Everybody with me so far?"

Geronimo responded with a barely perceptible nod. Alan and Preston were more vocal.

"Good," Gideon continued. "At that point one of two things will happen. If they still haven't sent a barge out to the *Ti Win,* we wait. I've already told Wormack not to panic if we shut down and break off all communications for a prolonged period. If that happens, we move only when Tillston gives us the coded signal confirming the fact that they've started off-loading the supplies from the freighter. Then we haul ass to the interception point, get ourselves in position, and lay low until the barge starts into the harbor. Then we tuck the nose of the *Indon* right up under the stern of that supply barge, let the tug's prop mask our presence, and follow her in.

"When we get in the harbor, Alan goes out first. Your job, Captain, is to locate and incapacitate as many of the gunboats as you can. You've got enough Pl-1 in that tac pak of yours to blow up Havana Harbor—just make damn certain you don't blow yourself up along with

Sarawak's boats. We've already lost two men, and I seriously question whether Nelson is worth a third."

"Your politics are showing, Colonel," Alan said with a grin.

Gideon grunted and turned toward Jessie. "Jessie, the minute you drop the three of us off, you haul ass to the designated coordinates and wait. If we've calculated this thing right, your take-up position should be some forty or fifty yards out from the main dock. All three of us will be leaving a trail of NL magnetic-pulse canisters to screw up their dockside communications. The only problem with that is, it'll screw up our communications as well. If we stay on schedule and keep cool, we'll come out of this smelling like a rose." Gideon paused. "Any questions?"

He studied each of their faces and waited. He sighed and slumped back against the cargo bulkhead of the Sikorsky's fuselage.

"No questions? Good—that means everyone knows what to do. Let's do it—and one last thing . . . " He paused again, this time for several seconds, before he added, "Good luck. We're going to need it."

Gideon Stone checked the time of the drop. It was 0302.07; they were seven minutes ahead of schedule. The *Indon* had disappeared into the black, angry waters below them some seven miles from the mouth of the Karimunjawa harbor.

The CH-53E's pilot gave them a position report, recited the coordinates, continued the countdown, and Gideon mouthed the numbers along with him. " . . . one thousand and five—one thousand and four—one thousand and three . . . " The muscles in his back tensed and his legs coiled. He gripped the rail frame around the cargo door with one hand on each side, and felt the wind buffet him.

"One thousand and two . . ."

The pilot's voice crackled through the cargo area.

For Gideon there was one final split-second hesitation. "It's like jumping into a damn tar pot—I can't see shit," he said. He knew the pilot was the only one who could hear him, and in turn Gideon could hear the man chuckle—a chuckle that only momentarily interrupted the rhythm of the count. Now it was more than five seconds, but the count continued.

"One thousand and one . . ."

He felt the pressure of Geronimo's hand on his back.

"Go."

Suddenly it all came rushing back to him. The first time Gideon Stone had jumped out of a helicopter into the opaque blackness of an ocean night, there had been a terrifying and spine-numbing awareness of his mortality. In real time, that awareness had been a mere speck, a nanosecond, a billionth of any appreciable measure, an increment far too small for the human brain to calculate. But it was there—and now it was back.

In was that billionth of a second when the heart seems to stop, the brain ceases to function—and the mind rejects all forms of reality. It was in this space, in this darkness, in this unmeasured gap in time, that Gideon Stone had first realized the human species could become not only helpless, but completely and totally disoriented.

He leaped and plummeted, feeling nothing except the sudden harsh unwelcome of turbulent water. Then his mind played a second trick on him—there was the welcome thought that all of this was a transitory thing—which, of course, it wasn't. He spiraled into the water and the air went out of him. There was an icy shock and the expected cochleating action that pulled him down into a water world with no dimension. Finally, the buoyancy compensator took over and he began the timeless claw back to the surface.

Then, in that same time vacuum, he was joined in his insanity; the rest of the team followed. Geronimo hit the water less that twenty feet from him. Jessie knifed into the water no more than fifty feet away—and finally the Apache pilot came down. He saw Jessie surface, clear her mask, and scramble up and onto the deck of the *Indon.* She had landed the closest. At the same time, Geronimo had captured the flotation collar and was hustling his way around the perimeter of the DSSRV to attach and inflate the device.

The scramble was on; the valves on the collar were designed to keep the *Indon* afloat just long enough to get everyone and the equipment on board. Timing was critical.

He heard a floundering, out-of-sync kind of splashing sound in the water behind him, and realized it was Jeris Alan. The Apache pilot had hit the surface harder than anticipated and dislodged his dive gear. He was struggling to keep his head above water as Gideon began swimming toward him. Rolling eight-to-nine-foot swells were swamping the pilot, swallowing him up, and corkscrewing him back to the surface again. Each time Gideon tried to grab him, Alan found a way to fight him off. Finally Gideon gave up, swam around behind him, and managed to get a headlock on him. Only then did Jeris Alan give up his struggle.

It took several more minutes for Gideon to swim back to the *Indon*, push the frantic pilot up and onto the deck where Alan could get a grip on the handle of the battery-access locker, and retrieve the man's tac pak. From there

Geronimo and Jessie were able to drag him to the access hatch. Jessie slipped down the adit, braced herself against the ladder, and helped Gideon guide the still-groggy pilot down into the personnel aperture. Then, while Gideon checked for damage topside, Geronimo emerged for a second time, dove back into the water, peeled away the last section of the temporary flotation device, shimmied up on the grid deck, and crawled into the tube. By the time he had cleared, Jessie Preston had already begun peeling out of her dive gear and was activating the computers. Moments later, she heard Gideon climb into the adit, seal the access hatch, and start down the ladder.

By the time Gideon was able to wiggle out of his dive gear, Jeris Alan was spread-eagled on the floor of the *Indon*'s control room and his breathing was gradually returning to normal. "How's he doing?" Gideon asked.

Jessie appraised the man a second time before she answered. "He's okay—he took in some water—but he'll be fine. All he needs now is a couple of minutes to get himself reoriented."

Gideon knew the feeling.

"At this very moment," Jessie continued, "he's probably convinced he swallowed half of the damn Java Sea."

Gideon was looking at Geronimo. "As soon as you can, get him propped up. Make sure his lungs are clear and his dive gear isn't broken."

Sheban Geronimo grabbed the officer under his arms, lifted him into a sitting position, and held his head back against the bulkhead. Alan's garbled protest was framed by a series of racking coughs and sputters.

Gideon, meanwhile, had taken his seat in the module's command chair and his fingers were already dancing through a maze of toggle switches on the A panel. From the time they had jumped until the *Indon* began springing to life, it had taken all of eleven minutes. The computers were up, the makeup air had begun whistling through the vents, and both the A and B panels were suddenly bathed in intricate compositions of vivid red, green, blue, and yellow lights. Finally, Gideon glanced over at Jessie Preston and pressed the button underneath the main chronometer. "Make a note, Preston," she heard him mutter. "When you get to be my age you're too old for this shit." In the same breath she heard him ask for the chrono reading.

Jessie Preston was still smiling as she counted, "03, 02, 01, all mark, 0321."

"Corrected. We stand at 0321LT, mission time 0011MT."

"Gottcha," Jessie repeated. "We're in sync."

"All systems?"

Again it took Jessie several seconds to scan the instrumentation on the B panel. "Just like in the training manual, Colonel, up and go—full function—all systems."

"Let's take her down to three-zero feet and get rid of the surface turbulence," Gideon said. "Then let's go find that supply barge."

"Change of plans?" Jessie asked.

"Un-huh. While I was thrashing around in that water out there, I had me one helluva idea."

"In all due respect, Colonel, this is no time to start improvising."

"You've heard that old saying about a better mouse trap?"

Jessie Preston nodded.

"Well, I just invented one."

Day 7: Time 0321LT
Karimunjawa

For Ketan Sabo, only three hours and twenty minutes into his stint as the base duty officer for the night, it had already been a long shift. Unable to sleep before coming on duty, he had since spent most of his time wandering through the Bandung headquarters complex, and twice visited the mess hall, where he had consumed three stiff cups of *kopi susu* in an effort to help him stay alert.

His most recent stop had been the building that housed the Bandung base ops and administration, and in the back, a makeshift detainment center where the American Vice President was being impounded.

At age twenty-seven, Ketan Sabo was the youngest of those that Bojoni Sarawak referred to as his staff of senior officers and advisors. A Hindu by birth, born in the mountain regions of Java in the shadow of the great volcano Gunung Bromo, he had gravitated west as a youth, became a student, studied engineering for two years at the Emoria, and there learned about and gradually became enchanted with the doctrines of the Communist Party, PKI. When that happened it was only a short time before he was recruited by Sarawak and given a commission in the Bandung. Now, five years later, he was a captain and considered to be one of the general's most trusted confidants.

It was shortly after two in the morning when he'd passed by the guard and unlocked the door leading to the small cluster of rooms where Franklin Nelson was being detained. To his surprise, the light was on and the hostage was awake, writing in what appeared to be an old journal. When he heard Sabo unlock his door, Nelson looked up without changing his expression.

"What do you want?" Nelson demanded. The little man was peering over the top of his half glasses and frowning.

Ketan Sabo wasn't quite certain he knew what he wanted. Did he have to admit that he had been wandering aimlessly for the last couple of hours and ended up in the confinement center out of boredom—or was he required to make up some reason for being there? He decided there was no reason to do either. Under what circumstances did the captor owe the captive anything, least of all an explanation for his actions?

Instead of answering, Sabo walked across the dimly lit room until he was standing in the light.

"You're the one Sarawak calls Sabo. Right?" Nelson said.

"I am," Sabo replied. It wasn't all that often that he had an opportunity to use the English he had learned at the Emoria, and he wondered if he would be able to adequately converse with the American official.

Nelson closed his journal. He looked tired. "Perhaps you can tell me. No one else seems to be able to. How long do you intend to keep me here?" Nelson asked. There was no longer any rancor in his voice—just weariness.

Ketan Sabo had been present during several of Nelson's interrogation sessions since the coup attempt. The little man—and he was quite little, Sabo had decided, especially when compared to the other Americans he had seen in the streets of Jakarta—always began each session with the same question. How long would he be detained as a hostage.

Unlike many of his fellow officers, Ketan Sabo had never had the money or the opportunity to travel. Consequently, he knew very little about America and what he often heard Sarawak refer to as its oppressive government. Even so, he realized that the man referred to as the American Vice President was a powerful individual in his own country. For that reason, and even though he realized that Nelson was the Bandung's prisoner, he felt as though he should accord the American official at least a small degree of respect.

"I do not know how long you will be detained," he admitted. "I suspect you will be held hostage until there is a satisfactory response to General Sarawak's broadcast." Sabo was curious whether he had used the right words and whether he had pronounced them properly. More than once during his academy days he had admitted to his instructors that it was difficult for him to master the difficult English language.

Nelson cleared his throat and laid his pen down on the journal. As far as Sabo was concerned, the American had a pale, somewhat sickly look that Sabo decided was much less pleasing to the eye than the dark complexion of his Javanese countrymen. He continued to study the captive, and decided it was the rimless half glasses that made him look almost pathetic. Ketan wondered why such a big and powerful country like the United States would be represented by an individual with such a maudlin and anemic appearance.

"You are comfortable?" Sabo inquired.

Nelson glanced around the room at his sparse accommodations. "I am dry, if that's what you mean."

"Can I get you anything?"

Nelson seemed surprised by the question. The young man standing less than ten feet from him was the first of the Bandung to inquire as to his well-being. For that reason, Nelson attempted to temper the tone of his voice when he answered. "I wish only to be released," he said.

"You will be released when the oppressive Kujon government steps down and when your government quits meddling in the affairs of the Indonesian people," Sabo said. He was pleased with how he had dispatched the small man's complaint.

Nelson removed his glasses and began to clean them with his shirttail. "You inquired if there was anything I needed."

"I did," Sabo confirmed.

"Then I would like something to read," Nelson said. "Anything would be appreciated, Captain, as long as it was printed in English. Unfortunately, it's the only language I ever mastered." He sounded almost apologetic in his admission.

Suddenly, Ketan Sabo realized he was seeing the American Vice President in a somewhat different light. The man was unshaven, disheveled, and exhausted after his ordeal, and there was little evidence of the bellicose demeanor he had exhibited in the early hours of the Bandung coup attempt. Now he appeared to be little more than a beaten man. Most certainly he was no longer the epitome of capitalist greed that the general had painted him to be.

Sabo considered the man's request for several moments before he responded. "I believe I know where there are some magazines and newspapers," he said. "I will see if I can find something for you."

Day 7: Time 0334LT
Karimunjawa

The dock area of Sarawak's Karimunjawa island stronghold was situated at the west end of a narrow four-mile-long inlet leading in from the Java Sea. In water shallow for a port of its size, it had been dredged and constructed at the far end of a harbor bordered on one side by the arsenal and a string of warehouses and service buildings as well as the barracks. On the opposite bank was the base fuel depot and storage tanks.

Ships with a draft of no more than eighteen feet could navigate in the channel and unload dockside. Anything larger than that had to be unloaded near the open sea mouth of the harbor and barged in.

It was in the dockmaster's shed at the end of the main pier that Sabo first learned that the *Ti Win*, a Chinese tanker, had been transferring cargo to one of the base supply barges for the past two hours.

Sabo picked up the clipboard, glanced at the manifest, and checked his watch as the young dock officer, a lieutenant, informed him that he had been in radiophone contact with both the captain of the tug and the deck officer of the *Ti Win*.

"How long will it take to complete the transfer?" Sabo asked.

"At least another hour or so," the lieutenant estimated. He went on to indicate that the tug captain was complaining about unloading cargo in such foul weather.

Sabo turned and looked out the window at what he could see of the waters in the harbor's docking area. Even in the sanctuary of the anchorage the winds were whipping the water into a frenzied chop.

"I would not care to be out there in weather like this," Sabo admitted. He checked the anemometer gauge on the panel in front of him for the third or fourth time. The analog instrument indicated that the unloading was being accomplished while the crews contended with a steady twenty-mile-per-hour wind, with occasional gusts to thirty. To make matters worse, there was a steady rain, at times wind-whipped into near-horizontal patterns as it slashed by the shed's windows. "In fact," he joked, "it is not difficult for me to think of any number of places I would rather be."

The young officer ignored Sabo's observation, lit a cigarette, and leaned on the instrument shelf to stare out at the rain. The smoke from his cigarette circled over his head as he finished recording his 0330 report. "Did you hear the general's radio broadcast?" he asked without looking at Sabo. Sabo nodded, and the man saw the gesture in the reflection in the window. "Do you really think he will launch the missiles against the Kujon strongholds in Surabaya and Yogyakata?"

Sabo detected the concern in the young Bandung officer's voice. "It troubles you because you come from that region or have family near one of Kujon's bases?"

"Near Surabaya," the man admitted, "a sister and her baby. It is the only family I have except for an aunt who is quite elderly."

"I am certain he will launch the missiles if Kujon does not respond," Sabo said. He tried to make it sound as if Sarawak had no choice. As an officer of the Bandung, he knew it was expected of him. Ketan Sabo had learned to be cautious in how he answered the questions of junior officers. Like the other members of the general's senior staff, he knew all too well that Bojoni Sarawak had been known to shoot men guilty of far less than improper statements.

There was an protracted silence while the dock officer considered Sabo's response. Finally, he turned to Sabo. "If the captain is tired," he offered, "there is a cot in the next room. I will be glad to wake the captain when the barge comes in."

Sabo nodded. "I could use a little sleep," he admitted.

Day 7: Time 0404LT
The Indon

By the time Gideon Stone and the crew of the *Indon* had picked up the tanker's signal and located the *Ti Win*, Jeris Alan had regained his equilibrium and the DSSRV was maneuvering approximately five hundred yards off the stern of the Chinese vessel. Less than ten minutes earlier, Jessie had acknowledged that she was picking up fragments of the radiophone exchanges between the off-loading tanker and the tug captain. Most of the exchanges were in Chinese, but periodically she was able to pick up splinters of Maylay conversations between the tug captain and a member of his crew. From those bits and pieces, Jessie Preston had been able to determine that the tug captain was estimating it would be another hour until the transfer was complete.

"Have they said anything about what they're off-loading now?" Gideon asked.

Jessie pressed the earphones tight to her head and listened. "If I understand what I'm hearing, Colonel, they've already transferred the gasoline; now it's aviation fuel. From the sound of things, they seem to have most of the fuel already aboard the barge—and now they're getting ready to retract the hoses. The Chinese captain is indicating still have quite a few oil drums to transfer."

"Aviation fuel?" Gideon repeated the words slowly, like a man who had just been handed the kind of information that would make him rich. Even in the dim cabin illumination cast solely by the cluster of instrument panel lights, Jessie could see a small smile starting to play at the corners of Gideon's mouth. Then he repeated it for the second time. "Aviation fuel, huh? This could get real interesting. This could work out even better then I had hoped."

Jessie continued to monitor the exchanges between the two vessels. From time to time she grimaced as she struggled to decipher a word.

Gideon kept his voice low as he turned to Alan. "How many of those Nl-7s's do we have on board?"

The Apache captain began sorting through the tac packs, counting as he did. "Altogether, ten," he finally said.

"What kind of timers?"

Alan checked each of the Nl-7s's a second time. "No fixed, all variable. All the fuses are electric."

Gideon's smile broadened as he stood up. "Take the controls, Preston. Just hold her steady, you've got a two-knot tow. Jeris, you take the B panel. Never mind what they're saying, but let me know the minute those guys quit talking to each other."

Jeris Alan crawled into the *Indon*'s second chair as Jessie moved over and Gideon crouched down beside Geronimo.

"All right, Corporal, I need a crash course in these little Nl-7s jewels we've been carting around. Just exactly what the hell do they do and how do they do it?"

Sheban Geronimo lifted one of the devices out of his tac pak and held it up for Gideon's inspection. At first glance it appeared to be nothing more than a fourteen-inch-long aluminum cylinder with a small timing device on one end. "Can't say as I know exactly how they work, Colonel, but I can tell you what they do."

Gideon hefted one of the batons and studied it. He judged it to weigh less than three pounds.

"Electromagnetic pulse canister," Geronimo said, "better known as the Nl-7s. The effective operating radius is thirty, maybe forty yards, Colonel. At that distance it'll knock out every electronic device within that range."

"Computers? A ship's radar? Navigational equipment?"

"Everything—all electronics systems," Geronimo repeated.

"For how long?"

Geronimo thought for a moment. "Well—until they figure out what the hell is causing the power loss and locate the canister—or until the canister power source gives up the ghost."

"How long does that give us?"

"How much do you need?"

"Two—maybe three hours."

"Piece of cake, Colonel." Geronimo twisted the end cap to demonstrate. "Twist, set the timer, plant it—and wait."

"Suppose I planted one of those little babies on the hull of the tug towing that barge?"

For Geromimo, Gideon's questions suddenly all made sense, and despite the fact the corporal's swarthy face was creasing into a broad grin, he managed to keep his voice barely above a hoarse whisper. "With no navionics, sir, and no way to guide her once that tug and barge enter the narrow channel between the mines, there's a mighty good chance that tug captain would be in for one helluva ride."

"But the tug and the barge have to get through the mines first in order for my plan to work," Gideon cautioned.

Geronimo was still grinning. "We can rig up a pulse fuse."

"Will it work?"

"Piece of cake."

Gideon sagged back, momentarily propping himself against the *Indon*'s bulkhead for support. "Boys and girls," he chuckled, "I think we've just worked out a way to ruin General Sarawak's little playhouse."

Alan and Preston were looking at him.

"Remember I said I had an idea, Preston? Well, try this one for size; one tug and one barge loaded with aviation fuel and oil suddenly go out of control in a narrow channel, after they pass through the minefield."

"I like it," Alan said.

"If that doesn't give our boy Sarawak one great big surprise, nothing will. Good idea," Jessie added.

"And that surprise is going to give us just exactly what we need," Gideon continued, "one great big diversion. While Sarawak is trying to figure out what went wrong, we slip ashore and retrieve ourselves a Vice President." Gideon paused. "Hell, it's better than good, it's brilliant. The more I think about it, the more I like it. Geronimo, my friend, let's you and me take ourselves a little swim."

The waters in the *Indon*'s dive chamber swirled up and around the two men until it swallowed them in a dark, cold, unfamiliar world. At the same time each of them could hear the *Indon*'s computer voice spitting out the obligatory series of predive environment readings followed by the equally obligatory systems checks.

"Do you read me?" Jessie's voice crackled in.

"Loud and clear. How do we look?"

"Check your vision aid," she instructed.

Gideon activated the IFO display and the night-vision device in his visor. "Got it," he confirmed.

"Okay, shut it down. Save your batteries. Run your intercom check with Corporal Geronimo."

"Read me, Corporal?"

"It's working," Geronimo verified, "clear as a bell."

"Good job, gentlemen; the A panel checks out in here. Captain Alan is checking your LS numbers." There was a delay before he heard her voice again. "Okay—readings verified; you're both looking good." Gideon waited until he heard the voice order a mission-time verification and the sound of the sea valves closing and the adit opening. They spiraled down and out.

Gideon gained his balance and began the systems check. "We're on 0003, make that 0004; working against 0030."

"VS okay," she verified. "Can you see each other out there?"

"Negative—it's murky as hell; get me oriented. We're still in the backwash of the aft prop," Gideon complained. "I can hear Geronimo but I can't see him."

"The imager indicates he's just a few feet in back of you—no more than twenty," Jessie reported. "I've got both of you on the NV screen. You're looking good. Your target should be straight ahead of you."

"How far?"

"Allowing for drift and tow, less than a hundred yards." The transmission was strong, and Jessie's voice was buzzing in his ear. "We're getting a CR reading. It looks like they've shut down the screws on the tanker. The only cavitation we're recording now is coming from the smaller target—that would be the tug. It sounds like the crew's working her engine pretty hard to keep the barge cozied up to that tanker."

As he moved out of the wash of the aft prop, the water began to clear and Gideon was finally able to get a visual on Geronimo. The corporal, a strong swimmer, was now less than ten feet off to his left. Directly ahead of them Gideon could see the evidence of increased agitation in the water from the props of the tug.

"Still murky, Colonel?" Jessie asked.

"Starting to clear. We're close enough that we'd better kill the OS light on the bow," Gideon said. "Shut her down, Jess. If we're lucky, the next time you hear from us, we'll be knocking on your front door."

Gideon heard her say, "Good luck." Then there was silence.

Seconds later the lights of the *Indon* went dark, and the only illumination he could see was coming from the aux lights on the barge where the work crew was unloading the tanker. Directly ahead of them, it appeared as little more than a blurry wash of quivering white-yellow. Gideon stopped until he knew precisely where Geronimo was. "Talk to me, Corporal. Where are you now?" Out of habit, he was keeping his voice low.

"Just off to your left, Colonel." The corporal's voice hissed through his headphones like a snake. "I've got you spotted; you lead, I'm a born follower. Otherwise I'd be an officer, right?"

Gideon stifled the inclination to chuckle, checked his air, and swam through a waist-high outcropping of seaweed and coral. The area was dotted with jagged clumps of lava rock inhabited by an occasional school of fish, species unknown. He was momentarily distracted by a fleeting thought of the fishing off of the rocks back in Largo, until he realized he could hear the sound of the tug's motor. He estimated the distance between them and the tug now at less than twenty-five yards.

Gideon stopped for a moment, crouching in the sand at the edge of the outcropping, and waited for Geronimo. He had opened the flap on the tac pak of his aux belt and removed one of the Nl-7s's. When Geronimo came into view, Gideon was already gesturing up at the rudder of the tug. He held one finger up in front of the mask to indicate silence. Geromimo acknowledged, removed one of the electromagnetic pulse canisters from the pouch on his belt, activated his NV, and spiraled up into the prop-excited waters above him.

Both Gideon Stone and Sheban Geronimo knew this was the stage of their mission when all the timing and careful step-by-step planning turned from strategy and scheme to chance and luck. Geronimo's job was to plant two Nl-7's, one on the stern near the prop, and one on the hull directly adjacent to the tug's engine housing, both above the conventional waterline. At Geronimo's suggestion, as an added precaution, both of the devices had been carefully double packaged in watertight, heat-soluble plastic containers to keep moisture from affecting the timing device.

The chance part of the operation came in the timing. Jessie Preston had heard the Bandung tug captain estimate that it would take another hour for the tanker to complete the transfer; thirty-seven minutes had elapsed since that transmission. As a result, the crew of the *Indon* was gambling on a fifty-five-minute window, all based on the voice-log recording received aboard the DSSRV at 0417LT.

Now, at 0440 and an MT of 0017, another thirty-three minutes had elapsed. From less than twenty feet under the hull of the tug, Gideon could still hear the tanker pumps laboring. But even with the depth chop caused by the monsoon winds on the surface, the Chinese vessel floated high like a cork in the water—an indication she had unloaded at least a significant part of her cargo.

The question Gideon couldn't answer was whether the *Ti Win* was off-loading everything she carried, or if she was destined for another port and another delivery. If she was, she could be closer to wrapping up the transfer than any of them were estimating. That could throw off the timing.

The second element of chance was whether or not the sedative grenades that Gideon intended to plant in addition to the Nl-7s's would be discovered, recognized, and disposed of before they could detonate. The plan called for them to go off eight to ten minutes before the Nl-7s's ignited. Collectively they had decided that the mark was 0044MT. That meant Gideon would time the sedative grenade for forty minutes and Geronimo was to set the timers on the Nl-7s's to go off eight to ten minutes later. The pulse detonation could delay the timing device no more than ten minutes. If the tug hadn't cleared the minefield by then, the *Indon,* following at close quarters, could be in a heap of trouble.

Gideon swam, then groped his way up along the bow of the tug until he broke the surface. A wave caught him and slapped him hard against the rusty steel plates of the hull.

He closed his eyes, righted himself, gave himself time to let his head clear, and stared up into the darkness at the tug's gunnel. He had guessed right, a series of old tires had been rigged along the side to serve as bumpers. He had come up on the starboard side slightly aft of the bow, the off side from where the tug was snugged up to the barge.

He dropped below the surface, twisted the dial and set the timer on the SG, resurfaced, took off his dive mask, waited for a swell, gripped the sedative grenades with one hand, and braced himself against the hull with the other. It would come—he knew it would. It was like waiting for the firecracker to go off after setting the fuse.

From that point on, Gideon knew it had very little to do with skill, with dexterity, or even with training. Those were the givens—if that was all there was to it, he was in. Now, in addition to everything else, he needed luck and timing and maybe a touch of athleticism. Because when the swell came, it would suck the breath out of him and he would forget to breathe even when he could. That was the way it happened that night when the *Rita Green* capsized in choppy waters six miles off the coast of Marathon. That was the way it would be now.

He knew when it came it would roar out of the darkness with sledgehammer force—and even though he knew it was coming, it would catch him off guard.

Then it came.

He caught the wave, felt it heave him up, and he reached skyward. When he came down—it was with a slam dunk. Charles Barkley would have been proud of him. His fingers caught momentarily on the edge of the tire, but the grenade was safely nestled in the cavity between the walls of the tire when he hit the water again. He dropped below the surface, righted himself, popped up, cleared his mask, rolled with the swell, shoved the mouthpiece back in his mouth, and disappeared beneath the surface.

As he began clawing his way back to the depths, he entertained his ongoing fantasy. In it, Jake Ruppert was handing him a check. This time the check was big enough to buy that boat and there was enough left over to pay a deck hand until his charter business got rolling.

It was exactly 0457LT, mission time 0051.32, when Jessie Preston disengaged the seal on the door to the *Indon*'s dive chamber and Gideon Stone and Sheban Geronimo stood grinning at her. Geronimo was holding his hand up with the thumb and forefinger forming a circle. "Welcome home, gentlemen," she said with a grin of her own.

"Too bad you don't have some coffee, Preston," Gideon gruffed. "I think there's cause for celebration."

"You planted the Nl-7s's?"

Geronimo nodded. "Right where we planned; one just above the prop, one near the tug's engine."

"What about the SG?"

"Where, if it works, it'll do the most damage—in the bumpers, by the wheelhouse. With any luck at all, the whole damn crew will be camped around the heater in that wheelhouse trying to dry out when those pulse canisters go off. The only problem is, they'll be dead to the world and they'll miss all the fireworks."

Jessie Preston, still smiling, turned, knelt down, and rummaged around in her sea pack. When she stood up and turned around again she was holding a thermos. "It's coffee, Colonel; made it back on the *Bo Jac*. Jake Ruppert said coffee, black and hot, would keep you going when nothing else would."

Gideon Stone took the thermos, poured himself a cup, and one for each of the others. He took a sip and held up his cup in toast. He was smiling. "Did I tell you how glad I am to have you aboard, Preston?"

Chapter Eleven

Day 7: Time 0527LT
The Bandung Tug

The night had been long and Apaca Tern, at age sixty-one, was near exhaustion. In the chop and chill of the Java Sea night, it had taken the four men on the supply barge and the four-man crew of the Bandung tug just over five hours to transfer the cargo from the *Ti Win*. But now, for Apaca and the rest of the men, there was a sense of accomplishment; the gear had been stowed, the winches secured, and only three small containers of a light lubricating oil had washed overboard. To Apaca's way of thinking, it was a small price to pay.

There were two oil heaters in the crew quarters, which the captain of the tug, Goron Ki, readily acknowledged weren't really crew quarters at all, but simply a place where the men could go when they were not needed on deck. Next to the heaters was a small makeshift galley with two hot plates where the men could make *kopi* and lace it with *susu*. Apaca had mixed himself a cup, located a small area between two storage cabinets, and more or less isolated himself from the rest of the confusion in the crowded room. His wife had packed a *martabak* for him, liberally lacing it with goat cheese and *mentimum,* and he was savoring it, carefully tearing off small pieces of the concoction as he ate.

The conversation in the cramped quarters was raucous and most of the men were laughing, boasting, and congratulating themselves, ignoring the pounding the tug was taking from the monsoon driven waves.

Icfon Jurawa had spied him earlier, and now wedged himself into the small space beside Apaca. "You no doubt have enough for a hungry shipmate?" the man teased. "I have no wife to take such good care of me as yours does you."

Apaca slipped a slice of the spiced cucumber out of his sandwich-like meal and handed it to the man. Icfon, much younger than Apaca, was a man who never appeared to be prepared for anything—meals as well as work. "Here," Apaca joked, "but next time tell your girlfriend to fix you something before you go to work."

Icfon stuffed the morsel in his mouth and laughed. "If I had a girlfriend," he admitted, "that is exactly what I would tell her to do. But—"

"I know, even if you had one," Apaca interrupted, "you would not be able to accommodate her on what the Bandung pays us."

"Precisely why I do not have one," Icfon said. "On

what Sarawak pays us, we are lucky to be able to keep body and soul together, let alone feed a woman or a family. Besides, what woman is willing to put up with having her man out of her bed at all hours of the night, never knowing where he is, never knowing whether or not he will come home?"

Apaca nodded, and this time tore off a larger piece of his *martabak* to hand to his friend. "There have been times when we could afford little more than sago or a small portion of *opor ayam*," he admitted. "Sometimes I think the general is testing our conviction—seeing how hard we are willing to work in return for so little."

Icfon, sitting close to the fire wall between the crew quarters and the engine compartment, listened for several moments to the tug's ancient engine struggle against the force of the waves. He was nodding agreement. "It is a difficult night," he observed. "I would not want to be Captain Ki. The channel is narrow enough without having to cope with angry waters."

"He is a master seaman," Apaca reminded his young friend. "I have seen his papers. He once received an commendation for his seamanship from Soekarno."

"Perhaps Soekarno should have told him it is unwise to take his ship out on a night like this," Icfon said with a laugh. "Or maybe Captain Ki should be given another commendation for seamanship if we make it back into the harbor safely."

"You are concerned?" Apaca inquired.

"I am," Icfon said. "Listen to the wind, then consider the mines that protect the entrance to the harbor. If Captain Ki makes an error in judgment, we could all be victims like the men who died in Jakarta."

Apaca Tern did not admit it, of course, but he had not given much thought to the recent failed coup attempt in the Javanese capital. Because of his age and the fact that he was not in good health, he had never considered becoming an actual member of the Bandung militia. He believed in what Sarawak was doing, and he supported the general—but becoming an actual militiaman who marched and carried a gun was something he had decided he had no calling for.

Still, he disputed what Icfon had to say. "They did not die in vain, my young friend," Apaca said. Again, the truth of the matter was he had not thought this matter through either; he was merely repeating what one of the staff officers had reported Sarawak as having said when the general returned to Karimunjawa.

This time Icfon did not answer him. Instead he cocked his head to one side and listened to the sounds of the laboring engine. "We are approaching the channel," he said. "This is always the time when I worry."

Apaca saw no reason to dwell on the danger of Ki's mission. He had ridden out storms on the tug on more than one occasion, and the ancient vessel had always negotiated the minefield with no difficulty. He finished his pancake sandwich, sipped his *kopi,* and turned his thoughts to other matters.

In the wheelhouse of the Bandung tug, Goron Ki stood at the helm of his laboring ship and watched the screen of his newly installed radar. Like so many other of the more modern navigational devices on his ship, it too had been salvaged—this one from the wreck of a Dutch tanker. In the thirty-seven years he had been a tug captain, the majority of which had been spent maneuvering craft in and out of the shallow waters of the inlet leading into the Karimunjawa harbor, this was the first time that he had been afforded the luxury of a RANG unit. To Goron Ki, at least, the thought that he might someday have radar-assisted navigation guidance had been little more than a dream. RANG was something he had only read about and would never know. But now, with new mine nets replacing the old percussion mines planted at random intervals in the inlet, and with winds much stronger then he normally encountered, the unit was not a luxury, it was a necessity. Tonight especially, he was grateful for the added precaution.

He watched the echo pattern, adjusted his heading when necessary, and muttered small obscenities when the barge was slow to respond. Out of the corner of his eye, a man he referred to as his first officer, for no other reason than the man had been with him for a long time and cherished the title, stood wide-eyed watching the shifting pattern of the mine nets and probably, Ki decided, praying for a safe entry like the others.

Ki lit a cigarette, offered his first officer one, stole a quick glance at the anemometer gage, and refocused his attention on the RANG screen. Their reentry was proving more difficult than he had anticipated. After the long, undulating waves in the open sea, the chop in the channel, combined with keeping the barge under control, was proving to be a significant challenge to his years of experience.

Day 7: Time 0549LT
The Indon

Gideon Stone caressed the sensitive controls of the *Indon* like the pistol grip on a hair-triggered automatic, and the control cabin, without personnel lighting, was awash in an eerie red-green glow. Next to him, Jessie Preston replicated his every move with the dual-guidance control mechanism, consciously ignoring everything but the OP computer where she double-checked the stream of alphanumerics trailing across the pale green screen.

Behind Gideon, peering over his shoulder, Jeris Alan watched the alpha indications on the screen waver tantalizingly close, only to dance away again and then repeat the cycle. "Each one of those little gems could put a hole in that damn tug and barge big enough for us to drive through," Gideon whispered. "Wanna try it, Captain?"

Alan forced a laugh. "You're doing just fine, Colonel. I'll stay right here and enjoy the show. Truth is, I'd rather be up on top where I can see what the hell is going on."

"You'd be watching the screen on that Apache of yours just like the colonel is," Jessie reminded him. "It's not much better up there than it is down here."

"To each his own," Alan quipped. "I'd feel a whole lot better if I'd grown a set of gills before we started this one."

Gideon Stone loosened his hold, flexed his fingers, arched his back, and took a deep breath before regripping the controls. In that short space of time the *Indon* had drifted two degrees. He looked over at Jessie Preston and asked for the readings. Her voice had gone monotone and she sounded flat, like the voice monitor on the computer.

"Batteries?" Gideon asked.

"Twenty percent of capacity on 1 pack." She glanced back at Geronimo to see if he had pulled the aux rack into position. "Looks like we're ready for the changeover anytime you are," she advised.

"We can milk some more out of 1," Gideon grunted. "Let's double-check what we've got so far. Read off your checklist one more time; is there anything else we can shut down? I want to be damn certain this baby has enough juice to get us out of here."

Jessie Preston was shaking her head before he finished.

"We're operating on min c-2 right now—she's giving us all she's got if we want to keep the four batteries in aux reserve."

Gideon listened, and fell silent for several minutes with his attention focused on the data being displayed on the A panel. Finally, his mouth formed a pencil-thin line and his eyes somehow darkened. "What do you think, Preston? Think you can get this little jewel out of here if . . . if for some reason Geronimo and I don't make it back in time?"

Jessie frowned. "Negative thinking, Colonel. You'll make it. What's that line from *Apollo 13*? 'Failure is not an option.' " Gideon was surprised at how convincing she sounded. Then she decided to add, "And yes, I can get us out of here. You're starting to sound like a chauvinist again."

There was another protracted period of time before Gideon began again. "Okay, gang, while we've still got a few minutes left, let's etch this little scenario in stone. With any luck at all, that tug and barge won't make it to the fuel pier—when those sedative grenades go off and the Nl-7s's kick in—it's bound to hit something. Pray for a bang—the bigger the bang, the better for us. Right now, simple all-out first-class chaos in that harbor would suit me just fine.

"Now then, the minute we hear the bang, Jessie will kill the power and I'll give the signal. That's when Jeris, Sheban, and I head out. When that happens, everyone, no exceptions, mark that 0000 on your Mickey Mouse. Got it?

"From that point on we've got exactly one hundred and twenty minutes to find Nelson and get the hell out of here. I want everyone strapped in and ready to go at MT0121. If one of us isn't back, you go anyway. Understand? Any questions?"

"If you don't make it back—" Jessie started to ask.

"Don't worry, we'll find a way out," Gideon assured her.

Gideon waited for more questions. There were none.

"All right, each of us knows what to do. Jessie, you get those damn computers reconfigurated. Use the mine profile we've been logging on inbound and reverse it—that's all you have to do." Gideon looked at his watch again. "You'll be pushed to get it done in that amount of time, but you can do it. You know the rest. When all your chicks come home to roost, get us the hell out of here."

Jessie nodded and continued to stare back at him. She had the knack of making people feel she was using her emerald-green eyes to see through their social veneer and into their soul. She knew it and she used it.

Gideon turned to the Apache pilot. "Jeris, the minute you get on the surface, get your bearings and start planting those Nl-7s's. If Wormack and Tillston's G2 on what we can expect in the way of a harbor inventory is anywhere near correct, you should have time enough to disable every damn gunboat in the harbor. If you run out of Nl-7s's, shoot up the damn controls. I don't care how you do it, but I don't want anything to be able to follow us out of the harbor. Got it?"

Jeris Alan repeated Gideon's instructions verbatim, and began strapping on his dive gear.

"Sheban," Gideon said, "it's you and me, babe. We gotta find us a Vice President and he could be anywhere on that damn base. We're hedging our bets, though, on what Tillston, Martin, and Kilborn all think. According to them, our best bet for finding Nelson is that long narrow building designated on Tillston's sketch as the base ops building. On the map that Tillston showed us it's the Ln-2 complex: the long, narrow, one story building south of the big warehouse. That's where we go first. If he's not there, we start searching—and we do a helluva lot of praying."

"What about Sarawak?" Jessie pressed.

Gideon shook his head. "According to Jake he's not our concern. If we get Nelson and get him home safe—we get an 'atta boy' from the President. Anything less and we haven't done the job."

"Suppose one of us runs across him?" Alan pressed.

Gideon held up his hand in a halting motion. "Don't go looking for him," he warned.

Geronimo, standing next to the dive chamber, managed a smile, held up his index finger, and carefully drew it horizontally across his throat. "Right?"

"Right," Gideon repeated. "All I'm saying is, don't go looking for him. If you stumble over him, all bets are off. He's fair game."

Day 7: Time 0613LT
The Bandung Tug

Apaca Tern closed his eyes and leaned his head back and to one side as he listened to the chunking, syncopated sound of the tug's diesel. What he noticed was less of a laboring sound and more sounds that indicated both the tug and its tow had now passed through the mine nets. It was a reassuring sound that under normal circumstances would have meant it would soon be time to go back to work.

To Apaca's surprise, however, Captain Ki had called for only three of the men to come up on deck. Perhaps, he decided, the waters in the harbor were calmer than any of them had expected—or it was an indication that the skipper did not anticipate difficulty maneuvering the eighty-foot fuel barge into the docks next to the fuel depot. Whatever the reason, Apaca was grateful he did not have to go back to work. He was tired; it had been a long night. He lit a cigarette, watched the smoke hang in the air, and rubbed his eyes.

Other than the sound of the tug engine, Apaca based much of his thinking on the sound of the wind. The monsoon winds, he had learned when he first went to sea, sounded different over water than they did over land. Because of that, he knew the tug and barge had already passed through the inlet and minefield and were now safe in the harbor.

"Do you hear that, Apaca?" Icfon asked. Neither had moved from the small alcove in the crew room next to the tug's engines, and both sat with their knees drawn up and their arms wrapped around them.

Apaca opened his eyes and listened. "I do not hear anything," he admitted, "but my hearing is not as good as it used to be." He laughed, if for no other reason than to demonstrate to Icfon that he could accept the infirmities that accompanied his mounting years.

"I hear a hissing sound," Icfon insisted, " . . . like a gas leak."

Apaca sniffed at the stale, smoky air in the room. "You are imagining things. The only thing I can smell is the *martabak*." He patted his stomach.

Icfon inclined his head to one side and nudged his friend with his elbow. "Maybe it is wishful thinking. Maybe it is nothing more than the—" He broke off in mid-sentence when he saw Apaca's head slump forward. "Hey, old man, they do not pay us . . . for . . . for sleep . . . sleeping." He tried to finish what he was saying, but he realized his words had begun to sound slurred. The words had barely managed to escape his lips, and now he was struggling to hold his head erect. As he looked around the room, Frante Achin, the only other member of the loading crew that had not been called up on deck with the rest of the detail, had, like Apaca, slumped over with his head on the table. His eyes were closed.

"Something is . . . is . . . something is wr-wrong," Icfon mumbled, and he too began to spiral into another world.

Goron Ki turned the wheel over to the only other man on his crew qualified to take the helm and leaned forward. He ignored the curtains of rain against the wheelhouse windows as he attempted to verify the instrument readings on the panel in front of him. "Quarter speed," he instructed as he looked ahead, straining to see the position of the barge.

The helmsman acknowledged his captain's command. His voice was partially muffled by the incessant sound of the wind and rain. At the same time, the young second officer noticed that his own eyes were heavy and that a slightly peculiar odor had permeated the cluttered wheelhouse.

Ki himself suddenly felt drowsy. He closed his eyes, opened them again, and realized how much effort it had taken to accomplish the task. Behind him, the three deckhands he had called topside were all sitting strangely still, and one of them had even slumped over as though he was sleeping.

Ki tried to form words, but they seemed to get tangled and distorted somewhere in the process of forming them. He felt dizzy and braced himself—but the effort proved futile. It was too late. He was already sagging to his knees. Over the ship-to-shore radio he could hear distant static, crackling sounds—half words, garbled words, fragments of instructions. The words made no sense.

Where were they coming from? Was it the young officer on the loading pier? He thought he recognized the fact that someone was shouting his name and the element of—what was the word—was it "urgency" in the man's voice?

In the hushed, dimly lit personnel pod of the *Indon,* Gideon Stone looked up at Jessie Preston when she held up her hand. "Listen—I think we're in, Colonel," she whispered. "The tug has come to full stop. Now we're picking up an idle." There was another pause before she confirmed the tug's diesel had chattered into reverse.

Gideon got to his feet, eyed the A panel, and glanced at his watch. "Ten to one says she's getting ready to maneuver into the fuel pier. All right, gentlemen, time to pull up your socks and drop your . . . " He let his voice trail off when he remembered there was a woman present. "Get your bib on and your tucker zipped up. With any luck at all, all hell will break loose up there in the next couple of minutes, and we'd better be ready to take advantage of it."

Jeris Alan was already on his feet, counting as he finished pulling on his dive hood and reached for his fins. " . . . one thousand and thirty—one thousand and twenty-nine—one thousand and twenty-eight . . . " He grinned at Geronimo. "How about it, Corporal, ready to go swimming?"

Sheban Geronimo nodded, finished pulling on his gloves, and secured the wrist straps on both his depth gauge and compass. He snugged the air hose up and over his right shoulder, and double-checked his purge valve before giving his mouthpiece one final bit of scrutiny. As usual, his face was void of expression.

Alan continued his count. " . . . one thousand and

twenty-one—one thousand and twenty—one thousand and nineteen . . . "

"Into the dive chamber," Gideon hissed. "Slam it and seal it, Preston. The minute you hear something definitive, open the floodgates."

"It's a shame we're going to miss the show up top, Colonel," she said. "It could be a dandy."

As Gideon pulled the compartment door shut behind him, Jessie Preston heard him mutter something about luck. She wasn't sure what he had said, but she had a good idea. It had taken a while, but Gideon Stone, the man she had heard so many stories about, was finally beginning to act and sound like he was back in charge and in his element.

She watched the door to the dive chamber slam shut, then heard the pressure lock engage and the hiss of the seal as the chamber went watertight. At the same time she was reaching for the sea valve and pressing the chamber control valve to "full open."

Ketan Sabo tried to shake off the effects of a sleep that had been both too short and too deep when he felt someone shaking him. "Captain. Captain Sabo," the voice repeated. The man was shouting at him in a heavy regional dialect, one that Sabo didn't understand. The words were little more than frenetic fragments, and his voice had taken on an almost hysterical dimension. " . . . something's wrong . . . "

Sabo sat up, rubbing his eyes. "What is it?" he demanded.

"The—the tug . . . " The young dock officer had turned away from him to look back through the window and he was shaking.

Sabo leaped to his feet, bolted to the window, and stared out at the dark, storm-battered Karimunjawa harbor. There was a momentary lull when all he could hear was the clamor of the wind and the noise of the rain—then there was an explosion, a full-throated rumble like an angry peal of violent thunder, quickly followed by a second, then a third. Finally the sound evolved into what seemed like an endless chain of salvos. The scene across the harbor had suddenly erupted in a turbulent orange-white panorama.

The window in the old harbor master's shed shattered, the walls buckled, and Ketan Sabo's world erupted in a spinning universe of razor-sharp splinters of glass and flying debris. Sabo could feel himself being bowled to the floor, and seconds later the harbor master's desk toppled over on him. The air rushed out of him, and he saw the young officer out of the corner of his eye. The man's face was a bloody montage, peppered with tiny splinters of glass and networked with lacerations that would have rendered him unrecognizable if Sabo had not been standing beside him at the time of the first blast. The man's mouth was distorted, twisted into the shape of a scream—but without a throat to convey it, he was unable to register his protest.

Sabo, pinned to the warped, water-soaked flooring of the old shed, watched helplessly as one brilliant flash of orange-red light after another ripped holes in the smothering combination of darkness, wind, and rain. The blackness was no longer black. The night was no longer night. Fleeting, demonic pyrotechnic displays competed to fill the voids in the darkness—all created by the searing, churning balls of flame.

The Bandung captain was transfixed. The chain of explosions had ripped a hole in the night and the harbor was on fire. With hands bloodied by flying broken glass, he tried to push the weight of the old desk off him. But the effort proved futile—he did not have the strength.

Goron Ki felt the oil-soaked decking of the tug heave, then buckle beneath him and the wall of angry flames engulf him. The inferno was swallowing him up, digesting him, and in those final seconds of his life there was a horrifying awareness of what was happening—of the journey—of the transition he was about to make—the migration between life and death. His lungs filled with the hot gas of the holocaust, and he flailed his arms in outrage and pain. Then, as if fate would deliver him, he felt himself being lifted up, catapulted by unseen forces, and finally cast into a dark, cold world where the fire was momentarily assuaged by the chill of harbor water. He opened his mouth and gulped in the ablution. Then he gyrated down and down until his lungs exploded.

Apaca Tern had been thrown clear by the first blast. Now he floundered in the water like a speared fish. Curiously, there was nothing to see—only to feel. He pulled himself through the water because it was the instinctive thing to do—he wasn't even certain he was clawing his way to the surface. Already his lungs ached and his brain hammered. Unseen, powerful forces dictated his response. He reached out, again and again, cupping his hands, drawing himself through the water, propelling, swimming; swimming stronger than he could ever remember.

Finally, he broke through. He gulped in the acrid, smoke-filled, oil-soaked air and began to cough. Then he opened his eyes—and through the watery, salty mist that blurred them, saw the fiery display that had once been the Karimunjawa docks. Explosion followed explosion—

until there were no longer distinguishable sounds; it was one continuous, rolling wall of amphibious thunder.

His hands were burnt, his face seared, and his body tortured—yet the aging deckhand somehow found the strength to orient himself. Behind him, on the bank opposite the burning wharfs, he could see the headlights of vehicles spearing their way through the darkness toward the dock area. Sandwiched in between the chain of explosions, he could hear the mournful drone of the base alert system and the ear-piercing, shrill sounds of emergency sirens.

He treaded water, swallowed it, coughed it up, and spat it out again only to have the cycle repeated. He felt the ache of his ordeal, and when he was certain he no longer had the strength to survive, he somehow found the courage to begin swimming again toward the shore.

Bojoni Sarawak felt the floor shake, heard the windows rattle, and squeezed his eyes shut. His first thought was that he was again plunging into another of the terrible dreams that accompanied the fever. Instinctively he reached up to mop away the mantle of sweat that he knew would be coating his forehead. But this time there was none. His forehead was dry and cool.

Instead of the fever, it was the lethargy he had to shake off. He opened his eyes to discover that the woman was already sitting up. A red-orange sheen played with her olive-colored skin, and in her nakedness she looked like one of the bronze statues on the peace monument in the park near the Cierbon in West Java. Despite it all, the only word to escape him was "What . . . " and then his voice trailed off.

From the very hill overlooking the harbor where Sarawak had established his Bandung headquarters and first planned his takeover of the government, he could see nothing but a ring of fire.

He leaped out of bed, pulled on his trousers, and reached for the telephone that connected him to the duty officer in the B-2 complex. "What happened?" he screamed.

The voice on the other end of the line was rattled and disoriented. "I—I don't know—don't know, General. The—the fuel—the fuel depot—fuel depot is on fire . . . "

Sarawak slammed the phone down, grabbed a shirt, and raced out on the balcony. Despite the incessant wind and rain, the low-hanging clouds over the Karimunjawa harbor were glazed in a surreal wash of red, orange, and yellow. He watched one explosion follow another, each one belching rockets of fire into the skies over the Bandung complex. Finally, the anesthetizing effect of what was happening began to pass, and he sprinted down to his car and headed for the harbor.

Jeris Alan was in luck. He had surfaced less than two hundred yards from the pier where the Bandung gunboats were moored on the far side of the harbor from the fire. He made a quick mental note to congratulate Tillston or whoever was responsible for accurate G2 information, and started swimming toward the slips where the gunboats were tied.

As he swam, images materialized and faded. He had experienced them before. They clicked on and off in his mind like computer screens; referencing, reinforcing, indexing. Wormack's briefing session had been thorough. Houjians were new. Houjians were fast. Houjians had replaced what? Was it the Huangfeng or Hegu-class missile boats? He mentally chided himself—why the hell was he worried about what they replaced? He had a missile—

and that mission now was going to be a helluva lot easier than it would have been without the diversion created by the fire.

Despite his good fortune, every fourth or fifth stroke he looked back. From where he was in the harbor, the fire appeared to be spreading. Good. Double good. Damn—it was happening. The high—the inevitable high was beginning. In a few seconds—or a few nanoseconds or however the hell they measured things like that—he would begin to experience it. He was ecstatic. He was free, free-as-a-goddamned-bird. What was it they called it—the *superman* syndrome? He was powerful, invincible, even more important, indestructible. Now it was happening. It was engulfing him—sweeping over him, the high—the rapture—just like always. Yeah, yeah; go, fire. Keep those bastards occupied.

His mind was racing—the inventory—back to the inventory. There was a combat-automation system, fire-control radar, twin SSM launchers—and in that forward gun housing a twin 37mm automatic machine gun—and two 30mm-type 69 AA guns. He'd put a crimp in their goddamn tail. One Nl-7s would do it. Just let those sons of bitches try to follow them out of the harbor. They'll get the surprise of their life.

Suddenly they—the gunboats—began to materialize—he could see one, then two; lined up like little clay ducks in a carnival shooting gallery. He was within fifty yards now of the first one.

Jeris Alan's brain was working at a fever pitch. He knew he had to get his bearings. Already one thought was telescoping into another—like a drill, invading, weighing one action against another. There was a chain of routine, first this—then that. Some of it was training, more of it, maybe even most of it, was impulse and intuition.

Then he saw it and his mind began cataloging and referencing again; there was something in the water straight ahead of him. What the hell was it? What was it Ensign Carbor said? That's it, whatever you do, wherever you go, regardless of the kind of mission, expect the unexpected. This was one Tillston hadn't said anything about. It loomed in the red-orange darkness just ahead of him, bigger than the fast Houjian attack boats he had been warned about. So much for Tillston and the thoroughness of his goddamn G2 briefing. Don't sweat it—it's just one more thing to contend with. He could handle it. Just let them try to stop him. He was a one-man, goddamn instrument of destruction. Get ready, Sarawak, you're about to experience your and your damn Bandung's worst nightmare.

He had experienced it all before. In a sense he was outside of himself—but still calling the shots, feeling himself and his invincibility—apart from himself—watching himself slice through the water; doing what he had been trained to do. Another stroke—then another—and another—until he could reach out and feel it; a hull, cold, wet, the feel of barnacle-crusted plates of steel.

Now, he thought, now we exercise caution—now we swim around—now we make certain—under the pier, under the stern, the screws, look for a foothold—not that far now, reach up. Get up and over that gunnel, Alan baby, and you're in—you're ready to wreak havoc.

Jeris Alan slithered up out of the water, grabbed the helston, and pulled himself into position where he could survey most of the foredeck. More luck, the deck was clear. Behind him, the wet grey darkness before dawn was being illuminated by the bank of flames devouring the entire infrastructure of the harbor's fuel depot.

He crawled over the gunnel, peeled out of his dive gear, and began working his way forward. The Houjian had been buttoned up for the night. There would be crew aboard—but no more than a handful. Somewhere up ahead of him he could hear voices, men's voices—they seemed to be coming from the port side of the vessel. He crouched and crawled cautiously past the gun turret until he could see them. They both were wearing slickers, bundled against the rain, staring in disbelief across the expanse of water at the conflagration on the other side of the harbor.

Behind him, the docks were deserted, and with the chaos created by the fire, it was reasonable to anticipate little or no interference. Still, he took time to scan up and down the length of the pier before straightening up, pinning his back to the wall of the gun turret, and slipping through the small maintenance opening to the port side of the attack vessel. That was where he waited until one of the crew men stepped back under the shelter of the wheelhouse overhang to light a cigarette. When he did, Jeris Alan made his move. He slipped up behind the crewman, reached around, clamped one hand over the man's mouth, circled his neck with the other, and gave it a violent twist to the right. It all happened so quickly the Bandung crewman didn't even have time to react. Alan brought his knee up square in the small of the man's back and jerked him backwards. Even over the din of what had now become a succession of minor explosions coming from across the water, Jeris Alan could still hear the ugly, snapping sound of a man's back breaking. The crewman went limp and Alan released his hold. When he did, the man slumped to the deck.

The Apache pilot pulled the body back into the turret cavity and waited. There was another explosion, one that sent streamers of hot, burning gas into the Karimunjawa sky, and when it did, Alan leaped from the shadows. He used his right hand like the blade of an ax, bringing it down hard against the back of the second man's neck just below the base of the skull. The Bandung crewman's body went limp and he slumped forward against the gunnel. In the same motion, Jeris Alan reached down, cupped his hands around the man's legs, and lifted him over the railing. He heard the body hit the water, waited to see if it would resurface, and when it didn't, headed for the wheelhouse. He had already checked the time. There were exactly eighty-one minutes and thirty-seven seconds left before he was scheduled to rendezvous with the *Indon*. With that in mind, he was already searching through his tac pak, reaching for one of the Ni-7s's and thinking about where he would stash it to do the most damage.

Chapter Twelve

Day 7: Time 0633LT
Karimunjawa Harbor

Gideon Stone came to the surface under the pilings of the central wharf. Directly overhead he could see the buckled remains of the pier and the rubble of what once had been some sort of shelter or shed. One wall had survived and was still standing. In the glow of the inferno raging on the far side of the harbor, the scene was chaos, like something he would have expected to see in a big-budget disaster movie. There was a discordant symphony of what had become muted explosions, accompanied by wailing fire sirens and men shouting. Despite the storm, the sounds of the turmoil on the far side of the harbor managed to careen across the water.

From what he was able to make out through the clouds of billowing smoke, the fire continued out of control and the row of Bandung fuel sheds had already been reduced to piles of tangled ruins. Plus, there was what Jake Ruppert would have considered a bonus; the flames continued to spread and were now consuming rows of warehouses. The fire appeared to be hopelessly out of control.

Less than ten feet behind him, in water still up to his chest, Sheban Geronimo was plowing his way into the shallows. He was towing the watertight tac pak behind him. He had already begun shedding his dive gear, and was pointing in the direction of a small row of buildings adjacent to the pier.

On shore, in the shadow of the pilings, both men began the systematic routine of stowing dive gear and checking their weapons. When they finished, Geronimo tucked the tac pak now containing their dive gear behind a pile of debris under the pier, and the two men started up a small incline toward a cluster of three service vehicles.

"It's like someone knew we were coming and wanted to make it easy for us," Gideon whispered. He instructed Geronimo to keep his eyes peeled while he crawled into a vintage forties Chinese Jeep, reached under the dash, disconnected the wires from the ignition, and started to hotwire it.

He was halfway through the process when he felt Geronimo's hand on his shoulder. "We got company," the corporal whispered, "—two of 'em. They're headed this way."

Gideon crouched down on the floorboard, rolled over on his back, coiled his knees, and waited. Geronimo squatted, moved quickly around to the other side of the vehicle, and hid in the shadows. The two men were close enough now that Gideon could hear them talking. From here on out, he knew it was all a matter of timing.

When the door swung open, Gideon kicked. It wasn't a direct hit, but it was close enough. Gideon had caught the man in the chest and he heard him let out a yelp. By the time the Bandung militiaman could regain his senses, Gideon had made his move. He jerked himself into a sitting position, gained some semblance of balance, vaulted forward, and launched himself headfirst at the still-stunned guard. It was even easier than he had anticipated. If Bojoni Sarawak had his men on a training regimen, it was obvious this one wasn't one of the general's poster boys. He was as wide as he was tall, and far too bulky to summon up any kind of agility when he needed it most. Before the man could scramble to his feet, Gideon had landed two more blows. The first rocketed the man's head backward, and the second buried itself in the folds of his stomach. Gideon could hear the wind erupt out of him, and there was the sudden heavy odor of garlic and a pathetic, pleading kind of moan.

Geronimo wasn't as fortunate. He leaped, but his man was quicker—a lot quicker. The man brought his knee up and his hand down in a karate chop that caught the corporal on the side of the neck. As Geronimo stumbled forward, there was another volley, a well-timed and well-placed one-two combination of knee and fist. The knee caught Geronimo flush in the mouth, and the fist landed on the side of his head just below the ear. Suddenly there were cheap rockets going off in his head and bile flooding his mouth. He slumped forward, off balance, and his adversary landed another blow, this one with the butt end of a .45 automatic.

Then, as Geronimo rolled over on his back, he saw something fly through the air. It was Gideon. The former lieutenant colonel had vaulted across the hood of the jeep and caught Geronimo's assailant by surprise. Both men went down in a tangle of arms and legs on the gravel surface between the two vehicles. But this time there was a difference; Geronimo's man had lost his advantage. Gideon reached out, grabbed the man's arm, slammed it against the door of the jeep, knocked the automatic out of his hand, and brought his knee up into the man's crotch, all in one maneuver. There was a momentary groan, an unexpected whimper, and it was over. Gideon pinned the man's arms with his knees, shoved the beam of his flashlight in the man's face, and took a look at him.

"Well, well, well, Corporal," Gideon snarled, "look what we have here. Damned if we didn't get ourselves one of Sarawak's officers."

Geronimo struggled to his knees, wiped the blood off his mouth, spat, and took out his own .45. "Move over, Colonel, it's my turn. Let me show you your tax dollars at work. I'll demonstrate the little impromptu persuasion technique we learned in our training sessions a couple of months ago." He cupped his hand over the Bandung officer's nose to shut off his breathing, clamped down on both sides of the man's face, forced his mouth open, and rammed the barrel of the automatic in his mouth.

Gideon winced as he watched the man's front teeth crack and break off.

"Now the second part of this little exercise comes under the heading of interrogation," Geronimo mumbled. "The guy that taught me this technique called it 'stress interrogation.' I think you can see why. Want me to demonstrate, Colonel?"

Gideon nodded, and watched as Geronimo's finger curled past the trigger guard and coiled around the trigger.

"Now, Colonel, what would you like me to ask him?"

"Ask him if he can speak English."

"You heard the colonel." Geronimo was hissing like a coiled rattler. "Now listen very carefully. Your head moves two ways, up-and-down and sideways. When one of us asks a question, you nod or shake your head and I'll interpret. But let me warn you. If you value your miserable fucking neck, soldier boy, I suggest you think real hard and come up with answers real fast."

The Bandung officer stared up into the blinding glare of the flashlight. His eyes were glazed and he was having trouble breathing. When he had waited as long as he thought he dared, his head inched up and down. The movement was so slight it was almost imperceptible—but Geronimo had his answer and he grinned.

"I think we got us an affirmative, Colonel. Next question."

"Ask him if he knows where his general is holding the American Vice President hostage."

Sheban Geronimo pressed down on the automatic, burying it deeper in the man's mouth. "You heard the colonel."

The Bandung officer started to gag. Finally he nodded.

"Now ask him where he is," Gideon said.

Geronimo cocked his head to one side. "Know how much pressure it takes to pull the trigger on one of these little jewels, soldier boy? Sure you do, but since everyone knows you're not supposed to talk with your mouth full, I'll tell you. The answer is little, damn little. In fact, I could slip real easy kneeling here in the gravel like I am, and if I did, I'd make one helluva mess out of what you're using for brains, soldier boy."

"Here's the deal," Gideon said, leaning over into the glare of the flashlight so that the Bandung officer could see him. "You show us where Sarawak is holding the hostage and you live. Stall, and they'll scoop up your brains with a damn shovel."

Geronimo pulled the gun out of the man's mouth, grabbed him by the front of his slicker, and pulled him into a sitting position. The rain continued to cascade down the man's face, creating rivulets of blood that traced their way through the creases, over his chin, eventually dripping down on his chest.

"I—I—will show—show you," the officer finally managed to reply.

Gideon's eyes darted in both directions and he got to his feet. "Tell Wonder Boy what happens next. Tell him he's going to get his skinny ass in that damn jeep and take us to where Sarawak is holding Nelson prisoner. If we get stopped, he talks in English and English only. Tell him you'll be driving and I'll be sitting right behind him with a 9mm semi-automatic about six inches from the back of his head. If I hear anything that even halfway sounds like he's trying to talk Maylay, I pull the trigger."

Geronimo assessed the battered face in front of him. The man was running his tongue over his broken teeth. "I get the feeling he understands," he said.

"You may also wish to tell our boy that I'm out of shape and a little edgy about this whole thing," Gideon added, "and you may also want to caution him that there's nothing worse than a nervous man with a nervous finger on the trigger of a 9mm semi-automatic."

Gideon continued to monitor the time. It was ten minutes later, with the windscreen wipers of the old Chinese M-7 ATNO struggling against the torrents of rain hammering down on them, when the Bandung officer cautiously raised his hand to point out the location of the headquarters complex. His mouth was bloodied and his voice sounded as if it had to be strained through layers of gauze before the words finally worked their way out. "There," he said, " . . . in there." He was gesturing toward a side entrance with a single light over the door.

"What do you think, Colonel?" Geronimo asked. "Think it's a setup?" "We'll have to chance it. Ask him how many guards."

The Bandung officer shrugged. *"Dua—tiga."*

"English, dammit," Gideon snarled. He shoved the barrel of the 9mm in the back of the man's neck to make his point.

"Two, maybe—maybe three," the officer estimated.

"Where?"

The man hesitated before he answered. He continued to spit blood. "There are—are three on duty. One or two—will be in the dayroom. One—one will be positioned outside of the door."

"How about it, Colonel?" Geronimo asked. "Buy it?"

Gideon eyed the eight-foot-high chain-link fence surrounding the headquarters compound and the lighted guard shack at the entrance. "Ask him if this is the only way in."

Despite his obvious discomfort, the Bandung officer was allowing the trace of a smile to play with the corner of his mouth. "All of the entrances are guarded," he informed them. From the tone in his voice, his answer had the ring of a minor victory.

"Tell soldier boy he's pushing his luck," Gideon said. "Tell him we're going through the main gate and it's up to him to get us through. If he doesn't, he buys the farm and the situation gets a whole lot messier."

Geronimo repeated his colonel's order, and stole a quick glance at the Bandung officer's face. As beleaguered as he was, he was getting braver by the moment.

"I don't like it, Colonel. I don't think we can trust this bastard."

"Stop at the gate," Gideon ordered, "but be ready for anything."

As Geronimo brought the ATNO to a halt, he saw one of the Bandung militiamen in the guard shack lean forward and try to peer through the steamy glass window.

Gideon began prodding the Bandung officer. "Your man is looking for a signal, soldier boy, better give him one—now. If he doesn't wave us through in the next ten seconds, Uncle Sarawak will be looking for a place to bury your scrawny bones."

Major Assasio Muta was playing a hunch. Moments after the initial explosion in the Karimunjawa fuel depot, he had dressed and driven to the Bandung headquarters complex. He knew his general well enough to know that Sarawak's reaction would be to go to the scene of the fire.

Muta, who had been with the Indonesian rebel forces for over fifteen years, and an officer for the last ten, was easily the most suspicious of Sarawak's senior staff. He had immediately suspected the possibility that what was happening could well be more than just an accident. While others were preoccupied with the fire, Muta followed his hunch and decided to check on the American hostage.

Now he was standing in the narrow corridor outside the room where Nelson was being detained, peering through a small observation port in the door, watching the man's very move. Two militiamen, both volunteers, stood next to him, one on each side. Like most of the men attracted to Sarawak's PRJ movement in recent years, they were young, poorly trained, and at the moment, clearly distracted by the fires raging out of control on the other side of the harbor.

As Muta watched, Nelson stood at his window, trying to get a better view of what was happening. "Has he said or done anything out of the ordinary?" Muta asked.

The two militiamen exchanged nervous glances before the taller of the two, the one wearing a corporal's insignia, tendered an answer. "I noticed nothing, sir, and I have been on duty since *delapan*."

The other militiaman nodded agreement. "Yes, since *delapan*," he confirmed.

"And for ten hours you have done nothing but stand guard here outside the prisoner's door?"

Again there was an exchange of glances before the two men assured Muta that they had been at their post throughout the period. "Except, that is, for the time when Captain Sabo was here," the tall one admitted.

"Sabo?" Muta repeated. "When was Captain Sabo here?" Like the others, Muta had heard the persistent rumors that someone, someone high within the ranks of the Bandung movement, was assisting the Americans in their efforts to undermine Sarawak's coup attempt and free Nelson. How else could the failure of the Jakarta plot be explained? Of course there was betrayal. Failure packaged in whispers of betrayal was easier for Sarawak's forces to accept.

At first Muta had dismissed the persistent whispers as mere gossip, something that could be expected when the coup attempt failed. After all, coup attempts did not fail without reason. It was never the fault of the leader of the coup. There had to be a reason, a reason that had nothing to do with underestimating the resolve of the incumbent, Sarni Kujon, or the outrage of the most powerful nation on earth.

"What did Captain Sabo say?" Muta pushed.

"He ordered us to find some reading material for the prisoner," one of the men offered.

"And did you?"

"No, but the captain went to the dayroom and returned with some magazines for the prisoner."

"Did you check to see if that was all he gave the prisoner?" Muta asked.

There was another hesitation before both men shook their heads. "No, Major Muta," the tall one admitted.

Suddenly, to Assasio Muta, the timing of Sabo's visit and the fuel depot explosions was simply too much of a coincidence. Perhaps the rumors were true. Perhaps there was a traitor in the Bandung staff. Now, hearing of Sabo's visit to the American, he suspected betrayal. Could it be that Sabo's visit was timed to inform the American Vice President that there would be an attempt to rescue him and that he should be ready? If that was the case, the explosions could have been designed as a diversion.

"You are fools," Muta seethed. "You should have checked to make certain there was nothing in those magazines."

"But it was Captain Sabo," the corporal protested.

Muta ordered one of the men to unlock the door, and when the man did, Muta shoved him aside and opened it. Nelson turned away from the window to look at him, blinking at the sudden intrusion of feeble light filtering in from the hall.

"Put your hands over your head and turn around," Muta ordered.

Nelson hesitated, then complied as the Bandung major turned on the single overhead light and crossed the room with his automatic drawn. "What is the meaning of this?" Nelson protested, but his tired voice lacked the indignation he had hoped for.

Muta kicked the stack of magazines aside and instructed the two militiamen to search the prisoner. The corporal, more zealous than his partner, obviously saw the order as an opportunity to at least partially redeem himself. He shoved Nelson up against the wall, kicked his legs apart, and hunted for anything that might possibly incriminate Sabo. When he finished, he looked back at Muta wearing an expression of disappointment. "I find nothing," the guard admitted.

"Exactly what did Captain Sabo say to you when he was here earlier?" Muta demanded.

Nelson tried to straighten himself. "The one you call Captain Sabo merely offered me the courtesy of a few magazines," he answered. "Nothing more than mere common courtesy."

Muta pressed forward until his face was no more than a few inches from Nelson's. "I do not believe you," Muta said. The tone of his voice mirrored his anger. "Do you know what I think? I think Captain Sabo came here for the express purpose of informing you that your American lackeys would make another of their ill-advised attempts to rescue you tonight."

Nelson tried to laugh. He managed to get out only one word, "Preposterous," before Muta reached back and slapped him across the mouth with the back of his hand.

The frail Vice President reeled backward and staggered. The blow had raised an instantaneous red welt across his face, and the Vice President's swollen lips betrayed the force of Muta's blow. For Assasio Muta, Nelson's protest had been too quick, too vehement, and not at all convincing. In the major's mind, the rumors were suddenly true. Now it was all beginning to make sense; someone had given the Americans inside information, someone had assisted them, otherwise the coup attempt would have been successful. Ketan Sabo, unlike the rest of Sarawak's men, had not been caught in the hotel fire. Where was he? Suddenly all of Sabo's actions seemed suspicious.

"Handcuff this man," Muta barked. "I will take the prisoner with me. If Captain Sabo has revealed where the prisoner is being detained, our American friends will be both surprised and disappointed when they come to release him."

The rangy Bandung corporal spun Nelson around, shoved him face against the wall, pulled his arms around behind him, and handcuffed him. When he turned back to look at Muta, the major was smiling.

Muta lit a cigarette and took several drags while he studied his prisoner. "Not only will they be disappointed and surprised, they will have blundered into our trap." He looked at the younger and smaller of the two men. "You," he said, "you will position yourself just outside of the door. The Americans will naturally assume that you are standing guard over the prisoner. You will allow them to subdue you. Meanwhile, Corporal, you will assemble your other men, keep them out of sight. Make certain they do not see you. You will wait. When you hear the scuffle outside the door, prepare to intercede. When the door opens, you will open fire."

As Muta finished outlining his plan, he took pleasure in the fact that both of the militiamen were smiling.

From the jump seat of the ATNO, Gideon Stone watched the militiamen in the guard shack laboriously shoulder his way into his rain poncho. They were the gestures of a man who was not at all pleased with the prospect of getting out in the rain to open the wire-mesh gate to the headquarters' main entrance.

Gideon again jabbed the young Bandung officer in the back of his neck with the barrel of his 9mm.

Finally the door to the guard shack opened, the man stepped out, gingerly avoided a puddle, and approached the vehicle. He had pulled his hood up, and was shielding his eyes from the glare of the headlights with his hand.

Gideon continued to exert pressure with the barrel of the 9mm. "This is it, soldier boy," he hissed. "Do what you're supposed to do and you may live long enough to tell your grandkids about it."

The guard stepped up and peered into the ANTO, and the young officer snarled, "Open the gate."

The guard hesitated.

"I am Lieutenant Pan, open the gate."

"But I have orders from—" the man protested.

"Open the gate," Pan demanded. "I do not care who gave you orders."

Gideon again nudged the barrel of the semi-automatic up behind the man's ear, and crouched low as the guard glanced past his officer at the ATNO's driver. Geronimo's face was hidden in the shadows, and Gideon held his breath. Apparently satisfied, the guard stepped back, started to turn, thought better of his actions, turned back again, and gave the lieutenant a salute. Finally he walked out in front of the vehicle to unlock the gate.

As Geronimo ran through the gears pushing the tired ANTO through the gate and under the lights, Gideon used the opportunity to check the time. They had already used more than thirty-one minutes of mission time. They were scheduled to rendezvous with Jessie and the *Indon* in exactly seventy-one minutes and thirteen seconds. They could still make it.

From the outset they had known that the batteries on the DSSRV were the limiting time factor in their mission.

Working backwards, he knew that when Jessie surfaced, she had ten minutes top time. Ten minutes max. If they weren't there by the designated time, her instructions were clear. Abort the muster and leave without them.

Now, for the first time, even though they were making progress, Gideon was beginning to experience the first tinges of doubt. So far everything, the surfacing, the rendezvous with Geronimo, locating Nelson, had all happened—but they had taken longer than Gideon had anticipated. Time, not finding Nelson, was rapidly becoming the critical factor in the equation. Added to all of that was the fact that it was fast approaching the hour when darkness would no longer be their ally. They were counting on darkness, but despite the continuing rain and the heavy smoke, an empty, gray, somber slit of daylight was beginning to materialize on the eastern horizon; proof that even in the monsoon season there was a daylight factor to contend with.

The sky to the east and the eroding time factor were the downside. The upside was the fact that they had located the compound where they were told Nelson was being detained—and they still had the rain. Rain was their other cover.

"Is there a CQ?" Gideon asked.

Pan was slow to answer.

Gideon nudged him with the barrel of the semi-automatic again. "Don't start thinking you're home free, cowboy. You're not off the hook until we have Nelson safe in hand."

"There will be a guard on duty," Pan finally admitted. It had taken all of fifteen seconds for the momentary display of bravado to waver.

"What about the side entrance?"

Pan shook his head. "One guard, no more," he said.

"You heard the man, Sheban. Head for the west end of the complex—and step on it."

It had taken the better part of the first twenty minutes after closing the valves on the dive pod to locate them, but Jessie Preston had finally discovered the harbor frequencies being used by the Bandung on the surface. She clamped the earphones tight to her head, trying to filter through a cacophony of fevered exchanges for anything that might give her some indication of what was happening on the surface.

She felt good about one thing—so far, everything had gone according to plan; the *Indon* was resting on the bottom of the Karimunjawa harbor in forty feet of water with only the most essential of the DSSRV's support systems activated. Makeup air had been cut back to 1.10, and the *Indon* was in what Gideon had termed a ready but stand-down position.

Still, in the last ten minutes, Jessie had become aware that the air quality inside the command pod was beginning to deteriorate. Her breathing, according to the personnel systems monitors, had become slightly more labored, and she found herself beginning to think more about her oxygen intake, pulse, and other vitals. According to the readouts she was still within the AR, but she realized she was already at the stage where she was constantly reminding herself to be alert to the potential of apnea.

Aware that she was functioning just inside acceptable performance parameters, she continually scanned the three critical gauges of the SMS on the A panel, constantly checking and verifying the *Indon*'s position, auditing battery usage, and monitoring the ET indicator on the CC chronometer.

Each time she did she leaned forward, rubbed her eyes,

and redoubled her intent to monitor her instrumentation. Likewise, each time there was a lull in the exchanges, she peeled the earphones away from her head so she could hear the sounds of the Bandung vessels racing back and forth across the harbor. Even at a depth of forty feet, the shallow-water vibrations continually buffeted the *Indon,* and in the eerie green light of the command pod it was easy to imagine the chaos on the surface.

At other times she closed her eyes to see if that would help her concentrate. That was when she remembered to check the gridscope and CLAW integrity. These were followed by two quick calculations to make certain she had not drifted out of position. According to the GS reading, she was still within forty feet of the pier—right where she was supposed to be.

Checking the time kept her alert. It was at fifty-nine minutes and thirty seconds before they were scheduled to rendezvous. If everything went according to their plan and she needed the full ten minutes surface time for the pickup, it would be exactly one hour and twenty-one minutes before she would be threading the *Indon* back through the harbor's minefield into open water. Then there was the matter of the rendezvous with the Stallion—would she have enough power? She decided she would worry about that later.

All of the calculations and reconfiguring, some for the third and fourth time, had been running through Jessie Preston's head when she was interrupted by the intermittent flashing of a red warning light on the B panel. She reached across, switched to the SMC, system monitoring computer, and saw the words "breach" flash on the screen.

She began scanning, indexing the computer through the schematic. Finally the words "breach in dive pod wt seal" scrolled up from the bottom of the screen. She ripped off the headphones, and opened the door to the dive pod. A thin stream of water had begun trickling into the dive chamber. More than two inches of seawater had already seeped in.

Sheban Geronimo brought the ancient ATNO to a halt less than twenty yards from the door at the west end of the complex, and Gideon Stone prodded the Bandung officer out of the vehicle ahead of him. Just as Pan had indicated, there was a single guard. A small man, he was standing back under the shelter of the building's overhang, huddled against the side of the building. From the outset it was obvious that the man recognized his Bandung lieutenant. He started to step forward, and Geronimo caught him with the stock of his HK. The blow, delivered to the man's midsection, sent him sprawling backward into the mud and he failed to get up.

At the door, Gideon motioned Geronimo to one side, positioned Pan directly in front of the door, and started to reach for the knob. If there was an alarm and guards were waiting, it was Pan who would be in the line of fire.

Gideon's voice was reduced to a hissing whisper. Twice within the last several minutes he had felt the throbbing sensation in his shoulder intensify. The painkiller was wearing off. He reached inside his slicker and slipped his hand under his shirt. The blood was starting to seep through the bandage. He saw Geronimo looking at him.

Once more he was aware they could be stepping into a trap. He continued to prod Pan. "Okay, cowboy, it's truth time. If there's an alarm on the door and you know how to deactivate it, now's the time. If your guards in there decide to shoot first and ask questions later, you're the one that gets your belly full first."

Pan glared back at him. The officer's expression failed to mask his rage. Again he waited until he heard the metallic click in Gideon's 9mm. When he did, he reached out and ran the tips of his fingers along the edge of the door frame until he made contact with the alarm trigger.

Gideon took a deep breath. "Don't do anything stupid," he warned.

Flanked by Gideon on one side and Geronimo on the other, the Bandung officer appeared to be vacillating. Finally, as though resigned to his fate, he reached out, pressed the button, and waited for the return buzz. Gideon held his breath until he heard the locking mechanism click.

"Wait," Gideon said. "Let's make damn sure."

"They will suspect nothing. They will think I am the morning officer reporting for duty," Pan volunteered.

"Who is *they* and where the hell are they?" Gideon pressed.

"There is a desk just inside the main entrance," the officer assured him. "They gather there when they have completed their rounds."

By the time Gideon realized Pan's sudden cooperation had nothing to do with the barrel of the semi-automatic pointed at his head, it was too late. For one split second, Gideon had gotten careless. He had dropped his guard. He had assumed too much—and it was about to cost him. The moment they stepped through the door, the Bandung officer dropped to his knees and Gideon saw the reason why. A hidden security camera had been recording their every move. Less than thirty feet away, in the semi-shadows of the long corridor, two Bandung militiamen stood poised with what Gideon immediately recognized as old but deadly Soviet PPsh 41 machine guns. Pan had turned and, despite his broken teeth and swollen mouth, was grinning up at him from the floor. "And now it is my turn." He stood up and motioned for the militiamen to move forward.

Out of the corner of his eye Gideon could see Geronimo hesitate and his finger tighten on the trigger of his 9mm. "We can take our chances, sir. Two of us, three of them; hell, them's the kind of odds I like."

Pan continued smiling as he got to his feet. He stayed close to the wall, making certain he was out of line of fire of the two militiamen. "Such a move would be very foolish," he said. "You see, there are two men behind you as well."

Gideon heard the shuffling footsteps of the men behind him. They had already disarmed Geronimo, and now one of them was reaching for his HK. The other grabbed him, spun him around, spread his legs, and shoved him up against the wall next to Geronimo.

"Now," the Bandung lieutenant said with a grin, "how is it you Americans say it? The shoe is on the other foot."

"Save yourself grief, Pan, all we want is Nelson," Gideon said.

Pan was preening. "Ah, yes—the one you call your Vice President. Another noble but ill-advised attempt to rescue one of your leaders. However, I am afraid that your efforts, as they have been in the past, are once again in vain. Now we not only have the one that you call your Vice President. Now we have you as well."

Gideon heard a snapping sound, and saw Geronimo's knees buckle and the corporal drop to the floor. Then it happened to him. He hit the floor face-first, and Pan's foot slammed down on the back of his neck.

"Shoot them?" one of the militiamen asked.

Pan hesitated. "Shoot them," Pan ordered, then hesitated. "No. Wait. Inform Major Muta that we have captured two of the Americans."

It took several minutes for Pan and his militiamen to herd Gideon Stone and Sheban Geronimo into a small room just outside the headquarters complex dayroom. Both men were bound with their hands behind their back and forced to lie on the floor. Pan pulled up a chair, turned it around, straddled it, sat down, lit a cigarette, exhaled a vaporlike gray-blue cloud of smoke, and studied his hostages for several moments before he spoke.

"I cannot help but be curious," he began. "Like many of my countrymen, I was a student in your country for a short time." He paused to wipe the blood off his mouth with his sleeve. "During that time I witnessed firsthand the excessive decadence in your society and the men who gain and exercise power by oppressing the masses."

"Spare me the rhetoric, Pan," Gideon snarled. His voice was muffled.

Pan laughed, then sobered. "Tell me," he continued, "why would men such as yourselves be willing to go to such lengths and take such great risks to free a man whose contributions are—"

The Bandung officer's tirade was interrupted by a knock at the door by one of the militiamen. He was a slight man who wore the worried expression of someone who wasn't at all certain that under the circumstances he was allowed to intrude. He addressed Pan by his rank and delivered his message in Maylay. Pan stepped out into the hall and picked up the telephone. The conversation lasted for no more than two or three minutes, and the only words Gideon was able to decipher were "Muta" and "Nelson."

When he returned to the room, Pan's demeanor included both a swagger and a peptic laugh. He sat down again and looked at his hostages. "Apparently you have gone to a great deal of trouble for nothing," he said. "Major Muta, like myself, is also aware of your senseless plot. The fires you set in our fuel depot were created to distract us, were they not?"

Gideon knew what Pan wanted. The lieutenant was looking for an opportunity to posture. He had spoken directly to the powerful Major Muta—and Muta, his men knew, was second in command only to the general himself. This was an occasion for Pan to demonstrate his importance. He had the audience; now all he needed was the reason. Gideon was determined not to give it to him. Instead of answering Pan's question, he bit his lip. At the moment, Pan was holding all the cards, and Gideon realized there was little to be gained by adding fuel to the fire.

Instead, he waited, playing to the man's weakness. It was all too apparent that Pan was pontificating for the benefit of his men. He had what he needed: the sound of his own voice and someone to listen—two Americans and a handful of Bandung militiamen as well. He dropped his cigarette on the floor and snuffed it out with the heel of his boot.

"There is great irony in all of this," Pan exclaimed. "It seems you and your colleague here have risked your lives to rescue the man you call your Vice President"—Pan paused for effect—"and he isn't even here. Major Muta informs me that he escorted your Vice President from these premises quite some time ago."

"Where is he?" Gideon demanded.

"His whereabouts is of little consequence to you," Pan replied. "Your concern now should be for your own safety. Major Muta informs me that your untimely arrival here on Karimunjawa is unfortunate for you—but quite fortunate for us. You and your colleague here will replace the members of the UN security delegation that escaped from the hotel in Jakarta.

"General Sarawak will again inform the world that one life will be sacrificed every six hours until Sarni Kujon steps down and turns over the reins of the Javanese government to the PRJ."

Pan walked slowly around the two prone hostages, glaring hard at both of them. There was venom in his voice when he fixed his stare on Gideon. "It should not surprise you that I will be most happy to recommend to the general that you be the first."

Chapter Thirteen

Day 7: Time 1811LT
Key Largo

Hooker Herman leaned his considerable bulk against the bar, ignored the crowd, and pretended to be listening intently to what the woman was saying. It went with the territory; women talking to bartenders was nothing new for Hooker. Over the years, more women than he could count had sat at his bar and bent his ear.

Hooker Herman complained about the amount of time it took, but he enjoyed his reputation as a good listener. On more than one occasion he had been overheard telling his male patrons that his popularity with the women was due to the fact he always had time for the ladies, always gave them the famous Hooker smile, and never, never repeated what they told him.

If the truth were known, however, Hooker seldom really listened to more than half of what they told him. Why? Because he figured half was what most of the confidences were worth. By the next morning the lady in question would have forgotten both what she had said and who she had told.

This one was different, though. This one had captured his attention. She was pretty, and more than pretty, she was charming. She was the kind of woman that make other women envious—and just a bit nervous.

What was it she said her name was? Carrie? Cristy? At any rate, this one was attractive enough that he found himself paying more attention than usual.

"We had a dinner engagement," the woman said, "but I couldn't make it. And he said he didn't have a telephone so there was no way to let him know." She glanced around the crowded bar and sighed. "I don't know why, but I never thought about calling him here."

"What did you say your name was?" Hooker ask.

"Carrie," the woman repeated, "Carrie Jordon."

Hooker rolled the name over in his mind, rubbed his chin, and suddenly the light went on. "Sure," he said, "now I remember, couldn't have been more than a week ago." He pushed himself away from the bar and stood back with his anvil-sized arms folded across his chest. "Wish I could tell you more, but the bottom line is, he just ain't here. He's been gone about a week now."

"Do you know where he went? When he'll be back? How I can get in touch with him?"

Hooker's big, expressive face softened. "Let me tell you something, lady. With Gideon Stone you never know.

Sometimes he's here. Sometimes he ain't. All I can tell you is sooner or later he'll come waltzing in, pull a stool up to the bar, order a margarita or scotch and water, and act like nothing has happened. If he feels like telling me where he's been and what he's been doing, he'll do it. If he doesn't, he won't."

Carrie Jordon nodded as though she understood. She hesitated for several moments, reached for her purse, opened it, rummaged through the contents, and finally emerged with a business card. She studied it and handed it to Hooker. "If and when you see him, give him that, will you?"

Hooker looked at the card. Carrie Jordon, more precisely, Dr. C. K. Jordon, was a psychiatrist from Miami. She had one of those business cards that listed everything but her measurements; office number, fax number, e-mail number, car phone, and if that wasn't enough, she had scribbled two more numbers on the back of the card.

"Tell him to keep trying until he reaches me. If he can't locate me through one of those numbers, I'm probably dead." She managed to work up an obviously disappointed smile.

"That would be a shame." Hooker sighed. He would have said more, maybe even asked her a question or two, but she was laying a twenty-dollar bill on the bar and closing her purse. He watched her stand up, shrug, and work her way through the crowd toward the door. It occurred to him that Gideon Stone, in Hooker's words, knew how to pick 'em.

Day 7: Time 1815LT
Washington

The Friday night ritual in the Ruppert house for more years than Jake could remember was to have his wife

Alice invite friends in for an intimate but casual dinner. Alice loved to cook. It was one of her passions—and it was an arrangement that worked well for her husband. Jake, however, in typical Jake Ruppert fashion, had tied one stipulation to his wife's end of the ritual; their dinner guests for the evening could have nothing to do with the Agency.

Now, less than ten minutes before Bob and Sue Thomas, both old school friends from Jake and Alice's days at Colgate, were due to arrive, the preparations were finally complete and Jake had time to drift into the Ruppert family room to catch the news. Instead he stood at the window for several minutes and monitored the progress of a line of thunderstorms that had been raking their Sherman Heights community for the better part of the past two hours. When he tired of that, he decided to turn on the television and try to coax their ten-year-old dachshund, Mary Catherine, out of his favorite chair. By the time he had accomplished the latter and the images on their aging Sony finally began to materialize, he found himself watching and listening to two commentators, both of whom he had been introduced to at a Washington Press Club luncheon earlier that week. It came as no surprise that they were talking about the man all Washington had been cussing and discussing for the past week, Bojoni Sarawak.

"I'm afraid you're right, Mel," one of the men was saying. "This latest threat by Sarawak comes on the heels of one earlier today when he indicated he would retaliate against the regime of Sarni Kujon by launching a missile attack at Kujon's installations in both Surabaya and Yogyakata."

That was all Jake Ruppert heard before he snatched up the telephone and dialed his office. "What the hell is this

I'm hearing about Sarawak making another threat?" he shouted.

"That you, Jake?" the voice asked. Ruppert recognized the voice of Sam Turley working the hot line in the office on the Agency's CRU night crew. "Glad you checked in, we've been trying to get through to you for the past thirty minutes. The phone company says the storms are playing havoc with the telephones. Apparently, though, that's everyone but Huntine. He's called in twice in the last thirty minutes. He's screeching like a cat in heat. . . ."

"Forget Huntine, what's this they're saying about Sarawak?"

"Radio Republik Indonesia carried another tape released by Sarawak within the past hour. CNN and the networks picked it up. He's claiming the Americans launched a sneak attack against his base in Karimunjawa, set fire to his fuel depot, burned down his warehouses, and killed a number of his militiamen. He's also claiming he has captured some of the American forces that—"

"Did he say how many?" Ruppert cut in.

Turley scanned the text of the transmission. "Negative, unspecified—but here's the kicker. He's claiming this whole thing is in the hands of the Americans now. He wants the President to put the heat on Kujon to step down now. Not only that, he claims, until he gets some kind of affirmative response from us, he's going to start executing the Americans he's captured in the raid. Needless to say, the President is pissed. Sarawak isn't giving him much time. Sarawak is saying if he doesn't get some indication Kujon is stepping down, he'll start the executions at sunset Karimunjawa time."

Ruppert looked at his watch. "Shit. That's less than ten hours from now." The voice on the other end of the line waited; he knew the acting Agency director wasn't finished. "What the hell makes that son of a bitch think we can get Kujon to start jumping through hoops now? Hell, it's the same Kujon who didn't take action against Sarawak even when he had the whole world warning him of the PKI threat."

Turley waited. Finally he said, "Any orders, sir?"

"Have you heard anything from Wormack?"

"Can't get through to him either," Turley admitted.

"Keep trying. If Huntine calls again, tell him I'm on my way down to Langley. He can get me on the car phone."

Sam Turley heard the phone click in his ear, and turned to answer the other telephone on his desk. Shuler Huntine was past the point of exchanging greetings. "Have you located Ruppert yet?"

"Give him ten minutes, then try his car phone," Turley said. "He said to tell you he's on his way in."

Day 7: Time 0831LT
Karimunjawa Harbor

When Jeris Alan was able to see through the clouds of swirling smoke, the scene was backdropped by a slate-colored sky that continued to belch torrents of water on the smoldering remains of the Karamunjawa warehouses. The bank of fires from the fuel storage area continued to rage, and there was still no indication that Sarawak's men were making headway bringing the flames under control.

From where he waited, using the pilings of the central pier for cover, he could see most of the activity in the harbor. The Bandung resources were focused on their miseries to the west, and there had been virtually no activity in the dock area where the gunships were moored. He had depleted his supply of Nl-7s's, using a variety of fuses: timers, sound sensitive, heat, and finally, frequency fuses that could be remotely detonated from the *Indon*. He had used all four kinds for the simple reason that there was always the chance a target scanner might intercept the electronic signal and give away the device's location. With the uncertainty resulting from the fires, a preset device guaranteed them nothing in the way of a systems malfunction if it had already been spent while the gunboats remained moored at the pier.

He continued to tread water as he waited, periodically checking his watch and continually scanning the crimson-tinted mercury-colored surface forty yards from the pier. He was already two minutes into the ten-minute window for the scheduled rendezvous, and there was no sign of either Gideon or Geronimo.

He pulled his mask down, cleared it, pulled it up over his face, turned on his penlight, checked his mouthpiece and the gauge on his compressed-air cylinder, before scanning the area around the wharf one last time and allowing his weight to pull him below the surface. Jeris Alan knew from years of experience that the muster on one of these missions was always the hard part. He had always considered getting everyone back and in one piece as the real test of a mission's success. In this one there was the added hazard of having to buddy the Vice President down to the *Indon*. If the man was familiar with dive procedures, it wouldn't be all that difficult. If he wasn't, just getting him aboard the DSSRV could be a struggle. He knew what he was doing—so did Geronimo. It was Stone he was concerned about. He had seen the definite evidence of rust in the way the former colonel responded.

He tried to put the thought out of his mind and focused instead on the plan. Jessie should be waiting forty yards out and forty feet down in the murky early light-of-day depths of a harbor that had been dredged out of rock and coral. Still, with each steady and even stroke that pulled him through the water, he was getting more apprehensive. The fact that Gideon and Geronimo hadn't made it back to the rendezvous point with the hostage was beginning to play with his mind. What if they didn't make it back? What then?

He stopped, checked his compass and depth gauge, groped down in the darkness, felt the bottom, and propelled himself ahead again. Under the circumstances, with all of the confusion on the surface, he wondered how likely it was that the *Indon* would have been detected. The chances seemed slim—but he couldn't gamble on *slim*. Still, there were a lot of things working in their favor. By now the Bandung had to be confused, running around in circles, wondering what the hell had happened. Who would have thought that the Americans would have the audacity to slip through a mine-seeded harbor and trigger the fires in the fuel depot?

He paused again, checked his position, turned on his helmet AR, and listened. Nothing. If there was activity on the surface, his AR wasn't picking that up either. So far, so good. He made one more check of the time; now there was just over four minutes left in the window. He swallowed and began swimming toward the rendezvous coordinates again. If Jessie Preston was where she was supposed to be and in a stand-down posture, he knew she couldn't be more than a few feet ahead of him.

Then he saw it. He had almost bumped into it; black on black, a shadowy image, a welcome, vague, surreal incarnation out of all concert with his surroundings. He reached out, touched it, then circled the hull of the DSSRV twice before he gave the signal: two raps on the hull near the personnel pod. When the acknowledgment came, he had already maneuvered his way under the dive locker compartment and was waiting for the hatch to open. It opened, and he wasted no time propelling himself up and in.

Moments later, while the battery-driven pumps labored to purge the water from the dive chamber, Jeris Alan began stripping out of his dive gear. He was waiting for the sound of the seals to disengage and release him from the compartment. When it did, he shouldered out of his air tanks and crawled through. He was already anticipating Jessie Preston's first reaction. It came right on cue.

"Where's Stone and Geronimo?"

Jeris Alan shook his head. Any hope that Gideon, Sheban, and the hostage might have made to the *Indon* even before the appointed rendezvous time had been dashed. "No sign of them," he admitted. "Looks like we'll have to extend the window."

Her answer came back at him like a shot. "Can't, we've got a problem." The usual composure in the woman's voice had eroded.

"What the hell do you mean can't?" Alan snapped. "We damn sure can't bail out of here without 'em."

Jessie gestured toward the power-reserve gauge on the A panel. Jeris Alan could see the red indicator light blinking.

"Looks like we'll switch over to the aux pack earlier than we anticipated," he speculated. "Both Gideon and I calculated we'd still have a twenty-percent reserve even when we get to the pickup point. We'll have to use some of that reserve now."

Jessie was shaking her head. "We're already on reserve. I had to switch over more than an hour ago. Our two-zero reserve is already spent."

"Spent? What do you mean, spent?"

"We've got a breach in hull integrity," Jessie said carefully. "According to the OB computers, we've somehow managed to put a hole in the hull in the vicinity of the starboard diving plane. The pumps are working overtime. Both electric drive motors, the primary and the standby, have shorted out and we continue to take on water in the dive chamber. I shut down everything I could, but I had to switch over to the aux pack almost seventy minutes before we planned to go to the backup system."

"You're certain?" Alan asked.

She nodded. "I've calculated the reserve seven ways from Sunday. By the time we purge the ballast tanks and pilot this thing back through the minefield, we'll be lucky to get out into open water."

Jeris Alan studied the A panel console, and felt the old familiar mission-ending sensation beginning to gnaw at his stomach. "Have you double-checked? Are we operating any onboard system that isn't absolutely essential?"

"Only if you consider breathing non-essential," Jessie quipped. "I've powered down everything I can think of. We still need the gyro, the props, the compensators, we need the tanks and we need the computers."

"Can you steer this thing back through the minefield without the starboard props?" Alan pressed.

Jessie hesitated before she answered. "I can try," she said. "I can lock us into the onboard Avoidance-Guidance System, but I don't know how this thing will respond with only the port props. The real question is, can the computers handle it?"

"Suppose we shut down the power to the AGS and manually try to slip her through?"

"How do we avoid the mines?"

Alan was going out on a limb and he knew it. "Suppose we had a set of eyes on the bow." He said it like a man who wasn't at all certain he even wanted to suggest it.

"Too dark," Jessie replied, "and your range from the forward obs ports is too restricted. The biggest port has only a five-inch opening. By the time you spotted the mine, *if* you spotted the mine, in these waters I wouldn't have enough time to correct our course."

"Would it work if I rode the bow and talked you through?"

Jessie's expression went blank. She was trying to picture what the Apache pilot was suggesting. "Are you saying you'd ride out there, straddling the cone, and try to guide us through?"

In Jeris Alan's mind it was a long shot—but it was also a scheme that just might work. "As I recall, this tub is equipped with a series of outside-vehicle communications ports, isn't it?"

Jessie nodded. "Four of them: fore, aft, starboard, and port."

"Theoretically at least . . . " Alan was being cautious. "If I plugged into the OVC and talked you through, we could make it. All we'd have to do is cut back on prop speed, keep it under two knots, and go black on everything inside the personnel pod. If we did all that and we had any luck at all, we just might have enough battery life to make it."

"Sounds risky." Jessie was shaking her head.

Jeris Alan wasn't smiling. "Hey, I don't like this little scheme any better than you do. But unless you've got a better idea . . . "

"It would be like riding a blind bull through a herd of very receptive heifers. Those mines are magnetized; get too close to them and they'll come cozying up to you like—"

Alan checked his watch. "Window's up. We're out of time. I say we carve out another fifteen minutes and give Gideon a chance. If he doesn't show by then, I crawl back into the air tanks and play cowboy."

Jessie Preston wasn't listening. She was already going over the checklist to see if there was anything else on the *Indon* that could be shut down.

Day 7: Time 0849LT
Karimunjawa

Gideon Stone was slowly becoming aware of two factors; the throbbing in his head and the darkness. He knew where the throbbing came from, a blow to the back of his skull by one of Sarawak's militiamen. The blackness, however, was a different kind of blackness. This was the totally opaque kind of blackness a man experiences when he is locked in a room with no windows and no light. This blackness was a nothingness—a void within a bigger void.

He lay there for several moments before he tried an experiment—the slightest movement of his head. When he did, his stomach went into instant rebellion. His brain was doing a crazy, disoriented kind of motionless dance—and the pain raced down—or was it up—the length of his spine, grating each nerve as it went. He tried again, this time shutting his unseeing eyes—this time counting—and even though the numbers were still inside his head, he immediately realized they had dissipated into a kind of surreal tangle of curious shapes and images. There was a throbbing sensation in his shoulder, and he imagined he could feel it bleeding again.

His world was gauze—a black gauze. He waited—then tried again—and was rewarded with the same litany of pain and confusion he had experienced earlier.

Then he heard it—a voice—distant, monosyllabic, laced with static. He knew better than to move his head yet another time; as jumbled and chaotic as his thoughts were, he understood now that any sort of movement was equated with pain.

"Colonel?" The one whispered word snaked through the absence of light and crawled like a thief into his hammering consciousness. He ignored it—but then he heard it again. "Colonel?" It was a hissing undertone—a barely audible buzz amidst the cacophony of confusing sounds ringing in his head. The voice repeated it, and this time when he heard it he knew it wasn't his imagination.

He managed to sneak out the word "Geronimo?" in reply.

"Here, Colonel," the voice came back at him. "Don't ask me where. The only thing I know is we're both in the same damn place."

Gideon was finally able to summon up the courage to open his eyes again. This time there were no rockets, no pyrotechnics, no lingering tortures—only a sharp pain at the base of his skull and a dull, thudding ache that encompassed his entire head. "Where—where are we?" he finally managed. "What—what the hell—happened?"

"They worked you over pretty good," Geronimo whispered, "some guy named Muta. He said it was Sarawak's orders. He wanted to know how many of us there were."

Gideon moved again, and this time the pain made it only halfway up his spine before his brain exploded. He squeezed his eyes shut and held his breath. He tried moving his fingers and then his hands—both seemed to work. Finally he found the courage to start inching his way toward the sound of Geronimo's voice.

"How—how long have—have we been here?"

"You've been out a while," Geronimo explained. "How long I don't know. I've lost track of time. Muta has had one of his goons check on us twice. I get the feeling they plan to haul you back in there for round two when you regain consciousness."

Gideon tried to order his thoughts. He had managed a quick look at his watch just before Pan had marched them into the building where Sarawak was supposedly waiting. Their mission time was down to thirteen minutes at that point. If Geronimo was anywhere near right in his estimate of time, the *Indon* was long gone by now. The question was, how far gone and had they made it out of the harbor?

He was close enough now that he could hear Geronimo's breathing. "How about you, are you okay?" Gideon asked.

"They must have figured you were in charge," Geronimo said, keeping his voice low. "They didn't pay any attention to me. One of Muta's men opened the door, cracked me across the back of the head, and shoved. I was in here a long time before they dumped you in."

"Could you make out anything they were saying?"

"Not much. Most of what they had to say was in Maylay. But I did get one thing out of it. This guy Muta thinks we must have had some help getting past their guards. He keeps repeating the name of some guy—I think his name is Sabo. From what I could make out, he's got a detail out looking for the guy."

Gideon Stone closed his eyes again, and as he did he heard the door open. When he opened them again, a heavyset man with a 9mm mini-Uzi dangling from his left hand was towering over him. The light from the corridor behind him was silhouetting him. "Ah," the man sneered, "the pig is awake, Major." The sneer was half laugh. "Now Major Muta can continue his interrogation." He punctuated his assessment with a kick. The blow caught Gideon in the ribs, the air went out of him, and his stomach began digging a hole again. Unlike him, it was looking for another hiding place.

Gideon was still sucking in, trying to force air back into his lungs, when the militiaman grabbed him by the front of his shirt and jerked him to his feet. In the same motion he shoved him into the corridor outside the room and pinned him against the wall.

"Bring him here," a voice hissed in English.

The guard pulled him away from the wall, prodding him ahead into a small room where a single incandescent bulb was hanging from the ceiling. There were four other people in the room, all men. A tall, black-haired man with a dark, square-jawed face that looked as though it had been chiseled out of stone stepped forward and motioned for Gideon to take a seat. "Name, please?" the man said. His English was impeccable.

Gideon hesitated. He recognized the man as Sarawak himself.

"You would be wise to answer my questions, American. Perhaps you should take notice of the fact that Major Muta standing over there is most eager to continue with your interrogation."

Gideon blinked in the stark light and looked across the room at a squat, bull-shouldered man with epaulets on his shoulders. The man's face was pockmarked and he wore his black hair combed straight back into an abbreviated ponytail. Most of his facial features were encased and partially hidden in the folds of his heavy jowls.

"Perhaps I should explain that Major Muta is my most skilled and effective interrogator."

Gideon was anticipating the worst. He waited.

"Once again. Who are you and who sent you?" Sarawak demanded. As he asked his question, he reached behind him and produced a small voice recorder. "Speak plainly, American."

"You know who I am and why I'm here," Gideon said.

"Why are you here?" Sarawak repeated.

"You know damn well why I'm here. I'm here because you are holding the Vice President of the United States hostage."

Sarawak smiled, nodded, and stepped back to make way for Muta. The Bandung major confronted Gideon for several seconds, then brought his hand around like a man chopping wood. It caught Gideon on the side of the head just below the ear and sent him sprawling backwards off the chair. He landed hard on his back with the salty, hot acid taste of blood instantly flooding his mouth. The pain came rocketing back.

Sarawak stepped forward, reached down, erased the tape in the recorder, and depressed the rewind button. "Get on your feet, American," Sarawak said.

Gideon worked his way to his knees, grabbed the back of the chair, and held on.

"Now, considering Major Muta's considerable abilities in this area, perhaps you would like to reconsider. You will find a certain amount of wisdom in answering my question."

Gideon Stone slumped to the floor again.

"I want a full confession from this man," he heard

Sarawak say. "Record every word. I will use the tape of his confession in my next radio broadcast. I want the world to hear his admission of American duplicity, and I want the world to be aware of their unwanted intervention in the affairs of a small nation struggling to throw off the yoke of an oppressive and decadent government."

Muta was smiling.

Gideon's eyes drifted shut and he spiraled back down again, escaping for the moment into a disconnected world where there was less pain and no reality. The words he heard were muted, but even in his half-aware universe he heard Sarawak droning out orders. "Throw him back in the room with the other one. When he regains consciousness, Major Muta, you will try again. . . . "

Gideon was able to record the shuffling of feet, the sound of muted voices, and the chill dampness associated with someone opening and closing a door. He thought he heard wind, and then the sound ceased.

The world of Gideon Stone had again gone silent.

Day 7: Time 0913LT
Karimunjawa

Ketan Sabo's face was swollen and bleeding when he was led into the room. Two Bandung militiamen reported they had found him wandering aimlessly near the Karimunjawa docks, and acting under Muta's orders, had driven him to the place where the major had been conducting his interrogation of the two captured Americans.

Muta, sitting behind a desk, looked up when Sabo entered. "Ah, Captain Sabo," Muta said, "I have been waiting for you. You will sit there." The Bandung major pointed to a chair directly in front of the desk.

Sabo was still confused. He sat down and before Muta

could continue, carefully began tracing the tips of his fingers over the meshwork of cuts and abrasions on his face. Muta's first question surprised him.

"Where were you when the fuel barge exploded, Captain?"

Sabo had to think for a moment. "I—I was in the harbor officer's post, Major, across the harbor from the fuel depot. Why do you ask?"

Muta scowled. "How convenient, Captain; you were across the harbor and you were out of danger, but you were in an excellent position to see everything that was happening."

"Convenient?" Sabo repeated. "I do not understand what you mean."

"On the contrary, Captain, I think you do. I think you understand exactly what I am getting at."

Sabo shifted in his chair and looked around the room. The room was filled with unsmiling faces. He recognized the sober-faced young lieutenant, the one called Pan, but he knew little about the other militiamen, other than the fact that two of them were usually in Muta's entourage.

"I was the night duty officer," Sabo volunteered, "I was making my rounds. . . . "

Muta stood up, folded his large hands behind his back, and began slowly pacing back and forth behind his desk. "Are you saying that you wish me to believe that you knew nothing of the American attempt to rescue the hostage tonight?"

Despite Sabo's swollen face, he wore the bewildered expression of one who had no idea of what was being implied. "Americans?" he repeated. "I know nothing of— are you saying that the explosions are the result of Americans?"

Muta stopped pacing and leaned forward now with his

hands on his desk. "Tell me, Captain Sabo, are you denying that you visited the American Vice President earlier this evening?"

"It was not, as you state it, a *visit,* Major Muta." He somehow managed to convey indignation in his voice. "I went to the compound to check on the prisoner early in my rounds."

Muta continued to glower. "Let me put it another way, Captain. The hostage's guards report that you went in to see the American by yourself. They also say that you were not accompanied by the guard outside his door. They report that you spoke to the hostage alone."

"That is true," Sabo acknowledged.

"I submit that the reason it was necessary for you to speak to him without the guard present was because you were warning him that the Americans would be making an attempt to rescue him at some point during the course of the night."

Sabo was stunned. He denied the charge. "It is true that I spoke to him alone, but the door was open. The guard could hear everything that was said."

Muta looked at one of the two militiamen that had been standing guard over Nelson earlier. "Is that true?" he asked. "Could you overhear the conversation between Captain Sabo and the hostage?"

The guard shook his head. "No, Major," he said.

Ketan Sabo could not believe what he was hearing. He tried to think back to his brief conversation with the American Vice President and what he had said that could be construed as passing along information about an impending attempt to rescue the man. Finally he said, "I offered to get him some reading material, that is all."

"And did you?" Muta pushed.

Sabo nodded.

"And what was in that so-called *reading material*?"

"It was merely some magazines," Sabo protested, "nothing more."

Muta straightened up and began prowling the room again. "If, as you say, it was nothing more than a few magazines, Captain, why did you not instruct one of the guards to obtain the material for you?"

"The reading material had to be printed in English. I thought I was better qualified to determine what the hostage would find interesting."

"You speak English, Captain?"

"Very little," Sabo admitted.

Muta's laugh was derisive. "A little," he repeated. "Again, very convenient. Do you know what I think, Captain Sabo? I think you went to find reading material because you needed time to devise some way of informing the hostage of the American attempt to rescue him. You passed along that information by enclosing it in the reading material."

"These charges are preposterous," Sabo protested. "I am loyal to the PKI and the Bandung movement."

"Are you? Then explain how it is that you were unable to locate the Americans that invaded the hotel in the first hostage rescue attempt?"

"I followed them into the old embassy," Sabo countered, "but in the smoke and confusion they managed to escape."

"I am told a different story, Captain. One of the militiamen reported that you followed the Americans into the street where you spotted a vehicle that was not authorized to be there. I am also told that when you saw that the driver was still in the vehicle, you instructed your man not to shoot that driver. You did this, of course, because you were part of the conspiracy. Is that not correct?"

Sabo shook his head. His voice was finding strength. "I instructed the man not to shoot because it would have been a senseless act—the driver was already dead."

Muta paused long enough to stop and stare out the window at the still-burning fuel-storage tanks on the hill. He had been witness to such sabotage before; it would be days before the fires could be brought under control. It would take years to rebuild their island fortress. Finally he turned around again to confront Sabo. "I have always wondered, what makes a man betray his country, Captain? Is it money? How much are the Americans paying you?"

Despite his condition, Sabo managed to measure his words. "If there is a conspiracy, Major, you are the one who has engineered it. I am guilty of none of these accusations. I am loyal to General Sarawak, and I do not understand your attempt to discredit me."

This time Muta moved around the desk and stood in front of him. His face was no more than a few inches from Sabo. "You are a liar, Captain, and your deceit and treason have been discovered. I shall inform General Sarawak that you are a traitor."

Sabo sagged back in his chair. He was bewildered by Muta's charges. He had sacrificed everything to become a member of the Bandung movement—and now he was accused of the heinous crime of sedition. He stared back at his accuser with tears in his eyes—but he could think of nothing else to say. He scanned the weary faces of the other men in the room, and he could tell by the way they looked at him that they were in concert with Muta.

Pan stepped forward. "What would you have me to do with this man?" he asked.

"What do you do with a dog that bites his master?"

Muta said. "The answer is quite obvious, Lieutenant, you take him out and shoot him."

Only then did Sabo realize that Sarawak had entered the room. He looked briefly at Sabo and turned his attention toward Muta. "You are most efficient, Major, and I agree with your assessment. Under most circumstances, that is what the unconscionable dog deserves. However, I have a much better idea. Captain Sabo has chosen to betray us and that makes him a traitor. The execution of a traitor should not be done in haste, especially when that execution can become an example for others whose loyalty may waver when circumstances become difficult. Therefore it would be prudent to see that as many men as possible have the opportunity to see what happens when they are tempted to be disloyal to our cause."

For a moment, Muta looked disappointed. Then he straightened again and squared his shoulders. "As the general wishes."

Sarawak smiled. "Very well, gentlemen, that settles that issue. In the meantime we have work to do." He turned his attention to Pan. "And now, Lieutenant, have your men put Captain Sabo in with our other guests. The Americans have a quaint saying. Birds of a feather flock together. Perhaps Captain Sabo's American consorts will wish to commiserate with him over another bungled attempt to deter us from our objective."

Pan, accompanied by one of the militiamen, jerked Sabo to his feet and shoved him ahead of him down the narrow corridor to the room where Gideon and Geronimo were being detained. While one guard unlocked the door and the other covered Sabo with a scarred 9mm Mk2 pistol, Pan shoved his former squadron officer stumbling into the darkened room with the two Americans.

"I trust you will find your accommodations most disagreeable, Captain Sabo," Pan said, "and I cannot help but add that I feel certain that before all of this is over you will plead with General Sarawak to allow Major Muta to finish his task."

Chapter Fourteen

Day 7: Time 1003LT
The Java Sea

Jessie Preston was convinced the *Indon* had given them everything it had. Now it corked on the surface of the storm-tortured waters of Tian Bay, with both the primary and aux batteries spent. The breach in its hull had been aggravated to the extent that the *Indon*'s dive deployment chamber and most of the systems in the aft section had been completely flooded out. Up until the very moment that the magnesium-hulled craft had broken through to the surface, the issue had been in doubt.

When it did, it was Jessie Preston's victory. She had tweaked and manipulated the DSSRV's computers, continually calculated and recalculated both their progress and position, and finally, when the batteries were spent, resorted to crossed fingers and hard prayer. In the end, Lady Luck had been with them; there was just enough juice left in the batteries for one final purge of the ballast tanks and they had surfaced, in her words, "reasonably close to the designated rendezvous coordinates." Now the only question left was whether "reasonably close to the designated rendezvous coordinates" was going to be close enough to get the job done.

For the first two hours after threading their way through the minefield in Karimunjawa harbor, it had been the Jessie Preston show; now it was Jeris Alan's turn. He scampered up the access ladder, opened the air lock entrance hatch, and pulled himself through, dragging the rubberized temporary flotation collar with him. He opened the scuttle lid, dropped over the side of the *Indon* into the churning water, pulled the R-Chain on the collar to begin the inflation, and began attaching it at several points along the hull; first to the towing fairlead, then the stabilizing keel, and finally to the air tanks over the stern. He managed to finish his chore just as Jessie crawled through the scuttle lid and grabbed the rim of the ballast ports to steady herself.

The gods were smiling on them; the rain had momentarily slackened, but the waves continued to twist and oscillate the cigar-shaped craft. Jessie reached out, grabbed the rim of the ballast tube, and held on. "By God, give the old girl credit," she shouted. "At least she got us this far."

"Close the air lock on the hatch," Alan screamed, straining to be heard above the sound of the waves.

Jessie cranked the valve until it would go no further. "Got it," she hollered back. The words were carried away by the wind.

"Collar secured," she heard Alan shout. She reached

out and grabbed his hand to steady him as he pulled himself out of the water and up unto the hull.

He moved close to her. "I sure as hell wouldn't take any bets on how long that damn flotation collar will keep this tub afloat." The words, most of which were carried by the howling wind, made it through to her in unintelligible bits and pieces.

Jessie Preston hooded her eyes from the rain. "It probably wasn't designed to keep this thing afloat when it's half full of water. That's why I brought these. . . . " She held up two life jackets. "Put it on. If she goes down, we don't want to go with her."

With one hand holding onto the mooring cleats, Jeris Alan unbuckled his safety harness, attached the snap to one of the D rings on the conning tower, slipped into the vest, and reattached the safety line. Jessie did the same, and looked up into the rain. "How long do you figure we can keep her afloat?"

"Ten—twenty minutes tops," Alan shouted. "If we don't hear that damn chopper in the next five minutes, we've got problems—big problems."

Jessie shielded her eyes again and looked up into the rain, searching for the chopper. "We won't hear it until it's almost on top of us."

Alan wiped the rain off his face and braced himself as a wave slammed him hard against the wall of the tower. "One consolation, they know what they're doing," he said. "I've been plucked out of situations worse than this."

"Tell me about it," she said with a grin. "Where and when? Right now I could use a little reassurance." The rest of what Jessie was attempting to say was washed away by another giant wave colliding with the *Indon*'s hull.

Alan leaned back into his safety harness and closed his eyes against the assault of the salt water. He was exhausted, and in the few minutes he had been topside he had started to chill. Within a matter of seconds that chill deteriorated into uncontrollable trembling—and for the first time for as long as Jeris Alan could remember, the element of fear was rapidly becoming part of his survival equation.

He opened his eyes against the salty spray and looked at the woman. Her eyes were closed, but her lips were moving as though she was mouthing the words to some mantra. Even as close as she was to him, they were words without sound. He decided she was praying. In return, the only words of encouragement he could think to offer her was a cryptic "Hold on, Jessie, we'll make it," and even then he couldn't be certain she had heard him.

He remembered reading an account of how the men survived the sinking of the *Indianapolis* after it had delivered the atomic bomb toward the end of World War II. After surviving the better part of three days in the shark-infested waters, the men said that the most terrifying time of the ordeal after they had been located was waiting for the rescue planes to pluck them out of the water. Jeris Alan understood that fear now.

He opened his eyes again to check on Jessie. She had locked her hands around the cleat in front of the conning tower. But she no longer appeared to be praying. "Hold on, Jessie," he repeated. "These guys know what they're doing. They'll be here any minute now."

Jessie opened her eyes and looked at him. Her face had drained of color, and she was trembling. Then, while he watched, her death grip on the cleat loosened and in what seemed like a slow-motion study in terror, she slipped silently over the side of the *Indon*'s hull into the water.

For the next few seconds, maybe minutes, of his life, Jeris Alan reacted out of instinct. He unsnapped his safety harness, peeled out of his life jacket, and dove into the water after the woman. The first few strokes consisted of little more than frantic flailing at the water. Finally he sucked in his breath, spun 360 degrees in the water, and went under. The salt water burned his eyes, but he somehow managed to keep them open. In microseconds his world went from the slate gray of the storm-tortured surface to a frothy, colorless under-universe where the sound of the storm was intensified. Twice he used the hull of the floundering *Indon* as a touchstone and came up for air.

Each time he renewed his search, he encountered a blinding kind of yellow-green opaqueness obscuring the hostile world where he couldn't breathe. His chest began to hammer. Each effort was the same. He clawed his way down through the water until there was nowhere else to go and started for the surface again. The only difference between the third and fourth efforts was that as he attempted to surface, he slammed into the hull of the DSSRV and became momentarily disoriented.

Otherwise each of the efforts was the same. He broke through to the surface, gulped twice, filled his lungs, and went down again.

After the fourth dive he was aware that time, not the obstructing confusion of a churning sea and its camouflaging, obscuring hostility, had become his enemy. Jessie Preston had been down too long. She had slipped into the worst of all possible worlds—a world where he couldn't see, and even worse, he couldn't breathe. He went down again, this time deeper than before. This time he felt something. His vision was blurry—but he continued to strain—and finally he could see what it was. It was Jessie. She was face-up, still connected by the safety harness, back arched, eyes open, and other than the undulating, eerie dance of a body caught in the agitation of the water, she was motionless.

Lungs ready to burst, Jeris Alan reached out, grabbed her by the hair, and began propelling himself upward. When he broke through to the surface, he was less than twenty feet from the *Indon* and he could hear the thumping sound of the helicopter's rotor.

Day 7: Time 2333LT
Washington

Shuler Huntine kept one phone nestled in the crook of his neck and shoulder, reached down and flipped the switch on his speaker phone—a device he hated and had been known to call the "son-of-a-bitch box," and waited. On one line he had Jake Ruppert. On the other would eventually be Fong Lu Chek.

It was his second attempt to get through to the Chinese official in the last ten minutes. On the earlier call he had been informed that Beijing's official off-the-record voice had retired early in the evening and did not wish to be disturbed. It had taken a second call, this time to Fong's private number, to convince his Chinese secretary that the matter was sufficiently urgent to awaken his employer. From the tone of the man's voice, it was obviously a chore he did not relish.

When Fong came on the line, however, his voice sounded like anything but a man who been inconvenienced. "Mr. Huntine," he began, "I hope I have not been discommodious. At my age, it sometimes takes a moment or two to be sufficiently alert."

"Not at all," Huntine assured him, "but we have a developing situation that the President believes you need to be aware of."

"I assume you are referring to the continuing situation with General Sarawak," Fong said.

"I am," Huntine confirmed. "I have Mr. Ruppert on my other line and he is prepared to give you an update. He has been in touch with the people closest to the situation several times in the past hour. On this end, President Weimer has been updated and he concurs that you should be made aware of what has transpired. Go ahead, Jake."

Jake Ruppert cleared his throat and wasted no time on amenities. "Earlier today, sir, a small contingent of Americans attempted to rescue Vice President Nelson from Sarawak's stronghold on the island of Karimunjawa. I won't burden you with the details of how this mission was configurated, but I am authorized to inform you that a series of non-aggressive diversionary actions were instigated, and a search for the Vice President was conducted. We now have been informed that the mission failed and we have every reason to believe that the Vice President is still being held hostage."

To Jake's surprise, Fong made no attempt to press for details.

"Concurrent with these events," Ruppert continued, "General Sarawak has released another tape through RRI. He is threatening to resume his executions. Now he says he will execute two captured members of the rescue effort as well as the Vice President." Jake paused to allow Fong to assimilate everything he was telling him. "This threat is in addition to his earlier warning today that he intends to launch missile attacks against two Kujon installations in Suryabaya and Yogyakata."

There was another pause, but again Fong remained silent.

Ruppert continued. "Perhaps I should also mention that two other members of the rescue force were recovered by one of our helicopters."

The delay on Fong's end of the line was an indication he had been taping their conversation. "And why does your President Weimer believe it is necessary to inform me of such matters? Has there been a change in his thinking since our Bethesda meeting?"

Huntine took over. "There has been," Huntine admitted, "and that is precisely why the President has instructed me to contact you, sir. As we speak, the President is meeting with high-ranking military officials and senior advisors to inform them of the situation."

"And?" Fong pressed.

"As you well know, the American aircraft carrier *Shenandoah* is currently operating in that area, and the President is ordering it and the necessary support vessels to proceed to the discussion zone for possible engagement with Sarawak forces."

"Such an action would be most unfortunate," Fong said carefully. Only then did Shuler Huntine believe he detected a minor crack in the man's otherwise always unerring demeanor. "You are aware of course that my government would consider—"

"At this point, Mr. Fong, President Weimer is doing what he believes is necessary to insure the rescue of Vice President Nelson. We are informing you and your government as a matter of diplomatic courtesy."

"Your President's decision, it is irrevocable?"

"It is unless you have a better idea. If you know a way to get those men out of there without any further bloodshed, then now is the time for your government to speak up."

"Unfortunately, Mr. Huntine, my government, unlike yours, sees this as a purely regional dispute between the current government of Sarni Kujon and the dissident factions of the PRI under the leadership of General Sarawak."

Huntine bit his lip before he continued. "And I submit then that your leaders are ignoring the fact that General Sarawak has already authorized the execution of three members of the United Nations delegation. Now he is threatening more executions."

"Perhaps it is your government that is at fault, Mr. Huntine. If your government had acted with more alacrity and decisivenesses when this situation was developing . . . "

"We have had no response from Kujon despite the—"

Fong said, "You will understand, of course, when I say a timetable must be established before any action is taken. My government must be informed and they must have time to respond to what I feel compelled to describe to them as both a hostile and irrational act on the part of the United States government. I will continue to advise them that a negotiated settlement can still be accomplished if all parties give this matter time."

"And our response to that is we don't have time. We are out of time. People are dying, and more will die if we fail to initiate some sort of action that will make Sarawak see the folly of his conduct."

"When are you proposing to take such actions?"

"Immediately. The *Shenandoah* is poised to respond as we speak. President Weimer is prepared to make the announcement to the American people within the hour."

Fong sighed. "Then I must contact my people and inform them of your intended course of action immediately. However, I must warn you that my government will view the consequences of any such actions as the responsibility of the government of the American people."

"Damn it, Fong, your people have a direct pipeline to this screwball. Your people in Beijing can defuse this situation before it erupts into something all of us regret." The second Huntine said it, he realized he had overstepped the delicate communication line that existed, as well as diplomacy itself. When Fong played the tape back for his superiors, it would sound as if the Americans were trying to implicate the Chinese. "I believe I've said everything I had to say, Huntine added. "This call is a matter of courtesy, not a call seeking concurrence."

Fong had regained his temporarily eroded decorum. "I trust we will talk again, Mr. Huntine." Then he hung up.

Ruppert's voice came through on the other line. "Who's in that meeting with the President?"

"Everyone that needs to be and probably a few who don't."

"You said the President is going to address the American people. At this hour?"

Huntine looked at his watch. "It's damn near midnight, but that probably won't stop him. But I'll tell you one thing for certain, Jake, it'll sure piss off the people if he interrupts David Letterman. Every time he does, we hear about it."

Day 8: Time 1211LT
Karimunjawa

Somehow Gideon realized it wasn't consciousness he was experiencing, it was a webby, twilight kind of sensation that defied description—a peculiar void where he could hide from pain and reality and at the same time allow an awareness of the fact that where he was he had no desire to be.

He had opened his eyes once or perhaps twice, but each time it was an act of futility. The world outside his pounding head was as dark as the one inside. Still, there was a force that seemed to compel him to take the final step and make the transition into a universe of wary sensibility.

In the darkness his shoulder ached, but he began to run his hand gingerly over his face, tracing his fingers over a myriad pattern of cuts, bruises, and contusions. Everything hurt. His lips were crusted with blood, his eyes, one of them at least, was nearly swollen shut, and his mouth was dry because he had been forced to divert his air supply away from what felt like a broken nose.

He tried groaning—and when he did, got a response. It was Geronimo.

"How you doin', Colonel?" Under the circumstances the question seemed unnecessarily solicitous. He could tell by the way Geronimo had asked it that there was nothing he could do about the situation.

Gideon tried propping himself up on his elbows. To his amazement, he was able to accomplish it. The only question that made any sense after he had achieved it was: "Where the hell are we?"

"Different time, same station, Colonel. But this time we got us some company."

Considering the way his head throbbed, Gideon was surprised anything Geronimo said made sense to him. "Alan?" he asked. The Apache pilot seemed like the only possibility. He was the only other one who had come ashore—unless, of course, something had gone wrong aboard the *Indon*. That was a possibility he didn't want to think about.

"Negative. No word on the captain. From what I've been able to get out of him so far, our guest is one of *them*. They dumped him in here a couple of hours ago."

Gideon stiffened. "What do you mean, dumped him in here?"

"I think it's legit, Colonel. I got a quick look at him when they opened the door. His face looks a helluva lot like yours did when they were through with you. He's pretty well busted up. If he's a plant, he took a whole lot of shit to make him look real."

Gradually Gideon was able to make out a slit of light creeping through under the door, and he could hear the Bandung guard shuffling around out in the hall. He managed to push himself into a sitting position and began taking inventory. It was the same accounting as before; everything hurt—but everything except the shoulder seemed to be working. Even then, it was the pounding in his head that hurt the most. "So who is this guy?" he whispered.

"He ain't much on talkin'," Geronimo said, "and he don't speak a helluva lot of English. Bits and pieces mostly—most of which don't make a helluva lot of sense. Mostly Maylay, I guess—but I got enough out of him to figure out that they must have thrown him in here with us because they think he's the one that tipped us off on how to get in the harbor."

Gideon's eyes had adjusted just well enough for him to make out the vague outline of the man. "What's his name?" Gideon grunted.

Sabo was shaking. Several times he started to speak, but each time the words locked up in his throat.

"Namo?" Geronimo repeated. "The colonel will be glad to know I figured out how to ask him that much at least."

Ketan Sabo hesitated long enough that Geronimo wasn't certain the Maylay had understood him. This was the enemy that was asking him questions—he was understandably wary. Like Gideon, he had been put through one of Muta's interrogation sessions, and he knew he wasn't in the best of shape to handle another one, especially the kind Muta could mete out. Finally, though, he tried. Gideon reasoned that the man had convinced himself there was even more danger in not responding. "Cap—tain—Cap—tain Ketan Sabo," he said in a quivering voice.

Gideon tried to clear his head. "Sabo," he repeated. Then he paused. "Okay, Sabo, that wasn't so hard, was it? Now, let's start with the simple stuff. First of all, where the hell are we?"

"Better keep your voice down, Colonel," Geronimo cautioned. "Every time that guard heard me and Sabo here talkin', he looked through that damn slot in the door and told us to be quiet. We might be better off if he didn't know you had rejoined the livin'."

Gideon lowered his voice. "Where are we?" he repeated.

Again there was a hesitancy in Sabo's answer. "You—you are in—in com-pound." It sounded as though he knew his English was shaky and he was searching for the right words. Then he added, "You are in the head—in the headquarters building."

"Good, you're on a roll. Don't stop now. Second question. What makes Sarawak think you're the one that tipped us off?"

"He—he be-be-lieves—I am guilty of treason. He—he be-lieves I have betrayed Bandung."

"Why?" Gideon pressed.

"Earlier—earlier this night I visit hostage, American

official hostage. I am able—able to"—he struggled to search for words—"ob-tain reading material for hostage. That is when—General Sarawak accuses me. Major Muta tells him he believes I passed along information about American attempt to rescue him."

It was obvious Sabo was trying to cooperate. Through it all he continued to search for the words that would enable the Americans to understand him.

"Go on," Gideon encouraged.

"He—he is con-vinced I give Americans information on how to—how to get into Karimunjawa without being detected."

Gideon slumped back against the wall to steady himself as he listened. Gideon was tempted to laugh at the part about how someone in the Bandung had helped them, but the thought of just how much he would hurt if he did laugh was more than enough to deter him. "You can tell your General Sarawak he doesn't give us enough credit, Captain. When you see him again, tell him I told you we figured out how to penetrate his little island stronghold all by ourselves."

If Ketan Sabo understood the attempt at humor in what Gideon had said, he gave no indication.

"All right, next question. Where is your General now?"

"I—I—I over-hear guards talking many times ago," Sabo tried. He was sifting each word, combing through a vocabulary he seldom used. "There was talk of speech—speech made by American President—a radio broadcast."

"What kind of speech?" Gideon pressed.

Sabo tried to answer but couldn't come up with the words.

"That speech—how long ago—since we've been in here?"

"I don't know, Colonel, it's been a while," Geronimo

cut in, "a couple of hours ago maybe. I've lost track of time. All I can tell you is there was a helluva lot of chatter goin' on out there in the hallway afterwards. It took a while before it all died down."

Gideon listened, and began rummaging through his inventory of aches and pains again. This time he took stock of the parts that worked and the parts that didn't. Then he began to feel his way across the room toward Geronimo. "Got any feel for how many guards they've got out there?"

"Can't tell. If there's more than one, they ain't been talkin," Geronimo said. "Why?"

"I'm still putting the pieces together," Gideon admitted, "but I think it's high time we started trying to find a way out of here. And we start by telling Sabo to keep his mouth shut and stay out of our way. Somehow we've got to get that guard to open that door."

Geronimo moved closer to him. "What's the plan?"

"It's the oldest trick in the book, but it just might work. We start by creating a little diversion. Make that guard think someone is sick in here. When you get to the door, I'll start making noise, banging on the wall and moaning. You start shouting. Tell him the one Muta's been pounding on is sick. Tell him he'd better get a doctor. Get close enough that when he opens that door you can take his feet out from under him."

Geronimo nodded, stood up, kept his back to the wall, and inched his way in the darkness toward the door. Then he stood back out of the line of sight so he wouldn't be seen when the guard looked through the observation slot. "Ready, Colonel," he whispered.

Gideon Stone counted to three and began moaning while he kicked and slapped the wall. Geronimo stood back. The ruse worked. Both men heard the guard stand up and walk toward the door. A thin, momentary stream of light penetrated the darkness when he opened the observation slot. *"Berhenti,"* the guard shouted.

"Here goes nothin'," Geronimo whispered. "Let's hope to hell I can pull this off. Please," he groaned aloud. "He's dying. Get a doctor."

"Tidak dokter," the guard insisted as he slid the dead bolt open on the door.

"He says no doctor," Geronimo whispered.

Gideon, curled into the fetal position, groaned and held his breath. If they were going to pull this one off, he knew it would have to be more convincing than a couple of well-timed moans. He heard the door creak slowly open. The guard was suspicious, but the only thing Gideon focused on was the silhouette of the man outlined against the light in the corridor. To Gideon Stone, the militiaman looked imposing and the Mk 2 pistol he was carrying looked like a cannon.

Gideon let out another groan, rolled over, and clutched his stomach. The guard was taking the bait. He took one step into the room and stopped, stabbed the beam of his flashlight down at Gideon, writhing on the floor, and studied him. When he saw Gideon curled up in pain, he reached around behind him for the light switch.

For one split second the militiaman had dropped his guard. For one split second he was off balance. That split second was all Geronimo needed; he made his move. It was a maneuver he had practiced a thousand times; his hand came down hard, like a man chopping wood, and his knee came up even harder. Both hit their target.

The karate chop caught the guard in the throat; the knee caught him in the crotch. There was the hollow, flat, revealing sound of air escaping and the trumpeting agony of a man who had been hit in his most vulnerable area. The

Bandung militiaman staggered forward, gasping for air and grasping his crotch. Then Geronimo finished him off. He landed two more blows; the second sent the guard to his knees. When Geronimo brought his knee up the second time, it was into the man's face and the guard pitched backward, eyes glazed. The Bandung guard hit the floor, twitched twice, groaned, and lost consciousness.

Gideon assessed Geronimo's handiwork, congratulated him, crawled to his knees, and finally managed to stand up. His legs were rubbery and his head was pounding. He leaned against the wall for support and looked at Sabo.

The man Sarawak had accused of being a traitor was still cowering in the corner of the room. In the half-light, Gideon was finally able to get a look at him; the Malayan's face looked like hamburger, it was swollen, latticeworked with bruises. He was squinting into the sudden wash of light.

While Gideon struggled to get his own equilibrium, Geronimo pounced on the fallen guard, stripped him of his automatic and his flashlight, used the guard's belt to tie his hands, went to the door, and glanced up and down the corridor. "So far, so good," he hissed.

Gideon was still wobbly. He pushed himself away from the wall and tried to steady himself. As he did, he motioned for Geronimo to get Sabo to his feet. "See if our Maylay friend here can stand up. If he can, we can use him. If he can't, we leave him here with his Bandung playmate."

Sheban Geronimo pulled the terrified Sabo to his feet, pinned him against the wall, and waved the muzzle of the guard's Mk 2 in his face. "Let me give you something to think about, soldier boy. If you think your Major Muta was tough to get along with, let me assure you—you ain't seen nothin' yet. Now—we want answers and we want 'em fast. For openers, where the hell are we and how do we get out of here?"

Ketan Sabo had reached the point where he was too terrified to talk. He had seen what had happened to the guard, and he feared the same. He pointed toward the door, choked, and eventually the words came spilling out. They were confused and garbled.

"All I'm gettin' from our boy is a bunch of gibberish, Colonel. It's like he somehow suddenly forgot how to talk. Let's leave him here. We can make better time without him."

Gideon was shaking his head. "I don't think so. Five will get you ten he knows where Sarawak is and how we can get to him. Sarawak is the key. If we find Sarawak—I think we'll find Nelson."

Geronimo's face was less than six inches from Sabo's. "Sounds like the colonel just granted you a temporary reprieve, soldier boy. But you better underline that word *temporary*. Because the reprieve is gonna last only as long as you cooperate. Got it?"

Sabo blinked and nodded.

"Ask him again, where is Sarawak keeping the hostage?"

Sabo appeared to understand. He pointed toward the door and gestured. "I can show you—in office."

"Show us," Gideon said.

Geronimo prodded the Bandung captain out of the room and down the corridor. Sabo stopped and opened a door. The room was cluttered, the ashtray was overflowing, and the place smelled of mildew and stale cigarette smoke. On one wall was a map of the Karimunjawa installation. "There," Sabo said, alternately pointing to two locations, "Sarawak either there or there."

Gideon studied the two locations and looked at Geronimo. Sabo had indicated a small alcove near the northwest tip of the island. It appeared to be the one Tillston had warned them about. The other location was near the airstrip. "What about the hostage?" Gideon repeated.

"If hostage alive—hostage with Sarawak."

"What do ya think, Colonel? Think this clown is jerkin' our chain? Leadin' us into a setup?"

Gideon studied the frightened Sabo for several moments. Beneath the network of cuts and bruises, the man's face was drawn and drained of color. His hands were shaking. "I think he's too damned scared to be lying. I say we go for it . . ."

Day 8: Time 1417LT
Karimunjawa

The officer's name was Kulit. He was, according to the insignia on his uniform, a lieutenant. Sarawak could not recall having seen him before. Now, with his face streaked with a sooty residue of oil and smoke, and his uniform stained with sweat, the lieutenant was standing at attention while he reported. "The fire has spread to the number *tujuh* oil-storage unit, General. I am afraid it is lost."

Bojoni Sarawak listened, bit his lip, sagged back in his chair, and closed his eyes. He remained that way for several moments, seemingly transfixed by the news before dismissing the man with a wave of his hand. He waited until the door closed behind the young officer before he looked at Muta and spoke.

"What is the latest on the American aircraft carrier?" Sarawak opened his cigarette case, took out a cigarette, tapped it on his desk, and lit it. When he exhaled, a thin veil of blue-gray smoke languished over his head like a portent.

Even Muta's normally gruff voice was subdued as he reported. "We have two small patrol boats, both masquerading as fishing vessels, patrolling the waters just outside the seven-mile limit, General. Both vessels report picking up transmissions between the American aircraft carrier and the two support vessels that accompany it."

"How close are they?"

"We are estimating they will be less than five kilometers off shore by dawn," Muta said.

Sarawak seemed almost pensive. "Then it is only a matter of time until they will be in position to send an exploratory force ashore," he speculated. He looked up, first through the thin membrane of smoke hovering near the ceiling, and finally at the torrents of unceasing rain washing against the window.

"Do you think they will risk coming ashore?" Muta asked.

"I am afraid it is inevitable."

Muta waited, not knowing what else there was to say. He realized what was happening. He had seen it before, in the early days of the movement when there had been setback after setback. This was the pensive, occasionally defeatist side of his general; a dimension of the complex man that seemed to manifest itself when times appeared to be darkest for the Bandung movement. When his men needed him most, Sarawak was prone to withdraw and question.

Almost as an afterthought Sarawak asked, "Have we failed?"

"I remember reading that failure, if that is how this is judged, is a temporary adjudication by men who have not lived through an event," Muta said. "It is subject to reevaluation in the dawn of every new day. Because of you, our island country has been born again, General." When he finished, he looked long and hard at the man who had been called a visionary by scholars in places as far away as Cuba, and a man who was viewed by his followers as the leader with a divine blueprint for his country's future.

Sarawak ignored Muta's attempt at an incantation. His mood was desperate. "You have assessed our loses?" he inquired.

Muta stood with his hands clasped behind his back. He was uncomfortable with his leader's occasional bouts of melancholia. "I have," he reported. "All warehouses on the western rim of the harbor have been destroyed. Those that are still standing have been gutted by fire—and the fuel depot, as Lieutenant Kulit has reported, continues to burn. I am afraid that with the burning of the warehouses we have lost the ability to repel any invasion attempt by even a small American expeditionary force."

Sarawak leaned forward with his arms on the desk. "I appreciate your pragmatism, Major. What about our manpower?"

Again Assasio Muta hesitated. This time he was even more reluctant to answer. "I am afraid," he said cautiously, "that many of the men believed that the Americans had already launched a full-scale offensive when the fuel depot was set on fire last night. Both Lieutenants Kulit and Pan report the majority of them have fled into the mountains. Those that remain are exhausted from fighting the fires."

"How many remain?" Sarawak pressed.

"No more than a hundred men—at the most a few more than that."

Bojoni Sarawak frowned, stood up, and walked across

the room to a window where he could see the oil fires on the distant side of the harbor. The skies were black, draped in a thick blanket of heavy oil-spawned smoke. "Our ability to retaliate with missiles is still intact?"

Muta nodded. "We still have the ability to launch the missiles," he confirmed.

"And thousands will die if we do," Sarawak reflected, "but for what purpose? Kujon remains in power."

"The dream of Karimunjawa can be rebuilt," Muta said stubbornly, "but it will take time. Tomorrow will dawn much as it has today, but when it does, the ruins will smolder less and it will be a time of rebirth. You must accept that."

Sarawak straightened. Muta interpreted the gesture as one of new resolve. "You are right in your thinking, Major," Sarawak declared. "We must view this night as nothing more than an unfortunate but temporary setback." Muta heard his general put the emphasis on the word *temporary*. "We must begin now to prepare for the day when the fires of Karimunjawa have cooled and been forgotten."

There was reason for Muta to smile. "Then you will accept the offer from our comrades in Beijing?"

"I will," Sarawak said.

For Bojoni Sarawak the implementation of the evacuation plan from Karimunjawa had at one time been unthinkable. Now, however, he was viewing it as, in Muta's words, a "plan for rebirth."

The move from the headquarters building to the secret bunker located near an obscure and seldom-used inlet some fifteen miles from the base proper was designed to be accomplished with only a small contingent of his most trusted officers and men. The only member of the ten-man entourage not included in the original plan was the hostage, the American Vice President. Nelson was moved to the bunker by two of Sarawak's most trusted militiamen. He was transferred in the back of a munitions truck along with several boxes containing documents that Sarawak was determined to destroy prior to their evacuation.

In the time it had taken them to make the move, it had become apparent to the men who accompanied the contingent to the bunker that Bojoni Sarawak was writing off his Jakarta plot and was already redefining his plan for the Bandung's future in the Javanese PKI.

The twenty-by-twenty-four-foot room where Sarawak assembled his staff had been built two levels below a nondescript block building less than five hundred feet from a small airstrip and the inlet. In the early days of the Bandung it had served as the movement's war room. The subterranean bunker was constructed with three-foot-thick, steel-reinforced concrete walls, and equipped with all of the necessary communications and survival gear.

By the time he arrived at the bunker, Sarawak was again in charge. He cleared his throat before he spoke to his men. When he began, the words were near-messianic. The tone of his voice had recaptured the element of incantation. "The unprovoked attack by the American forces on Karimunjawa may have succeeded in reducing our once-proud island fortress to ruins—but like the Egyptian phoenix we too will be renewed, rising from the ashes of Karimunjawa to a new immorality.

"We have had the opportunity to view firsthand the devastation that can be rendered by superior numbers. We will learn from this and we will recruit in the villages, the mountains, the rural areas, and the cities—and our numbers will swell. When that new day dawns, we will be strong—we will be ready."

When he finished, he looked around the room. "And now, Lieutenant Pan, if you will, step forward, please."

Muta braced himself as the young officer who had been instrumental in capturing the two Americans smiled and moved toward Sarawak. The man was expecting to be commended for his actions, but for it to happen so quickly and in the presence of some of his superior officers and men was beyond his expectations. He saluted his general and stood at attention.

Sarawak appraised him. As usual, Muta had been right. Pan appeared to be approximately the same height and weight as the general. The only real difference was in their ages.

"And now, Lieutenant, you will be so kind as to change into this uniform," Sarawak said.

Pan's smile changed to a frown. The uniform was like that worn by his general, right down to the epaulets and the star on the collar of the tunic. "I am flattered, but I do not understand, General," Pan said. "This looks like your uniform."

"Indeed it does. You are most observant, Lieutenant," Sarawak complimented him. "But I assure you, this uniform is quite appropriate for what you are about to contribute."

Muta and two of his aides had moved forward until they were standing beside the young officer. Still perplexed, Pan continued to frown.

"You may thank Major Muta for this, Lieutenant. You see, it was Major Muta that I instructed to develop a contingency plan in the event it became necessary for us to temporarily abort our Bandung mission here on

Karimunjawa. I believe you will find that he has accomplished his task in a most Machiavellian manner.

"At this very moment, the American aircraft carrier *Shenandoah* is on its way toward Karimunjawa with two support vessels. Within hours we expect the Americans to be in a position to launch an offensive against us."

Pan's expression had evolved from one of expectation to confusion, and finally apprehension. "But I do not—"

Sarawak interrupted him before he could finish. "When the Americans arrive, they will find the two men you captured earlier as well as Captain Sabo, who, Major Muta has regrettably learned, aided the Americans in their sneak attack on our base. Fortunately, that plays right into our hand; Captain Sabo knows of this facility and he eventually will lead them here."

Pan started to draw back, but felt Muta's hand on his shoulder.

"When they arrive, the Americans will find the bunker in ruins—and, of course, the body of what they believe to be General Bojoni Sarawak, burned beyond recognition after having committing suicide. Diabolically clever, would you not agree?"

Pan began to struggle.

"Come, come, Lieutenant. Major Muta assures me that you are committed to the cause. Surely you are willing to step forward in our hour of retrenchment." Sarawak paused and lit a cigarette. "By now you have no doubt figured out that the body they discover will be that of none other than Lieutenant Tidek Pan. Quite ingenious, don't you think?"

Pan knew it was futile to struggle. He was aware of the barrel of Muta's automatic pressed against the base of his skull. "But—but I have served you well, General. There must be others who can—"

"Indeed you have," Sarawak said, "and in death you will continue to do so. You will be a hero. Your sacrifice will enable the Bandung to re-emerge stronger than ever. The Americans, when they find your body, will believe they have eliminated Sarawak. They will no longer continue to search for me and you can rest assured that, perhaps in a less flamboyant fashion, the work of the Bandung will continue."

Pan tried to pull away, and Muta's grip tightened.

"Take him away," Sarawak ordered. "Put the uniform on him."

Chapter Fifteen

Day 8: Time 0301LT
Washington

Jake Ruppert had often declared that when he retired from the Agency there would be no telephones in his house. But that day hadn't as yet arrived and now, in the small hours of the morning, he was aware that the telephone was ringing—and he was doing his best to ignore it. He felt Alice nudge him, rolled over, buried his head under the pillow, and pulled the covers up in a final, feeble, and futile effort to escape the incessant noise.

But the annoying ringing continued, and he finally gave up. He reached out, slapped at the offender, and waited to see if his response had been sufficient. For a moment there was silence; then he heard the tape on the answering machine spring into action.

It recited the number the caller had reached and concluded with: "*. . . if you'll leave your name and number, we will return your call as soon as we are available.*"

What followed was inevitable. "Goddamn it, Jake, pick up the phone," the caller thundered. It was Shuler Huntine.

Jake rolled over, inched his tired legs over the edge of the bed, ran his fingers threw his thinning hair as though the gesture would clear away the cobwebs of an interrupted sleep, and reached for the receiver. "For Christ's sake, Shuler," he growled, "don't you ever sleep?"

"I'll sleep when I'm not up to my ass in alligators," Huntine snapped. "Right now you're number one on my need-to-know list. So listen up."

Ruppert switched on the night-light beside his bed and put on his glasses as though the glasses would help him. "At this hour this could only be about Sarawak, right?"

"Indirectly. We just got a call from Fong."

Ruppert sighed. "Hell, Shuler, I already know what you're going to tell me. I could have predicted it. He's warning you that the boys in Beijing are up in arms over Weimer's decision to send the *Shenandoah* into Karimunjawa waters, correct?"

"On the contrary," Huntine countered, "the old boy is bending over backwards to help us; this time he's the one that's passing along information. According to Fong, there was a contingency plan in case Sarawak's coup attempt failed. It appears that plan is being implemented. Fong's government is making arrangements for one of their submarines to rendezvous with Sarawak."

"Rendezvous with Sarawak?" Ruppert repeated. "What the hell is that supposed to mean?"

"It means that Sarawak is folding his tent. He's jumping ship. Less than an hour ago he advised his contacts in Beijing that he's calling off the dogs. According to Fong there has been a contingency plan all along—a plan to assist Sarawak in an evacuation in the event that the coup attempt failed. Our best thinking is he's heard about the President sending in the *Shenandoah* and he intends to bail out while he can still get out."

Despite the hour, Jake Ruppert was allowing a half-smile to creep over his face. Then it dissipated. "That takes care of Sarawak, but what about the Vice President?"

"That's the unknown in this equation. And it's a big one. No sign and no word on Nelson. He may be dead for all we know. I've been in touch with your night man, Turley. He says Wormack hasn't heard anything since they picked up Agent Preston and Captain Alan earlier in the day. So based on what we know so far, we're assuming the Vice President, your man Stone, and Sheban Geronimo are still Sarawak's prisoners. At this point we don't know whether Sarawak intends to carry through on his threat to assassinate the hostages or what. At the same time, some of the President's advisors are warning him this whole thing could be a trap. We're advising Colonel Hastings aboard the *Shenandoah,* the man in charge of the detachment being sent ashore, that there is a strong possibility that Sarawak still has a few tricks up his sleeve."

"But no word on Stone or the corporal?"

"None," Huntine confirmed, "and no way to get word to them if they're still alive. If they're in the wrong place at the wrong time when Hastings puts his people down . . . " Huntine's voice trailed off, but Jake Ruppert knew what he meant.

"What time are they going ashore?"

"Six o'clock Washington time. That would be eighteen hundred Karimunjawa time. The weather boys are indicating we can expect somewhat of a break in the weather late in the day."

Jake Ruppert was seldom at a loss for words, but this was one of those times. He realized that the President's decision to send in the *Shenandoah* took the matter out of his hands. There was nothing to say—no protest to register. Even if Sarawak had abandoned his plan to dispose of the hostages, it didn't look good for Gideon and the young corporal. Ruppert knew Hastings and he knew his reputation. Jack Hastings was the kind who would shoot up the place first and the interrogation would be an afterthought—and only if there happened to be survivors. Hastings's idea of a clean operation was an operation where none of the opposition was left standing.

"What do we do, Shuler, just stand by and let this happen?" he finally asked.

"That's why Fong warned us that his people would be picking up Sarawak with one of their subs. The Chinese don't want any interference, and they sure as hell don't want one of our jet jockeys blowing their sub out of the water when it surfaces. As nasty as it is right now, if that happens, this situation could get a whole lot nastier."

Jake Ruppert had a gnawing sensation in the pit of his stomach. It was the kind of feeling a man gets when he knows bad things are about to happen and there isn't a damn thing he can do about it. "What can I do?" he asked. The question came out sounding feeble and purposeless.

"Wait for orders. The President is calling the shots now. You and I become the relay team. If Turley hears from Wormack, I want to know about it," Huntine said. "In other words, keep me informed. I'll do likewise."

Ruppert heard the receiver click in his ear, and nestled the telephone back in its cradle.

"What was that all about?" he heard Alice ask. She was sitting up in bed, looking at him.

"That was Huntine," he mumbled, "Shuler Huntine." There was a protracted, somber silence before he continued. "The day I talked Gideon Stone into this mess, he was telling me how much he enjoyed living down there in Largo. Maybe that's what you and I should do."

Day 8: Time 1552LT
Karimunjawa

It had taken Assasio Muta and two of his militiamen no longer than ten minutes to insure that everything in the bunker was saturated with gasoline. Sarawak had supervised the entire operation. Now, as he looked around a room cluttered with reams of discarded files and debris, he was finally satisfied.

"Bring in the lieutenant," he told Muta. "Order two of your men to stay and send the others away."

Assasio Muta left the room, and returned with two of his men. They were half-leading, half-carrying the young officer. Tidek Pan had been drugged to the point that he could barely walk. With the aid of the two remaining militiamen supporting his weight, Pan was guided to a long leather couch adjacent to the very desk where Bojoni Sarawak had spent the better part of ten years meticulously designing his plan for the Bandung takeover of the Javanese government.

"Seat him at the end of the couch," Sarawak ordered, and waited until the groggy Pan was propped in position with one hand resting on the armrest. "We must make it appear that General Sarawak's final troubled moments were ones of deep reflection and dismay." Sarawak laughed. "After all, we want our adversaries to think he has failed. Right, Major? The Americans must be reassured that I have departed from this life—otherwise our little scenario will not be convincing."

Pan's head lolled to one side, and there was an anguished but drug-aborted attempt at speaking. His eyes were open but glazed.

Sarawak studied the scene much as a director would analyze a stage setting. He walked over to an ornate teak cabinet on the far side of the room, opened the door, and took out a bottle. "And now, for the final touch, a drink of *tuak* for our unfortunate stand-in." He looked at Muta. "It has been well publicized that Bojoni Sarawak prefers *tuak* to other alcoholic beverages, has it not?"

Muta was impressed with Sarawak's thoroughness. The man had a reputation for paying attention to the smallest detail. He nodded. "So it has been written," he confirmed.

"Then it is appropriate that he should appear to have died leaving nothing to chance and at the same time indulging himself."

Sarawak walked quickly back across the room, placed the glass in Pan's hand, and set the bottle next to Pan on the floor.

"And now, Major Muta, if you will . . . "

Assasio Muta did not hesitate when he was given an order. He walked over to the couch, unholstered his .45-caliber automatic, released the safety, bent down, and with his left hand forced Pan's mouth open. Then, with his right hand, he shoved the barrel into Pan's mouth and pulled the trigger. Finally, the automatic was placed in

Pan's hand with his finger on the trigger. The entire process had taken less than fifteen seconds.

Muta stepped back to appraise his work, then looked at Sarawak. Bojoni Sarawak was smiling. "That should be sufficient, Major. My compliments, a task well done. Between your handiwork and the fire, it will indeed be difficult for anyone to prove that a disenchanted Bojoni Sarawak, unwilling to accept his failure, did not take his own life. Would you not agree?"

Again Muta nodded.

Sarawak waited for Muta to exit, walked to the door, turned on the ventilation fan to the concrete-walled room, took out a cigarette, lit it, and threw the still-burning match back into the room. As he closed the heavy steel door to the bunker, he heard the muffled explosion.

Day 8: Time 1447LT
Karimunjawa

Gideon Stone hung back in the shadows out of a steady monsoon-fostered rain that within the last hour had run the gamut from heavy downpour to little more than a light rain. Now it was raining hard again as he waited for Geronimo to come out of the last building. When the corporal emerged he was shaking his head.

"No one, Colonel, not a damn soul. Where the hell do you figure they all disappeared?"

"You tell me." Gideon glanced out at the carryall they had commandeered outside of the headquarters building. "Our boy Sabo is running out of options."

"Think he's stallin' us, Colonel?"

Gideon shook his head. "Under the circumstances, I don't think so—he's too damn scared."

The two men walked back to the ATNO, where Sabo was tied. He was slumped over in the seat. Gideon again picked up the map they had taken from the offices in the building where they had been detained. Geronimo was looking over his shoulder when Gideon began pointing to the one remaining set of buildings. "Here by that inlet, the ones Tillston told us about in the briefing. They're the only ones we haven't checked out."

When he looked at Geronimo, the corporal was staring off at what was left of the still-burning fuel depot. The chain of explosions had ceased, but even though the fires had diminished, they were still raging out of control. It was apparent now that most, if not all, of the Bandung efforts to control the fire had become a thing of the past. The handful of Sarawak's men that remained had turned their attention from fighting the fires to looting. Gideon and Geronimo could see the militiamen carting off everything the Bandung rebels believed useful and disappearing into the surrounding hills with their bounty.

Geronimo lit a cigarette and cupped it in his hand. "What happens if we don't find the Vice President, Colonel?"

Gideon allowed his aching body to sag back against the fender of the ATNO. "First of all, we don't give up until we've worked our way through that cluster of buildings down by the inlet. Then, if we don't find him there, I guess we write him off. Plus, we don't get an 'atta boy' from the President."

"Then we better get our butts in gear, Colonel," Geronimo said with a grin. "I'm counting on that 'atta boy' to get me another stripe. The question is, where the hell is this unmarked inlet Tillston was talking about? He said it was all but hidden."

Gideon shrugged. "According to the map it's due west

of here, and we've got our soldier boy here in the ANTO to show us the way."

To their surprise, Ketan Sabo cooperated. Geronimo managed to negotiate the winding road leading out of the Karimunjawa headquarters area to a small cluster of buildings near the inlet. The road itself culminated in a steep hill that dropped down into a clearing. The last several hundred yards were little more than a muddy, rutted trail that tested the old ATNO as well as Geronimo's driving skills.

"Just like everything else around here, it looks deserted, Colonel," Geronimo observed. He had pulled the aging four-wheeler into the clearing and brought it to a halt.

Gideon looked around. The location on the map was marked Chebay Inlet, and it looked abandoned. "Remember what my pappy said, 'Looks can be deceiving.' We play it close to the vest until we're certain."

Gideon turned around in his seat and poked at Sabo until the belabored Bandung captain lifted his head. "Okay, soldier boy, where's this bunker your boss is so secretive about?"

Ketan Sabo was slow to come around. He lifted his head, squinted, and tried to scan the area. One eye was almost swollen shut, and the other wasn't much better. It was obvious he was still struggling to get his bearings. He had been to this place that Muta and one or two other senior officers referred to as Sarawak's "bunker" on only one other occasion. Now, in the rain and smoke, it looked different. He pointed to a gray-green Quonset hut on the far side of the building. "I think it's there—there beneath the . . . "

Geronimo crawled down out of the ATNO, released the

safety on his 9mm, crouched, worked his way through the mud across the clearing, and pinned his back against the side of the building. Gideon knew he was counting. Geronimo glanced back at the ATNO, kicked the door open, and jumped back out of the line of anticipated fire. It wasn't what he was expecting. Instead of encountering resistance, two Bandung militiamen, neither wearing shoes, both with terrified expressions on their face, stood with their hands up. When one of the men saw Geronimo, he dropped to his knees with his hands covering his face. The other, seemingly more terrified than the first, could do little more than mutter, *"tolong, tolong."*

"Surprise, Colonel, looks like we caught us a couple of looters."

Gideon pulled Sabo down out of the ATNO and pushed the Bandung officer ahead of him across the clearing toward the Quonset hut. Twice Sabo lost his footing and slipped to his knees in the mud.

"You're in luck, soldier boy. Looks like we just keep finding reasons to keep your skinny ass alive. Now you get a chance to play interpreter for us." Gideon shoved the Bandung captain through the door ahead of him and stepped in out of the rain behind him. Geronimo had the two militiamen pinned up against the wall with their hands high over their heads.

The looters had somehow managed to commandeer a small burro and a cart. The cart was already half full. Thus far they had managed to round up a spool of copper wire, some tubing, a box of shells, two rifles, several cartons of canned goods, and a two-way radio.

"Looks like you two were making quite a haul," Gideon quipped.

Neither of the militiamen responded.

Gideon turned to Sabo. "Okay, first question, ask them if either of them speaks English."

Sabo was trembling. *"Bisa—bisa berbicara bahasa Ingriss?"* he stammered.

This time both men shook their heads.

"Neither speaks English," Sabo confirmed.

Gideon moved closer. "All right, ask them what they know about hostages. If they tell you they don't know, ask them where the bunker is."

Sabo repeated the questions in Maylay. Other than a series of shrugs, neither of the rebels responded, and Sabo looked at Gideon. In the meantime Geronimo had moved closer to the two men, and they could hear the metallic sound of his 9mm as he again released the safety. He prodded the older of the two, poking the barrel of the MP-5N in the small of the man's back.

Gideon's voice sounded brittle. "Try again, ask them where the hell Sarawak's bunker is."

Sabo repeated Gideon's question in Maylay and the older of the two, having considered the alternative, began to mutter and point.

"He says—says he can show us," Sabo indicated.

With Geronimo immediately behind him, repeatedly nudging him with the barrel of his automatic, the militiaman led them through a small access door at the back of the building, across another clearing, and gestured down an incline at a small shed built into the side of a hill. It was entirely surrounded by a thick growth of chepek and gum trees.

"He says the entrance to the bunker is in the back of the shed," Sabo said.

"Tell him to lead the way," Gideon barked.

It took several minutes for Gideon and Geronimo to

prod their three frightened Bandung captives through the wet undergrowth and down the hill. At the base of the hill Geronimo took over. The wooden door was nothing more than a prop. He kicked it open. Beyond it was a set of steps leading down to a heavy steel door.

"Now, ask him if Sarawak is still down there," Gideon whispered. Sabo translated, and the militiaman nodded.

As he did, Geronimo tried the door to the bunker. His hand recoiled, and he moved back toward Gideon. "Got a problem, Colonel, that door is hot as hell. The damn thing could be rigged—it could be a booby trap."

Gideon turned to Sabo again. "Tell your man to open it," he hissed, "and when you do, remind him that if his boss, Sarawak, has the damn thing rigged, it's his ass right along with ours. So if he knows something, now is the time to speak up."

Sabo repeated the command as Geronimo prodded the man toward the door. The militiaman hesitated, and the trembling became even more pronounced. Twice he glanced back at his fellow militiaman. He was stalling. When he had waited as long as he believed he could, he reached for the latch and his hand recoiled from the heat.

"Open it," Geronimo growled. Again the man hesitated before starting to fumble with the tail of his shirt. He tore off a piece, wrapped it around his hand, and again forced himself to reach for the latch.

The door rocketed open, and a backdraft of thick, acrid, choking smoke and intense heat billowed out. Gideon and Geronimo hit the floor. The others weren't as lucky. Gideon saw two of the men crumple while one tried to escape up the steps. He made it only as far as the third step.

Gideon rolled over and covered his face, but it was too little, too late. A searing, acid-like sensation clawed its way into his lungs and he plummeted headfirst into unconsciousness.

Day 8: Time 1541LT
Inggres Bay
Karimunjawa

Bojoni Sarawak huddled under a rocky outcropping, watching as Asassio Muta worked his way up a small rocky incline toward him. Both men were exhausted.

At the water's edge, a third man, older and formerly a member of the militia, stood next to a twenty-foot dory, tending the ancient Mercury outboard. The old man was hunch-shouldered, and wore a slicker to protect himself from the rain. Sarawak did not know his name.

"It is almost time," Muta informed his leader.

Sarawak took time to grind out his cigarette before he stood up. Despite his fatigue, he wore the expression of a man who refused to acknowledge his failures. He pushed back his sleeve and glanced at his watch. Muta was right, the rendezvous time was 1800 hours. If all went according to the careful prearranged plan, any moment now the Chinese submarine would surface some five hundred yards offshore, he would be taken aboard, and he would begin again to plan for the day when he would force the Kujon government to step down.

"Do you hear them?" Muta asked.

Sarawak turned his eyes up toward the man who had been with him since the inception of his inspired plan to overthrow the Kujon regime. "What is it that you hear, comrade?"

"It sounds like helicopters," Muta assessed. "It can only be the Americans. No doubt they are from the American aircraft carrier."

Sarawak looked down again and studied the pebbles at his feet. He had not said as much to Muta, but he was again enduring the ravages of the fever. He wiped the sweat from his forehead and felt the cooling ablutions of the rain. "The Americans," he mused, "are a curious lot. They would risk all-out war to save the life of one of their own."

Muta nodded, and again urged his general to get up. "It is time," he reminded Sarawak.

Sarawak sighed, stumbled to his feet, and with Muta's assistance began to work his way down the rocky incline toward the shore and the dory. He was shivering again—the fever had not subsided.

Muta paused once to look up, scanning the leaden skies to see if he could see the American helicopters. The thumping sound of the rotors, for the moment at least, seemed to be at some distance from them. All of the sounds came from east of the tiny inlet, and he presumed they were now over the Karimunjawa base proper. "What if they spot the submarine, General?"

Sarawak looked up, assessing the thick canopy of black smoke that hovered over them. Even the strong monsoon winds were unsuccessful in their attempt to clear away the polluted residue of the fuel depot fires.

"They will not suspect such a rendezvous," Sarawak responded. "What they are not looking for they will not find. It is the nature of such regimented men."

The boatsman looked up as Muta and Sarawak lumbered into the shallow craft. Then he pushed the vessel out and away from shore, crawled in, and started the motor. It coughed and sputtered several times before it accepted its fate and came to life.

The water in the normally peaceful inlet came at them in repeated spasms, and the tiny craft bobbed up and down even in the alcove that sheltered it. Sarawak crawled under the cover of a large gray canvas, and Muta worked his way back to the helm. "You know the coordinates of the rendezvous point?" he asked. The old man nodded. If he thought it was foolish for the ones that called themselves Bandungs to attempt such an endeavor in such unwelcoming waters, his expression revealed nothing of it. "I have fished here for many years," he replied. "I know these waters well." He pointed to a barely visible outcropping of rocks and then to another point on the shore. "We will go there, just beyond the shallows . . . and wait."

Muta could feel the tiny craft heave and pitch in waves that often crashed over the sideboards. The slicker was of little use to him now: the water was assaulting him from every direction. He tried to shield his eyes from the ever-present onslaught of the salt spray, and scrutinized the horizon for some sign of the submarine. Then, like some kind of ghostly aberration, he saw it. It loomed no more than two hundred yards off the small craft's bow, "There it is," he shouted, pointing into the turgid darkness.

Sarawak pushed away the shielding canvas and peered in the direction Muta was pointing. The old man had already swung the bow of the dory around and was heading for the low cigar-shaped silhouette just ahead of him.

Within a matter of seconds the features of the Chenya-class sub became apparent. Both Sarawak and Muta were able to make out the vessel's conning tower, the unusually large snorkel mast, and finally the vague profile of two men. As the dory approached, Sarawak could hear the men shouting instructions and see them gesturing.

The old man brought the nearly swamped dory along the port-side hull of the giant sub, and waited for the sub's personnel to scamper down the ladder from the control tower and drop mooring lines down to the tiny vessel. Sarawak stood up, braced himself, and grabbed hold of one line while Muta caught hold of the other.

It had come down to this. Sarawak extended his hand to his long-time comrade and pulled the man to him. The embrace was brief and the words hurried. "Good fortune to you, my comrade and colleague," Sarawak said. There was emotion in their farewell.

"We will meet again, General, and . . . " Muta's words were carried away by the wind.

While one of the Chinese sailors dropped the rope boarding ladder down, a third figure appeared on the tower. "You are Sarawak?" he asked in perfect Maylay.

Bojoni Sarawak saluted and held up his hand with his fist clenched. "I am General Sarawak," he confirmed.

The hands of the officer on the control tower suddenly appeared above the tower's welt. In them he cradled a 9mm submachine gun, and he opened fire. A furious hail of laserlike bullets erupted, raking the sub's grid decking. In one continuous motion, the man swept the barrel of his rapid-fire weapon back and forth until the rain of bullets swallowed up their prey.

A stunned Asassio Muta saw Sarawak pitch face-forward, his bullet-riddled body twitching and convulsing. But before he could react or even register a protest, the gunman had turned his attention to him. Muta saw the tracerlike pattern of fire, and instantaneously felt the hot lead rip holes in his body. There was a microsecond or two when the outrage equaled the pain and the inevitability of what was about to happen had time to register. He groped frantically at the gaping holes in his body and opened his eyes one final time. The old man who had delivered them to their rendezvous was already dead.

Muta's eyes followed the silhouettes of the men on the

deck of the submarine as they scurried up the ladder to the control tower and disappeared. Moments later the great, grey, ominous beast gracefully slid beneath the agitated waters of the tiny bay and vanished. It was the last thing Asassio Muta ever saw.

Day 10: Time 1437LT
The Shenandoah

In a military career that encompassed over fifteen years of active duty, Gideon Stone had never been much on social graces or protocol. This, however, was one of those rare occasions when he wished he knew what was appropriate. He had never met a Vice President before, and didn't know what to call him. His nurse, a tall, awkward-looking woman wearing an ensign's insignia, had indicated that she'd heard others aboard the carrier refer to him as Mr. Vice President. Gideon decided that was the way he would greet the man until he was instructed otherwise.

When the door to the small wardroom at the end of the corridor opened and the Vice President was wheeled in by a ramrod-straight full bird colonel, Gideon was taken aback. The man in the wheelchair was smiling, extending his hand.

"Mr. Vice President," Gideon mumbled, "it's a pleasure to meet you, sir."

"On the contrary, Colonel Stone, *I* am the one who's pleased to meet *you*. If it hadn't been for you and Colonel Hastings here, I might never have had this opportunity."

Hastings walked around from behind the Vice President's wheelchair and introduced himself. His reputation had preceded him; he appeared to be everything Gideon had heard about him. He was a strapping six-footer with an ingratiating smile.

"So, Mr. Vice President—" Gideon began again.

"I wish you'd call me Frank," the Vice President said. "After all, any two men who have been to hell and back together should be on a first-name basis, don't you think?"

Gideon was relieved. The protocol question had been resolved and the Vice President seemed to be inclined to keep their conversation on a personal level.

Hastings finally spoke and when he did, his voice completed the package. It was deep and resonant. "I tagged along with the Vice President because I heard that the minute you got out from under the oxygen mask you started asking questions. I thought just maybe I might be able to answer a few of those questions for you."

Hastings was right. It had been almost forty-eight hours since he and Geronimo had been rescued from Sarawak's bunker. Outside of the fact that Hastings's men had recovered them and they had been immediately transported to the sick bay aboard the *Shenandoah,* Gideon had learned little else.

"How about Corporal Geronimo?" Gideon asked.

"He's doing fine," Hastings assured him. "A little the worse for the wear and tear of these last few days, but he's recovering. Like you, he's getting up close and personal with an oxygen mask until we're sure his lungs are okay. It appears that you two got hit pretty hard when you opened the door to Sarawak's bunker."

"And you, Mr. Vice President?"

Franklin Nelson pursed his lips. "I am most fortunate; the gods were smiling on me this time." His voice was scratchy and weak. "I'm not at all certain I have the names right, but a Major Muta, I believe that's his name, had me moved to another location immediately after a series of explosions in the rebel fuel depot. When it became apparent that Sarawak's men were abandoning their posts, I overheard Sarawak and this Muta fellow discussing what they called their 'bunker plan.' I have no idea what the specifics of that plan were, but I apparently became a bit too much of a nuisance at that point and Sarawak instructed his people to get rid of me. They tried, and I must admit that on the surface at least, it looked pretty bleak. They shot me twice and threw me down a small ravine. I think they thought I was dead. Fortunately, neither wound was fatal, and the worst of it was I broke my leg when I landed."

"Fortunate is right," Hastings interjected. "The Vice President took one in the side and one in the thigh; that's why we're pushing him around in a wheelchair."

"I heal fast for an old man," Nelson quipped, "but even with that, the doctors tell me it will be several weeks before I'll feel like going back to work."

Gideon Stone was more than surprised. First of all, the frail-appearing little man with the thick glasses about whom he had heard and read so many derogatory comments wasn't all that frail. Second, he was proving to be candid, open, and charming. Gideon decided the man had been and still was worth the effort—not factoring in, of course, the misery Ruppert's assignment had put him through in the last ten days.

"So, any other questions?" Hastings asked.

"What about Sarawak?"

Hastings and the Vice President exchanged glances. "It appears General Sarawak couldn't face his failure," Nelson said. "His remains were found in the bunker. Under the circumstances, there wasn't a great deal left of him."

"Are we certain it was Sarawak?" Gideon pressed.

"We're still running tests," Hastings admitted, "but there isn't much doubt on our people's part. A good set of dental records would enable us to tie a nice tidy bow around this whole episode, but unfortunately, those records aren't available."

Gideon permitted a slow smile to materialize. "Well, I guess despite all the bangs and bumps then, we can call the mission a success, huh?"

Nelson frowned. "On balance, yes, but I would be remiss if I did not acknowledge the fact that the world community lost some good men in the process. I refer, of course, to my colleagues on the Security Council."

"Any more questions?" Hastings asked.

"One or two," Gideon said. "How about the folks on the *Bo Jac*?"

"All present and accounted for. One of them, a J. Preston, wanted to be sure I conveyed the following message. It says, 'I told you I could get us out of there, and stay in touch.' "

Gideon smiled. "One last question. When do I get to go home?"

"I'll be going home tomorrow. You can ride back with me if you like," Nelson offered.

Day 15: Time 1420LT
Bethesda, Maryland

"I thought it curious," Fong began, "when Mr. Huntine asked for this meeting, Mr. Ruppert. After all, from everything I have observed in the past few days, I must conclude that what started out to be a rather unsavory situation has been satisfactorily resolved. Is that not the case?"

"For the most part it is," Ruppert admitted, "but there are still a few unanswered questions."

The three men were walking through a window-lined corridor that connected the club's health facilities to the club's conference rooms. As they walked, Shuler Huntine occasionally glanced out at the club's sprawling lawn, now decorated with skiffs of snow. He was waiting for Ruppert to continue.

"If I can answer any of your questions, Mr. Ruppert, I will be most happy to accommodate you," Fong said.

Jake Ruppert paused. "You will recall that as events on Karimunjawa were winding down, you informed us that one of your submarines was making arrangements to rendezvous with General Sarawak. You asked, and we agreed, not to interfere. Is that the way you remember it?"

Fong smiled. "And you want to know why that rendezvous never occurred, correct?"

"Precisely," Ruppert said.

"Fate intervened," Fong replied. "For whatever reason, General Sarawak chose to take his own life. If he had not chosen to do so, by now he would be someplace in China. Perhaps I should also add that I find your question rather intriguing. Have I not seen and heard accounts on your American television and in your American newspapers which describe the conditions under which General Sarawak died?"

"You have," Ruppert acknowledged.

"It may also interest you to know, Mr. Ruppert, and you may have suspected this, that despite the apparent collapse of General Sarawak's stronghold on Karimunjawa, my government still has sources that are, and will continue to be, close to that situation."

"The entire matter boils down to this, Mr. Fong. Our forensic experts are among the best in the world, and even though they have investigated the situation thoroughly, we are still seeking definitive proof that the remains we found in that bunker are those of General Sarawak."

"And you think I may be able to provide some insight into this matter?"

"I don't *think*, sir. I'm simply saying my government *hopes* you can."

Fong smiled. "My sources are quite reliable, Mr. Ruppert. They assure me General Sarawak is dead. These are sources I trust implicitly."

Shuler Huntine knew Fong as well as anyone, and he understood that his Chinese colleague was giving Jake Ruppert what he considered to be the final word on the matter. "That's good enough for me, Jake," he concluded.

The three men walked past the row of private conference rooms and stepped into the club's lobby. As they shook hands, Huntine and Ruppert thanked Fong for his time and cooperation.

Then, as the two Americans donned their coats and started for the door, Fong smiled. "It is written that when a master can no longer rely upon his servant, it is best to discharge his servant from his duties."

Huntine smiled. "Did Confucius say that?"

Fong's implacability was betrayed by his own small smile. "There are many wise men and prophets in my country beside Confucius, Mr. Huntine. It is the wise man that listens to them."

Day 20: Time 1742LT
Key Largo

Gideon Stone busied himself taking inventory. The bullet hole in his shoulder was healing, he could breathe without any discomfort, and the assortment of other little irritants resulting from his sojourn were all but forgotten. He was back where he was supposed to be.

He had spent the morning fishing for yellow jack, and the afternoon nursing several of Hooker's margaritas. He had concluded along about mid-afternoon that if pressed to determine which of the two had given him the most pleasure, it would have been impossible for him to decide.

However, he acknowledged that the thing that had made this a supremely wonderful day, and vastly different from other equally delightful days in Largo, was a simple piece of paper. Carefully tucked away in his pocket was a deposit slip for the sum of thirty-five thousand dollars, courtesy of the United States government. He kept the deposit slip close at hand, and from time to time took it out to admire it.

Late in the afternoon, he had moved around to Hooker's west deck, the one that afforded him a view of the Gulf, situated himself so that he would be able to watch the sunset, and waited for what Hooker referred to as "God's ultimate blessing."

Suddenly he was aware of a fragrance, a delightful sensation that even the gratifying surroundings of Key Largo wouldn't otherwise offer him. He looked up, and there she stood.

"Remember me?" she said. Her voice was musical, the kind of music he liked. "Hooker was supposed to give you my card and you were supposed to call me."

"Hooker never was very dependable," Gideon said.

"So I've learned. At any rate, you and I were going to have dinner together, remember?"

"I do indeed."

"Well, since I had to break that date, maybe I could make amends by buying dinner for you. Would that put me back in your good graces?"

"It would indeed."

"I know a great little Indonesian restaurant just up the highway. Sound appealing?"

Gideon Stone winced. "Let's not do Indonesian tonight," he said.